FIVE RED HERRINGS

Also by Dorothy L. Sayers and available in
the NEL series:

FIVE RED HERRINGS

Dorothy L. Sayers

NEW ENGLISH LIBRARY/TIMES MIRROR

First published in Great Britain by
Victor Gollancz Ltd. in March 1931

First published as a Four Square Edition 1959
Reprinted March 1960
Reprinted August 1960
Reprinted June 1962
Reissued in this NEL edition July 1968
New edition November 1969
New edition June 1972
New edition April 1975
Reissued October 1976
This new edition September 1979

NEL Books are published by
New English Library from
Barnard's Inn, Holborn,
London EC1N 2JR.
Made and printed in Great Britain by
C. Nicholls & Company Ltd.
The Philips Park Press, Manchester
45003845 9

FOREWORD

To my friend Joe Dignam,
kindliest of landlords

Dear Joe,—

Here at last is your book about Gatehouse and Kirkcudbright. All the places are real places and all the trains are real trains, and all the landscapes are correct, except that I have run up a few new houses here and there. But you know better than anybody that none of the people are in the least like the real people, and that no Galloway artist would ever think of getting intoxicated or running away from his wife or bashing a fellow-citizen over the head. All that is just put in for fun and to make it more exciting.

If I have accidentally given any real person's name to a nasty character, please convey my apologies to that person, and assure him or her that it was entirely unintentional. Even bad characters have to be called something. And please tell Provost Laurie that though this story is laid in the petrol-gas period, I have not forgotten that Gatehouse will now have its electric light by which to read this book.

And if you should meet Mr. Millar of the Ellangowan Hotel, or the station-master at Gatehouse, or the booking-clerks at Kirkcudbright, or any of the hundred-and-one kindly people who so patiently answered my questions about railway-tickets and omnibuses and the old mines over at Creetown, given them my very best thanks for their assistance and my apologies for having bothered them so.

Give my love to everybody, not forgetting Felix, and tell Mrs. Dignam that we shall come back next summer to eat some more potato-scones at the Anwoth.

DOROTHY L. SAYERS.

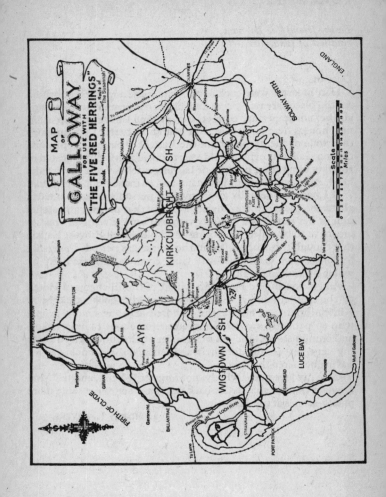

CAMPBELL QUICK

IF one lives in Galloway, one either fishes or paints. 'Either' is perhaps misleading, for most of the painters are fishers also in their spare time. To be neither of these things is considered odd and almost eccentric. Fish is the standard topic of conversation in the pub and the post-office, in the garage and the street, with every sort of person, from the man who arrives for the season with three Hardy rods and a Rolls-Royce, to the man who leads a curious, contemplative life, watching the salmon-nets on the Dee. Weather, which in other parts of the Kingdom is gauged by the standards of the farmer, the gardener, and the week-ender, is considered in Galloway in terms of fish and paint. The fisherman-painter has the best of the bargain as far as the weather goes, for the weather that is too bright for the trout deluges his hills and his sea with floods of radiant colour; the rain that interrupts picture-making puts water into the rivers and the lochs and sends him hopefully forth with rod and creel; while on cold dull days, when there is neither purple on the hills nor fly on the river, he can join a friendly party in a cosy bar and exchange information about Cardinals and March Browns, and practise making intricate knots in gut.

The artistic centre of Galloway is Kirkcudbright, where the painters form a scattered constellation, whose nucleus is in the High Street, and whose outer stars twinkle in remote hillside cottages, radiating brightness as far as Gatehouse-of-Fleet. There are large and stately studios, panelled and high, in strong stone houses filled with gleaming brass and polished oak. There are workaday studios – summer perching-places rather than settled homes – where a good north light and a litter of brushes and canvas form the whole of the artistic stock-in-trade. There are little homely studios, gay with blue and red and yellow curtains and odd scraps of pottery, tucked away down narrow closes and adorned with gardens, where old-fashioned flowers riot in the rich and friendly soil. There are studios that are simply and solely barns, made beautiful by ample proportions and high-pitched rafters, and habitable by the addition of a tortoise stove and a gas-ring. There are artists who have large families and keep domestics in cap and apron; artists who engage rooms, and are taken care of by landladies; artists who live in couples or alone, with a woman who comes in to clean; artists who live hermit-like and do their own charing. There are painters in oils, painters in water-colours, painters in pastel, etchers and illustrators, workers in metal; artists of every variety, having this one thing in common – that they take their work seriously and have no time for amateurs.

Into this fishing and painting community, Lord Peter Wimsey was received on friendly and even affectionate terms. He could make a respectable cast, and he did not pretend to paint, and therefore, though English and an 'incomer', gave no cause of offence. The Southron is tolerated in Scotland on the understanding that he does not throw his weight about, and from this peculiarly English vice Lord Peter was laudably free. True, his accent was affected and his behaviour undignified to a degree, but he had been weighed in the balance over many seasons and pronounced harmless, and when he indulged in any startling eccentricity, the matter was dismissed with a shrug and a tolerant, 'Christ, it's only his lordship.'

Wimsey was in the bar of the McClellan Arms on the evening that the unfortunate dispute broke out between Campbell and Waters. Campbell, the landscape painter, had had maybe one or two more wee ones than was absolutely necessary, especially for a man with red hair, and their effect had been to make him even more militantly Scottish than usual. He embarked on a long eulogy of what the Jocks had done in the Great War, only interrupting his tale to inform Waters in parenthesis that all the English were of mongrel ancestry and unable even to pronounce their own bluidy language.

Waters was an Englishman of good yeoman stock, and, like all Englishmen, was ready enough to admire and praise all foreigners except dagoes and niggers, but, like all Englishmen, he did not like to hear them praise themselves. To boast loudly in public of one's own country seemed to him indecent – like enlarging on the physical perfections of one's own wife in a smoking room. He listened with that tolerant, petrified smile which the foreigner takes, and indeed quite correctly takes, to indicate a self-satisfaction so impervious that it will not even trouble to justify itself.

8

Campbell pointed out that all the big administrative posts in London were held by Scotsmen, that England had never succeeded in conquering Scotland, that if Scotland wanted Home Rule, by God, she would take it, that when certain specified English regiments had gone to pieces they had had to send for Scottish officers to control them, and that when any section of the front line had found itself in a tight place, its mind was at once relieved by knowing that the Jocks were on its left. 'You ask anybody who was in the War, my lad,' he added, acquiring in this way an unfair advantage over Waters, who had only just reached fighting age when the War ended, 'they'll tell you what they thought of the Jocks.'

'Yes,' said Waters, with a disagreeable sneer, 'I know what they said, "they skite too much." '

Being naturally polite and in a minority, he did not add the remainder of that offensive quotation, but Campbell was able to supply it for himself. He burst into an angry retort, which was not merely nationally, but also personally abusive.

'The trouble with you Scotch,' said Waters, when Campbell paused to take breath, 'is that you have an inferiority complex.'

He emptied his glass in a don't-careish manner and smiled at Wimsey.

It was probably the smile even more than the sneer which put the final touch to Campbell's irritation. He used a few brief and regrettable expressions, and transferred the better part of the contents of his glass to Waters' countenance.

'Och, noo, Mr. Campbell,' protested Wullie Murdoch. He did not like these disturbances in his bar.

But Waters by this time was using even more regrettable language than Campbell as they wrestled together among the broken glass and sawdust.

' "I'll break your qualified neck for this,' he said savagely, 'you dirty Highland tyke.'

'Here, chuck it, Waters,' said Wimsey, collaring him 'don't be a fool. The fellow's drunk.'

'Come away, man,' said McAdam, the fisherman, enveloping Campbell in a pair of brawny arms. 'This is no way to behave. Be quiet.'

The combatants fell apart, panting.

'This won't do,' said Wimsey, 'this isn't the League of Nations. A plague on both your houses! Have a bit of sense.'

'He called me a —,' muttered Waters, wiping the whiskey

from his face. 'I'm damned if I'll stand it. He'd better keep out of my way, that's all.' He glared furiously at Campbell.

'You'll find me if you want me,' retorted Campbell, 'I shan't run away.'

'Now, now, gentlemen.' said Murdoch.

'He comes here,' said Campbell, 'with his damned sneering ways—'

'Nay, Mr. Campbell,' said the landlord, 'but ye shuldna ha' said thae things to him.'

'I'll say what I damn well like to him,' insisted Campbell.

'Not in my bar,' replied Murdoch, firmly.

'I'll say them in any damn bar I choose,' said Campbell, 'and I'll say it again – he's a—.'

'Hut!' said McAdam, 'ye'll be thinkin' better of it in the morning. Come away now – I'll give ye a lift back to Gatehouse.'

'You be damned,' said Campbell. 'I've got my own car and I can drive it. And I don't want to see any of the whole blasted lot of ye again.'

He plunged out and there was a pause.

'Dear, dear,' said Wimsey.

'I think I'd best be off out of it too,' said Waters, sullenly. Wimsey and McAdam exchanged glances.

'Bide a bit,' said the latter. 'There's no need to be in sic a hurry. Campbell's a hasty man, and when there's a wee bit drink in him he says mair nor he means.'

'Ay,' said Murdoch, 'but he had no call to be layin' them names to Mr. Waters, none at all. It's a verra great pity – a verra great pity indeed.'

'I'm sorry if I was rude to the Scotch,' said Waters, I didn't mean to be, but I can't stand that fellow at any price.'

'Och, that's a'richt,' said McAdam. 'Ye meant no harm, Mr. Waters. What'll ye have?'

'Oh, a double Scotch,' replied Waters, with rather a shame-faced grin.

'That's right,' said Wimsey, 'drown remembrance of the insult in the wine of the country.'

A man named McGeoch, who had held aloof from the disturbance, rose up and came to the bar.

'Another Worthington,' he said briefly. 'Campbell will be getting into trouble one of these days, I shouldn't wonder. The manners of him are past all bearing. You heard what he said to Strachan up at the golf-course the other day. Making himself out the boss of the whole place. Strachan told him if he saw him on the course again, he'd wring his neck.'

The others nodded silently. The row between Campbell and the golf-club secretary at Gatehouse had indeed become local history.

'And I would not blame Strachan, neither,' went on McGeoch. 'Here's Campbell only lived two seasons in Gatehouse, and he's setting the whole place by the ears. He's a devil when he's drunk and a lout when he's sober. It's a great shame. Our little artistic community has always gotten on well together, without giving offence to anybody. And now there are nothing but rows and bickerings – all through this fellow Campbell.'

'Och,' said Murdoch, 'he'll settle down in time. The man's no a native o' these parts and he doesna verra weel understand his place. Forbye, for all his havers, he's no a Scotsman at a', for everybody knows he's fra' Glasgow, and his mother was an Ulsterwoman, by the name of Flanagan.'

'That's the sort that talks loodest,' put in Murray, the banker, who was a native of Kirkwall, and had a deep and not always silent contempt for anybody born south of Wick. 'But it's best to pay no attention to him. If he gets what is coming to him, I'm thinking it'll no be from anybody here.'

He nodded meaningly.

'Ye'll be thinking of Hugh Farren?' suggested McAdam.

'I'll be naming no names,' said Murray, 'but it's well known that he has made trouble for himself with a certain lady.'

'It's no fault of the lady's,' said McGeoch, emphatically.

'I'm not saying it is. But there's some gets into trouble without others to help them to it.'

'I shouldn't have fancied Campbell in the rôle of a home-breaker,' said Wimsey, pleasantly.

'I shouldn't fancy him at all,' growled Waters, 'but he fancies himself quite enough, and one of these days—'

'There, there,' said Murdoch, hastily. 'It's true he's no a verra popular man, is Campbell, but it's best to be patient and tak' no notice of him.'

'That's all very well,' said Waters.

'And wasn't there some sort of row about fishing?' interrupted Wimsey. If the talk had to be about Campbell, it was best to steer it away from Waters at all costs.

'Och, ay,' said McAdam. 'Him and Mr. Jock Graham is juist at daggers drawn aboot it. Mr. Graham will be fishing the pool below Campbell's hoose. Not but there's plenty pools in the Fleet wi'out disturbin' Campbell, if the man wad juist be peaceable aboot it. But it's no his pool when a's said and dune – the river's free – and it's no to be expectit that Mr. Graham will pay ony heed to his claims, him that pays nae heed to onybody.'

'Particularly,' said McGeoch, 'after Campbell had tried to duck him in the Fleet.'

'Did he though, by Jove?' said Wimsey, interested.

'Ay, but he got weel duckit himsel',' said Murdoch, savouring the reminiscence. 'And Graham's been fushin' there every nicht since then, wi' yin or twa of the lads. He'll be there the nicht, I wadna wonder.'

'Then if Campbell's spoiling for a row, he'll know where to go for it,' said Wimsey. 'Come on, Waters, we'd better make tracks.'

Waters, still sulky, rose and followed him. Wimsey steered him home to his lodgings, prattling cheerfully, and tucked him into bed.

'And I shouldn't let Campbell get on your nerves,' he said, interrupting a long grumble, 'he's not worth it. Go to sleep and forget it, or you'll do no work to-morrow. That's pretty decent, by the way,' he added, pausing before a landscape which was propped on the chest of drawers. 'You're a good hand with the knife, aren't you, old man?'

'Who, me?' said Waters. 'You don't know what you're talking about. Campbell's the only man who can handle a knife in this place – according to him. He's even had the blasted cheek to say Gowan is an out-of-date blunderer.'

'That's high treason, isn't it?'

'I should think so. Gowan's a real painter – my God, it makes me hot when I think of it. He actually said it at the Arts Club in Edinburgh, before a whole lot of people, friends of Gowan's.'

'And what did Gowan say?'

'Oh, various things. They're not on speaking terms now. Damn the fellow. He's not fit to live. You heard what he said to me?'

'Yes, but I don't want to hear it again. Let the fellow dree his own weird. He's not worth bothering with.'

'No, that's a fact. And his work's not so wonderful as to excuse his beastly personality.'

'Can't he paint?'

'Oh, he can paint – after a fashion. He's what Gowan calls

12

him – a commercial traveller. His stuff's damned impressive at first sight, but it's all tricks. Anybody could do it, given the formula. I could do a perfectly good Campbell in half an hour. Wait a moment, I'll show you.'

He thrust a leg out from the bed. Wimsey pushed him firmly back again.

'Show me some other time. When I've seen his stuff. I can't tell if the imitation's good till I've seen the original, can I?'

'No. Well, you go and look at his things and then I'll show you. Oh, Lord, my head's fuzzy like nothing on earth.'

'Go to sleep,' said Wimsey. 'Shall I tell Mrs. McLeod to let you sleep in, as they say? And call you with a couple of aspirins on toast?'

'No; I've got to be up early, worse luck. But I shall be all right in the morning.'

'Well, cheerio, then, and sweet dreams,' said Wimsey.

He shut the door after him carefully and wandered thoughtfully back to his own habitation.

Campbell, chugging fitfully homewards across the hill which separates Kirkcudbright from Gatehouse-of-Fleet, recapitulated his grievances to himself in a sour monotone, as he mishandled his gears. That damned, sneering, smirking swine Waters! He'd managed to jolt him out of his pose of superiority, anyhow. Only he wished it hadn't happened before McGeoch. McGeoch would tell Strachan and Strachan would redouble his own good opinion of himself. 'You see,' he would say, 'I turned the man off the golf-course and look how right I was to do it. He's just a fellow that gets drunk and quarrels in public-houses.' Curse Strachan, with his perpetual sergeant-major's air of having you on the mat. Strachan, with his domesticity and his precision and his local influence, was at the base of all the trouble, if one came to think of it. He pretended to say nothing, and all the time he was spreading rumours and scandal and setting the whole place against one. Strachan was a friend of that fellow Farren too. Farren would hear about it, and would jump at the excuse to make himself still more obnoxious. There would have been no silly row that night at all if it hadn't been for Farren. That disgusting scene before dinner! That was what had driven him, Campbell, to the McClellan Arms. His hand hesitated on the wheel. Why not go back straight away and have the thing out with Farren?

13

After all, what did it matter? He stopped the car and lit a cigarette, smoking fast and savagely. If the whole place *was* against him, he hated the place anyhow. There was only one decent person in it, and she was tied up to that brute Farren. The worst of it was, she was devoted to Farren. She didn't care twopence for anybody else, if Farren would only see it. And he, Campbell, knew it as well as anybody. He wanted nothing wrong. He only wanted, when he was tired and fretted, and sick of his own lonely, uncomfortable shack of a place, to go and sit among the cool greens and blues of Gilda Farren's sitting-room and be soothed by her slim beauty and comforting voice. And Farren, with no more sense or imagination than a bull, must come blundering in, breaking the spell, putting his own foul inter-pretation on the thing, trampling the lilies in Campbell's garden of refuge. No wonder Farren's landscapes looked as if they were painted with an axe. The man had no delicacy. His reds and blues hurt your eyes, and he saw life in reds and blues. If Farren were to die, now, if one could take his bull-neck in one's hands and squeeze it till his great staring blue eyes popped out like — he laughed — like bull's eyes — that was a damned funny joke. He'd like to tell Farren that and see how he took it.

Farren was a devil, a beast, a bully, with his artistic tempera-ment, which was nothing but inartistic temper. There was no peace with Farren about. There was no peace anywhere. If he went back to Gatehouse, he knew what he would find there. He had only to look out of his bedroom window to see Jock Graham whipping the water just under the wall of the house — doing it on purpose to annoy him. Why couldn't Graham leave him alone? There was better fishing up by the dams. The whole thing was sheer persecution. It wasn't any good, either, to go to bed and take no notice. They would wake him up in the small hours, banging at his window and bawling out the number of their catch — they might even leave a contemptuous offering of trout on his window-sill, wretched little fish like minnows, which ought to have been thrown back again. He only hoped Graham would slip up on the stones one night and fill his waders and be drowned among his infernal fish. The thing that riled him most of all was that this nightly comedy was played out under the delighted eye of his neighbour, Ferguson. Since that fuss about the garden-wall, Ferguson had become absolutely intolerable.

It was perfectly true, of course, that he had backed his car into Ferguson's wall and knocked down a stone or two, but if

14

Ferguson had left his wall in decent repair it wouldn't have done any damage. That great tree of Ferguson's had sent its roots right under the wall and broken up the foundations, and what was more, it threw up huge suckers in Campbell's garden. He was perpetually rooting the beastly things up. A man had no right to grow trees under a wall so that it tumbled down at the slightest little push, and then demand extravagant payments for repairs. He would not repair Ferguson's wall. He would see Ferguson damned first.

He gritted his teeth. He wanted to get out of this stifle of petty quarrels and have one good, big, blazing row with somebody. If only he could have smashed Waters' face to pulp – let himself go – had the thing out, he would have felt better. Even now he could go back – or forward – it didn't matter which, and have the whole blasted thing right out with somebody.

He had been brooding so deeply that he never noticed the hum of a car in the distance and the lights flickering out and disappearing as the road dipped and wound. The first thing he heard was a violent squealing of brakes and an angry voice demanding:

'What the bloody hell are you doing, you fool, sitting out like that in the damn middle of the road right on the bend?' And then, as he turned, blinking in the glare of the headlights, to grapple with this new attack, he heard the voice say, with a kind of exasperated triumph:

'Campbell. Of course. I might have known it couldn't be anybody else.'

CAMPBELL DEAD

'DID ye hear aboot Mr. Campbell?' said Mr. Murdoch of the McClellan Arms, polishing a glass carefully as a preparation for filling it with beer.

'Why, what further trouble has he managed to get into since last night?' asked Wimsey. He leaned an elbow on the bar and prepared to relish anything that might be offered to him.

'He's deid,' said Mr. Murdoch.

'Deid?' said Wimsey, startled into unconscious mimicry.

Mr. Murdoch nodded.

'Och, ay; McAdam's juist brocht the news in from Gatehouse. They found the body at 2 o'clock up in the hills by Newton-Stewart.'

'Good heavens!' said Wimsey. 'But what did he die of?'

'Juist tummled intae the burn,' replied Mr. Murdoch, 'an' drooned himself, by what they say. The pollis'll be up there now tae bring him doon.'

'An accident, I suppose.'

'Ay, imph'm. The folk at the Borgan seed him pentin' there shortly after 10 this morning on the wee bit high ground by the brig, and Major Dougal gaed by at 2 o'clock wi' his rod an' spied the body liggin' in the burn. It's slippery there and fou o' broken rocks. I'm thinkin' he'll ha' climbed doon tae fetch some watter for his pentin', mebbe, and slippit on the stanes.'

'He wouldn't want water for oil-paints,' said Wimsey, thoughtfully, 'but he might have wanted to mix mustard for his sandwiches or fill a kettle or get a drop for his whiskey. I say, Murdoch, I think I'll just toddle over there in the car and have a look at him. Corpses are rather in my line, you know. Where is this place exactly?'

'Ye maun tak' the coast-road through Creetown to Newton-Stewart,' said Mr. Murdoch, 'and turn to the richt over the brig and then to the richt again at the signpost along the road to Bargrennan and juist follow the road till ye turn over a wee brig on the richt-hand side over the Cree and then tak' the richt-hand road.'

'In fact,' said Wimsey, 'you keep on turning to the right. I think I know the place. There's a bridge and another gate, and a burn with salmon in it.'

'Ay, the Minnoch, whaur Mr. Dennison caught the big fish last year. Well, it'll be juist afore ye come to the gate, away to your left abune the brig.'

Wimsey nodded.

'I'll be off then,' he said, 'I don't want to miss the fun. See you later, old boy. I say – I don't mind betting this is the most popular thing Campbell ever did. Nothing in life became him like the leaving it, eh, what?'

It was a marvellous day in late August, and Wimsey's soul purred within him as he pushed the car along. The road from

Kirkcudbright to Newton-Stewart is of a varied loveliness hard to surpass, and with a sky full of bright sun and rolling cloud-banks, hedges filled with flowers, a well-made road, a lively engine and the prospect of a good corpse at the end of it, Lord Peter's cup of happiness was full. He was a man who loved simple pleasures.

He passed through Gatehouse, waving a cheerful hand to the proprietor of the Anwoth Hotel, climbed up beneath the grim blackness of Cardoness Castle, drank in for the thousandth time the strange Japanese beauty of Mossyard Farm, set like a red jewel under its tufted trees on the blue sea's rim, and the Italian loveliness of Kirkdale, with its fringe of thin and twisted trees and the blue Wigtownshire coast gleaming across the bay. Then the old Border keep of Barholm, surrounded by white-washed farm buildings; then a sudden gleam of bright grass, like a lawn in Avalon, under the shade of heavy trees. The wild garlic was over now, but the scent of it seemed still to hang about the place in memory, filling it with the shudder of vampire wings and memories of the darker side of Border history. Then the old granite crushing mill on its white jetty, surrounded by great clouds of stone-dust, with a derrick sprawled across the sky and a tug riding at anchor. Then the salmon-nets and the wide semi-circular sweep of the bay, rosy every summer with sea-pinks, purple-brown with the mud of the estuary, majestic with the huge hump of Cairnsmuir rising darkly over Creetown. Then the open road again, dipping and turning – the white lodge on the left, the cloud-shadows rolling, the cottages with their roses and asters clustered against white and yellow walls; then Newton-Stewart, all grey roofs huddling down to the stony bed of the Cree, its thin spires striking the sky-line. Over the bridge and away to the right by the kirkyard, and then the Bargrennan road, curling like the road to Roundabout, with the curves of the Cree glittering through the tree-stems and the tall blossoms and bracken golden by the wayside. Then the lodge and the long avenue of rhododendrons – then a wood of silver birch, mounting, mounting, to shut out the sunlight. Then a cluster of stone cottages – then the bridge and the gate, and the stony hill-road, winding between mounds round as the hill of the King of Elf-land, green with grass and purple with heather and various with sweeping shadows.

Wimsey pulled up as he came to the second bridge and the rusty gate, and drew the car on to the grass. There were other cars there, and glancing along to the left he saw a little group of men gathered on the edge of the burn forty or fifty yards from the road. He approached by way of a little sheep-track, and found himself standing on the edge of a scarp of granite that shelved steeply down to the noisy waters of the Minnoch. Beside him, close to the edge of the rock, stood a sketching easel, with a stool and a palette. Down below, at the edge of a clear brown pool, fringed with knotted hawthorns lay something humped and dismal, over which two or three people were bending.

A man, who might have been a crofter, greeted Wimsey with a kind of cautious excitement.

'He's doon there, sir. Ay, he'll juist ha' slippit over the edge. Yon's Sergeant Dalziel and Constable Ross, mekkin' their investigation the noo.'

There seemed little doubt how the accident had happened. On the easel was a painting, half, or more than half finished, still wet and shining. Wimsey could imagine the artist getting up, standing away to view what he had done – stepping farther back towards the treacherous granite slope. Then the scrape of a heel on the smooth stone, the desperate effort to recover, the slither of leather on the baked short grass, the stagger, the fall, and the bump, bump, bump of the tumbling body, sheer down the stone face of the ravine to where the pointed rocks grinned like teeth among the chuckling water.

'I know the man,' said Wimsey. 'It's a very nasty thing, isn't it? I'll think I'll go down and have a look.'

'Ye'll mind your footing,' said the crofter.

'I certainly will,' said Wimsey, clambering crablike among the stones and bracken. 'I don't want to make another police-exhibit.'

The Sergeant looked up at the sound of Wimsey's scrambling approach. They had met already, and Dalziel was prepared for Wimsey's interest in corpses, however commonplace the circumstances.

'Hech, my lord,' said he, cheerfully. 'I dooted ye'd be here before verra long. Ye'll know Dr. Cameron, maybe?'

Wimsey shook hands with the doctor – a lanky man with a non-committal face – and asked how they were getting on with the business.

'Och, well, I've examined him,' said the doctor. 'He's dead beyond a doubt – been dead some hours, too. The rigor, ye see, is well developed.'

'Was he drowned?'

'I cannot be certain about that. But my opinion – mind ye, it is only my opinion – is that he was not. The bones of the temple are fractured, and I would be inclined to say he got his death in falling or in striking the stones in the burn. But I cannot make a definite pronouncement, you understand, till I have had an autopsy and seen if there is any water in his lungs.'

'Quite so,' said Wimsey. 'The bump on the head might only have made him unconscious, and the actual cause of death might be drowning.'

'That is so. When we first saw him, he was lying with his mouth under water, but that might very well come from washing about in the scour of the burn. There are certain abrasions on the hands and head, some of which are – again in my opinion – post-mortem injuries. See here – and here.'

The doctor turned the corpse over, to point out the marks in question. It moved all of a piece, crouched and bundled together, as though it had stiffened in the act of hiding its face from the brutal teeth of the rocks.

'But here's where he got the big dunt,' added the doctor. He guided Wimsey's fingers to Campbell's left temple, and Wimsey felt the bone give under his light pressure.

'Nature has left the brain ill-provided in those parts,' remarked Dr. Cameron. 'The skull there is remarkably thin, and a comparatively trifling blow will crush it like an egg-shell.'

Wimsey nodded. His fine, long fingers were gently exploring head and limbs. The doctor watched him with grave approval.

'Man,' he said, 'ye'd make a fine surgeon. Providence has given ye the hands for it.'

'But not the head,' said Wimsey, laughing. 'Yes, he's got knocked about a bit. I don't wonder, coming down that bank full tilt.'

'Ay, it's a dangerous place,' said the Sergeant. 'Weel, noo, doctor, I'm thinkin' we've seen a' that's to be seen doon here. We would better be getting the body up to the car.'

'I'll go back and have a look at the painting,' said Wimsey, 'unless I can help you with the lifting. I don't want to be in the way.'

'Nay, nay,' said the Sergeant. 'Thank you for the offer, my lord, but we can manage fine by oorsel's.'

The Sergeant and a constable bent over and seized the body.

19

Wimsey waited to see that they required no assistance, and then scrambled up to the top of the bank again.

He gave his first attention to the picture. It was blocked in with a free and swift hand, and lacked the finishing touches, but it was even so a striking piece of work, bold in its masses and chiaroscuro, and strongly laid on with the knife. It showed a morning lighting – he remembered that Campbell had been seen painting a little after 10 o'clock. The grey stone bridge lay cool in the golden light, and the berries of a rowan-tree, good against witchcraft, hung yellow and red against it, casting splashes of red reflection upon the brown and white of the tumbling water beneath. Up on the left, the hills soared away in veil on veil of misty blue to meet the hazy sky. And splashed against the blue stood the great gold splendour of the bracken, flung in by spadefuls of pure reds and yellows.

Idly, Wimsey picked up the palette and painting-knife which lay upon the stool. He noticed that Campbell used a simple palette of few colours, and this pleased him, for he liked to see economy of means allied with richness of result. On the ground was an aged satchel, which had evidently seen long service. Rather from habit than with any eye to deduction, he made an inventory of its contents.

In the main compartment he found a small flask of whiskey, half-full, a thick tumbler and a packet of bread and cheese, eight brushes, tied together with a dejected piece of linen which had once been a handkerchief but was now dragging out a dishonoured existence as a paint-rag, a dozen loose brushes, two more painting-knives and a scraper. Cheek by jowl with these were a number of tubes of paint. Wimsey laid them out side by side on the granite, like a row of little corpses.

There was a half-pound tube of vermilion spectrum, new, clean and almost unused, a studio-size tube of ultramarine No. 2, half-full, another of chrome yellow, nearly full, and another of the same, practically empty. Then came a half-pound tube of viridian, half-full, a studio-size cobalt three-quarters empty, and then an extremely dirty tube, with its label gone, which seemed to have survived much wear and tear without losing much of its contents. Wimsey removed the cap and diagnosed it as crimson lake. Finally, there was an almost empty studio-size tube of rose madder, and a half-pound lemon yellow, partly used and very dirty.

Wimsey considered this collection for a moment and then

dived confidently into the satchel again. The large compartment, however, yielded nothing further except some dried heather, a few shreds of tobacco and a quantity of crumbs, and he turned his attention to the two smaller compartments.

In the first of these was, first, a small screw of greaseproof paper on which brushes had been wiped; next, a repellent little tin, very sticky about the screw-cap, containing copal medium; and, thirdly, a battered dipper, matching the one attached to the palette.

The third and last compartment of the satchel offered a more varied bag. There was a Swan Vesta box, filled with charcoal, a cigarette-tin, also containing charcoal and a number of sticks of red chalk, a small sketch-book, heavily stained with oil, three or four canvas-separators, on which Wimsey promptly pricked his fingers, some wine-corks and a packet of cigarettes.

Wimsey's air of idleness had left him. His long and inquisitive nose seemed to twitch like a rabbit's as he turned the satchel upside down and shook it, in the vain hope of extracting something more from its depths. He rose, and searched the easel and the ground about the stool very carefully.

A wide cloak of a disagreeable check pattern lay beside the easel. He picked it up and went deliberately through the pockets. He found a pen-knife, with one blade broken, half a biscuit, another packet of cigarettes, a box of matches, a handkerchief, two trout-casts in a transparent envelope, and a piece of string.

He shook his head. None of these was what he wanted. He searched the ground again, casting like a hound on the trail, and then, still dissatisfied, began to lower himself gingerly down the smooth face of the rock. There were crannies here into which something might have fallen, clumps of bracken and heather, prickly roots of gorse. He hunted and felt about in every corner, stabbing his fingers again at every move and swearing savagely. Small fragments of gorse worked their way up his trouser-legs and into his shoes. The heat was stifling. Close to the bottom he slipped, and did the last yard or so on his hinderparts, which irritated him. At a shout from the top of the bank he looked up. The Sergeant was grinning down at him.

'Reconstructing the accident, my lord ?'

'Not exactly,' said Wimsey. 'Here, wait just a moment, will you ?'

He scrambled up again. The corpse was now laid as decently as possible on a stretcher, awaiting removal.

'Have you searched his pockets ?' panted Wimsey.

'Not yet, my lord. Time enough for that at the station. It's purely a formality, ye ken.'

'No, it's not,' said Wimsey. He pushed his hat back and wiped the sweat from his forehead. 'There's something funny about this, Dalziel. That is, there may be. Do you mind if I go over his belongings now ?'

'Not at all, not at all,' said Dalziel, heartily. 'There's no sic a great hurry. We may as weel dew't first as last.'

Wimsey sat down on the ground beside the stretcher, and the Sergeant stood by with a notebook to chronicle the finds.

The right-hand coat pocket contained another handkerchief, a Hardy catalogue, two crumpled bills and an object which caused the Sergeant to exclaim laughingly, 'What's this, lip-stick ?'

'Nothing so suggestive,' said Wimsey, sadly, 'it's a holder for lead-pencil – made in Germany, to boot. Still, if that's there, there might be something else.'

The left-hand pocket, however, produced nothing more exciting than a corkscrew and some dirt; the breast-pocket, only an Ingersoll watch, a pocket comb and a half-used book of stamps; and Wimsey turned, without much hope, to the trouser-pockets, for the dead man wore no waistcoat.

Here, on the right, they found a quantity of loose cash, the notes and coins jumbled carelessly together, and a bunch of keys on a ring. On the left, an empty match-box and a pair of folding nail-scissors. In the hip-pocket, a number of dilapidated letters, some newspaper cuttings and a small notebook with nothing in it.

Wimsey sat up and stared at the Sergeant.

'It's not here,' he said, 'and I don't like the look of it at all, Dalziel. Look here, there's just one possibility. It may have rolled down into the water. For God's sake get your people together and hunt for it – now. Don't lose a minute.'

Dalziel gazed at this excitable Southerner in some astonishment, and the constable pushed back his cap and scratched his head.

'What would we be lookin' for ?' he demanded, reasonably.

(Here Lord Peter Wimsey told the Sergeant what he was to look for and why, but as the intelligent reader will readily supply these details for himself, they are omitted from this page.)

'It'll be important, then, to your way o' thinking,' said Dalziel, with the air of a man hopefully catching, through a forest of obscurity, the first, far-off glimmer of the obvious.

'Important ?' said Wimsey. 'Of course it's important. Incredibly, urgently, desperately important. Do you think I should be sliding all over your infernal granite making a blasted pincushion of myself if it wasn't important ?'

This argument seemed to impress the Sergeant. He called his forces together and set them to search the path, the bank and the burn for the missing object. Wimsey, meanwhile, strolled over to a shabby old four-seater Morris, which stood drawn well up on the grass at the beginning of the sheep-track.

'Ay,' said Constable Ross, straightening his back and sucking his fingers, preliminary to a further hunt among the prickles, 'yon's his car. Maybe ye'll find what ye're wantin' in it, after all.'

'Don't you believe it, laddie,' said Wimsey. Nevertheless, he subjected the car to a careful scrutiny, concentrated for the most part upon the tonneau. A tarry smear on the back cushions seemed to interest him particularly. He examined it carefully with a lens, whistling gently the while. Then he searched further and discovered another on the edge of the body, close to the angle behind the driver's seat. On the floor of the car lay a rug, folded up. He shook it out and looked it over from corner to corner. Another patch of grit and tar rewarded him.

Wimsey pulled out a pipe and lit it thoughtfully. Then he hunted in the pockets of the car till he found an ordnance map of the district. He climbed into the driver's seat, spread out the map on the wheel, and plunged into meditation.

Presently the Sergeant came back, very hot and red in the face, in his shirt-sleeves.

'We've searched high and low,' he said, stooping to wring the water from his trouser-legs, 'but we canna find it. Maybe ye'll be tellin' us now why the thing is so important.'

'Oh ?' said Wimsey. 'You look rather warm, Dalziel. I've cooled off nicely, sitting here. It's not there, then ?'

'It is not,' said the Sergeant, with emphasis.

'In that case,' said Wimsey, 'you had better go to the coroner – no, of course, you don't keep coroners in these parts. The Procurator-Fiscal is the lad. You'd better go to the Fiscal and tell him the man's been murdered.'

'Murdered ?' said the Sergeant.

'Yes,' said Wimsey, 'och, ay; likewise hoots! Murrrderrrt is the word.'

'Eh!' said the Sergeant. 'Here, Ross!'

The constable came up to them at a slow gallop.

'Here's his lordship,' said the Sergeant, 'is of opeenion the man's been murdered.'

'Is he indeed?' said Ross. 'Ay, imph'm. And what should bring his lordship to that conclusion?'

'The rigidity of the corpse,' said Wimsey, 'the fact that you can't find what you're looking for, these smears of tar on the Morris, and the character of the deceased. He was a man anybody might have felt proud to murder.'

'The rigidity of the corpse, now,' said Dalziel. 'That'll be a matter for Dr. Cameron.'

'I confess,' said the doctor, who had now joined them, 'that has been puzzling me. If the man had not been seen alive just after 10 o'clock this morning, I would have said he had been nearer twelve hours dead.'

'So should I,' said Wimsey. 'On the other hand, you'll notice that that painting, which was put on with a quick-drying copal medium, is still comparatively wet, in spite of the hot sun and the dry air.'

'Ay,' said the doctor. 'So I am forced to the conclusion that the chill of the water produced early rigor.'

'I do not submit to force,' said Wimsey. 'I prefer to believe that the man was killed about midnight. I do not believe in that painting. I do not think it is telling the truth. I know that it is absolutely impossible for Campbell to have been working here on that painting this morning.'

'Why so?' inquired the Sergeant.

'For the reasons I gave you before,' said Wimsey. 'And there's another small point – not very much in itself, but supporting the same conclusion. The whole thing looks – and is meant to look – as though Campbell had got up from his painting, stepped back to get a better view of his canvas, missed his footing and fallen down. But his palette and painting-knife were laid down on his stool. Now it's far more likely that, if he were doing that, he would have kept his palette on his thumb and his knife or brush in his hand, ready to make any little extra touch that was required. I don't say he might not have laid them down. I would only say it would have looked more natural if we had

24

found the palette beside the body and the knife half-way down the slope.'

'Ay,' said Ross. 'I've seen 'em dew that. Steppin' back wi' their eyes half-shut and then hoppin' forward wi' the brush as if they was throwin' darts.'

Wimsey nodded.

'It's my theory,' he said, 'that the murderer brought the body here this morning in Campbell's own car. He was wearing Campbell's soft hat and that foul plaid cloak of his so that anybody passing by might mistake him for Campbell. He had the body on the floor of the tonneau and on top of it he had a push-cycle, which has left tarry marks on the cushions. Tucked in over the whole lot he had this rug, which has tar-marks on it too. Then I think he dragged out the corpse, carried it up the sheep-track on his shoulders and tumbled it into the burn. Or possibly he left it lying on the top of the bank, covered with the rug. Then, still wearing Campbell's hat and cloak, he sat down and faked the picture. When he had done enough to create the impression that Campbell had been here painting, he took off the cloak and hat, left the palette and knife on the seat and went away on his push-bike. It's a lonely spot, here. A man might easily commit a dozen murders, if he chose his time well.'

'That's a verra interesting theory,' said Dalziel.

'You can test it,' said Wimsey. 'If anybody saw Campbell this morning to speak to, or close enough to recognise his face, then, of course, it's a wash-out. But if they only saw the hat and cloak, and especially if they noticed anything bulky in the back of the car with a rug over it, then the theory stands. Mind you, I don't say the bicycle is absolutely necessary to the theory, but it's what I should have used in the murderer's place. And if you'll look at this smear of tar under the lens, I think you'll see traces of the tread of a tyre.'

'I'll no say ye're no richt,' said Dalziel.

'Very well,' said Wimsey. 'Now let's see what our murderer has to do next.' He flapped the map impressively, and the two policemen bent their heads over it with him.

'Here he is,' said Wimsey, 'with only a bicycle to help or hinder him, and he's got to establish some sort of an alibi. He may not have bothered about anything very complicated, but he'd make haste to dissociate himself from this place as quickly as possible. And I don't fancy he'd be anxious to show himself in Newton-Stewart or Creetown. There's nowhere much for him to go northward – it only takes him up into the hills round Larg and the Rhinns of Kells. He could go up to Glen Trool, but there's not much point in that; he'd only have to come back the same way. He might, of course, follow the Cree back on the eastern bank as far as Minniegaff, avoiding Newton-Stewart, and strike across country to New Galloway, but it's a long road and keeps him hanging about much too close to the scene of the crime. In my opinion, his best way would be to come back to the road and go north-west by Bargrennan, Cairnderry, Creeside and Drumbain, and strike the railway at Barrhill. That's about nine or ten miles by road. He could do it, going briskly, in an hour, or, as it's a rough road, say an hour and a half. Say he finished the painting at 11 o'clock, that brings him to Barrhill at 12.30. From there he could get a train to Stranraer and Port Patrick, or even to Glasgow, or, of course, if he dumped the bicycle, he might take a motor-bus to somewhere. If I were you, I'd have a hunt in that direction.'

The Segreant glanced at his colleagues and read approval in their eyes.

'And whae d'ye think, my lord, wad be the likeliest pairson to hae committed the crime ?' he inquired.

'Well,' said Wimsey, 'I can think of half a dozen people with perfectly good motives. But the murderer's got to be an artist, and a clever one, for that painting would have to pass muster as Campbell's work. He must know how to drive a car, and he must possess, or have access to, a bicycle. He must be fairly hefty, to have carried the body up here on his back, for I see no signs of dragging. He must have been in contact with Campbell after 9.15 last night, when I saw him leave the McClennan Arms alive and kicking. He must know the country and the people pretty well, for he obviously knew that Campbell lived alone with only a charwoman coming in, so that his early morning departure would surprise nobody. He either lives in the same way himself, or else had a very good excuse for being up and out before breakfast this morning. If you and a man who fulfils all these conditions, he's probably the right one. His railway-ticket, if he took one, ought to be traceable. Or it's quite possible I may be able to put my finger on him myself, working on different lines and with rather less exertion.'

'Och, weel,' said the Sergeant, 'if ye find him, ye'll let us know.'

'I will,' said Wimsey, 'though it will be rather unpleasant, because ten to one he'll be some bloke I know and like much better than Campbell. Still, it doesn't do to murder people, however offensive they may be. I'll do my best to bring him in captive to my bow and spear – if he doesn't slay me first.'

FERGUSON

ON his way back to Kirkcudbright, it occurred to Wimsey that it was more than time for tea, and while voraciously filling himself up with potato-scones and ginger-cake, made out a rough list of possible suspects.

At the end of the meal, the list stood as follows:

Living in Kirkcudbright:

1. Michael Waters – 28 – 5 foot 10 inches – unmarried – living in lodgings with private latch-key – landscape painter – boasts of being able to counterfeit Campbell's style – quarrelled with Campbell previous night and threatened to break his neck.

2. Hugh Farren – 35 – 5 foot 9 inches – figure and landscape painter – particularly broad in the shoulder – married – known to be jealous of Campbell – lives alone with a wife who is apparently much attached to him.

3. Matthew Gowan – 46 – 6 foot 1 inch – figure and landscape painter, also etcher – unmarried – house with servants – wealthy – known to have been publicly insulted by Campbell – refuses to speak to him.

Living in Gatehouse-of-Fleet:

4. Jock Graham – 36 – 5 foot 11 inches – unmarried – staying at Anwoth Hotel – portrait painter – keen fisherman – reckless – known to be carrying on a feud with Campbell and to have ducked him in the Fleet after being assaulted by him.

5. Henry Strachan – 38 – 6 foot 2 inches – married – one child, one servant – portrait painter and illustrator – secretary of golf-club – known to have quarrelled with Campbell and turned him off the golf-course.

The list had reached this stage when the landlord of the hotel came in. Wimsey gave him the latest news of the Campbell affair, without, however, referring to the murder theory, and remarked that he thought of running along to Campbell's house, to see if anything was known there about his movements.

'I doot ye'll no be hearin' much there,' said the landlord. 'Mrs. Green that does his work is away home, but she knows juist naething at a', except that when she arrived this mornin' at 8 o'clock to put the place in order, he had went oot. And Mr. Ferguson that lives next to him was away to Glasgow by the first train.'

'Ferguson?' said Wimsey. 'I think I've met him. Didn't he do those mural paintings for the town hall at some place or other?'

'Ay, he's a verra gude penter. Ye'll have seen him gaun aboot in his wee Austin. He has the stujo next to Campbell's every summer.'

'Is he married?'

'Ay, but his wife's away the noo, visitin' wi' friends in Edin-bro'. I believe they du not get on so verra weel tegither.'

'Who, Ferguson and Campbell?'

'No, no, Ferguson and Mrs. Ferguson. But the ither's true, too. He and Campbell had an awfu' quarrel aboot a bit of wall of Ferguson's that Campbell knocked down wi' his car.'

'I wonder if there is a single person in the Stewartry that Campbell didn't have a row with,' thought Wimsey, and made an addition to his list:

6. John Ferguson – about 36 – about 5 foot 10 inches – grass-widower – landscape and figures – row about a wall.

'By the way,' he went on, 'is Jock Graham anywhere about?'

'Och, Jock – he's away oot. He didna come hame last nicht at a'. He said he might be fishin' up at Loch Trool.'

'Oho!' said Wimsey. 'Up at Loch Trool, is he? How did he go?'

'I couldna say. I think the factor had invitit him. He'll ha' spent last nicht in Newton-Stewart, maybe, and went up wi' the factor in the mornin'. Or he will ha' been fishin' the loch all nicht.'

'Will he, though?' said Wimsey. This put a new complexion on the matter. An active man might have driven the body up to the Minnoch and walked back to Newton-Stewart in time to keep his appointment, if that appointment was not an early one. But it would have to be, of course, for a day's fishing, and Jock Graham liked to work by night.

'Will he be back tonight, Joe ?'

'I couldna say at all,' said the landlord, scattering his hopes at a blow. 'They'll maybe tak' twae nichts if the fishin's gude.'

'H'm!' said Wimsey. 'And very nice, too. Well, I'll be getting on.'

He paid his bill and came downstairs, accompanied by the landlord.

'How's Andy ?' he asked, casually.

'Och, fine,' said the other. 'He's in a great way, though, to-day. Some fellow's pinched his push-bike. An' the worst is, he had juist fitted it wi' new tyres on both wheels.'

Wimsey, with his thumb on the self-starter, paused, electri-fied.

'How's that ?'

'It's his ain fault. He will go leavin' it aboot the place. It'll be some o' these trampin' fellows that sells carpets, verra like. There's naebody in Gatehouse wad du sic a thing.'

'When did he miss it ?'

'This mornin', when he was aff to schule. It's a gude thing it wasna the motor-bike he's always after me to be givin' him.'

'I daresay somebody's just borrowed it,' said Wimsey.

'That's so. It may turn up yet. Well, gude day to your lord-ship.'

Wimsey did not cross the bridge, but turned up the road to the railway station. He passed the turning on the left leading past Anwoth Old Kirk to the Creetown road, and followed the course of the Fleet till he came to a small lane on the right. At the end of this stood two little detached cottages, side by side, looking over a deep pool – in fact, the famous disputed pool in which Jock Graham had ducked the deceased Campbell.

Under normal circumstances, Wimsey would have expected to find both doors confidingly on the latch, but today the lower cottage, which was Campbell's, had been locked – probably by the police. Wimsey peered in through all the ground-floor windows in turn. Everything seemed peaceful and in order as the charwoman had left it that morning. There was a sitting-room of bachelor appearance in front and a kitchen behind – the

29

usual but and ben with a bedroom over. In addition, a glass-roofed studio had been built out beyond the kitchen. At the right-hand side, the shed that had housed the Morris stood empty, a fresh set of tyre-tracks in the dust showing where the car had been taken out that morning. Just beyond, a wooden gate led into an untidy little garden. From the end of the studio a party-wall of rough stone ran down, separating the yard and garden from those belonging to the other cottage, and Wimsey noticed a breach in the wall and the pile of debris which marked where Campbell had backed injudiciously while turning into the garage, and given cause for so much unneighbourly feeling.

Ferguson's cottage was the mirror-image of Campbell's, but his garden was neatly cared-for, and his garage was brand-new and built, regrettably, of corrugated iron. Wimsey pushed open the door and was confronted by a new and shining two-seater of a popular type.

This surprised him for a moment. Ferguson had taken the early train to Glasgow, and Gatehouse Station is six and a half miles from the town. Why had Ferguson not taken the car? He could easily have left it at the station till his return. It appeared to be a new toy; perhaps he had not cared to leave it in strange hands? Or perhaps he meant to be away a long time? Or perhaps— ?

Wimsey lifted the bonnet thoughtfully. Yes, that was the explanation. A gap and some loose connections showed that the magneto had been taken away. Quite probably Ferguson had carried it off with him to Glasgow for repairs. How, then, had Ferguson got to the station? A friendly lift? the 'bus? Or a bicycle? The simplest way was to go and ask. At a small country station no passenger goes unnoticed, and one might as well make sure that Ferguson really had travelled by that train.

Wimsey closed the bonnet and shut the garage-door carefully after him. The house-door was open and he walked in and glanced around. It was as neat and non-committal as any house could be. Everything had been swept, dusted and tidied up by Mrs. Green, including the contents of the studio; for when the artist is away the charwoman will always play among the paint-pots, and no amount of remonstrance will prevent it. Wimsey glanced at some figure-studies piled against the wall, squinnied up his eyes at an elaborate and mannered piece of decorative landscape on the easel, noted casually that Ferguson got his painting materials from Roberson's, glanced along a row of

30

detective novels on the sitting-room bookshelf, and tried the lid of the writing-bureau. It was unlocked, and disclosed an orderly row of pigeon-holes, with everything in its place. Wimsey put down Ferguson as a man of an almost morbidly exact mentality. There was nothing here to throw any light on Campbell's death, but he became all the more anxious to get hold of Ferguson. The way in which the cottages were built, detached and sharing one common entrance yard, ensured that everything which was done in the one could be overlooked from the other. If anything unusual had happened to Campbell the previous night, Ferguson could scarcely have failed to see something of it. And, on the other hand, if Ferguson had not seen it, then nobody had, for the two little houses stood remote from all the other neighbours, hidden at the bottom of the rough, leafy lane, with the Water of Fleet lipping by at the bottom of the gardens. If Jock Graham, indeed, had been fishing Standing-Stone Pool that night – but no! He was supposed to have gone to Loch Trool. Ferguson was the man. It would be advisable to get quickly upon the track of Ferguson.

Wimsey went back to his car and started away up the long hill road to Gatehouse Station, which lies at the edge of the Galloway hill-country, looking away over the Fleet Valley and the viaduct and frowned on by the lofty scarp of the Clints of Dromore.

The railway-station at Gatehouse is approached by one of those gates so numerous in the Border Country, which provide some slight restraint upon straying cattle but to the impatient motorist appear an unmitigated nuisance. As usual, however, at this point, an obliging old gentleman emerged from the little group of cottages by the wayside and let Wimsey through.

Immediately beyond the gate, the road branches right and left into a rough, stony track, of which the left-hand side goes deviously down to Creetown, while the right-hand side wanders away to Dromore and ends abruptly at the railway viaduct. Wimsey crossed this road and kept straight on down a steep little approach, heavily masked by rhododendrons, which brought him to the station.

The line from Castle-Douglas to Stranraer is a single one, but boasts of two sets of rails at Gatehouse Station, for the better convenience of passengers and to allow of the passing of trains. Wimsey approached the station-master, who was profiting by a

31

slack period between two trains to study the *Glasgow Bulletin* in his office.

'I've been trying to find Mr. Ferguson,' said Wimsey, after the usual greetings, 'to fix up a fishing-party at Loch Skerrow, but I'm told he went away this morning by the 9.8. Is that so ?'

'Ay, that is so. I saw him mysel'.'

'I wonder when he'll be back. Was he going to Glasgow, do you know, or only to Dumfries ?'

'He mentioned he was gaun to Glasgow,' said the station-master, 'but he'll maybe be back the nicht. Angus here will be able to tell ye if he took a return ticket.'

The booking-clerk, who shared the station-master's office, remembered Mr. Ferguson very well, because he had taken a first-class return to Glasgow, an extravagance somewhat unusual among the artist community.

'But of course,' said Wimsey, 'the ticket is available for three months. He's not bound to return today. Did he leave his car here, I wonder ?'

'He didna come by car,' said the clerk. 'He tell't me the magneto was broken down, and he was obliged to take the train from here, instead o' drivin' to Dumfries.'

'Oh, then he bicycled up, I suppose,' said Wimsey, carelessly.

'Nay,' said the station-master, 'he'll have come with Campbell's 'bus. He arrived aboot that time, did he no, Angus ?'

'He did that. He was talkin' with Rabbie McHardy when he came in. He'll maybe have told him how long he thocht to be stayin' in Glasgow.'

'Thanks,' said Wimsey. 'I'll have a word with Rabbie. I wanted to charter a boat for tomorrow, but if Ferguson isn't going to be back, it's not much use, is it ?'

He chatted for a few minutes more, giving them a suitably censored account of the Campbell affair, and then took his leave. He had not got very much farther, except that he seemed to have more or less eliminated Ferguson from his list of suspects. He would have to check him up, of course, and see that he really had arrived in Glasgow. This might present a little difficulty, but it was merely routine work for Dalziel and his myrmidons.

Wimsey looked at his watch. Jock Graham was at present the most promising candidate for criminal honours, but since he had disappeared, there was nothing to be done about him for the present. There was, however, still time to go and interview Strachan, and so round off his inquiries in Gatehouse.

STRACHAN

STRACHAN lived in a pleasant, middle-sized house handily situated for him a little way out of Gatehouse on the road that goes up to the golf-course. The neat maid who came to the door smiled kindly upon the visitor and said that the master was at home and would his lordship please step in.

His lordship stepped accordingly into the sitting-room where he found Mrs. Strachan seated by the window instructing her small daughter Myra in the art of plain knitting.

Wimsey apologised for calling just before dinner, and explained that he wanted to fix up with Strachan about a foursome.

'Well, I don't quite know,' said Mrs. Strachan, a trifle doubtfully. 'I don't think Harry is likely to be playing for a day or two. He's had rather a tiresome – oh, well! I really don't know. Myra, dear, run and tell Daddy Lord Peter Wimsey is here and wants to talk to him. You know, I never like to make any sort of arrangements for Harry – I *always* manage to put my foot in it.'

She giggled – she was rather a giggly woman at the best of times. Nervousness, Wimsey supposed. Strachan had an abrupt manner which tended to make people nervous, and Wimsey more than suspected him of being a bit of a domestic tyrant.

He said something vague about not wanting to be a nuisance.

'Of *course* not,' said Mrs. Strachan, keeping an uneasy eye on the door, 'how *could* you be a nuisance ? We're always so *delighted* to see you. And what have you been doing with yourself this beautiful day ?'

'I've been up to the Minnoch to see the body,' said Wimsey, cheerfully.

'The body ?' cried Mrs. Strachan, with a little squeal. 'How dreadful that sounds ! What *do* you mean ? A salmon, or something ?'

'No, no,' said Wimsey. 'Campbell – Sandy Campbell – haven't you heard ?'

'No, what?' Mrs. Strachan opened her large baby blue eyes very wide indeed. 'Has anything happened to Mr. Campbell?'

'Good Lord,' said Wimsey, 'I thought everybody knew. He's dead. He tumbled into the Minnoch and got killed.'

Mrs. Strachan gave a shrill shriek of horror.

'Killed? How perfectly dreadful! Was he drowned?'

'I don't quite know,' said Wimsey. 'I think he bashed his head in, but he may have been drowned as well.'

Mrs. Strachan shrieked again.

'When did it happen?'

'Well,' said Wimsey, cautiously, 'they found him about lunchtime.'

'Good gracious! And we never knew anything about it. Oh, Harry' – as the door opened – 'what *do* you think? Lord Peter says poor Mr. Campbell has been killed up at the Minnoch!'

'Killed?' said Strachan. 'What do you mean, Milly? Who killed him?'

Mrs. Strachan shrieked a third time, more loudly.

'Of course I don't mean that, Harry. How absurd and how horrible! He fell down and cut his head open and got drowned.'

Strachan came forward rather slowly and greeted Wimsey with a nod.

'What's all this about, Wimsey?'

'It's perfectly true,' said Wimsey. 'They found Campbell's dead body in the Minnoch at 2 o'clock. Apparently he had been painting and slipped over the edge of the granite and cracked his skull on the stones.'

He spoke a little absently. It was surely not his fancy that his host looked exceedingly pale and upset, and now, as Strachan turned his face round into the full light of the window, it was obvious that he was suffering from a black eye – a handsome and well-developed black eye, rich in colour and full in contour.

'Oh!' said Strachan. 'Well, I'm not surprised, you know. That's a very dangerous spot. I told him so on Sunday, and he called me a fool for my pains.'

'Why, was he up there on Sunday?' said Wimsey.

'Yes, making a sketch or something. You remember, Milly, just on the other side of the burn from where we were picnicking.'

'Goodness!' exclaimed Mrs. Strachan, 'was *that* the place? Oo! how perfectly horrid! I'll never go there again, never. You may say what you like. Wild horses wouldn't drag me.'

'Don't be ridiculous, Milly. Of course you needn't go there if you don't want to.'

'I should always be afraid of Myra falling in and being killed,' said Mrs. Strachan.

'Very well, then,' said her husband, impatiently. 'Don't go there. That settles that. How did all this happen, Wimsey?'

Lord Peter told the story again, with such detail as he thought desirable.

'That's exactly like Campbell,' said Strachan. 'He walks about – that is, he used to walk about – with his eyes on his canvas and his head in the air, never looking in the least where he was going. I shouted out to him on Sunday to be careful – he couldn't hear what I said, or pretended he couldn't, and I actually took the trouble to fag round to the other side of the stream and warn him what a slippery place it was. However, he was merely rude to me, so I left it at that. Well, he's done it once too often, that's all.'

'Oh, don't speak in that unfeeling tone,' exclaimed Mrs. Strachan. 'The poor man's dead, and though he wasn't a very nice man, one can't help feeling sorry about it.'

Strachan had the grace to mutter that he *was* sorry, and that he never wished any harm to the fellow. He leaned his forehead on his hand, as if his head was aching badly.

'You seem to have been in the wars a bit yourself,' remarked Wimsey.

Strachan laughed.

'Yes,' he said, 'most ridiculous thing. I was up on the golf-course after breakfast when some putrid fool sliced a ball about a thousand miles off the fairway and got me slap-bang in the eye.'

Mrs. Strachan gave another small squeak of surprise.

'Oh!' she said, and then subsided swiftly as Strachan turned his parti-coloured eyes warningly upon her.

'How tiresome,' said Wimsey. 'Who was the blighter?'

'Haven't the faintest idea,' replied Strachan, carelessly. 'I was completely knocked out for the moment, and when I pulled myself together again and went to spy out the land, I only saw a party of men making off in the distance. I felt too rotten to bother about it I simply made tracks for the club-house and a drink. I've got the ball, though – a Silver King. If anybody comes to claim it I shall tell him where he gets off.'

'It's a nasty knock,' said Wimsey, sympathetically, 'A beautiful specimen of its kind, but uncommonly painful, I expect. It's come up nicely, hasn't it ? When exactly did you get it ?'

'Oh, quite early,' said Strachan. 'About 9 o'clock' I should think. I went and lay down in my room at the club-house all morning, I felt so rotten. Then I came straight home, so that's why I hadn't heard about Campbell. Dash it all, this means a funeral, I suppose. It's a bit awkward. In the ordinary way we send a wreath from the Club, but I don't quite know what to do under the circumstances, because last time he was here I told him to send in his resignation.'

'It's a nice little problem,' said Wimsey. 'But I think I should send one, all the same. Shows a forgiving spirit and all that. Keep your vindictiveness for the person who damaged your face. Whom were you playing with, by the way ? Couldn't he have identified the assassins ?'

Strachan shook his head.

'I was just having a practice round against bogey,' he said. 'I caddied for myself, so there were no witnesses.'

'Oh, I see. Your hand looks a bit knocked about, too. You seem to have spent a good bit of your time in the rough. Well, I really came in to ask you to make up a foursome tomorrow with Waters and Bill Murray and me, but I don't suppose you'll, so to speak, feel that your eye is in just yet awhile ?'

'Hardly,' said Strachan, with a grim smile.

'Then I'll be popping off,' said Wimsey, rising. 'Cheerio, Mrs. Strachan. Cheerio, old man. Don't bother to see me off the premises. I know my way out.'

Strachan, however, insisted on accompanying him as far as the gate.

At the corner of the road Wimsey overtook Miss Myra Strachan and her nurse taking an evening stroll. He stopped the car and asked if they would like a little run.

Myra accepted gleefully, and her attendant made no objection. Wimsey took the child up beside him, packed the nurse into the back seat and urged the Daimler Double-Six to show off her best paces.

Myra was delighted.

'Daddy never goes as fast as this,' she said, as they topped the tree-hung rise by Cally Lodge and sailed like an aeroplane into the open country.

Wimsey glanced at the speedometer-needle, which was

flickering about the 85 mark, and took the corner on a spectacular skid.

'That's a fine black eye your Dad's got,' he remarked.

'Yes, isn't it ? I asked him if he'd been fighting, and he told me not to be impertinent. I like fighting. Bobby Craig gave *me* a black eye once. But I made his nose bleed, and they had to send his suit to the cleaners.'

'Young women oughtn't to fight,' said Wimsey, reprovingly, 'not even modern young women.'

'Why not ? I like fighting. Oo! look at the cows!'

Wimsey trod hastily on the brake and reduced the Daimler to a lady-like crawl.

'All the same, I believe he *was* fighting,' said Myra. 'He never came home last night, and Mummy was ever so frightened. She's afraid of our car, you know, because it goes so fast, but it doesn't go as fast as yours. Does that cow want to toss us ?'

'Yes,' said Wimsey. 'It probably mistakes us for a pancake.'

'Silly! Cows don't eat pancakes, they eat oil-cake. I ate some once, but it was very nasty, and I was sick.'

'Serve you right,' said Wimsey. 'I'd better put you down here, or you won't be back by bed-time. Perhaps I'd better run you part of the way home.'

'Oh, please do,' said Myra. 'Then we can drive the cows and make them run like anything.'

'That would be very naughty,' said Wimsey. 'It isn't good for cows to run fast. You are an impertinent, bloodthirsty, greedy and unkind young person, and one of these days you'll be a menace to society.'

'How lovely! I could have a pistol and a beautiful evening dress, and lure people to opium-dens and stick them up. I think I'd better marry you, because you've got such a fast car. That would be useful, you see.'

'Very,' said Wimsey, gravely. 'I'll bear the idea in mind. But you might not want to marry me later on, you know.'

WATERS

It amused Lord Peter to lead the simple life at Kirkcudbright. Greatly to the regret of the hotel-keepers, he had this year chosen to rent a small studio at the end of a narrow cobbled close, whose brilliant blue gate proclaimed it to the High Street as an abode of the artistically-minded. His explanation of this eccentric conduct was that it entertained him to watch his extremely correct personal man gutting trout and washing potatoes under an outside tap, and receiving the casual visitor with West End ceremony.

As he clattered down the close, picking his way past the conglomeration of bicycles which almost blocked the entrance, Wimsey perceived this efficient person waiting upon the doorstep with an expression which, though strictly controlled, might almost have been called eager.

'Hullo, Bunter!' said his lordship, cheerfully. 'What's for dinner ? I'm feeling uncommonly ready for it. There's a beautiful corpse up at Creetown.'

'I apprehended, my lord, that your lordship would be engaged in investigation. Not being certain of the exact hour of your lordship's return, I thought it wiser, my lord, to prepare a dish of stewed beef with thick gravy and vegetables, which could, in case of necessity, be kept hot without deterioration.'

'Excellent,' said his lordship.

'Thank you, my lord. I understand from the butcher that the portion of the animal which I have been accustomed to call shin of beef is termed in these parts the – er – hough.'

'I believe you are right, Bunter.'

'I did not take the man's word for it,' said Bunter, with melancholy dignity. 'I inspected the carcase and ascertained that the correct cut was removed from it.'

'You are always so thorough,' said Wimsey, appreciatively.

'I do my best, my lord. Would your lordship desire me to refer to the comestible as – er – hough – during our residence in this country ?'

'It would be a graceful concession to national feeling, Bunter, if you can bring yourself to do it.'

'Very good, my lord. I presume that the leg of mutton will again pass under the appellation of jiggot, as on the occasion of your lordship's previous visit ?'

'Certainly, Bunter.'

'Yes, my lord,' Bunter sighed deeply. 'Whatever is correct I will endeavour to do to your lordship's satisfaction.'

'Thank you, Bunter. We must try to be correct under all circumstances.'

'Yes, my lord. Dinner will be served in twenty minutes, as soon as the potatoes are ready.'

'Right-ho!' said his lordship. 'I'll just run across the close and have a chin-wag with Miss Selby till dinner-time.'

'Pardon me, my lord. I understand that the ladies have gone away.'

'Gone away ?' said Wimsey, rather taken aback.

'Yes, my lord. I was informed by the young person who attends upon them that they had gone away to Glasgow.'

'Oh!' said Wimsey, 'they're away to Glasgow. But that probably only means that they are out for the day. It does not necessarily imply, as it does down South, that they have packed up bag and baggage and departed on a long visit. Well, I'll go and hunt up Mr. Waters. I rather want to see him. I may bring him back to dinner.'

'Very good, my lord.'

Wimsey crossed the High Street and knocked upon the door of Waters' lodgings. The landlady answered his knock and in reply to his inquiry observed that 'Mr. Waters was away just now.'

'When will he be back ?'

'I couldna say, my lord, but I'm thinkin' he'll be stayin' the nicht in Glasgow.'

'Everybody seems to have gone to Glasgow,' said Wimsey.

'Och, ay. They'll all have went tae the Exhibition. Mr. Waters was away by the first train.'

'What! the 8.45 ?' said Wimsey, incredulously. From what he had seen of Waters the previous night he had hardly expected such energy.

'Ay,' said the landlady, placidly. 'He had his breakfast at 8 o'clock and was away with Miss Selby and Miss Cochran.'

Wimsey felt rather relieved. He had been afraid for the

moment that this early activity might have something a little sinister about it. But, chaperoned by Miss Selby and Miss Cochran, Waters could scarcely have got into mischief. One more of his six suspects seemed to be safely eliminated. He left a message that he would like to see Mr. Waters as soon as he got back and returned to Blue Gate Close.

He had finished his savoury stew, and was enjoying an admirable cheese soufflé, when there was a sound of two pairs of heavy boots labouring over the cobbles, followed by that of a voice inquiring for his lordship.

'Hullo!' said Wimsey, 'is that you, Dalziel?'

'Yes, my lord.' The Sergeant shouldered his way through the narrow doorway and stood aside to allow his companion to pass. 'I've been reportin' this matter to Sir Maxwell Jamieson, the Chief Constable, an' he has been gude enough to come round wi' me for a word wi' your lordship.'

'Splendid,' said Wimsey, heartily. 'Delighted to see you both. We haven't met before, Sir Maxwell, but that's not to say I don't know you well by reputation, as I fancy, you know me. There was a trifling complaint of speeding last year, I believe, in which justice was rather more than tempered with mercy. Have a drink.'

'Well,' said Dalziel, when Wimsey's proffered hospitality had been accepted, with suitable signs of appreciation. 'I've been makin' inquiries along the line in accordance wi' the theory, but I'm no sae verra weel satisfied t'ane way or t'ither. But first of a', I'd have ye ken I've interviewed the folk at Borgan, and they tell me young Jock saw Campbell pentin' there at ten minutes past ten when he gaed oot tae tak' a message to a wumman at Clauchaneasy, and he was still sittin' there when Jock returned at five minutes past eleven. Sae ye see, he couldna ha' left the place till a few minutes past eleven at the airliest.'

'When you say he saw Campbell, do you mean that he knew it was Campbell or that he only thought it was?'

'Nay, he disna ken Campbell, but he saw a man in a big black hat and a plaid cloak, like Campbell was wearin'. An' he thinks there was a big plaid or rug liggin' by the side of him.'

'Then it may have been the murderer.'

'Ay, so it may, but it's the time o' day I wad dra' your attention to. Ye'll admit that, murderer or no murderer, he couldna ha' left yon place till past eleven?'

'That seems clear enough.'

'Well, then, we come tae the investigations consairnin' the railway. There's no sae mony trains in the day between Stranraer and Girvan stops at Pinwherry or Barrhill.'

The Sergeant pulled an L.M.S. time-table from his pocket and smacked it out upon the table.

'Let's tak' the trains tae Stranraer first. The murderer micht verra likely be thinkin' o' escapin' by the boat fra' Stranraer, ye ken, and if so, it's in Ireland we'll have to be lookin' for him.'

He pulled out a thick pencil and jotted the times down on a sheet of paper.

	a.m.	p.m.
Girvan	10.45	2.16
Pinmore	11.1	2.31
Pinwherry	11.8	2.39
Barrhill	11.18	2.50
Glenwhilly	11.33	3.6
New Luce	11.41	3.13
Dunragit	11.52	3.26
Castle Kennedy	12 noon	3.33
Stranraer	12.7	3.39

Wimsey shook his head.

'He couldn't catch the first train – not on a bicycle, at any rate. Barrhill is his nearest point, and, if you give him only five minutes to pack his traps and get started, that leaves a bare eight minutes for ten miles or so. It's just conceivable that he might do it by car if he blinded like hell and the train happened to be late, but how could he have got the spare car along? Of course he could have hung about somewhere in the hills and taken the 2.50, or he could have ridden farther and picked the same train up at another station, but that would give him a very poor alibi.'

'That's so, my lord,' said Dalziel. 'I hadna overlookit the possibeelity. Noo, there's a report come in fra' the station-master at Pinwherry that there was a gentleman tuk the 2.39 at Pinwherry. He paid particular attention to him because he was a stranger and appeared out of the ordinar' nairvous and excited.'

'Where did he book to?'

'That's juist the interesting part of the matter. He tuk his teeckit to Stranraer—'

'Why, of course,' said Wimsey, with his eye on the time-table. 'That explains why he waited for that train. That's the one that makes the connection with the boat to Larne. It's a rotten connection at that – over three hours to wait in Stranraer – but it's apparently the only one there is.'

'I was aboot to tell ye,' said the Sergeant, 'the gentleman inquired maist anxiously aboot the connection and seemed sair disappointit to learn that there was no boat before 7 o'clock.'

'That fits in all right,' said Wimsey, 'though it's queer he didn't find out about the boats earlier, while he was thinking this crime out so carefully. What was this fellow like ?'

'Juist a youngish body in a grey suit and soft hat, they tell me, an' carryin' a wee attaché-case. Rather tall than short, wi' a sma' dark moustache. The station-master wad ken him again.'

'Did he give any particular account of himself ?'

'He said somethin' o' havin' misread the time-table and thocht there was a boat at 3.50.'

'Well, that's perfectly possible,' said Wimsey. 'You see there are three lines at the bottom of the page showing the steamer connections from Stranraer Pier to Larne and Belfast, and just above them, three lines showing the train-connection between Stranraer, Colfin and Port Patrick. It's easy to mistake the one for the other. But look here, Dalziel, if there was no boat for him before 7, you must have been in time to catch him.'

'That's a fact, my lord, and so soon as I had the report I telephoned through tae the pollis at Stranraer to have a sairch made; but I got their answer juist before comin' over here, and it was tae the effect that there was no sic a pairson on the boat.'

'Damn it!' said Wimsey.

'They are conducting an inquiry in Stranraer, in case he should be in hidin' there, and are stoppin' all cars enterin' and leavin' the toon, and naiturally they will keep a strict eye on tomorrow's boat. But it is no unthinkable that the felly isna mekkin' for Larne at a'. That may ha' been juist a blind.'

'Did he actually go to Stranraer ?'

'It seems so. The teeckets ha' been checkit, and the third-class teecket issued at Pinwherry, was duly given up at Stranraer. Unfortunately, the porter whae collectit it is no obsairvin' body and canna say what like the mon was that handit it tae him.'

'Well, you seem to have done pretty well on that part of the business,' said Wimsey, 'considering the shortness of the time. And it looks as though we really had got on to something. By the way, did the stationmaster at Pinwherry mention whether the passenger had a bicycle ?'

'Nay, he hadna a bicycle. I askit him how he came there, but naebody had noticed him come. It seems he juist walkit intae the station.'

'Well, of course, if he was taking the Irish boat, he would probably get rid of the bicycle first. He had plenty of time to hide it up in the hills. Well – that looks rather hopeful. Still, we mustn't rely on it too much. How about the trains in the other direction – the ones going to Glasgow ?'

Dalziel turned over a couple of pages, licked the thick pencil and produced a new list.

		a.m.	p.m.	p.m.
Stranraer	dep.	11.35	12.30 (from Stranraer Pier)	4.5
Castle Kennedy		11.42	...	4.12
Dunragit		11.52	12.42	4.20
New Luce		12.7 p.m.	...	4.33
Glenwhilly		12.19	...	4.45
Barrhill		12.35	...	5.0
Pinwherry		12.43	...	5.8
Pinmore		12.56	...	5.18
Girvan	arr.	1.6	1.37	5.28
	dep.	1.11	1.42	5.36

'There are opportunities there, too,' said Wimsey. 'How about the 12.35 ? He could catch that easily and go on to Glasgow, and from there he could get anywhere.'

'Ay, that's so. That was what I thocht masel'. I telephoned tae the station-master at Barrhill, but there was only four passengers by thet train, an' he knowed them a' pairsonally.'

'Oh!' said Wimsey. 'I see. That rather puts the lid on that, then.'

'Ay. But there's anither thing. I didna rest satisfied wi' that. I pursued my inquiries at the ither stations along the line an' I found there was a gentleman wi' a bicycle tuk the 1.11 train at Girvan.'

'Was there, by Jove!' Wimsey pulled out his map of the district and studied it intently.

'It could be done, Dalziel, it could be done! Barrhill is nine miles from the scene of the crime and Girvan is, say, twelve miles further on – call it twenty-one miles altogether. If he started at 11.10 that would give him two hours, which means just over ten miles an hour – easy enough for a good cyclist. Was the train punctual, by the way ?'

'It was. Ay, he could ha' done it.'

'Did the station-master give any description of him ?'

'He said that accordin' tae the porter he was juist an ordinary gentleman of thirty or forty years of age, in a grey suit and a check cap pu'd weel doon. Clean-shaven, or nearly so, and of middling size, and he was wearin' big glasses wi' they tinted lenses.'

'That's suspicious,' said Wimsey. 'Would the porter be able to identify him, do you think ?'

'Ay, I'm thinkin' he wad. He said the gentleman spoke like an Englishman.'

'Did he ?' Wimsey considered his six suspects. Waters was a Londoner and spoke standard public-school English. Strachan, though a Scot, habitually spoke with an English accent, having been educated at Harrow and Cambridge. He, however, was a noticeably tall man. It could hardly be he. Gowan was double-tongued; he spoke English with Wimsey and the broadest Scots with the natives – but then, Gowan's grand silky beard which had never known a razor was pointed out to visitors as one of the local sights of Kirkcudbright. Graham was completely Londonised, and his English would pass muster at Oxford. His astonishing blue eyes were his one really memorable feature – was this the explanation of the tinted glasses ? Farren – his Scots tongue was unmistakable; nobody, surely, could mistake him for an Englishman. His whole person was noticeable, too – the wide, ridgy shoulders, tumbling fair hair and queer, light eyes, temperish, pouted mouth and heavy jaw. Ferguson, too, was Scottish in accent, though not in idiom, and in feature might be almost anything.

'Did the gentleman give any particular account of himself ?' asked Wimsey, coming rather suddenly out of his abstraction.

'No, he only got tae the station as the train was standin' at the platform, but he said somethin' aboot startin' late fra' Ballantrae. He tuk his ticket for Ayr and the machine was labelled according.'

'We may be able to trace that,' said Wimsey.

'Ay, that's so. I hae sent an inquiry to Ayr and to Glesga'. They'll maybe remember 't.'

44

'And maybe not,' said Wimsey. 'Well, now, Dalziel, I also, as the lady said, have not been idle.'

He produced his list of suspects.

'Mind you,' he said, warningly, 'this list may not be complete. But we know the man we are looking for is a painter, which narrows the field considerably. And all these six people are known to have had it in for Campbell in one way or another, though some of the motives may seem pretty inadequate.'

The Sergeant peered thoughtfully at the list, and so did Sir Maxwell. The latter's jurisdiction extended over both Kirkcud-brightshire and Wigtownshire, and he knew all the artists more or less well, though not with any great intimacy, his own interests being military and sporting.

'Now,' said Wimsey, 'two of these people have alibis. Fergu-son was duly seen on to the 9.8 from Gatehouse. He had no bicycle with him, and he booked to Glasgow. There's a picture exhibition on there, and no doubt that's what he was making for. Waters also departed for Glasgow by the 8.45 from Kirkcud-bright, in company with Miss Selby and Miss Cochran. If they all met at the show they will prove each other's alibis all right. Strachan was out all night and came home at lunch-time with a black eye, and what is more, he is telling lies about it.' He gave a brief summary of his conversations with Strachan and Myra.

'That looks bad,' said Dalziel.

'Yes; we mustn't pin all our faith to the cyclist at Girvan, or even to the mysterious passenger at Pinwherry; they may both be perfectly genuine travellers. Strachan might quite well have been painting up the Minnoch at 11 o'clock and ridden back to Gatehouse by lunch-time. It's only twenty-seven miles. It would be dangerous, because he might be recognised, but people who commit murders must take a few risks. Besides, he might have hidden his car somewhere on the road the day before, and picked it up on his way back, bringing the bicycle with him. Did I mention to you, by the way, that there's a bicycle disap-peared from the Anwoth Hotel at Gatehouse ?'

Dalziel shook his head.

'It's a case wi' a great number of possibeelities,' he said. 'Always supposin' that it *is* a case. We havena got the doctor's opeenion yet.'

'That'll come tomorrow, I suppose ?'

'Ay. The maitter has been laid before the Fiscal, and there will be a post-mortem examination. There's Campbell's sister

45

expectit to-nicht – it seems she's his only relation – an' they'll maybe wait till she has seen the corpse, forbye the licht will be better for the doctor in the mornin'.'

After the Sergeant and his companion had gone, Wimsey remained smoking thoughtfully for some time. He was worried about Waters. He had left him the night before in a dangerous mood. The last train from Glasgow got in to Kirkcudbright at 9.00. If Waters had really gone to see the Exhibition, it was not reasonable to expect him back that night. He would only have got into Glasgow at 2.16, and would have had to leave again at 5.30. Nobody would go all that way in order to spend a bare three hours in the town. Except, possibly, to establish an alibi. Could one establish an alibi that way ?

Wimsey turned to the time-table again. Kirkcudbright depart 8.45. That was capable of proof by witnesses. Tarff 8.53. Brig-of-Dee, 9.2 – nothing to be done from there, except by car. Castle-Douglas 9.7. That was different. Castle-Douglas was a junction. From there one might turn back in the direction of Newton-Stewart. Yes. There was a train. This was ridiculous, of course, because Waters had travelled with the two women, but there was no harm in working it out. Castle-Douglas 9.14, Newton-Stewart 10.22. Wimsey breathed a sigh of relief. If the murderer had been seen painting at 10 o'clock, that let out Waters. He could not have got even so far as Newton-Stewart by that time.

But all this depended on the doctor's report. If both Wimsey and he had been mistaken about the rigor – then it was possible that Campbell himself had been painting at the Minnoch till five minutes past eleven. In which case – Wimsey thumbed the time-table again.

In which case a train reaching Newton-Stewart at 10.22 might prove very handy to an intending murderer – supposing the murderer knew already that Campbell meant to paint that day at the Minnoch. A car from Newton-Stewart would bring him to the scene of the crime in twenty minutes – time enough and to spare. And though Waters had no car, such things can be hired. There would be a risk, certainly, for in country districts people know one another, and indeed, who would hire out a driverless car to a man he did not know, without making careful inquiries ? Yet, if the deposit were big enough, he might take the risk. It would not do to cross Waters off the list too promptly.

At this point Wimsey cursed himself for a fool. It was as certain as anything could be that Waters had travelled peacefully to Glasgow under the eyes of his friends, and would return peacefully with them the next day.

He looked at his watch. It was not possible, of course, that Waters had returned by the 9 o'clock train. Still, it would do no harm to go and see.

He walked along the High Street. There was no light either in Waters' sitting-room or in his bedroom, both of which faced upon the street. The landlady would think him daft if he made any more inquiries. There was Waters' studio – a big converted barn up a turning off the Tongland Road. If he had come back, he certainly would not be working there at this hour. Still, when one is restless, any excuse will serve to take a little walk.

Wimsey made his way past the Castle, up the little flight of steps and over the green by the harbour. The tide was dropping, and the long mud-flats of the estuary glimmered faintly in the pale midsummer night. The yacht that had come in that morning still lay close against the harbour wall, her spars and rigging making a bold foreground of interlaced verticals and horizontals against the galumphing curves of the ugly concrete bridge. Wimsey crossed the open space where the 'buses congregate by day, plunged down the little alley by the gasworks and came out past the station on to the Tongland Road.

Crossing the street, he turned off again to the right and found himself in a happy backwater, with an ancient overshot water-mill, a few cottages and a wide open space, grassy and forlorn, surrounded by sheds and derelict out-buildings.

Waters' studio was approached by a little winding path among overgrown bushes and lush grass. He pushed open the gate and tried the door. It was locked, and there was no sign of life about the place. The silence was intense. He heard some small animal move in the grass, the plop, plopping from the wooden trough over the paddles of the mill-wheel; far off, somewhere in the town, a dog barked hoarsely.

Wimsey turned to go. As he went, the stony path creaking under his feet, the door of one of the cottages was flung suddenly open, letting a long bar of light stream suddenly across the ground. Framed in the door he saw the silhouette of a woman peering out anxiously into the silvery darkness.

It occurred to Wimsey suddenly that this was Farren's house, and he paused, half-decided to stop and speak. But as he hesi-

47

tated, somebody laid a hand on the woman's shoulder and drew her in, shutting the door. There had been something quick and stealthy about the action that banished Wimsey's plan, half-formed. The second figure had been a man's, but it was taller and bigger than Farren's. He felt sure that it was not Farren, and that, if he knocked, the door would not open to his knocking.

FARREN

SIR MAXWELL JAMIESON was not a man to rush into precipitate action. Sound and cautious, with a reputation for taciturnity, he preferred to know exactly where he stood before committing himself to stirring up scandal by vexatious inquiries. He was not over-pleased to find Wimsey palpitating on his doorstep the next morning, shortly after breakfast, when he himself had barely had time to read the paper.

He was too wise to ignore Wimsey and his theories. He knew that Lord Peter had an uncanny nose for a crime, and that his help was valuable, but he did not care for this English habit of rushing into situations on a high tide of chatter and excitement. It was true that Wimsey had shown a certain amount of tact in coming to him. There was no telephone in Blue Gate Close, and if Wimsey must have the latest intelligence piping hot, it was better that he should apply for it in private than interrogate Sergeant Dalziel over the line in a hotel bar.

But Sir Maxwell was not yet perfectly convinced that there was any murder to be investigated. All this talk about missing objects and bicycles was well enough, but it was a small basis on which to rear so threatening a structure of accusation. Doubtless, if the things were more carefully searched for, they would be found, and the whole murder theory would collapse. Certainly, there was that awkward point about the rigor, but Sir Maxwell, turning over the pages of Taylor and Glaister, felt convinced that it was not possible to lay down any very exact or reliable laws about the onset of rigor.

He frowned over Wimsey's list of suspects – a disagreeable document, he thought, and savouring strongly of the libellous.

48

All these people were highly respected citizens. Take Gowan, for instance – a leading inhabitant of Kirkcudbright for over fifteen years, well known and well liked, in spite of his small vanities and somewhat overbearing manner. He was wealthy, kept a good house, with an English butler and housekeeper, and owned two cars, with a chauffeur to drive them when required. Was it likely that he would be found knocking his fellow-artists on the head and tumbling them into salmon-rivers in the neighbouring county ? What possible motive could he have for it ? There had been talk of some disagreement about a picture, but, in Sir Maxwell's experience, artists frequently disagreed about pictures, with no more consequences than a little cold-shouldering or the formation of a clique. Waters, again – a pleasant young man enough, though inclined to irritate his neighbours by his South-country mannerisms. It was unfortunate that he should have fallen out with Campbell, but surely he was not the man to harbour murderous resentment for a hasty word spoken over a drink. And Farren—

Sir Maxwell paused there, in justice to Wimsey. Where women were concerned, you never knew. Campbell had been rather a frequent visitor at the cottage by the old mill. It was said – there had been talk – threats had been uttered. If there was anything in it, there might be some difficulty in getting at the truth here. Farren's suspicions had probably been quite unfounded, for one could hardly look at Mrs. Farren and believe evil of her. Still, wives tell lies and provide alibis, even for the most unreasonable of husbands, and indeed, the more virtuous the wife, the more obstinate the liar, under such conditions. With considerable discomfort, Sir Maxwell admitted to himself that he could not undertake to say that the Farrens were, in the nature of things, clear of all suspicion.

Then, of course, there were those people over at Gatehouse. Jock Graham – a harum-scarum, word-and-a-blow fellow if ever there was one. Clever, too. If it came to picking the man with the brains to plan an ingenious crime and the coolness to carry it through, then Graham was the man for his money, every time. Graham had had plenty of practice in the execution of practical jokes, and he could tell a circumstantial lie, looking you square in the eyes with the face of an angel. Ferguson was notoriously on bad terms with his wife. Sir Maxwell knew nothing else to his disadvantage, but he noted it, in his upright Presbyterian mind, as a discreditable fact. Strachan – well, Strachan was

49

secretary of the golf-club and weel-respectit. Surely Strachan, like Gowan, could be ruled out.

The telephone rang. Wimsey pricked up his ears. Sir Maxwell raised the receiver with irritating deliberation. He spoke; then turned to Wimsey.

'It's Dalziel. You had better listen in on the extension.'

'Is't you, Sir Maxwell? ... Ay, we have the doctor's report ... Ay, it supports the theory of murder richt enough. There was nae water in the lungs at a'. The mon was deid before he got intae the burn. 'Twas the scart on the heid that did it. The bone is a' crushed intae the brain. Och, ay, the wound was made before death, and he must ha' deid almost immediately. There's a wheen mair blows to the heid an' body, but the doctor thinks some o' them will ha' been made after death, wi' the body pitchin' doon the burnside an' washin' aboot amang the stanes.'

'What about the time of the death?'

'Ay, Sir Maxwell, I was juist comin' to that. The doctor says Campbell will ha' been deid at least six hours when he first saw the body, an' mair likely twelve or thirteen. That'll pit the time o' the murder in the late nicht or the airly mornin' – at ony rate between midnicht and nine o'clock. And a verra suspeecious an' corroboratin' circumstance is that the man had nae food in his wame at a'. He was kilt before he had ta'en ony breakfast.'

'But,' said Wimsey, cutting in on the conversation, 'if he had had his breakfast early, it might have passed out of the stomach before lunch-time.'

'Ay, that's so. But it wadna ha' passed oot o' him a'-'gither. The doctor says his interior was as toom as a drum, an' he will stake his professional credit he hadna eaten onything sin' the previous nicht.'

'Well, he ought to know,' said Wimsey.

'Ay, that's so. That's his lordship speakin', is't no? Your lordship will be gratified by this support for our theory.'

'It may be gratifying,' said Jamieson, 'but I wish very much it hadn't happened.'

'That's so, Sir Maxwell. Still, there's little doot it has happened and we maun du the best we can by it. There is another remarkable circumstance, an' that is that we can find no recognisable finger-prints upon the artistic paraphernalia, and it has the appearance as if the user of them had been doin' his pentin' in gloves. An' the steerin'-wheel o' the car is wiped as clean as a whistle. Ay, I'm thinking the case is weel substantiated. Is it your opeenion, Sir Maxwell, that we should mak' the fact o' the murder public?'

'I hardly know, Sergeant. What do you think yourself? Have you consulted with Inspector Macpherson?'

'Weel, sir, he thinks we maun gie some gude reason for makin' our inquiries ... Ay, we'll best gae cannily aboot it, but there's folk talkin' a'ready aboot the quarrel wi' Waters ... ay, an' wi' Farren ... ay ... ay ... an' there's a story about Strachan bein' over in Creetown the nicht of the crime speirin' after Farren ... I doot we'll no be able to keep the thing hushed up.'

'I see. Well, perhaps we had better let it be known that there is a possibility of foul play – that we are not quite satisfied, and so on. But you'd better not tell anybody what the doctor says about the time of the death. I'll be over presently and have a word with the Fiscal. And meanwhile I'll get the Kirkcudbright police on to making a few inquiries.'

'Ay, sir, 'twill be best for them to sort it their end. I've a report here fra' Stranraer I'll hae to deal wi' masel'. They've detained a young fellow that was boardin' the Larne boat ... ay, weel, I'll ring ye again later, Sir Maxwell.'

The Chief Constable hung up the receiver, and confronted Wimsey with a dour smile.

'It certainly looks as though you were right,' he admitted reluctantly. 'But,' he added, more cheerfully, 'now that they've traced the man at Stranraer, it will probably all be cleared up this morning.'

'Maybe,' said Wimsey, 'but I rather doubt whether the man who fixed that accident up so cleverly would be fool enough to give himself away by making a belated bolt to Ireland. Don't you?'

'That's a fact,' said Jamieson. 'If he'd wanted to escape he could have taken yesterday morning's boat. And if he wanted to play the innocent, he could do it better at home.'

'H'm!' said Wimsey. 'I think, you know, the time has come to talk of many things with Farren and Gowan and Waters – only he's disappeared – and, in fact, with all the good people of Kirkcudbright. A little tactful gossip, Sir Maxwell, by a cheerful, friendly, inquisitive bloke like myself, may do wonders in a crisis. Nothing unusual in my making my morning round of the studios, is there? Nobody minds me. Why, bless you, I've got some of 'em so tame, they'll let me sit round and watch 'em paint. An official personage like you might embarrass them,

51

don't you know, but there's no dignity about me. I'm probably the least awe-inspiring man in Kirkcudbright. I was born looking foolish and every day in every way I am getting foolisher and foolisher. Why, even you, Chief, let me come here and sit round on your official chairs and smoke a pipe and look on me as nothing more than an amiable nuisance – don't you ?'

'There may be something in what you say,' agreed Jamieson, 'but you'll be discreet, mind. There's no need to mention the word murder.'

'None whatever,' said Wimsey. 'I'll let them mention it first. Well, toodle-oo!'

Wimsey may not have been an awe-inspiring person to look at, but his reception at Farren's house did not altogether justify his boast that 'nobody marked him.' The door was opened by Mrs. Farren, who at sight of him, fell back against the wall with a gasp which might have been merely surprise but sounded more like alarm.

'Hullo!' said Wimsey, breezing cheerily over the threshold, 'how are you, Mrs. Farren ? Haven't seen you for an age – well, since Friday night at Bobbie's, but it seems like an age. Is everything bright and blooming ? Where's Farren ?'

Mrs. Farren, looking like a ghost painted by Burne-Jones in one of his most pre-Raphaelite moments, extended a chill hand.

'I'm very well, thank you. Hugh's out. Er – won't you come in ?'

Wimsey, who was already in, received this invitation in his heartiest manner.

'Well – that's very good of you. Sure I'm not in the way ? I expect you're cooking or something, aren't you ?'

Mrs. Farren shook her head and led the way into the little sitting-room with the sea-green and blue draperies and the bowls of orange marigolds.

'Or is it scarves this morning ?' Mrs. Farren wove hand-spun wool in rather attractive patterns. 'I envy you that job, you know. Sort of Lady of Shalott touch about it. The curse is come upon me, and all that sort of thing. You promised one day to let me have a twirl at the wheel.'

'I'm afraid I'm being lazy today,' said Mrs. Farren, with a faint smile. 'I was just – I was only – excuse me one moment.'

She went out, and Wimsey heard her speaking to somebody at the back of the house – the girl, no doubt, who came in to do the rough work. He glanced round the room, and his quick eye noted its curiously forlorn appearance. It was not untidy, exactly; it told no open tale of tumult; but the cushions were crushed, a flower or two here and there was wilted; there was a slight film of dust on the window-sill and on the polished table. In the houses of some of his friends this might have meant mere carelessness and a mind above trifles like dust and disorder, but with Mrs. Farren it was a phenomenon full of meaning. To her, the beauty of an ordered life was more than a mere phrase; it was a dogma to be preached, a cult to be practised with passion and concentration. Wimsey, who was imaginative, saw in those faint traces the witness to a night of suspense, a morning of terror; he remembered the anxious figure at the door, and the man – yes. There had been a man there, too. And Farren was away. And Mrs. Farren was a very beautiful woman, if you liked that style of thing, with her oval face and large grey eyes and those thick masses of copper-coloured hair, parted in the middle and rolled in a great knot on the nape of the neck.

A step passed the window – Jeanie, with a basket on her arm. Mrs. Farren came back and sat down in a high, narrow-backed chair, looking out and past him like a distressed beggar-maid beginning to wonder whether Cophetua was not something of a trial in family life.

'And where,' said Wimsey, with obtuse tactlessness, 'has Farren disappeared to ?'

The large eyes shadowed suddenly with fear or pain.

'He's gone out – somewhere.'

'The gay dog,' said Wimsey. 'Or is he working ?'

'I – don't quite know.' Mrs. Farren laughed. 'You know what this place is. People go off, saying they'll be back to dinner, and then they meet a man, or somebody says the fish are rising somewhere, and that's the last you see of them.'

'I know – it's shameful,' said Wimsey, sympathetically. 'Do you mean he didn't even come home to his grub ?'

'Oh – I was only speaking generally. He was home to dinner all right.'

'And then barged out afterwards, saying he wanted some cigarettes and would be back in ten minutes, I suppose. It's disheartening, isn't it, the way we behave ? I'm a shocking offender myself, though my conscience is fairly easy. After all, Bunter is paid to put up with me. It's not as though I had a devoted wife warming my slippers and looking out of the front-door every five minutes to see if I'm going to turn up.'

Mrs. Farren drew in her breath sharply.

'Yes, it's terrible, isn't it?'

'Terrible. No, I mean it. I do think it's unfair. After all, one never knows what may happen to people. Look at poor Campbell.'

This time there was no doubt about it. Mrs. Farren gave a gasp of terror that was almost a cry; but she recovered herself immediately.

'Oh, Lord Peter, do tell me, what really *has* happened? Jeanie came in with some dreadful story about his being killed. But she gets so excited and talks such broad Scotch that I really couldn't make it out.'

'It's a fact, I'm afraid,' said Wimsey, soberly. 'They found him lying in the Minnoch yesterday afternoon, with his head bashed in.'

'With his head bashed in? You don't mean—'

'Well, it's difficult to say quite how it happened. The river is full of rocks just there, you see—'

'Did he fall in?'

'It looks like it. He was in the water. But he wasn't drowned, the doctor says. It was the blow on the head that did it.'

'How dreadful!'

'I wonder you hadn't heard about it before,' said Wimsey. 'He was a great friend of yours, wasn't he?'

'Well – yes – we knew him very well.' She stopped, and Wimsey thought she was going to faint. He sprang up.

'Look here – I'm afraid this has been too much of a shock for you. Let me get some water.'

'No – no—' She flung out a hand to restrain him, but he had already darted across the passage into the studio, where he remembered to have seen a tap and a sink. The first thing he noticed there was Farren's sketching-box, standing open on the table, the paints scattered about and the palette flung down higgledy-piggledy among them. An old painting-coat hung behind the door, and Wimsey inspected it inside and out with some care, but seemed to find nothing in it worthy of attention. He filled a cup at the tap, with his eyes roving about the room. The studio-easel stood in its place with a half-finished canvas upon it. The small sketching-easel was propped against the sink, strapped up. Farren had not gone out to paint, evidently.

The water, splashing on his hand, reminded him of what he was supposed to be there for. He wiped the cup and turned to leave the studio. As he did so, he caught sight of Farren's fishing-tackle standing in the corner behind the door. Two trout-rods, a salmon-rod, net, gaff, creel and waders. Well, there might be a fourth rod, of course, and one can fish without creel or waders. But, standing there so quietly, the things had a look of settled completeness.

He returned to the sitting-room. Mrs. Farren waved the cup impatiently aside.

'Thank you – I don't need it. I told you I didn't. I'm quite all right.' Her worried and sleepless eyes belied her. Wimsey felt that he was being a brute, but somebody would be asking questions soon enough. As well he as the police, he thought.

'Your husband ought to be here soon,' he said. 'The news will be all over the country by now. It's surprising, really, he hasn't got back already. You don't know at all where he is ?'

'I haven't the faintest idea.'

'I mean, I'd gladly take a message or do anything like that.'

'Why should you ? Thank you all the same. But really, Lord Peter, you talk as though the death were in my family. We knew Mr. Campbell very well, of course, but after all, there's no reason for me to be so prostrated as all that . . . I'm afraid I may sound callous—'

'Not at all. I only thought you looked a bit upset. I'm very glad you're not. Perhaps I misunderstood—'

'Perhaps you did,' she said in an exhausted voice. Then she seemed to gather up her spirits a little, and turned upon him almost eagerly.

'I was sorry for Mr. Campbell. He was a bitterly unpopular man, and he felt that more than people ever realised. He had a perpetual grudge against everybody. That's unattractive. And the more you hate everybody for hating you, the more unattractive you grow and the more they go on hating you. I understood that. I don't like the man. One couldn't. But I tried to be fair. I daresay people did misunderstand. But one can't stop going what's right because people misunderstand, can one ?'

'No,' said Wimsey. 'If you and your husband—'

'Oh,' she said, 'Hugh and I understood one another.'

Wimsey nodded. She was lying, he thought. Farren's objections to Campbell had been notorious. But she was the kind of woman who, if once she set out to radiate sweetness and light, would be obstinate in her mission. He studied the rather full, sulky mouth and narrow, determined forehead. It was the face

55

of a woman who would see only what she wished to see – who would think that one could abolish evils from the world by pretending that they were not there. Such things, for instance, as jealousy or criticism of herself. A dangerous woman, because a stupid woman. Stupid and dangerous, like Desdemona.

'Well, well,' he said lightly. 'Let's hope the truant will turn up soon. He promised to show me some of his stuff. I'm very keen to have a look at it. I daresay I shall meet him as I buzz about the country. On his bike, as usual, I suppose ?'

'Oh, yes, he's got his bicycle with him.'

'I think there are more bicycles per head of the population in Kirkcudbright than in any town I ever struck,' said Wimsey.

'That's because we're all so hardworking and poor.'

'Just so. Nothing is so virtuous as a bicycle. You can't imagine a bicyclist committing a crime, can you ? – except of course, murder or attempted murder.'

'Why murder ?'

'Well, the way they rush about in gangs on the wrong side of the road and never have any brakes or bells or lights. I call it murder, when they nearly have you into the ditch. Or suicide.'

He jumped to his feet with an exclamation of concern. This time Mrs. Farren had really fainted.

GRAHAM

LORD PETER WIMSEY, having rendered first aid to Mrs. Farren, left her comfortably reclining on the couch in the sitting-room and went in search of Jeanie. He discovered her in the fishmonger's and dispatched her home with the tidings that her mistress was unwell.

'Ay,' said Jeanie, philosophically. 'I'm no surprised. She's troubled in her mind aboot Mr. Farren. And nae wonder, wi' him mekkin' a' that disturbance and gaein' aff that gate an' never comin' back for twa nichts.'

'Two nights ?' said Wimsey.

'Ay. Nicht before last it was he went aff on his bicycle,

swearin' somethin' awfu' an' nae ward tae say whaur he was gaein' nor what he was gaein' to du.'

'Then he wasn't at home last night for dinner ?'

'Him ? Hame for's denner ? 'Deed no, nor ony time o' the day. Monday nicht it was he come back an' fund Campbell i' the hoose an' sent him packin', an' after that there was sic a collie-shangie it nigh frighted my brither's wife into a fit an' her verra near her time, tu. An' out he gaes and away, wi' Mistress Farren runnin' oot o' the door after him wi' the tears fallin' doon her cheeks. I dinna ken for why she takes on so aboot the man. I'd let him gae an' be daumed tae him, wi' his jealousies an' his tempers.'

Wimsey began to see why Jeanie had been sent out on an errand in such a hurry. It was foolish, though, for nobody could expect the girl to hold her tongue over so fine a piece of gossip. Sooner or later, the tale would have to come out to somebody. Even now he observed that curious glances were following them down the street.

He asked a few more questions. No. Jeanie's brother's wife could not say exactly what the quarrel was about, but she had witnessed it from her bedroom window. Mr. Campbell had been in about 6 o'clock, and then Mr. Farren had come in and Mr. Campbell had gone away almost immediately. She could not say there had been any dispute between Farren and Campbell. But then Mr. and Mrs. Farren had talked about an hour in the sitting-room and Mr. Farren had walked about the room and waved his hands a great deal, and Mrs. Farren had cried. Then there had been a shouting and a kind of a skelloch, and Mr. Farren had run out of the door cramming his hat over his eyes, and had snatched up his bicycle. And Mrs. Farren had run out to stop him and he had shaken her roughly off and ridden away. Nor had he been home syne, for Jeanie's brother's wife had kept a look-out for him, being interested to see what might happen.

That was Monday and this was Wednesday; and on the Tuesday, Campbell had been found dead up at the Minnoch.

Wimsey said good-bye to Jeanie, with a caution against talking too much about her employer's affairs, and turned in the direction of the police-station. Then he changed his mind. No need to make trouble before it was wanted. There might be other developments. It would not be a bad idea to run over to Gatehouse. There was a question he wanted to ask Mrs. Green who did the charing for Campbell. Also, something might have been found at Campbell's house – letters, papers or what-not. In any case, a wee run in the car would do him no harm.

Passing over the bridge at Gatehouse, with these intentions, he was arrested by the sight of a tall man standing outside the Anwoth Hotel in conference with the local constable. The man, who was very shabbily dressed in an ancient burberry, dilapidated plus-fours, disreputable boots and leggings and a knapsack, waved a hand in violent greeting. Wimsey pulled up with reckless haste, nearly slaying the hotel cat, and waved violently back.

'Hullo – ullo – ullo!' he cried. 'Where d'you spring from, you old ruffian ?'

'That's just what everybody seems anxious to know,' said the untidy man, extending a large, raw-boned hand. 'I don't seem to be allowed to go away on a little private matter without a hue and cry. What's it all about ?'

Wimsey glanced at the constable, who shook his head mysteriously.

'Having received order,' he began, 'to make an inquiry—'

'But you haven't received orders to make a mystery, have you ?' said the untidy man. 'What's the matter ? Am I supposed to have committed a crime ? What is it ? Drunk and disorderly, eh ? or riding a push-bike without a tail-light ? or driving to the public danger, or what ?'

'Weel, now, Mr. Graham, sir – in the matter of the bicycle, I wad be glad to know—'

'Not guilty this time,' said Mr. Graham promptly. 'And in any case borrowing isn't stealing, you know.'

'Have you been borrowing push-bikes ?' asked Wimsey, with interest. 'You shouldn't. It's a bad habit. Push-bikes are the curse of this country. Their centre of gravity is too high, for one thing, and their brakes are never in order.'

'I know,' said Mr. Graham, 'it's shameful. Every bicycle I borrow is worse than the last. I often have to speak quite firmly about it. I nearly broke my neck the other day on young Andy's.'

'Oh!' said the landlord, who had come up during this conversation, 'it's ye, is't, Mr. Graham, that's got the lad's bicycle ? Ye're welcome eneugh tae't. I'm no sayin' the contrary, but the lad's been a bit put out, not knowin' whaur it had disappeared tae.'

'It's gone again, has it ?' said Mr. Graham. 'Well, I tell you it's not me this time. You can tell Andy I'll never borrow his

58

miserable machine again till he has the decency to put it in order. And whoever did take it, God help him, that's all I can say, for he'll probably be found dead in a ditch.'

'That may be, Mr. Graham,' said the constable, 'but I'd be glad if ye wad tell me—'

'Damn it!' said Jock Graham. 'No, I will not tell you where I've been. Why should I?'

'Well, it's like this, old dear,' said Wimsey. 'You may possibly have heard in your mysterious retreat, that Campbell was found dead in a river yesterday afternoon.'

'Campbell? Good Lord! No, I hadn't heard. Well, well, well. I hope his sins are forgiven him. What had he done? Taken too many wee halves and walked over the dock at Kirkcudbright?'

'Well, no. Apparently he had been painting and slipped on the stones and bashed his head in.'

'Bashed his head in? Not drowned, then?'

'No, not drowned.'

'Oh! Well, I always told him he was born to be hanged, but apparently he's got out of it another way. Still, I was right about his not being drowned. Well, poor devil, there's an end of him. I think we'd better go in and have one on the strength of it, don't you? Just a little one to the repose of his soul. He wasn't a man I liked, but I'm sorry in a way to think I'll never pull his leg again. You'll join us, officer?'

'Thank you, sir, but if ye'd kindly—'

'Leave it to me,' murmured Wimsey, jogging the constable's elbow and following Graham into the bar.

'How have you managed not to hear about it, Jock?' he went on, when the drinks had been served. 'Where have you been hiding the last two days?'

'That's telling. You're as inquisitive as our friend here. I've been living a retired life – no scandal – no newspapers. But do tell me about Campbell. When did all this happen?'

'They found the body about two o'clock,' said Wimsey. 'He seems to have been seen alive and painting at five past eleven.'

'They didn't lose much time about it, then. You know. I've often thought that one might have an accident up in the hills about here and be lost for weeks. Still, it's a fairly well-frequented spot up there at the Minnoch – in the fishing season, at any rate. I don't suppose—'

'And how did ye ken, might I ask, sir, that the accident took place up at the Minnoch?'

'How did I— ? Oh-ho! To quote an extremely respectable and primly-dressed woman I once happened to overhear conversing with a friend in Theobald's Road, there's bloody more in it than meets the bloody eye. This anxiety about my whereabouts and this bash on Campbell's head – do I understand, constable, that I am suspected of having bashed the good gentleman and tumbled him into the stream like the outlandish knight in the ballad ?'

'Well, not exactly, sir, but as a matter of routine—'

'I see.'

'Och, now!' exclaimed the landlord, on whom a light had been slowly breaking. 'Ye're not meanin' tae tell as the puir man was murdered ?'

'That's as may be,' said the constable.

'He does mean it,' said Graham. 'I read it in his expressive eye. Here's a nice thing to happen in a quiet country spot.'

'It's a terrible thing,' said the landlord.

'Come now, Jock,' said Wimsey. 'Put us out of our misery. You can see the suspense is telling on us. How *did* you know Campbell was up at the Minnoch ?'

'Telepathy,' said Graham, with a wide grin. 'I look into your minds and the picture comes before me – the burn full of sharp stones – the steep slope of granite leading down to it – the brig – the trees and the dark pool under them – and I say, "The Minnoch, by Jove!" Perfectly simple, Watson.'

'I didn't know you were a thought-reader.'

'It's a suspicious circumstance, isn't it ? As a matter of fact, I'm not. I knew Campbell was going to be up at the Minnoch yesterday because he told me so.'

'He told you so ?'

'Told me so. Yes, why not ? I did sometimes speak to Campbell without throwing boots at him, you know. He told me on Monday that he was going up the next day to paint the bridge. Sketched it out for me, grunting all the time – you know his way.'

Graham pulled a piece of chalk from his pocket and set to work on the bar counter, his face screwed up into a life-like imitation of Campbell's heavy jowl and puffed lips, and his hand roughing in outlines with Campbell's quick, tricky touch. The picture came up before their eyes with the conjuring quickness of a lightning-sketch at the cinema – the burn, the trees, the bridge and a mass of bulging white cloud, so like the actual

60

canvas Wimsey had seen on the easel that he was thoroughly startled.

'You ought to be making a living by impersonations, Jock.'

'That's my trouble. Too versatile. Paint in everybody's style except my own. Worries the critics. "Mr. Graham is still fumbling for an individual style" – that kind of thing. But it's fun. Look, here's Gowan.'

He rubbed out the sketch and substituted a vivid chalk impression of one of Gowan's characteristic compositions – a grim border-keep, a wide sweep of coast, a boat in the foreground, with muscular fishermen bending over their nets.

'Here's Ferguson – one tree with decorative roots, one reflection of same in water – dim blue distance; in fact, general blues all over – one heap of stones to hold the composition up. Here's Farren – view of the roofs of Kirkcudbright complete with Tolbooth, looking like Noah's Ark built out of nursery bricks – vermilion, Naples yellow, ultramarine – sophisticated *naïveté* and no cast shadows. Waters – "none of these charlatans take the trouble to draw" – bird's-eye view of a stone-quarry with every bump identifiable – horse and cart violently foreshortened at the bottom, to show that he can do it. Bless you' – he slopped some beer on the counter and wiped the mess away with a ragged sleeve – 'the whole bunch of them have only got one gift between them that I lack, and that's the single eye, more's the pity. They're perfectly sincere, I'm not – that's what makes the difference. I tell you, Wimsey, half those damned portraits people pay me for are caricatures – only the fools don't know it. If they did, they'd rather die than sign the cheques.'

Wimsey laughed. If Graham was playing for time, he was doing it well. If he was trying to avert suspicion from his dangerous gift of imitation, his air of careless frankness could not possibly be better done. And his explanation was plausible enough—why, indeed, should Campbell not have mentioned where he was going – to Graham or to anyone?

The constable was registering impatience.

'As a matter of routine,' he murmured.

'Oh!' said Mr. Graham. 'This lad's one of the bulldog breed.'

'Obviously,' said Wimsey, 'like St. Gengulphus. They cried out, "Good gracious! How very tenacious!" It's no good old man. He means to have his answer.'

'Poor fellow!' said Graham. 'Want must be his master, as

61

nurses said in the good old days before Montessori was heard of. I was not up at the Minnoch. But where I was is my affair.'

'Weel, sir,' said the constable, nonplussed. Between the Judges' Rules, the Royal Commission, his natural disinclination to believe anything wrong about Mr. Graham, and his anxiety to pull off a coup, he felt his position to be a difficult one.

'Run along, laddie,' said Graham, kindly. 'You're only wasting your time. You've only to look at me to know I wouldn't hurt a fly. For all you know, the murderer's escaping while you and I exchange merry quips over a pint of bitter.'

'I understand,' said the constable, 'that ye refuse cateegoorically tae state whaur ye were on last Monday nicht.'

'Got it at last!' cried Graham. 'We're slow but sure in this country, Wimsey. That's right. I refuse categorically, absolutely, *in toto* and entirely. Make a note of it in case you forget it.'

The constable did so with great solemnity.

'Ah, weel,' he said, 'I'll hae tae be reportin' this tae the authorities.'

'Right,' said Graham. 'I'll have a word with them.'

The constable shook his head doubtfully and departed with slow reluctance.

'Poor devil,' said Graham. 'It's a shame to tease him. Have another, Wimsey?'

Wimsey declined, and Graham took himself off rather abruptly, saying that he must go down and see to things at his studio.

The landlord of the Anwoth followed him with his eyes.

'What's behind that?' said Wimsey, carelessly.

'Och, it will be some tale or anither,' replied the landlord. 'He's a perfect gentleman, is Graham, and a great lad for the leddies.'

'Quite so,' said Wimsey. 'And that reminds me, Rob, I've got a new limerick for you.'

'Have ye noo?' said the landlord, and carefully closed the door between the inn-parlour and the bar.

Having delivered himself of his limerick and taken his leave, Wimsey turned his attention again to business. Mrs. Green, the charwoman, lived in a small cottage at no great distance. She was making bannocks when Wimsey arrived, but having dusted the flour from her hands and transferred the bannocks to the girdle, was willing enough to talk about the sudden death of her gentleman.

Her Scots was broad and her manner excitable, but after putting his questions two or three times, Wimsey succeeded in understanding her replies.

'Did Mr. Campbell take any breakfast before he went out on Monday morning ?'

Yes, he did. There had been the remains of some bacon and eggs on the table and a used teapot and cup. Forbye, the loaf and butter had diminished, by comparison with the previous night, and there had been slices cut from the ham.

'Was that Mr. Campbell's usual breakfast ?'

Ay, fried eggs and bacon were his breakfast, as regular as clockwork. Two eggs and two rashers, and that was what he had taken that morning, for Mrs. Green had counted.

'Did Mr. Ferguson eat his breakfast that morning also ?'

Yes, Mr. Ferguson had taken a kipper with a cup of coffee. Mrs. Green had herself brought in a pair of kippers for him on Saturday, and he had had the one on Sunday morning and the other on Monday morning. There had been nothing unusual about either cottage, that she could see, and so she had told the policeman when he called upon her.

Wimsey turned these matters over in his mind as he ran back to Kirkcudbright. The doctor's report made those two eggs and rashers a suspicious circumstance. Somebody had breakfasted in Campbell's cottage, and the person who could do that most easily was Ferguson. Alternatively, if it was not Ferguson, Ferguson might have seen whoever it was. Tiresome of Ferguson to have gone off to Glasgow like that.

As for Graham, apparently he had not been at Glen Trool. His silence might have half a dozen different explanations. 'The leddies' was the most obvious; it would be well, in Graham's own interests, to discover whether he had any local attachment. Or he might merely have discovered some remote river, rich in trout which he wished to keep to himself. Or he might just be doing it to annoy. One could not tell. Beneath all his surface eccentricity, Graham was a man who kept his wits about him. Still, in a country place, where everybody knows everybody, it is impossible to keep one's movements altogether secret. Somebody would have seen Graham – that is, if somebody chose to speak. But that was as doubtful as everything else about the case, for your country-dweller is a master of pregnant silences.

Wimsey called at Sir Maxwell Jamieson's to make his report about the eggs and bacon, which was received with an 'Ay, imph'm' of the driest kind. There had been no further news from Dalziel, and he went home, first calling across the way, only to ascertain that Waters had not yet returned.

Bunter received him with a respectful welcome, but appeared to have something preying on his mind. On inquiry, however, this turned out to be merely the discovery that the Scots were so lost to all sense of propriety as to call a dish an 'ashet' – obviously with the deliberate intention of confusing foreigners and making them feel like bulls in china-shops.

Wimsey sympathised and, to take Bunter's mind off this mortifying experience, mentioned his meeting with Jock Graham.

'Indeed, my lord ? I was already apprised of Mr. Graham's reappearance. I understand, my lord, that he was in Creetown on Monday night.'

'Was he, by Jove ? How do you know ?'

Bunter coughed.

'After the interview with the young person at the china-shop, my lord, I stepped for a few moments into the McClellan Arms. Not into the public bar, my lord, but into the bar-parlour adjacent. While there, I accidentally overheard some persons mention the circumstance in the bar.'

'What sort of persons ?'

'Roughly dressed persons, my lord. I apprehend that they might have been engaged in the fishing-trade.'

'Was that all they said ?'

'Yes, my lord. One of them unfortunately glanced into the bar-parlour and discovered my presence, and after that they said nothing further about the matter.'

'Who were they, do you know ?'

'I endeavoured to ascertain from the landlord, but he said no more than that they were a bunch of lads from the harbour.'

'Oh! And that's all you will ever hear, I expect. H'm. Did you manage to see any of them ?'

'Only the one who looked in at the door, and him only for a brief interval. The rest had their backs to the bar door when I emerged, my lord, and I did not care to appear inquisitive.'

'No. Well – Creetown is on the way to Newton-Stewart, but it's a far cry from there to the Minnoch. Did they mention the time at which they saw Mr. Graham ?'

'No, my lord, but, from the circumstance that they alluded

64

to the number of drinks he consumed, I apprehend that it would be before closing-time.'

'Ah!' said Wimsey. 'An inquiry among the Creetown pubs might settle that. Very well, Bunter. I think I shall go out and clear my wits with a round of golf this afternoon. And I'll have a grilled steak and chips at 7.30.'

'Very good, my lord.'

Wimsey had his round of golf with the Provost, but without much satisfaction beyond that of beating him five up and three to play. He deduced from this victory that the Provost was not altogether easy in his mind, but he failed altogether to draw him on the subject of Campbell. It was 'an unfortunate occurrence,' and the Provost thought that 'it might be a wee while before they got to the bottom of it' – and after that the conversation was firmly led away to the quoiting match at Gatehouse, the recent regatta at Kirkcudbright, the shortage of salmon and depredations of poachers in the estuary, and the problems of sewage-distribution in tidal waters.

At half-past nine, when Wimsey had absorbed his grilled steak and rhubarb tart, and was dreaming over some old numbers of *The Gallovidian*, he was aroused by a clatter of feet upon the cobblestones of the close. He was just rising to look out of the window, when there was a knock upon the door, and a cheerful female voice called: 'May we come in ?'

Miss Selby and Miss Cochran occupied adjacent cottages and were continually to be found taking tea in each other's living-rooms or bathing together on the sands at the Doon. Miss Selby was tall, dark, rather angular, rather handsome in an uncompromising kind of way and painted rather good, strong, angular and handsome figure-studies in oils. Miss Cochran was round, cheerful, humorous and grey-haired; she illustrated magazine stories in line and wash. Wimsey liked them both, because they had no nonsense about them, and they liked him for the same reason, and also because they found Bunter extremely amusing. Bunter was always distressed to see them cooking their own dinners and putting up their own curtains. He would step reproachfully to their assistance, and take the hammer and nails from their hands, with a respectful, 'Allow me, miss'; and would obligingly offer to look after stews and casseroles during their absence. They rewarded him with gifts of vegetables and flowers from their garden – gifts which Bunter would receive with

65

a respectful, 'Thank you, miss. His lordship will be greatly obliged.' While Wimsey was greeting his visitors, Bunter now advanced unobtrusively and inquired, as soon as there was a pause in the conversation, whether the ladies would take supper after their journey.

The ladies replied that they were quite well-fed, but a little investigation showed that they had indeed had nothing since tea-time except a few sandwiches on the train. Wimsey promptly ordered omelettes, a bottle of claret and the remains of the rhubarb-tart to be brought forward, and, when Bunter had withdrawn to prepare the feast, said:

'Well, you've missed all the excitement.'

'So they told us at the station,' said Miss Cochran. 'What is it all about ? Is it true that Mr. Campbell is dead ?'

'Quite true. He was found in the river—'

'And now they're saying he's been murdered,' put in Miss Selby.

'Oh, they're saying that, are they ? Well, that's true, too.'

'Good gracious!' said Miss Selby.

'And who is it they're saying has done it ?' demanded Miss Cochran.

'They don't know yet,' said Wimsey, 'but there's a kind of an idea that it was a premeditated job.'

'Oh, why ?' asked Miss Cochran, bluntly.

'Oh, well, because the symptoms point that way, you know, and there doesn't seem to have been any robbery from the person, or anything – and – in fact, several things.'

'And in fact you know more than you think you ought to tell us. Well, it's fortunate we've got an alibi, isn't it, Margaret ? We've been in Glasgow ever since yesterday morning. It was on Tuesday it happened, wasn't it ?'

'It seems so,' said Wimsey, 'but just to make sure, they are checking up everybody's whereabouts from Monday night onwards.'

'Who's everybody ?'

'Well – the people who knew Campbell best, and so on.'

'I see. Well, you know we were here on Monday night, because we said good-night to you when you came in, and we went off by the 8.45 yesterday morning and we've got any amount of witnesses to show that we were in Glasgow between then and now, so I imagine we're all right. Besides it would have taken

66

more powerful people than Mary or me to tackle Mr. Campbell. What a relief to know that we can't possibly be suspected!'

'No – you two and Waters are out of the running all right, I fancy.'

'Oh ? Where was Mr. Waters ?'

'Wasn't he with you ?'

'With us ?'

They stared at one another. Wimsey apologised.

'I'm sorry. Mrs. Doings – his landlady, what's her name ? – told me Waters had gone with you two to Glasgow.'

'She must have got hold of the wrong end of the stick. He said on Sunday evening at Bob Anderson's that he might possibly turn up, but he didn't, so we thought he'd changed his mind. Anyhow, we didn't really expect him, did we, Mary ?'

'No. But isn't he here then, Lord Peter ?'

'Well, as a matter of fact, he's not,' said Wimsey, aghast.

'Oh, well, he must be somewhere,' said Miss Cochran comfortably.

'Naturally,' said Wimsey, 'but he certainly went off at about 8.30 yesterday morning, saying he was going to Glasgow. Or at least, he seems to have left that impression behind him.'

'Well, he certainly never came to the station,' said Miss Selby, decidedly. 'And he wasn't at the show either day, that I could see. But of course he may have had other fish to fry.'

Wimsey scratched his head.

'I must interview that woman again,' he said. 'I must have misunderstood her. But it's exceedingly odd. Why should he get up and go out early if he wasn't going to Glasgow ? Especially—'

'Especially what ?' said Miss Cochran.

'Well, I shouldn't have expected it,' said Wimsey. 'He was a bit lit-up the night before, and as a rule it takes a lot to get Waters out of bed at the best of times. It's rather unfortunate. Still, we can't do much till he turns up.'

'We ?' said Miss Selby.

'The police, I mean,' said Wimsey, blushing a little.

'You'll be helping the police, I expect,' said Miss Cochran. 'I was forgetting that you had such a reputation as a Sherlock. I'm sorry we don't seem able to help. You'd better ask Mr. Ferguson. He may have run across Mr. Waters somewhere in Glasgow.'

'Oh, Ferguson was there, was he ?'

Wimsey put his question carelessly, but not so carelessly as to deceive Miss Cochran, who darted a shrewd glance at him.

'Yes. He was there. I believe we can give ye the precise time we saw him.' (As Miss Cochran became more emphatic, she became more Scottish in her accent. She planted her plump feet squarely on the ground and leaned forward with a hand on each knee, like an argumentative workman in a tram.) 'That train of ours gets in at 2.16 – it's a bad train, stops at every station, and we'd have done better to wait and take the 1.46 at Dumfries, only we wanted to meet Margaret's sister Kathleen and her husband and they were away to England by the 4 o'clock train. They came to the station to meet us, and we went into the hotel and had a bit of lunch, for we hadn't had anything since 8 o'clock – there's none served on that train – and the hotel was as good a place as any to have our bit of talk in. We saw them off at 4 o'clock, and then we had a little argument whether we should go straight on to my cousin's where we were staying, or look in at the Gallery first. I said it was too late to do anything, but Margaret said it would be a good idea just to go down and see where they'd hung the different things, and then to come back next day and have our proper look at them; and I agreed that was a sensible notion. So we took the tram and we got into the Exhibition just about half-past four, or a few minutes earlier, and in the first room, whom should we see but Mr. Ferguson, just coming away. So of course we spoke to him and he said he'd been through the rooms pretty thoroughly once and was coming back next day. However, he went round once again with us.'

Wimsey, who had been trying to hold the whole local time-table in his head and was hurriedly calculating arrivals and departures, broke in at this point.

'I suppose he really *had* been through the place already ?'

'Oh, yes. He told us beforehand where everything was, and mentioned the ones he liked. He'd come in on the same train as we did – only I suppose he would go straight up to the Exhibition.'

'On your train – the 2.16. Yes, of course, he would join it at Dumfries. It leaves there at 11.22, doesn't it ? Yes, that's right. Did you see him at Dumfries ?'

'No, but that doesn't mean he wasn't there. He'd travel smoking, anyway, and we made for a nice, old-fashioned Ladies' Compartment, not being great smokers in confined spaces. Anyhow, he saw us at Glasgow if we didn't see him, because the

68

first thing he said when we met him was, "I saw you at the station, but you didn't see me. Was that Kathleen and her good man with you?" And then he mentioned that he had been in the same train.'

'Pretty good,' said Wimsey. 'Well, as you say, we'll have to see Ferguson — I mean, the police will have to see him.'

Miss Cochran shook her head.

'You can't deceive me,' she said. 'You're in it up to the eyes. If the truth were told, I dare say you did it yourself.'

'No,' said Wimsey. 'This is about the only murder I couldn't possibly have committed. I haven't the technical skill.'

GOWAN

INSPECTOR MACPHERSON of Kirkcudbright was one of those painstaking and unimaginative people for whom no hypothesis is too far-fetched to be investigated. He liked material clues. He paid no attention to such a trivial consideration as psychological improbability. The Chief Constable had put before him the ascertained facts about Campbell's death, and he saw that they pointed to the guilt of some artist or other. He liked them. The medical evidence was what he liked best; good, solid, meaty stuff about rigor and the alimentary canal. The business about trains and time-tables pleased him too; it lent itself to being set out in tabular form and verified. The bit about the picture was less satisfactory: it depended on technical matters which he did not personally understand, but he was open-minded enough to accept expert opinion on such matters. He would, for instance, have taken his Cousin Tom's advice on electricity or his sister Alison's opinion about ladies' underwear, and he was not unprepared to admit that a gentleman like Wimsey might know more than he did about artists and their paraphernalia.

Accordingly, he perceived that all artists were, for his purpose, suspect, no matter how rich, respectable or mild-mannered they might be, and whether they were known to have quarrelled with Campbell or not. Kirkcudbright was his district, and his job was to collect alibis and information from every artist in

Kirkcudbright, young or old, male or female, virtuous or wicked, indiscriminately. He went about the thing in a conscientious manner, not omitting Marcus McDonald, who was bedridden, or Mrs. Helen Chambers, who had only just settled in Kirkcudbright, or old John Peterson, who was ninety-two, or Walter Flanagan, who had returned from the Great War with an artificial leg. He noted the absence of Waters and Farren, though he did not get as much out of Mr. Farren as Lord Peter had done; and during the afternoon he presented himself at Mr. Gowan's front-door, notebook in hand and rectitude upon his brow. He had left Gowan to the last, because it was well-known that Mr. Gowan worked in the mornings and resented interruptions before lunch, and Inspector Macpherson had no notion of making difficulties for himself.

The English butler opened the door, and in reply to the Inspector's inquiry, remarked briefly:

'Mr. Gowan is not at home.'

The Inspector explained that his business was official, and again requested an interview with Mr. Gowan.

The butler replied loftily.

'Mr. Gowan is h'out.'

The Inspector begged to know when Mr. Gowan would be in again.

The butler condescended to explain further.

'Mr. Gowan is away.'

To the Scottish mind, this expression has not the same finality that it has to the English mind. The Inspector asked whether Mr. Gowan would be back that evening.

The butler, driven to be explicit, announced imperturbably:

'Mr. Gowan has gone to London.'

'Is that so?' said the Inspector, annoyed with himself for having put off his visit for so long. 'When did he go?'

The butler appeared to think this catechism ill-bred, but nevertheless replied:

'Mr. Gowan left for London on Monday night.'

The Inspector was startled.

'At what time on Monday night?'

The butler appeared to undergo a severe internal struggle, but answered, with great self-control:

'Mr. Gowan took the h'eight forty-five train from Dumfries.'

The Inspector thought for a moment. If this was true, it left Gowan out altogether. But it must, of course, be verified.

'I think,' he said, 'that I had best step in for a moment.'

The butler appeared to hesitate, but, seeing that a number of inhabitants from the close opposite had come out to stare at the Inspector and himself, he graciously gave way and let Macpherson into the handsome panelled entrance-hall.

'I am investigatin',' said the Inspector, 'this maitter o' the death o' Mr. Campbell.'

The butler bowed his head silently.

'I will tell ye, wi'oot circumlocution, that there is mair than a suspeecion that the puir gentleman was murdered.'

'So,' said the butler, 'I h'understand.'

'It is important, ye ken,' went on Macpherson, 'that we should get all possible information from those that saw Mr. Campbell of late.'

'Quite so.'

'And as a matter of routine, ye understand, that we should ken whaur everybody was at the time the calamity occurred.'

'Exactly,' said the butler.

'Nae doot,' pursued the Inspector, 'if Mr. Gowan were at hame, he wad be anxious tae gie us a' the assistance in his power.'

The butler was sure that Mr. Gowan would be only too happy to do so.

The Inspector opened his notebook.

'Your name is Halcock, is't no ?' he began.

The butler corrected him.

'H'alcock,' he said, reprovingly.

'H, a, double-l ?' suggested the Inspector.

'There is no h'aitch in the name, young man H'ay is the first letter, and there is h'only one h'ell.'

'I beg your pardon,' said the Inspector.

'Granted,' said Mr. Alcock.

'Well, noo, Mr. Alcock, juist as a pure formality, ye understand, whit time did Mr. Gowan leave Kirkcudbright on Monday night ?'

'It would be shortly after h'eight.'

'Whae drove him ?'

'Hammond, the chauffeur.'

'Ammond ?' said the Inspector.

'Hammond,' said the butler, with dignity. 'H'albert Hammond is his name – with a h'aitch.'

'I beg your pardon,' said the Inspector.

'Granted,' said Mr. Alcock. 'Perhaps you would wish to speak to Hammond ?'

'Presently,' said the Inspector. 'Can you tell me whether Mr. Gowan had seen Mr. Campbell at a' on the Monday ?'

'I could not undertake to say.'

'Mr. Gowan was friendly with Mr. Campbell ?'

'I could not undertake to say.'

'Has Mr. Campbell visited at the house recently ?'

'Mr. Campbell has never visited this house to my knowledge.'

'Indeed ? Imph'm.' The Inspector knew as well as Mr. Alcock that Gowan held himself very much aloof from the rest of the artistic population, and seldom invited anybody except for a stately bridge-party now and again, but he felt it his duty to put these questions officially. He ploughed on conscientiously.

'Noo, I'm only juist checkin' up on this maitter, ye ken, wi' a' Mr. Campbell's acquaintances. Can ye tell me what Mr. Gowan did on the Monday ?'

'Mr. Gowan rose at 9 o'clock according to custom and breakfasted at 9.30. He then took a turn in the garden and retired to his studio in the customary manner. He partook of luncheon at the usual time, 1.30. H'after luncheon, he was again engaged on his h'artistic pursuits till 4 o'clock, when tea was served in the library.'

The butler paused.

'Ay ?' said the Inspector, encouragingly.

'H'after tea,' went on the butler, more slowly, 'he went out for a run in the two-seater.'

'Did Hammond drive him ?'

'No. When Mr. Gowan takes the two-seater, he is accustomed to drive himself.'

'Ah ? Ay. Whaur did he go ?'

'I could not undertake to say.'

'Weel, when did he return ?'

'About 7 o'clock.'

'And then ?'

'Mr. Gowan then made the h'observation that he had decided to go to town that night.'

'Had he said anything aboot that airlier ?'

'No. Mr. Gowan is in the habit of making occasional journeys to town.'

'Without previous notice ?'

The butler bowed.

'It didna strike ye as unusual in any way ?'

'Certainly not.'

'Ay, imph'm. Did he dine before leaving ?'

'No. I understood Mr. Gowan to say that he would be dining on the train.'

'On the train ? Ye say he took the 8.45 from Dumfries ?'

'So I was given to understand.'

'But, man, are ye no aware that the 8.45 disna mak' ony connection wi' London ? It arrives in Carlisle at 9.59, which is verra late tae get dinner, and after that there's nae train tae London till five meenuts past twelve. Wherefore did he no tak his dinner here an' catch the 11.8 at Dumfries ?'

'I could not undertake to say. Mr. Gowan did not h'inform me. Possibly Mr. Gowan had some business to transact at Carlisle.'

The Inspector gazed at Mr. Alcock's large, white, imperturbable face, and said:

'Ay, that may be. Did Mr. Gowan say how long he would be away ?'

'Mr. Gowan mentioned that he might be h'absent for a week or ten days.'

'Did he give you any address ?'

'He desired that letters should be forwarded to his club.'

'And that is ?'

'The Mahlstick, in Piccadilly.'

The Inspector made a note of the address, and added:

'Have ye heard from Mr. Gowan since his departure ?'

The butler raised his eyebrows.

'No.' He paused, and then went on less frigidly. 'Mr. Gowan would not write unless he had occasion to mention any special h'instructions.'

'Ay, that's so. Then so far as ye ken, Mr. Gowan is at this moment in London.'

'For all I know to the contrary, he is.'

'Imph'm. Weel, noo — I wad like tae speak a word wi' Hammond.'

'Very good.' Mr. Alcock rang the bell, which was answered by a young and rather pretty maid.

'Betty,' said Mr. Alcock, 'h'inform Hammond that his presence is required by the H'Inspector.'

'Juist a moment,' said Macpherson. 'Betty, ma lass, whit time did Mr. Gowan leave here o' Monday nicht ?'

'Aboot 8 o'clock, sir,' said the girl, quickly, with a little glance at the butler.

'Did he dine before he went ?'

'I – I canna juist charge ma memory, sir.'

'Come, my girl,' said Mr. Alcock, magisterially, 'surely you can remember that. There's nothing to be frightened about.'

'No-n-no, Mr. Alcock.'

'No,' said Mr. Alcock. 'You are quite sure about that. Mr. Gowan did not dine at home on Monday ?'

'No.'

Mr. Alcock nodded.

'Then run and give Hammond my message – unless the Inspector wants to ask you anything further ?'

'No,' said Macpherson.

'Has – onything happened ?' asked Betty, tremulously.

'Nothing whatever, nothing whatever,' replied the butler. 'The Inspector is just making some routine inquiries, as I understand. And, Betty, just you give that message to Hammond and come straight back. No stopping and chattering. The Inspector has his work to get through same as you and me.'

'Yes – I mean, no, Mr. Alcock.'

'A good girl,' said the butler, as Betty ran out, 'but slow in the uptake, if you understand me.'

'Imph'm,' said Inspector Macpherson.

Hammond, the chauffeur, was a small, perky man, mongrel in speech, but betraying a strong streak of the fundamental cockney. The Inspector reeled off his preliminary speech about routine inquiries, and then came to the point.

'Did ye drive Mr. Gowan onywhere on Monday last ?'

'That's right. Drove 'im ter Dumfries.'

'What time ?'

'Eight o'clock for the 8.45.'

'In the two-seater ?'

'Naow, in the saloon.'

'What time did Mr. Gowan come in wi' the two-seater ?'

''Baht a quarter past seven, might be earlier, might be later. I was 'avin' me supper at 'alf-past seven, and the Riley was in the garridge w'en I come back there.'

'Did Mr. Gowan tak ony luggage wi' him ?'

'Bit of a bag, like. One 'er they 'tashy cases – 'baht so long.'

He indicated a spread of about two feet.

'Ay, imph'm. Did ye see him get into the train ?'

74

'Naow. 'E walked into the station and told me ter cut along 'ome.'

'What time was that ?'

'Eight thirty-five as near as makes no difference.'

'And ye cam' straight back tae Kirkcudbright ?'

'Sure thing. Naow. Wait a mo. I brought a parcel o' stuff back with me.'

'Ay ? An' whit stuff wad that be ?'

'Two pictures of Mr. Gowan's, what belonged to a gentleman in Dumfries. The boss didn't want 'em sent by train, so I picked 'em up at the house. They was all done up waitin' to be collected.'

'Ye went tae this hoose after ye had left Mr. Gowan at the station ?'

'That's right. Gentleman name of Phillips. Want 'is address?'

'Ay – ye may as weel gie't me.'

The chauffeur gave it.

'Did Mr. Gowan mek ony mention o' whaur he was gaein' ?'

''E only said 'e wanted ter catch the train for Carlisle.'

'Carlisle ?'

'That's right.'

'He didna say for London ?'

'Not ter me. Train for Carlisle, 'e says.'

'Ay – and when did he first gi' ye the order ?'

'Mr. Alcock comes down w'en I was 'aving me supper, and says Mr. Gowan wanted the saloon round at 8 o'clock ter tike 'im ter Dumfries. And I says, "Right-oh!" I says, "an' I can pick up them there pitchers at the same time." That's what I says and that's what I done.'

'Ay, verra guid. That's quite clear. Thank you, Mr. Hammond. This is naething at a', ye understand, but juist a simple formality.'

'Thet's all right. Finni ?'

'What's that ?'

'I says, finni ? meaning, is that O.K. ? complete ? 'ave yer done ?'

'Oo, ay, there's nae mair wantin' from ye at the moment.'

'Well, cheerio, then,' said the chauffeur.

'Did you wish to see Mrs. Alcock ?' inquired the butler, politely, but with the air of one prepared to endure all things.

'Oh, no – I'm thinkin' it'll no be necessary. Thank ye verra much, Mr. Alcock.'

'Don't mention it,' said the butler. 'I trust that you will soon have the miscreant by the heels. Very happy to have been of use, I am sure. There are two steps h'up to the front door. A beautiful h'evening, is it not ? Reelly, the sky is quite a poem. Good h'evening, Inspector.'

'A' the same,' said the Inspector to himself, 'it'll no be amiss tae make inquiries at Dumfries. They'll no have forgotten Gowan, wi' his big black beard. It's a queer thing he should suddenly be wantin' tae spend two-three hours in Carlisle waitin' for a train tae London. He micht verra weel ha' hired anither car tae fetch him hame.'

He considered a little, as he wandered thoughtfully towards the police-station.

'Forbye,' he continued, 'yon lassie didna seem juist sae ready wi' her replies as they twa.'

He pushed back his cap and scratched his head.

'Nae maitter,' said he, cheerfully. 'I'll sort it yet.'

MRS. MACLEOD

THINGS were lively in the Close that night. Wimsey had escorted his visitors to their doors, and was thinking of turning in, when the sudden opening of the blue gate and the cries of a fellow-creature entangled and in pain urged him to go to the assistance of the Chief Constable, who had become involved with the bicycles in the narrow passage.

'I don't mind telling you,' said Sir Maxwell, when at length he was safely seated in Wimsey's armchair and comforted with Scotch, 'that I am greatly disturbed about all this business. If I could see any clear line to follow up, it would be more satisfactory. Even supposing that your list of suspects comprises the whole of the possibilities (which at present, mark you, I am not disposed to grant) – even then, I simply do not know where to start an inquiry. That one or two of them should have no good alibis is only what one might expect – but that practically all of them should be open to suspicion really bewilders me.'

'Dear me!' said Wimsey.

'Graham and Strachan,' went on the Chief Constable, 'were both out all night, as you know, and have no explanations. Ferguson appears, from what you say, to be all right, but he has not been interrogated yet, and really, after today's experiences, I am beginning to doubt whether anybody's movements will bear investigation. Farren's disappearance is so suspicious that, if it were not for the extraordinary behaviour of the rest, I should get out a warrant for him straight away. Gowan —'

'Surely not Gowan, too ?'

'Gowan has gone to England, and there are points in Inspector Macpherson's report—'

'I haven't heard that yet.'

'No.' The Chief Constable gave the gist of the Inspector's interview with the servants, and resumed:

'There are undoubtedly points there that need looking into. And now comes a most infernal business about Waters.'

'Unbosom yourself,' said Wimsey. 'Trouble shared is trouble halved.'

'Well,' said Sir Maxwell, 'when Waters didn't turn up today with the ladies yonder, Inspector Macpherson made a few inquiries of Mrs. McLeod, who seems to have misled you – though, I think and hope, unintentionally. And these inquiries brought to light a very remarkable circumstance.

'Apparently Waters did ask to be called early on the Tuesday morning and did make the remark that he rather thought of going to Glasgow. On the Monday night, Mrs. McLeod heard him come in with you and go up to bed. Then you went out again. She puts this at about 10.30. Is that right ?'

'Meaning, did I leave about 10.30 ? Yes, that's near enough.'

'Well, then, some time between 11 and midnight, Mrs. McLeod heard somebody throwing pebbles at Waters' bedroom window. Her room is next but one to his, and they both look out on the High Street. She looked out, and saw a man down below. She couldn't make him out very well, but he seemed to be shortish and broad, well wrapped up in an overcoat and muffler. She was just going to shout down and tell him to shut up, when Waters' window opened, and she heard Waters say angrily:

'What the devil do you want ?'

'The man in the street said something which she did not catch, and then Waters said:

'"Well, don't make that blasted row. I'm coming down."

'She then leaned out a little further and saw a four-seater car standing a few yards down the street. Waters came down presently in some sort of outdoor togs – a sweater and trousers – she thinks – and he and the man went into Water's sitting-room. They talked there for a bit, and Mrs. McLeod went back to bed. Presently she heard somebody run up to Waters' bedroom and down again, and the front door was opened and shut. Mrs. McLeod looked out once more, and saw both men climb into the car and move off. In about three-quarters of an hour – being thoroughly wakened up by that time – she heard the door open softly again, and footsteps tiptoeing up the stairs into Waters' bedroom.

'Nothing more happened after that, and at 7.30 she knocked on Waters' door as arranged, with his shaving-water, and at 8 o'clock she put his breakfast in the sitting-room. She then went out to the back of the house to do some household work, and at 8.20, when she came in again, Waters had eaten a sketchy sort of breakfast and gone.

'Now, there are two more interesting points. First of all, Waters went – ostensibly to see an exhibition in Glasgow – in an old sweater, a pair of grey flannel bags, tennis-shoes and an old burberry. And secondly, he took his bicycle with him.'

'What ?' cried Wimsey.

'He took his bicycle with him. Or rather, to be accurate, his bicycle, which stands just inside the front door, was there on the Monday night and was gone at 8.20. The presumption is that Waters took it.'

'Good Lord!'

'What do you make of that ?' demanded the Chief Constable.

'What you want me to make of it,' said Wimsey, slowly, 'is that the man in the street was Campbell, come back to finish out his row with Waters. That they went off together to fight it out. That in the row, Campbell got his head bashed in. That Waters then concealed the body somewhere. Then he came home, in order to look as ordinary as possible. That he then thought out a plan of concealment, and that next morning he went off at the time previously appointed, put the body and the bicycle in Campbell's car, and hared off to the Minnoch to fake the accident.'

'Can you make anything else of it ?'

'I *might* make fifty things,' said Wimsey, 'but – not to practise

78

any mean concealment – I will admit that the circumstances seem to fit the crime. Except, perhaps, for one point.'

'Yes, I thought of that. What did he do with the body between midnight and 8 a.m.?'

'No,' said Wimsey. 'No – I see no difficulty about that. All he had to do was to put the body in the car and run it along to his studio. There is plenty of open space there where people stand cars and carts, and nobody would take any notice of an old car with junk in it, covered with a rug. It's not as if he'd left it in Piccadilly Circus. People leave cars in the street all night in this place, and nobody bothers. No, that's not what's puzzling me.'

'Well?'

'Well! If all that is true, where is Waters? He ought to have been here yesterday, blatantly establishing his entire innocence. What's the good of concocting an elaborate fake like that, and then drawing suspicion on yourself by running away?'

'Perhaps he got cold feet when he'd done it. Anyhow, your objection applies to them all, except Strachan and possibly Ferguson.'

'That's true. Well, Chief, I think you'll have to send out the hue and cry after Waters.'

'I suppose I shall. Will this mean Scotland Yard, do you suppose?'

'Well, you'll have to get help in tracing these people all over the country. They may be anywhere. But I'm still inclined to think that it's a case where local knowledge can make the running best. But I'm not in a position to pronounce, don't you know.'

'Of course, I'd rather we could work it ourselves. Macpherson is a good man and so is Dalziel.'

'That reminds me,' said Wimsey, 'how about the young man they detained at Stranraer?'

Sir Maxwell groaned.

'A wash-out. He turns out to be a perfectly respectable stranger employed in a linen manufactory at Larne. Apparently he had leave to visit his family, who live in some obscure farm near Pinwherry. He was given a long week-end, finishing up on Monday night. It seems there was some kind of jollification on the Monday night, and the lad was over-persuaded to stay on for it. On Tuesday, as soon as he had recovered his senses, he bolted off to the station, thinking he could get back that afternoon, but mistook the time-table and then found he could get no boat before 7 o'clock that evening.'

'Having, of course, missed the morning boat.'

'Exactly. That was what he originally intended to catch, of course, but owing to the jollification, he didn't. Well, having got to Stranraer, he decided that there was no point in returning that night, and that he might as well stay over and take the 6.10 boat on Wednesday morning. Consequently, Dalziel's message to the Stranraer police caught him as he was boarding this morning's boat. Dalziel has been working like a nigger all day, getting him identified by his family and by the station-master at Pinwherry and by the people at Larne, and the upshot of it is that his story is perfectly straight, and that he's guilty of nothing worse than being too drunk to go back to work on Monday night. Confound the fellow! He's wasted a whole day of our best man's time, and left us exactly where we were before. I hope he's sacked, that's all.'

'Oh, don't be vindictive,' said Wimsey. 'He couldn't know how inconvenient he was going to be. He "maun ha' gotten a rare fricht," as the man in Ian Hay's book said about the lice in his blanket.'

The Chief Constable grunted.

'Any more news of the man with the bicycle who took the train at Girvan ?'

'No, except that they've checked the tickets and decided that he went to Ayr all right.'

'How about the bicycle ?'

'The bicycle-ticket appears to have been given up too, though we can't trace any ticket-collector who remembers anything about it. It would be much easier if we knew what kind of bicycle we were looking for.'

'M'm. Yes. It wouldn't be a bad idea to get hold of some exact descriptions. Mrs. McLeod ought to know what Waters' bike looked like. I bet Andy could tell you every scratch and scrape on his old crock. It's got new tyres on, by the way. That ought to be a help.'

'And then there's Farren's bicycle.'

'So there is. And there's a very fine collection of bicycles, male and female, up our close. Anybody who urgently wanted to borrow one in Gatehouse or Kirkcudbright wouldn't have very great difficulty. And they all look much alike – honest, hardworking bicycles, half as old as time. For all we know, the murderer's bicycle, if he was a murderer, and used one, may have come peacefully back home by this time.'

'That's a fact,' said the Chief Constable. 'But we'll circulate those descriptions all the same.'

SERGEANT DALZIEL

ON the Thursday morning, Sergeant Dalziel woke unrefreshed and irritable. He had rather counted upon the young man at Stranraer. To have a murder reported at lunch-time on Tuesday, and to catch the murderer at 6.30 the next morning would, he felt, have been a smart piece of work. Now he had to start all over again. The voluminous, contradictory and confusing reports from Kirkcudbright worried him. Also he felt dissatisfied about the bicyclist at Girvan. Surely it must be possible to trace him and his bicycle. These inquiries by telephone were never satisfactory. There was nothing for it, he supposed, but to go himself. With a grunt of annoyance, he tucked himself into his shabby car, collected Police Constable Ross to act as his aide-de-camp, and set out to collect descriptions.

He began with the Anwoth Hotel. Here he had the advantage of interviewing the outraged owner of the missing bicycle. Information was forthcoming in abundance. He had to look for a six-year-old Raleigh, with two new Dunlop tyres. The frame was painted black; one of the handle-bar grips was slightly broken; the bell was missing and the brakes defective. There was a tool-bag containing a repair outfit; a pump on the cross-bar, and a carrier at the back. The Sergeant wrote down all the particulars, promised his best attention and passed on his way.

At Waters' lodgings, his task was more difficult. Mrs. McLeod had seen the bicycle week after week standing in her front passage, but, like most people of her type and sex, had only the very vaguest idea of its appearance. It was 'an auld yin,' it was of 'the ordinar' colour,' she 'couldna charge her memory' as to its fittings, though she thought there was, or had been, a lamp on it, because she had once had occasion to complain of drips on her floor. As for the maker's name, it had not occurred to her to look for it.

Her small son, however, proved more observant. He declared that it was a very old Humber, very rusty, and that it had neither bell nor lamp nor pump. 'But there's Mr. Waters' name on a wee luggage label,' he added, pleased to supply so helpful a clue.

'Ay, but I doot it'll no be there the noo,' said the Sergeant.

He passed on to Mrs. Farren's. Here he at first drew a complete blank. Mrs. Farren 'had not the faintest idea' what was the make of her husband's bicycle. She apologised for being so unpractical, and gave the Sergeant the impression that such details were beneath an artist's notice.

'I'm sure,' she added, 'I couldn't even tell you what make my own is.'

'H'm,' said the Sergeant, struck by an idea, 'could ye let me have a look at your own bicycle, ma'am ?'

'Oh, certainly.' She led the way to an outhouse, and indicated a clean, well-kept Sunbeam, not new, but well-oiled, and with all its parts in good condition.

'Ye keep it verra nice,' said Dalziel, approvingly.

'I like to have everything orderly and clean,' said Mrs. Farren. 'There is a real beauty in cleanliness and decency. Even inanimate things may breathe out a kind of loveliness if they are well cared-for. Do not you think so ?'

'Nae doot, Mistress Farren, nae doot, ma'am. Wad this machine and your husband's have been bought at the same time ?'

'Oh, no – his is newer than this.'

'Ah!' said Dalziel, disappointed. 'Imph'm. Aweel, nae doot Mr. Farren'll be returnin' home before verra long. Ye ha' heard naething from him, I suppose ?'

'No. But that's not really surprising. He does go off like this sometimes for days together. You know what men are – especially artists and fishers.'

'Och, ay,' said Dalziel, comfortably. 'Weel, if we should meet wi' him onywhere, we'll tell him he's expectit hame. Could I speak a bit word wi' the lassie ? She'll maybe ken what kind o' bicycle it is.'

'Jeanie ? Oh, certainly – though I doubt if she'll know much about it. I am always telling her she should be more observant – though I'm afraid I'm a bad example to follow. By the way, Sergeant, do you mind telling me why—'

She stopped and laid her hand on her throat as if the words were difficult to say, or as though, while feeling bound to ask the question, she were reluctant to hear the answer.

'Why what, were ye aboot tae say ?'

'Why all this fuss about my husband's bicycle ?'

The Sergeant looked hard at her for a moment, then turned his eyes away and answered pleasantly:

'Och, 'tis naething. But there's several bicycles missin' lately, and we've found a dealer at Castle-Douglas wi' twa-three machines he disna seem able tae gie a verra gude account on. Sae we're juist mekkin' a sort o' round-up throughout the district, tae see if we can identify ony o' them. However, ye're quite sure, Mr. Farren has his bicycle wi' him ?'

'So far as I know. Why not ? He – went away on it. But – I don't know of course – he may have left it somewhere – how should I know ? He might have had it stolen since Monday, anywhere, by anybody. I – have you found it anywhere ?'

Under Dalziel's steadfast eye, she was fumbling and stammering.

'I'll tak' ma aith,' said Dalziel to himself, 'she kens fine there is some importance tae be attached tae the bicycle, and she disna ken whether tae say her man had it or no. Wha could ha' tell't her ? It's no that Lord Peter, for he's clever, wi' a' his bletherin' talk. And it's no Macpherson, he'd never let oot a word. There's some yin is expectin' yon bicycle tae be found in a queer place, I reckon.'

Jeanie proved, indeed, to know as little about the bicycle as was to be expected, and produced no information beyond the fact that Mr. Farren was accustomed to clean both machines himself, and took 'a wheen o' trouble' over them. A man who cared for his tools, evidently, and particular in certain matters, though he was an artist.

A bicycle-shop in the town was more helpful. The machine was a Raleigh, not new, but in very good condition, black, with plated handle-bars. The shop had fitted a new Dunlop tyre to the back wheel a few weeks previously; the front tyre was of the same make and about six months old. Bell, brakes, lamps and brackets were all in good order.

Armed with these particulars, the Sergeant made his way to Girvan Station. Here he found the porter concerned, a middle-aged man named McSkimming, who repeated to him, in rather more detail, the account he had already given to the station-master.

The train from Stranraer was due in at 1.6, and on the Tuesday it had come in well up to time. It had just entered the station, when a gentleman had come in hurriedly, wheeling a bicycle. He had called to McSkimming, and the man had noticed the high, affected English voice, with its 'Heah, portah!' The gentleman had told him to label the bicycle for Ayr, quick, and the porter had wheeled the machine to the little case containing luggage-labels. While he was labelling it, the gentleman was undoing a strap which held a small leather case to the carrier, saying that he would take it in the carriage with him. As time was short, he had pulled out a note-case from his pocket and sent McSkimming off to buy him a third-class ticket and bicycle-ticket for Ayr. Running back with these, the man had seen his passenger standing at the door of a third-class smoker. He had handed over the tickets and received his tip, and had then placed the bicycle in the rear van. The train had moved out almost immediately afterwards.

No, he had not noticed the gentleman's face particularly. He was wearing a grey flannel suit and a check cap, and he had passed his handkerchief over his face from time to time, as though he were very hot with bicycling in the sun. As he gave the tip he had said something about being glad he had caught the train, and that it was a stiff pull from Ballantrae. He wore slightly tinted spectacles – the sort that is used to shield the eyes from sun-glare. He might have been clean-shaven, or he might have had a small moustache. McSkimming had had no time to notice details, forbye he had been feeling very unwell at the time with the awful pain in his stomach. If anything, he was feeling still worse today, and dooted that handling heavy luggage on a hot day did a man no good.

Dalziel sympathised and asked whether he thought he would be able to identify the man or the bicycle if he saw them again.

The porter did not know – he thought not. The bicycle had been old and dusty. He had not noticed the make. It was not his business. His business was to label it for Ayr, and he had so labelled it and put it in the van, and there was an end of it.

So far, so good. The bicycle had had a carrier, but then, many bicycles had that. It had looked old, and therefore was not very likely to have been Farren's, but it might have been either of the other two. There seemed to be no doubt that passenger and bicycle, whoever and whatever they might be, had safely travelled by the 1.11 to Ayr.

Dalziel thanked and rewarded the porter and returned to his car. Consulting the time-table, he saw that the train stopped only once before Ayr, and that was at Maybole. It would be worthwhile to call and see if, by any chance, the passenger had left the train there, instead of going on to Ayr.

At Maybole he interviewed the station-master, and learned that only two passengers had alighted from the Stranraer train on the Tuesday. Both were women and neither had a bicycle. This was only what he might have expected. The station-master added that the tickets of all passengers for Ayr by the train in question would be collected at Maybole. Eight third-class tickets had been given up – as was proved by a reference to the booking-clerk's returns – including a third-class ticket from Girvan. Any discrepancy between the number of tickets issued and collected would be checked at the Audit Office at Glasgow and reported within three days, so that if there was anything wrong about these tickets, they might expect to hear about it by the next day. The bicycle-ticket of a passenger travelling to Ayr would not be collected at Maybole; it would be retained by him until he claimed the machine at Ayr.

Dalziel left instructions that any query arising about tickets should be at once reported to him, and the two policemen then made their way to Ayr.

Ayr is a good-sized station, acting as a junction for several lines of traffic. The main line from Stranraer to Glasgow runs straight through the station. On the east side of the main line is the principal platform, containing the booking-hall, bookstall and station entrance, with a number of bays for branch lines.

Here Dalziel directed his first inquiries to the question of the bicycle ticket. A reference to the records showed that a ticket issued from Girvan to cover a twenty-five mile journey had been duly given up at Ayr. The next question was, to whom had the ticket been handed? Since the passenger-tickets had all been collected at Maybole, there would have been no collector at the barrier on that particular occasion. Therefore, presumably, the ticket would have been given up to the porter who removed the bicycle from the van.

Dalziel and Ross interviewed the porters in turn, but all were quite positive that they had not taken any bicycle out of the Stranraer train on the Tuesday. One of them, however, recalled something about the ticket. After seeing a number of passengers out of the train, he had gone back to the rear brake to deal with the luggage. The guard had then handed him a bicycle ticket, saying that it belonged to a gentleman who had taken his bicycle out himself and wheeled it away. The porter had considered this a shabby trick to avoid giving a tip, but he supposed that the traveller had been in a hurry, since the guard had seen him briskly wheeling the machine away in the direction of the exit. By that time the passenger would, of course, have left the station. People were often mean about tips, bicyclists especially. With times so hard and money so tight you didn't get twopence nowadays where once you would have got sixpence or a shilling. Call this a Socialist Government. Things were harder than ever for a working man, and as for Jimmy Thomas, he had sold himself, lock, stock and barrel, to the capitalists. If he (the porter) had had the right treatment, he would have been something better than an ordinary porter long before this, but with everybody getting at you all at once—

Dalziel cut short this jeremiad by asking whether the same guard would be travelling on the train that afternoon. The porter said, Yes, he would, and Dalziel determined to wait and interview him when he arrived. In the meantime he thought he and Rose might as well get some lunch, after which they would have to find somebody who had seen the bicyclist leave the station.

Over a hasty meal in the refreshment-room, the two officers discussed their campaign. It might take some time to trace the movements of their quarry after leaving Ayr Station, and it was necessary that Dalziel should be back at Newton-Stewart as early as possible, to keep in touch with Macpherson. There were a number of routine inquiries to be made at Glasgow, and it would, he felt be advisable to get hold of photographs of all the persons at present under suspicion, in order that the bicyclist might be identified, if possible. Since all the men were well-known artists, it seemed likely that an inquiry among the leading Glasgow newsagencies would produce the photographs, and this would be a far better plan than asking for them directly at Gatehouse and Kirkcudbright, which would have the effect of putting the suspects on their guard. It was therefore decided that Dalziel should board the train from Stranraer when it came in, and proceed to Glasgow, interviewing the guard on the way. Ross should keep the car and pursue his investigations as and how he could, reporting to Newton-Stewart from time to time. If he got on the bicyclist's track, he was to follow where it led and, if necessary, detain the man when he found him.

At 1.48, the train came in, and Dalziel got into it, after ascertaining that the guard was, in fact, the same man who had been in charge on the Tuesday. As it drew away from Ayr, he observed Ross engaged in conversation with the bookstall clerk. Ross was an energetic and enthusiastic man, and the Sergeant felt sure that he would not be slack in his investigations. He rather wished that he had felt justified in himself taking over the more adventurous and entertaining side of the inquiry, but he reflected that there was, after all, no certainty that the elusive bicyclist had anything to do with the crime, and that it would not do for him, in his position, to lose himself indefinitely on what might prove to be a wild-goose chase. He made his way along the train to the guard's van.

The guard perfectly remembered the incident of the bicycle. The train had scarcely drawn up at the station before a passenger – a youngish man in a check cap and grey flannel suit and wearing Crookes' glasses – had come running along the platform to the van. He had addressed the guard, saying that he wanted his bicycle got out immediately, as he had no time to lose. The porters were all up in front, and the guard had himself opened the van and handed out the bicycle first glancing at the label to make sure that it was the right one. It was labelled to Ayr correctly enough, and he remembered its being put in at Girvan. The gentleman thrust the ticket into his hand together with a shilling tip, and immediately walked away with the bicycle in the direction of the exit. The guard further recollected that the passenger had been carrying a small attaché-case. He had not seen him actually leave the station, because he had had to see to the coupling of the Pullman Restaurant Car, which was put on at Ayr. Before leaving the station, he had handed the bicycle-ticket over to a porter to be sent to headquarters in the usual way.

Dalziel asked next for a personal description of the traveller. This was not so easy to get. The guard had only seen him for about half a minute. He thought he would be between thirty and forty, of middle height, and either clean-shaven or wearing a small, fair moustache. Not a dark moustache – the guard felt sure he would have noticed that. His hair was almost invisible beneath his cap, but the guard's general impression was of a fairish man with a fresh complexion. He might perhaps have been mouse-coloured or sandy. His eyes, beneath the glasses, were at any rate not noticeably dark – blue, grey or hazel, possibly. The guard, like the porter at Girvan, had particularly noticed the high, affected English voice. He thought he might recognise a photograph of the man if he saw it, but he really could not be sure. Everything about the man, with the exception of the voice and the glasses, might be called nondescript. The bicycle was an old and shabby one. The guard had not observed the make, but he had noticed that the tyres were comparatively new.

Dalziel nodded. He knew better than to expect a recognisable description of a man in a cap and glasses, seen only for a few seconds by a busy official at a railway station. He went back to his compartment and passed the time making notes of the case until the train, after only a brief halt at Paisley, Gilmour Street, drew in to St. Enoch Station.

Here there was nothing for him to do except to inquire whether all tickets collected on the Tuesday had already been forwarded to the Audit Office. Being assured that this was so, he betook himself thither and was soon closeted with the head official there.

His business here was the purely routine matter of checking the tickets issued and collected on the Tuesday between Gatehouse and St. Enoch and Kirkcudbright and St. Enoch respectively. He found that these had already been made up and found to agree perfectly with the returns sent in by the issuing clerks. Wimsey's vague suggestion that Waters might have started from Kirkcudbright with a Glasgow ticket and disappeared *en route* was evidently incorrect. If, unseen by either the officials or by Miss Selby and Miss Cochran, he had indeed taken the 8.45 from Kirkcudbright, he must have booked to some intermediate station. But there seemed no reason at all to suppose that he had ever started by that train at all. Waters had simply disappeared and taken his bicycle with him. Was this, or was it not, the bicycle which had travelled to Ayr. The Sergeant, remembering that young Andrew had fitted new tyres not long before, was more inclined to think that this might be the Anwoth Hotel bicycle, but then he had no evidence about the condition of Waters' tyres.

He inquired for Ferguson's ticket, which was readily identified, being the only first-class ticket issued from Gatehouse to Glasgow that day. It had been duly punched at Maxwelltown, between Gatehouse and Dumfries, and again at Hurlford and Mauchline, between Dumfries and St. Enoch, thus affording definite proof that Ferguson had made the whole journey as he had purported to do.

Not satisfied with this, Dalziel demanded a check of all tickets issued on Tuesday on all lines within a fifty-mile radius of Newton-Stewart, in case some interesting discrepancy of some sort should turn up somewhere, and then departed for the Central Police Station at Glasgow.

Here he set on foot inquiries for a bicyclist seen travelling over the road between Bargrennan and Girvan between 11 a.m. and 1.11 p.m. on Tuesday morning, as also for any bicyclist seen in the neighbourhood of Ayr on the Tuesday afternoon, or travelling on any line out of Ayr or any of the neighbouring stations on Tuesday afternoon or Wednesday. For it readily occurred to him that the bicyclist might have ridden from Ayr to some near-by station and re-booked there, after, perhaps, disguising his appearance in some way. He then remembered that the compromising bicycle might have been abandoned in some convenient spot, and sent out a further call to search station-cloakrooms for unclaimed bicycles and report any bicycle left derelict by the roadside round about Ayr and the neighbourhood. He gave a general description of the three missing bicycles, asking, however, that reports should not be confined to these two makes, but extended to include any bicycle found abandoned during the prescribed period.

Having put the machinery of the law in motion, he turned his attention to the matter of the photographs. He had little difficulty in collecting what he needed among the newspaper offices of the city, and finished up at 6 o'clock with a fine collection of portraits of all six artists. He then discovered that he had missed the last train to Newton-Stewart, and that his only hope of getting back that night was to go to Girvan or Lockerbie and drive home.

His own car was, of course, at Ayr. Wearily, the Sergeant went to the 'phone and rang up the Ayr police to discover if Constable Ross was still in the town. But luck was against him. Ross had been in and left a message that he was following up a clue in the direction of Kilmarnock and would report again.

Cursing his fate – though somewhat cheered by the thought of a clue – Dalziel then rang up Kirkcudbright. Inspector Mac-pherson answered him. Yes, a great deal of new evidence had

come in. Yes, the Inspector thought Dalziel had better get back
that night if he could. What a pity he had now just missed the
6.20 to Girvan. (Sergeant Dalziel gritted his teeth.) Well, it
couldna be helped. Let him take the 7.30, getting in at 9.51, and
a car would be sent to meet him.

The Sergeant replied, with a certain grim satisfaction, that the
9.51 only ran on Saturdays and the 9.56 only on Wednesdays,
and that, this being a Thursday, they would have to meet him at
8.55 at Ayr. The Inspector retorted that in that case he had
better hire a car at Ayr. Finding that there was no help for it,
Sergeant Dalziel abandoned all hopes of a comfortable night of
dinner, talkie and bed at Glasgow, and reluctantly retired to the
refreshment-room for an early supper before catching the 7.30.

INSPECTOR MACPHERSON

At headquarters, meanwhile, the market in evidence was looking up. At least, as Wimsey observed to the Chief Constable, it
was not looking up so much as looking about in all directions.

The first piece of excitement was provided by a young farmer,
who presented himself rather diffidently at Kirkcudbright police-
station and asked to see Inspector Macpherson.

It appeared that he had been having a drink at the Murray
Arms in Gatehouse at about 9 o'clock on the Monday night,
when Mr. Farren had come suddenly into the bar, looking very
wild and queer, and had asked in a loud peremptory tone,
'Where's that b—— Campbell?' On perceiving that Campbell
was not anywhere in the house, he had calmed down a little, and
ordered two or three whiskies in quick succession. The witness
had tried to find out what the trouble was about, but had extracted nothing from Farren but a few vague threats. Presently,
Farren had again started asking where Campbell was. Witness,
who had lately come in from Kirkcudbright, and knew for a fact
that Campbell was in the McClellan Arms, formed the opinion
that Farren was in a dangerous mood and, in order to avert an
encounter, had said, untruthfully, that he fancied he had seen
Mr. Campbell in his car taking the road to Creetown. Farren
had then muttered something about 'getting him yet,' adding a

number of abusive epithets, from which witness gathered that the quarrel had something to do with Mrs. Farren. He (Farren) had then hurried out of the bar and witness had seen him ride off, not, however, in the direction of Creetown, but towards Kirkcudbright. Witness had not felt satisfied and had run out after him. When, however, Farren had got as far as the War Memorial, he had turned off to the left along the road to the golf-links. Witness had then shrugged his shoulders and dismissed the matter from his mind.

On Wednesday, however, when it became clear, through the activities of the police, that Campbell was considered to have been murdered, the incident presented itself in a more sinister light. He (witness) had consulted with the barman at the Murray Arms and with one or two men who had been in the bar with him during Farren's visit, and they had decided that the police ought to be told. Witness had been chosen as spokesman, and here he was. Witness had been reluctant to get Mr. Farren into trouble, but murder was murder and there you were.

Macpherson thanked the farmer and immediately put an inquiry through to Creetown, to find out whether Farren had, after all, followed the false trail in that direction. It was puzzling that he should have turned off by the golf-links. He had left Campbell in Kirkcudbright some three hours previously, and it was likely enough that, failing to find him in Gatehouse, he should have gone back to search for him on the Kirkcudbright road. But why the golf-links? Unless—

Unless he had gone to visit Strachan. Strachan and Farren were well known to be particularly friendly. Had there been some sort of complicity here? Had Strachan been at home between 9 and 10 on Monday night? That was comparatively easy to ascertain. The Inspector telephoned to Gatehouse for information and waited.

Then came the second excitement of the day – much more definite and encouraging. It presented itself in the shape of a small and very timid child of about ten, hauled along by a determined mother, who incited her offspring to speech by alternately shaking her and offering to 'skelp her ower the lug' if she did not do as she was told.

'I kenned fine,' said the mother, 'as she'd been up tae some mischief an' I wadna rest while I'd got it oot o' her. (Blow your nose an' speak civil to the policeman, or he'll hae ye locked up.) She's a bad girl, stravaiguin' about the country wi' the laddies when she should be in her bed. But they'll no listen tae their mithers these days. Ye canna do onything wi' them.'

The Inspector expressed his sympathy, and asked the lady's name.

'Mrs. McGregor, I am, an' we have our cottage between Gatehoose and Kirkcudbright – ye'll ken the place – near by Auchenhaye. Me an' my man was away tae Kirkcudbright last Monday nicht, an' Helen was alone at hame. An' no sooner are we away than she's away oot, leavin' the door open behind her as like as not for onybody tae come in—'

'Jist a moment,' said the Inspector. 'This wee lassie will be Helen, I'm thinkin'.'

'Ay, that's Helen. I thought it best tae bring her, seein' as this puir Mr. Campbell has been pit oot of the way, so the postman says. An' I says tae George, if Mr. Campbell was fightin' on the road Monday night, then the pollis ought tae know it. An' George says—'

The Inspector interrupted again.

'If your wee Helen can tell us onything aboot Mr. Campbell, we wad like fine tae hear it. Now, Mistress McGregor, will ye jist let the lassie tell us her ain tale fra' the beginning. Come along, Helen, dinna be frightened, now. Speak up.'

Helen, thus encouraged, began her story, which, between her own agitation and her mother's interruptions, was rather a tangled one. However, by dint of coaxing and the gift of a bag of sweeties which a constable was sent out to procure, the Inspector eventually succeeded in getting the tangle straightened out.

Mr. and Mrs. McGregor had gone over to Kirkcudbright on the Monday evening in a neighbour's car, to visit some friends, leaving Helen with strict instructions to lock the cottage door and put herself to bed. Instead of this, the abandoned child had gone out to play with some little boys belonging to a neighbouring farm. They had strayed down the road to some fields about half a mile away, where the boys were going to set some highly illegal rabbit-snares.

The Inspector shook his head slightly at this, but gave his promise that nothing dreadful should be done to the marauders, and Helen, who seemed to have been more troubled by this thought than by her mother's threats of punishment, went on more coherently with her story.

The place where they were looking for rabbits was about half-way between Gatehouse and Kirkcudbright, at a point where the road makes a very sharp and dangerous S-bend between two stone walls. It was a fine night, not dark, but dusk, and with a slight ground-mist lying in streaks on the hill. The boys had wandered well away into the fields and were intending to stay out much later, but at about a quarter to ten Helen, remembering that her parents would soon be home, had left them and started to go back by the road. She knew it was a quarter to ten, because one of the boys had a new watch which his grandfather had given him.

She crossed the fields and was just about to climb over the wall into the road, when she noticed a man in a car, drawn up stationary by the roadside and headed towards Gatehouse. The engine was running, and at that very moment, the driver pulled the car out across the road as though he was about to turn. At the same time, she heard another car approaching fast from the direction of Gatehouse.

She described the spot very exactly. It was not the sharpest and most dangerous part of the bend, where the walls are high on either side, but was what might be described as the lower bend of the S – the bend nearer Kirkcudbright. Here the turn is shallower and wider, and the wall on the side where she stood is a sunk wall, with gorse bushes and brambles beneath it. The approaching car came very quickly round the upper bend, just as the first car turned across the road, blocking the way. There was a sharp squeal of brakes, and the second car stopped, slewing violently to the right and avoiding a crash by a miracle. The driver had shouted out something and the first man had replied, and then the driver of the second car had said in a loud and angry tone, 'Campbell! Of course! It would be Campbell' – or words to that effect.

Then there had been a sharp exchange of abuse, and Campbell had stopped his engine and got out. She had seen him jump on the other man's running-board. There was some sort of struggle and then, all in a moment, both men were out on the road, fighting and struggling. There were blows and a great deal of foul language. She could not see exactly what was going on, because the men were on the far side of the two cars. They had fallen to the ground and seemed to be rolling over one another. Nor could she say what the cars were like, except that Campbell's was a four-seater and the other a large two-seater with very bright lights.

When the struggle had gone on for some little time, she got a bad fright. A big spanner was flung suddenly into the air. It just missed her head and fell close beside her. She cowered down again under the wall, afraid to stay where she was and yet anxious to find out what was happening. She heard horrid sounds as though somebody was being thumped and throttled. After a little time she peered up again and saw something which frightened her still more. A man was getting up from the roadside, and over his shoulders he had got the body of another man. From the limp way in which it hung she thought the man must be dead. She didn't scream, because she was afraid if she did that the terrible man would hear her and kill her too. He carried the body over to the two-seater car and slumped it into the passenger's seat. This was the car which stood nearest to Gatehouse. She didn't see the face of the living man, because it was all bent down under the burden he was carrying, but as he passed in front of the lights of the four-seater to get to the other car she caught a glimpse of the dead man's face and it looked very dreadful and white. She couldn't describe it, except that she thought it was clean-shaven and the eyes were shut. The terrible man then got into the driver's seat and backed the two-seater away round the bend in the direction of Gatehouse. She heard the engine change its note, and the lights moved backwards and forwards as though the car were turning round. Then she heard it move off again, and the noise of the engine gradually died away.

When it had gone, she climbed up over the wall, and thought she would have a look at the four-seater car, which was still standing half-across the road. It was headed towards Gatehouse, and its lights were turned towards the off-side of the road. Before she could examine it, however, she heard footsteps coming along from the direction of Gatehouse. She hoped it was somebody who would look after her and take her home, and then, suddenly, for no reason, it came over her that this was the bad man coming back to kill her. She was dreadfully alarmed, and started to run home as fast as she could. Then she heard an engine started up and hid herself in the bushes, thinking that the bad man was pursuing her in the car. Nothing came, however, and after a time she ventured out again and hurried home. Just as she got inside her own gate, a car flashed past at a furious pace towards Kirkcudbright. She got into the cottage just as the kitchen clock was striking ten. She rushed into the bedroom and jumped into bed, just as she was, and pulled the clothes over her head.

Mrs. McGregor then took up the tale. She and her husband had got home at 10.30, and found the child shivering and crying in bed with all her clothes on. She was so terrified that they could get nothing out of her. All they could do was to scold her soundly, undress her and put her to bed properly, give her a hot drink and stand by till she fell asleep from sheer exhaustion. All next day she refused to tell them anything, but the next night she had woken them up three times by crying out in her sleep that the bad man was coming to kill her. On Wednesday evening, her father, who made a great pet of the child, succeeded in getting the story out of her, and when they heard the name of Campbell mentioned they decided that the police ought to be told. In answer to a question of the Inspector's, Mrs. McGregor said that their kitchen clock was five or six minutes slow.

The Inspector thanked them both very much – and felt that he had indeed good reason to be grateful. He told Helen that she was a brave lassie, begged her mother not to punish her, in view of the great importance of her story, and ended the interview with a strongly-worded caution against passing the story on to anybody else.

When they had gone, he sat back to think it out. The times agreed fairly well with the doctor's report, except that he was now obliged to place the actual moment of the murder rather earlier than he had expected. As he interpreted it, Campbell and the other man had met and quarrelled, and Campbell had been killed in the struggle. The murderer must then have pushed Campbell's body into the two-seater car and concealed it somewhere at the side of the road. Then he had come back, fetched Campbell's car, and driven it back to Gatehouse, where it would, of course, be wanted to stage the fake accident. At some later time, he must have come back, collected his own car with the body in it, and – well, what? Driven it back to Gatehouse?

The Inspector grunted. There were difficulties here. Why in the world had not the murderer put Campbell's body straight away into Campbell's Morris and driven off with it there and then? Why court discovery by leaving the body by the roadside for anyone to find during the time it would take him to drive the Morris back to Gatehouse and return on his bicycle? For he must have come back on a bicycle or on foot, if he was going to take his own car away. A bicycle was the obvious thing for him to use, and he might quite well have brought it back in the dickey of the two-seater. But the difficulty remained; why had he left the corpse behind him ?

It was possible, thought Macpherson – indeed, it was more than possible – that the murderer had not at that time thought out the scheme of the alibi and the faked accident. Perhaps that explained it. He meant simply to drive away as though nothing had happened, and it was only afterwards that, having worked out his elaborate plan, he had returned to collect the corpse. But no! that would not work. It was Campbell's car that he had driven away with. The only explanation of that was that he had already planned the faked accident in his own mind. But that seemed simply incredible. Taking the child's account as reliable, which it appeared to be, it seemed obvious that the encounter between Campbell and the other man was fortuitous. Surely, in those few brief moments after the struggle, it would hardly have been possible for the murderer to work out his elaborate plan of escape.

And yet – *had* the meeting been, after all, fortuitous ? Campbell's behaviour, if you came to think of it, suggested the exact contrary. He had planted his car in the road at the exact point where it was most difficult for two vehicles to pass, and when he had heard the other car coming, he had actually drawn out so as to block the way still further. A crazy thing to do, since it was more likely to provoke a fatal accident than any other kind of encounter. Still, it was known that Campbell was drunk at the time, and this might have blinded him to the risk of a collision.

But, if the witness was to be trusted (and, after all, he could not pick and choose, believing one bit of evidence and rejecting another to suit his own theories), then it was clear that, whoever had expected the meeting, it was not the murderer. And if the murderer had not foreseen the meeting, he could not have premeditated the crime, and so could not have prepared the faked alibi beforehand.

'Ay,' said the Inspector to himself, 'but that doesna follow, by no manner of means. He might weel ha' premeditated the alibi, intendin' tae commit the murder at some ither place or time. Then, meetin' wi' Campbell in that verra convenient manner, he may ha' carrit oot his nefarious design forthwith.'

There still remained the difficulty about the car. And there was the account of the man who had driven so furiously along towards Kirkcudbright a short time after the encounter. Was he the murderer ? Impossible, if the murderer was taking Camp-bell's car to Gatehouse. If he was somebody else, who was he ? He must have passed the murderer on the road. He would have to be found. After a little further thought, the Inspector gave up this part of the problem as insoluble for the moment, and turned to another aspect of the matter.

How did his story fit in, if at all, with the evidence about Farren ? And here, suddenly, the Inspector gave a great smack with his hand upon the table. Of course ! the times fitted perfect-ly, and here was the explanation of why Farren had turned up the road to the golf-links. Evidently he had seen through the young farmer's well-meant lie about Creetown. He had searched Gatehouse for Campbell and, failing to find him there, had come to the conclusion that he must still be in Kirkcudbright. He had then hurried off to see Strachan, obviously for the purpose of borrowing Strachan's car. Whether or not Strachan was an accomplice was not quite plain. Probably not. No, again the Inspector smacked the table with enlightenment. This explained the whole thing – the taking of the wrong car, the leaving the body and everything. Farren's original idea had been to put the guilt of the murder on Strachan. The body was to have been found in Strachan's car and the inference was to have been that Strachan had decoyed Campbell away and murdered him.

A very poor plan, of course. Strachan would immediately tell the story of how he had lent the car to Farren. Probably he would be able to produce witnesses of the transaction. Moreover, the thing would in itself have a very unlikely appearance. What man would be fool enough to leave his own car lying about with a murdered body in it ? This was, in fact, the very point which had immediately struck the Inspector himself, and Farren, when he thought over what he had done, could not fail to see how un-reasonable his first idea was. But while driving Campbell's car back to Gatehouse, he would have time to think matters over. A better idea would occur to him – the idea of faking the acci-dent at the Minnoch. What then ? What would he do ?

He would first, of course, take Campbell's car back and put it in the garage. Then he would have to go and collect his own bicycle from Strachan's house. At that time of night it would be easy enough to do so without being seen, supposing, as was possible, that he had left the machine somewhere handy – say, just inside the garden gate.

With considerable excitement, the Inspector drew a pad of

paper towards him, and began to jot down a schedule of times, heading the document boldly: 'The Case against Hugh Farren.'

Monday.

6 p.m. Farren returns home and finds Campbell there. Turns him out of the house. (Jeanie's sister's evidence.)

7 p.m. After a quarrel with his wife, during which she presumably makes some damaging admission about Campbell, Farren departs on his bicycle.

9 p.m. Farren enters the Murray Arms, looking for Campbell. (The farmer's evidence.)

9.15 p.m. (about). Farren goes to Strachan's house and borrows car.

9.45 p.m. (about). Meeting with Campbell on the Kirkcudbright road. Murder of Campbell. (Helen McGregor's evidence.)

9.55 p.m. Farren plants the body in Strachan's car.

10 p.m. (or thereabouts). Farren starts back in Campbell's car.

10.10 p.m. Farren arrives in Gatehouse (say five miles) and garages Campbell's car.

10.30 p.m. Farren arrives on foot at Strachan's house to fetch bicycle.

11 p.m. Farren arrives on bicycle at the scene of the crime.

11.10 p.m. Farren is back with the body at Campbell's house. Hides the body in the house or garage.

11.20 p.m. Farren returns car to Strachan's house.

11.40 p.m. Farren is back at Campbell's house to prepare evidence of Campbell's having spent the night and breakfasted there.

The Inspector gazed with some complacency upon this schedule. Some of the times were, of course, only approximate, but the essential points corresponded well enough, and, making every allowance for Farren's being a slow walker, or bungling parts of his procedure, he had ample time to carry out all these manoeuvres before Tuesday morning.

Encouraged by this, the Inspector proceeded, rather more tentatively, with the rest of his theory.

According to the evidence of 'young Jock' at Borgan, the

spurious Campbell had been seen sitting by the Minnoch at 10.10 on the Tuesday morning. This, therefore, gave the latest possible moment for Farren's arrival there. Actually, the Inspector thought it would probably have been earlier. Farren would certainly not have risked hanging about in Campbell's cottage very late in the morning. He would have been up and away well before 8 a.m., when Mrs. Green was due to arrive. On the other hand, he would not have started ridiculously early, because of Ferguson. It would be necessary that Ferguson, if he happened to hear Campbell's car go out, should be able to swear that it left at a reasonable hour in the morning. Accordingly, the Inspector put down at a venture:—

7.30   Farren leaves Campbell's house, wearing Campbell's hat and cloak, with the body tucked away on the floor of the car and the bicycle on top, all covered by the rug.

8.35   (say). Farren arrives at the Minnoch, hides the corpse and starts on his painting.

10.10   Farren (disguised as Campbell) seen by Jock for first time.

11.5   Farren seen by Jock for the second time.

Here the Inspector paused uncertainly. Was two-and-a-half hours too long to allow for the painting of that picture? He knew very little about artists, and the thing had seemed to him a rough and sketchy affair. He must ask somebody who knew.

But there! What a thick-headed fool he was! Of course, Farren could not begin to paint till the light was good. He mightn't know much, but he did know that. He thoughtfully shook a few blots from his fountain-pen and continued.

It now seemed very probable that Farren was the passenger at Girvan. The schedule would therefore run on:—

Tuesday.

11.10 a.m.   Farren throws body into the river, puts on cap and overcoat and starts for Girvan on his bicycle.

1.7 p.m.   Arrives at Girvan. Has bicycle labelled for Ayr.

1.11 p.m.   Takes train for Ayr.

1.48 p.m.   Arrives Ayr.

Here, for the moment, the Inspector's deductions came to an end. Dalziel, he knew, was following up the trail of the bicycle. It would be better to wait for his report before carrying the schedule any further. But he had not done so badly. He had at last succeeded in fixing the crime definitely upon one person, and in producing a plausible time-scheme to which to work. Fortunately, also, it was one that was susceptible to confirmation at several points.

He glanced over his paper again.

If Farren had been searching for Campbell in Gatehouse between 8 o'clock and 9.15, there ought to be evidence of other calls besides that at the Murray Arms. Inquiries would have to be made at the Angel and the Anwoth. But surely, before asking at public houses, Farren would have tried Campbell's house. If so, it was almost impossible that he should not have been seen. For one thing, he would have had to cross the bridge twice, and there is no hour of the day at which the bridge at Gatehouse is not occupied by at least one idler. The bridge is the common club and gathering-place of the Gatehouse population, who meet there for the exchange of gossip, the counting of passing cars and rising trout, and the discussion of local politics. Even if, by a miracle, the bridge should have been clear on both occasions, there was the long bench outside the Anwoth Hotel, on which fishermen sit to tie knots, pat Bounce the dog and inquire of Felix the cat how many rats he has killed during the day. Lastly, supposing Farren to have escaped notice at both these points, there was always the possibility that Ferguson had been at home and had seen him come to the cottage.

Then, if Strachan's car had been taken out, surely somebody would know of it. Strachan himself might refuse information or lie stoutly in defence of his friend, but there still remained Mrs. Strachan, the child and the maid. They could not possibly all be in the plot. According to the theory, Farren had called three times at Strachan's – at about 9.15, to borrow the car; at about 10.40, to fetch the bicycle; at about 11.30 to return the car. The first and last of these visits at any rate ought to have left traces behind them.

Next, there were the three night visits to Campbell's house – the first, to garage Campbell's car; the second, to bring in the body; the third, on foot, to fake the evidence. No, that was not necessarily correct. There might have been only two visits. It was more likely that on the first occasion the car had been left somewhere, to be picked up on the final visit. That would reduce the risk very considerably. In fact, the body might have been transferred to Campbell's car at some quiet spot, thus doing away with the necessity of entering Campbell's place twice in two different cars – a proceeding bound to arouse suspicion. The transfer could not, naturally, have taken place in Gatehouse itself – that would have been the act of a madman. But it might have been done anywhere between Kirkcudbright and Gatehouse, or on the unfrequented piece of road between the War Memorial and Strachan's house. Or, if Strachan was indeed involved, it might have been done still more quietly and safely at Strachan's house itself.

The Inspector made an alteration or two in his time-table to correspond with this new theory, and made a note to advertise for any passer-by who might have seen a Morris car with Campbell's number-plates stationary at any point on the route.

Finally, the Tuesday morning's journey could now be corroborated. If his calculations were exact, Campbell's car must have passed through Gatehouse a little after 7.30; through Creetown about 8 o'clock; and through Newton-Stewart at about 8.15. Somebody must undoubtedly have seen it. The Newton-Stewart police were, in fact, already investigating this point, but now that he could give them the approximate times, his task would be easier.

Inspector Macpherson put a call through to Newton-Stewart and another to Gatehouse, and then turned back with renewed appetite for a fresh bite at his problem.

And now he suddenly realised, what he had momentarily overlooked in working out his times, that he had one piece of hugely important evidence lying ready to his hand. With any luck at all, he had the weapon!

That heavy spanner, which had hurtled through the air and nearly laid out the unfortunate little Helen – what else could it be but the blunt instrument which had crashed in Campbell's skull? It was perhaps odd that it should have drawn no blood, but much depended on the kind of spanner it was. Anyway, the great thing was to get hold of it. The doctor would tell him if it was a suitable weapon to have inflicted the blow. How fortunate that the corpse was still above ground! It was to be buried next day. He must get hold of that spanner instantly. The Inspector was simmering with suppressed excitement as he pulled on his cap and hastened out to his car.

FERGUSON'S STORY

ON the same Thursday morning that took Sergeant Dalziel and
Constable Ross to Ayr and set Inspector Macpherson to work
at time-schedules, Lord Peter Wimsey presented himself at the
farther of the two cottages at Standing Stone Pool.

The door was opened by Mr. Ferguson in person, palette in
hand, and dressed in a pair of aged flannel bags, an open shirt
and a shapeless and bulging jacket. He seemed a little disconcerted at the sight of an early visitor. Wimsey hastened to explain
himself.

'I don't know if you remember me. My name's Wimsey. I
fancy we met once at Bob Anderson's.'

'Yes, of course. Come in. When I heard you knock I thought
you were going to be a pound of sausages or the man from the
greengrocer's. I'm afraid the place is in rather a mess. I've been
away for a couple of days and Mrs. Green seized the opportunity to tidy up, with the result that I've had to spend a couple
of hours untidying it again.' He waved his hand towards a litter
of canvases, rags, dippers, bottles and other paraphernalia. 'I
never can find anything I want in a tidy studio.'

'And now I've come bargin' in and interrupting you just as
you were settling down to work.'

'Not a bit. It doesn't worry me. Have a drink ?'

'No, thanks, I've just had one. You carry on and don't mind
me.'

Wimsey cleared a number of books and papers from a chair
and sat down, while Ferguson returned to the contemplation of
a large canvas, in which Wimsey recognised the typical Ferguson
of Graham's malicious description – the tree with twisted roots,
the reflection, the lump of granite and the blue distance and the
general air of decorative unreality.

'Been in Glasgow, haven't you ?'

'Yes. Ran up to look at the show.'

'Is it a good one ?'

'Not bad.' Ferguson squeezed out some green paint on to his

palette. 'Craig's got some fine studies, and there's a good thing of Donaldson's. The usual allowance of duds, of course. I really went to see the Farquharsons.'

He added a blob of scarlet vermilion to the semi-circle of colours, and appeared to think that his palette was made up, for he took up a bunch of brushes and began to mix two or three paints together.

Wimsey asked a few more questions about the Exhibition, and then remarked carelessly:

'So you've lost your next-door neighbour.'

'Yes. I don't care to think too much about that. Campbell and I were not exactly on the best of terms, but — I wish he could have departed some other way.'

'It's all rather queer,' said Wimsey. 'I suppose you've had the police round, asking the usual questions.'

'Oh, yes. Apparently it's just as well I had an alibi. I say, Wimsey — you know all about this kind of thing — I suppose it's a fact that he was — that it wasn't an accident?'

'That does seem to be the case, I'm afraid.'

'What makes them think so?'

'Oh, well, I'm an outsider, you know, and of course the police aren't giving their game away. But I think it was something to do with his being dead before he got into the river and all that kind of guff, don't you know.'

'I see. I heard something about a bash on the head. What's the idea? That somebody snooped up behind and did him in for his money?'

'Something like that, I dare say. Though, naturally, the police can't tell if he was robbed till they know how much he had on him. They're making inquiries at the bank and all that, I expect.'

'Funny sort of place for a tramp to hang around, isn't it?'

'Oh, I dunno. There might have been some fellow sleepin' up there in the hills.'

'H'm. Why couldn't he just have hit his head on the stones in falling?'

Wimsey groaned within himself. This perpetual parrying of pertinent questions was growing wearisome. One after another, everybody wanted to know the same thing. He replied, vacuously:

'Couldn't say. Seems on the whole the likeliest idea, don't it? If I were you, I'd ask the doctor johnnie.'

'He wouldn't say, any more than you.'

Ferguson went on for a few minutes dabbing paint on to his canvas in silence. Wimsey noticed that he seemed to be working at random, and was not surprised when he suddenly threw the palette on to the table and, turning round, demanded suddenly:

'Look here, Wimsey. Tell me one thing. It's not good your pretending you don't know, because you do. Is there any doubt at all that Campbell died the same morning that he was found?'

Wimsey felt as though he had suddenly received a jolt in the solar plexus. Whatever made the man ask that – if it was not the self-betrayal of a guilty conscience? Not being very sure how to answer, he asked, quite simply, the question he had just asked himself.

'Whatever makes you ask that?'

'And why ever can't you give me a straightforward answer?'

'Well,' said Wimsey, 'it seems such a damn funny question. I mean – oh, well, of course – perhaps they didn't tell you about the picture?'

'What picture?'

'The picture Campbell had been painting. The paint was still wet on it. So he must have been alive that morning, or he couldn't have painted it, could he?'

'Ah!' Ferguson let out a long breath, as though his mind were relieved of some anxiety. He picked up his palette again. 'No, they didn't tell me that. That settles it, of course.'

He stepped back a couple of paces and regarded his canvas with head cocked and eyes half-shut.

'But what made you ask?'

'Well,' said Ferguson. He took up a palette-knife and began scraping off all the paint he had just put on. 'Well – the police have been asking questions. I wondered – See here' – his face was close to the painting and he went on scraping without looking at Wimsey – 'perhaps you can tell me what I ought to do about it.'

'About what?' said Wimsey.

'About the police. The first thing they did was to go into my movements, starting from Monday night. That was simple enough, as far as Tuesday went, because I took the 9.8 to Glasgow and was there all day. But I had to admit that I was here all Monday night, and they became – damnably inquisitive.'

'Did they? Well, I'm blessed.'

'That was why I wanted to know, don't you see? It's extremely unpleasant if – well, if there's any doubt about Campbell having been alive on the Tuesday morning.'

'Yes, I see your point. Well, so far as I know – mind, I don't pretend to know everything – but so far as I know, anybody who has a complete alibi for Tuesday morning is perfectly safe.'

'I'm glad of that. Not so much for my own sake, though naturally one isn't keen on being suspected of things. But – the fact is, Wimsey, I didn't quite know what to say to those fellows.'

'Oh ?' said Wimsey, his eyes all over the place. 'I say, I like that thing over there, with the white cottage and the heather in the foreground. It sits very nicely up against the slope of the hill.'

'Yes. It isn't so bad. I'll tell you what, Wimsey, after what you've said, I don't so much mind – that is, when those fellows were here, I thought there might possibly be something in it, so I – reserved judgment, so to speak. But perhaps I'd better spill the beans to you, and then you can say whether I ought to mention it. I'm not particularly anxious to make trouble. On the other hand, you know, I don't want to be an accessory to anything.'

'If my opinion is worth anything,' said Wimsey, 'I'd say, cough it up. After all, if anybody did do the poor devil in, it's rather up to one to get it detected, and so on.'

'I suppose it is, though one can't bring people to life again unfortunately. If one could, of course, one wouldn't hesitate. Still—'

'Besides,' said Wimsey, 'you never know which way evidence is going to work. People sometimes hang on to information with the bright idea of shieldin' their husbands or sons or best girls, and give the police a hell of a time, and when it does come out, it proves to be the one thing in the world that was wanted to save their necks – the husbands' and sons' and best girls' necks, I mean, of course.'

Ferguson looked dissatisfied.

'If I only knew why they wanted to know about Monday night,' he said, slowly.

'They want to find the last person who saw the man alive,' said Wimsey, promptly. 'It's always done. It's part of the regular show. You get it in all the mystery stories. Of course, the last person to see him never commits the crime. That would make it too easy. One of these days I shall write a book in which two men are seen to walk down a cul-de-sac, and there is a shot and one man is found murdered and the other runs away with a gun in his hand, and after twenty chapters stinking with red herrings, it turns out that the man with the gun did it after all.'

'Well, nine times out of ten he has done it – in real life, that is – hasn't he? Well, I don't know.'

'What *have* you told the police, anyhow?' asked Wimsey, losing patience a little, and fiddling with a tube of white paint.

'I said I'd been at home all evening, and they asked if I had seen or heard anything suspicious next door. I said I hadn't, and I can't say exactly that I did, you know. They asked if I'd seen Campbell come home and I said I hadn't seen him, but I'd heard the car come in. That was a little after 10. I heard it strike, and thought it was about time I pottered off to bed, as I had to catch a train next morning. I'd had a last drink and tidied up and picked out a book to read and had just toddled upstairs when I heard him.'

'Was that the last you heard of him?'

'Ye—es. Except that I had a hazy kind of idea that I heard the door open and shut again shortly afterwards, as if he had gone out again. But I can't say for certain. He must have come back again later, if he did go out, because I saw him go out again in his car in the morning.'

'Well, that's valuable. What time was that?'

'Some time between 7.30 and 7.45 – I can't say to the moment. I was just finishing dressing. I had to get my own breakfast, you see, so as to catch the 'bus for the 9.8. It's six and a half miles to that bally station.'

'You actually saw Campbell in the car?'

'Oh, yes, I saw him all right. At least, I suppose if I had to go into the witness-box, I could only swear to his clothes and general appearance. I didn't see his face. But there was no doubt it was Campbell all right.'

'I see.' Wimsey's heart, which had missed a beat, calmed down again. He had seen the handcuffs closing on Ferguson. If he had sworn to seeing Campbell alive at an hour when Wimsey knew him to have been dead—! But things were not made as easy as all that for detectives.

'What had he got on?'

'Oh, that hideous check cloak and the famous hat. There's no mistaking them.'

'No. Well, what is it you didn't let up about?'

'One or two other things. First of all – though I don't see that that can have had anything to do with it – there was a sort of a hullabaloo about 8 o'clock on Monday evening.'

'Was there ? I say, Ferguson, I'm so sorry, I've burst a perfectly good Winsor & Newton tube. It's my beastly habit of fidgeting. It's all bulged out at the end.'

'Has it ? Oh, it doesn't matter. Roll it up. Here's a rag. Did you get it on your coat ?'

'No, thanks, it's all right. What sort of hullabaloo ?'

'Fellow came round banging on Campbell's door and using language. Campbell was out – rather fortunately, because I gathered there was a perfectly good shindy brewing.'

'Who was the fellow ?'

Ferguson glanced at Wimsey, then back at his canvas, and said in a low tone:

'As a matter of fact, I'm afraid it was Farren.'

Wimsey whistled.

'Yes. I stuck my head out and told him not to make such a filthy row and he asked me where the something-or-other that what-d'ye-call-it Campbell was. I said I hadn't seen him all day and advised Farren to remove himself. So then he started some rigmarole about always finding the so-and-so hanging round his place and he wanted to have it out with him, and if once he laid hands on Campbell he would do all kinds of nasty things to him, inside and out. Of course, I paid no attention to it. Farren's always going off the deep end, but he's like the Queen of Hearts – never executes nobody, you know. I told Farren to forget about it, and he told me to go and do this and that to myself, and by that time I'd got fed up. So I retorted that he could go away and hang himself, and he said that was exactly what he was going to do, only he must slay Campbell first. So I said, Righto! but not to disturb hard-working people. So he hung about a bit and then took himself off.'

'On his two legs ?'

'No, on a bicycle.'

'Oh, yes, of course. He could hardly have walked from Kirkcudbright. I say, Ferguson, how much is there in that business about Mrs. Farren ?'

'Damn all, if you ask me. I think Campbell was fond of her in his way, but she's much too high-minded to get herself into trouble. She likes to do the motherly business – inspiration, you know, and influence of a pure woman. Do good, and never mind what the rude world says. Sweetness and beautiful lives and all that rot. Dash it! What have I done with the cobalt? Can't stick the woman, you know, never could. Oh! I've got it in my pocket, as usual. Yes. As you may know, my wife and I don't live together, and Gilda Farren takes it upon herself to lecture me. At least, I've choked her off now, but she once had the impertinence to try and "bring us together." Blast her cheek! She created a damned embarrassing situation. Not that it matters now. But I can't stick those interfering, well-meaning bitches. Now, whenever she meets me, she looks mournfully and forgivingly in my eyes. I can't stand that kind of muck.'

'Beastly,' agreed Wimsey. 'Like the people who offer to pray for you. Did Farren depart altogether, or did he by any chance come back?'

'I don't know. That's just the point. *Somebody* came later on.'

'When was that?'

'Just after midnight, but I didn't get up to see who it was. Somebody knocked at the door and presently whoever it was went in, but I didn't bother to get up and look. And then I went off to sleep.'

'And didn't hear the person go?'

'No. I've no idea how long he – or she – stayed.'

'She?'

'I say he or she, because I really haven't the least idea which it was. I don't think it was Farren, though, because I fancy I heard a car. You might give me that rag, if you've finished with it. I'm really frightfully vague about the whole business. To tell the truth, I thought it was Jock Graham up to his games again.'

'That's quite likely. H'm. If I were you, Ferguson, I think I'd mention it.'

'What? Just that midnight visitor, do you mean? Or Farren as well?'

'Farren too. But particularly the midnight person. After all, he apparently *was* the last to see Campbell alive.'

'What do you mean? I saw him in the morning.'

'Saw him to speak to,' said Wimsey. 'He might be able to give the police valuable help, if they could get hold of him.'

'Why hasn't he come forward, then?'

'Oh, Lord! a hundred reasons. He may have been selling illicit salmon, or, as you say, he may have been she. One never knows.'

'True. All right. I'll come clean, as they say. I'd better do it at once, or they'll think I know more than I do.'

'Yes,' said Wimsey. 'I shouldn't waste any time.'

He wasted none himself, but drove straight back to Kirkcudbright, where he met Inspector Macpherson just stepping into his car.

LORD PETER WIMSEY

'HULLO – ullo – ullo!' cried Wimsey. 'Where are you off to? I've got something for you.'

The Inspector clambered out of the car again and greeted Wimsey cordially.

'Weel, noo,' said he, 'I had something tae show ye, too. Wull ye step intae the station a wee while?'

The Inspector was in no way sorry to get someone to admire his time-schedule, and Wimsey applauded generously. 'What's more,' said he, 'I can fill up a blank or two for you.'

He unfolded his budget, while the Inspector sat licking his lips.

'Ay,' said the latter, ''tis a' clear as daylight. Puir Farren – he must ha' been in a rare way tae go and do such a thing. Peety we ha' lost sae much time. It's a hundred to one he's oot o' the country by noo.'

'Out of the country or out of the world,' suggested Wimsey.

'Ay, that's a fact. He said he wad hae 't oot wi' Campbell an' then mak' away wi' himsel'. They often says it an' doesna' do't, but whiles they do't a' the same.'

'Yes,' said Wimsey.

'I'm thinking,' pursued Macpherson, 'we'll no be far wrang if we send a search-party up into them hills beyond Creetown. Ye'll mind the sad affair there was a year or two ago, with the puir woman as threw hersel' doon one o' the auld lead-mines. Where there's been trouble once there may be again. It wad be a terrible thing if the puir man's body was to be lying up yonder and us not tae find it. Ay, d'ye ken, my lord, I'm thinkin' this'll juist be the verra thing that Mistress Farren's fearin', though she disna like tae say so.'

'I absolutely agree,' said Wimsey. 'I think she believes her husband's killed himself, and daren't say so because she suspects he may have done the murder. You'd better get your sleuth-hounds out at once, Inspector, and then we'll pop along and have a hunt for this spanner.'

'There's a terrible deal of work tae be done,' said Macpherson. 'I'll doot we'll no have men enough for a' these investigations.'

'Cheer up,' said Wimsey. 'You've pretty well narrowed it down now, haven't you?'

'Ay,' replied the Inspector, cautiously, 'but I'm no countin' upon it. There's mony a slip, an' I'm no losin' sight o' ony o' my suspectit pairsons, juist yet awhile.'

Wee Helen had described the site of Campbell's encounter with the man in the car so exactly that there was no necessity to take her along with them to point it out. 'We'll be mair comfortable and private-like on our own,' observed Macpherson, and heaved himself with a sigh of contentment into the front seat of Wimsey's huge Daimler. Six or seven minutes brought them to the bend. Here Wimsey deposited the Inspector, and here, after stowing the car out of the way of other travellers, he joined him in his search.

According to Helen's story, she had taken up her position beneath the sunk wall, on the left-hand side of the road going towards Gatehouse. Wimsey and Macpherson therefore started, one at either end of the bend, searching within a couple of yards from the wall and working gradually towards one another. It was back-breaking exercise, for the grass was rather long, and as he groped, Wimsey found himself versifying after the manner of the old man sitting on a gate.

> 'But I was scheming to devise
>   A wheeze to catch the spanner,
> With magnets of uncommon size,
>   And sell it for a tanner,
> Or train a pack of skilful hounds
>   To scent it like a rabbit,
> And something, something, something – ounds
>   And something, something habit.'

He paused and straightened his spine.

'Not very lively,' he mused; 'better, I think, for a Heath Robinson picture.

> *Or purchase half a ton of flints*
> *And hurl them in the dark*
> *And something or the other ending in glints,*
> *And a last line ending in see the spark.*

I ought to have brought Bunter. This is menial toil. It's really beneath the dignity of any human being, unless one is like the army of Napoleon which is popularly reputed to have marched on its belly. Hullo! hullo! hullo!'

His walking-stick – which he carried with him everywhere, even in the car, for fear that by some accident he might be obliged to stagger a few steps when he got to places – struck against something which gave out a metallic noise. He stooped, looked, and let out a loud yell.

The Inspector came galloping up.

'Here you are,' said Wimsey, with conscious pride.

It was a big King Dick spanner, slightly rusty with the dew, lying within a couple of feet of the wall.

'Ye've no touched it ?' asked the Inspector, anxiously.

'What do you take me for ?' retorted Wimsey, hurt.

Macpherson knelt down, drew out a tape-measure and solemnly measured the distance of the spanner from the wall. He then peered over the wall into the road and, drawing out his notebook, made a careful plan of the exact position. After that, he took out a large jack-knife and thrust it in among the stones of the wall, by way of making the indication still more precise, and only after performing these rites did he very gingerly lift the spanner, covering his fingers with a large white handkerchief and wrapping the folds of the linen tenderly about it.

'There might be finger-prints, ye ken,' said he.

'Ay, there might,' agreed Wimsey, in the language of the country.

'And then we've only tae get the prints of Farren and compare them. How will we do that now ?'

'Razor,' said Wimsey, 'palette-knife, picture-frames, pots – anything in his studio. Studios are never dusted. I suppose the actual riot took place on the other side of the road. There won't be much trace of it now, I'm afraid.'

The Inspector shook his head.

'It's no likely, wi' cars and cattle passin' up and doon. There was no bloodshed, an' this dry grass takes no marks, mair's the pity. But we'll tak' a look round.'

The tarmac itself betrayed nothing, and the indications in the grass were so vague that nothing could be made of them. Presently, however, Wimsey, beating about among a tuft of bramble and bracken, uttered a small astonished noise.

'What's that?' asked Macpherson.

'What indeed?' said Wimsey. 'It's one of these problems, Inspector, that's what it is. Did you ever hear of the Kilkenny cats that fought till only their tails were left behind them? Now here are two gentlemen having a fight, and both of them spirited away, leaving only a tuft of hair. And what's more, it's the wrong colour. What do you make of that?'

He held up in his hand a tuft of curly blackness suggestive of an Assyrian wall-painting.

'That's a queer thing,' said Macpherson.

'Cut off, not torn out,' said Wimsey. He pulled a lens from his pocket and examined the trophy carefully. 'It's soft and silky, and it's never been trimmed at the distal end; it might come from one of those sweet old-fashioned long-haired girls, but the texture's a bit on the coarse side. It's a job for an expert, really, to say where it does come from.'

The Inspector handled it carefully and peered through the lens with as much intelligence as he could assume on the spur of the moment.

'What makes ye say it's never been trimmed?' he enquired.

'See how the points taper. Is there a female in the country with hair so black and so curly, that's never been shingled or bingled? Were our blokes wrestling for a love-token, Inspector? But whose? Not Mrs. Farren's unless she's turned from a Burne-Jones to a Rossetti in the night. But if it isn't Mrs. Farren's, Inspector, where's our theory?'

'Hoots!' said the Inspector. 'Maybe it has naething tae do wi' the case at a'.'

'How sensible you are,' said Wimsey, 'and how imperturbable. Calm without something or other, without o'erflowing, full. Talking of that, how soon will the pubs be open? Hullo! here's another bunch of hair. Some love-token! I say, let's trot home with this and interview Bunter. I've a notion it may interest him.'

'Ye think so?' said Macpherson. 'Weel, that's no a bad idea, neither. But I'm thinkin' we'll better be away tae Newton-Stewart first. We'll have tae find the doctor and get the undertaker tae open the coffin. I've a great fancy tae see how this spanner fits yon wound in the heid.'

'Very good,' said Wimsey, 'so have I. But just a minute. We'd better have a look first and see if we can find out what happened to the body. The murderer stuck it into his car and drove off towards Gatehouse with it. He can't have gone far, because he very soon came back for Campbell's Morris, so there ought to be a gate about here somewhere. In fact, I fancy I remember seeing one.'

The search did not take long. About fifty yards farther along the bend they came to a rusty iron gate on the right-hand side. This led into a grassy lane which, after about thirty yards, turned abruptly to the left and was hidden behind some bushes.

'Here's the place,' said Wimsey. 'There's been a car up here lately. You can see where the wing scraped the post. The gate has a hook and chain – easy enough to undo. He must have backed it in up to the bend. Then, if he turned the lights off, it would be absolutely invisible from the road. There's no difficulty about that, and there's no other possible hiding-place for a mile or so, I'm certain of that. Well, that's uncommonly satisfactory. I gloat, as Stalky says. Back we go to the car, Inspector. Spit on your hands and grasp the coachwork firmly. I'm feeling sprightly, and I'm going to break all records between here and Newton-Stewart.'

Dr. Cameron was greatly interested in the spanner, and experienced so much difficulty in keeping his hands off it, that it was thought best to have it tested for finger-prints before any-things else was done. By the combined exertions of the police-staff, the local photographer and Wimsey, this was done. A magnificent thumb-print made its appearance after a dusting with mercury-powder, and a perfectly good negative was 'secured,' to use the journalist's pet phrase.

In the meantime, a constable had rounded up the undertaker, who arrived in great excitement, swallowing the last fragments of his tea. A slight further delay was caused by its occurring to somebody that the Fiscal should be notified. The Fiscal, for-tunately enough, happened to be in the town, and joined the party, explaining to Wimsey as they drove along to the mortuary that it was the most painful case he had handled in the whole of his experience, and that he had been much struck by the superi-ority of the Scots law to the English in these matters, 'For,' said he, 'the publicity of a coroner's inquest is bound to give much unnecessary pain to the relations, which is avoided by our method of private investigation.'

'That is very true,' said Wimsey, politely, 'but think of all the extra fun we get from the Sunday newspapers. Inquests are jam to them.'

'We then proceeded,' ran Inspector Macpherson's official notes on this occasion, 'to the mortuary, where the coffin was unscrewed in the presence of the Fiscal, Dr. Cameron, James McWhan (the undertaker), Lord Peter Wimsey and myself, and the body of Campbell extracted. On comparison of the spanner formerly mentioned with the wounds upon the head of the corpse, Dr. Cameron gave it as his opinion that a contused area upon the left cheek-bone agreed exactly in contour with the head of the said spanner and had in all probability been inflicted by that or by a similar instrument. With regard to the larger contused area upon the temple, which had occasioned death, Dr. Cameron could not speak with certainty, but said that its appearance was consistent with the use of the said spanner.'

After this triumphant entry, which bears the marks of considerable literary effort, appears another.

'Acting upon the suggestion of Lord Peter Wimsey' (the Inspector was a just man, giving honour where it was due, regardless of his own lacerated feelings), 'the finger-prints of the corpse were then taken.' (This last phrase is erased, and a better locution substituted), 'a record was then secured of the finger-prints of the corpse. On comparison of this record with the thumb-print found upon the spanner, these were both found to be identical. Acting upon instructions, I despatched both records to Glasgow for expert scrutiny.'

In this stately paragraph, nothing is said of the bitter disappointment experienced by the Inspector. It had seemed to him, with that finger-print in his hands, as though his case were concluded, and now, suddenly, he was taken up and cast down into the old outer darkness of uncertainty and gnashing of teeth. But his behaviour was handsome to the last degree.

'It's a great maircy,' said he to Wimsey, 'that your lordship should ha' taken the notion tae have that done. It wad never have entered my heid. We might have eliminated a' six suspects on the strength o' that deceivin' finger-print. It was a gran' notion of yours, my lord, a gran' notion.'

He sighed deeply.

'Cheer up,' said Wimsey. 'It's all the luck of the game. Come and have a spot of dinner with me at the Galloway Arms.'

Now that was an unlucky suggestion.

The gathering in Bob Anderson's studio was well attended that night. Bob was an artist, the geniality of whose temperament is best vouched for by the fact that it had never for one moment occurred to anybody engaged on the case that he could by any chance have hated Campbell, damaged Campbell, or been mixed up for a single moment in the Campbell mystery. He had lived in Kirkcudbright for nearly as many years as Gowan, and was extremely popular, not only with all the artists, but also with the local inhabitants, particularly with the fishermen and the men employed about the harbour. He seldom visited anybody, preferring to be at home every evening in the week, and all the news of the town was bound to filter through Bob's studio in time.

When Wimsey poked his long nose round the door on that Thursday evening, he found a full house already assembled. Miss Cochran and Miss Selby were there, of course, and Jock Graham (in a remarkable costume, comprising a fisherman's jersey, a luggage strap, riding-breeches and rope-soled deck-shoes), and Ferguson (rather surprisingly, for he did not as a rule go out of an evening), the Harbour-master, the doctor, Strachan (his black eye almost faded out), a Mrs. Terrington, who worked in metal, a long, thin, silent man called Temple, of whom Wimsey knew nothing except that his handicap was five at St. Andrews, and finally Mrs., Miss and a young Mr. Anderson. The babble of conversation was terrific.

Wimsey's entrance was greeted by a welcoming shout.

'Here he is! Here he is! Come away in! Here's the man to tell us all about it!'

'All about what?' said Wimsey, knowing only too well. 'What to back for the Leger?'

'Leger be damned. All about this business of poor Campbell. It's terrible the way the police come running in and out of one's house. One doesn't feel safe for a moment. Luckily I've got a cast-iron alibi, or I'd begin to feel I was a criminal myself.'

'No, Bob, not you,' said Wimsey.

'Oh, ye never know these days. But very fortunately I was at dinner with the Provost Monday night and didn't get home till midnight, and on Tuesday morning I was showing myself up and down St. Cuthbert's Street. But tell us, Wimsey, you that's hand in glove with the police—'

'I'm not allowed to tell anything,' said Wimsey, plaintively. 'You mustn't tempt me. It's not fair. I could not love thee, Bob, so much, loved I not honour more. Besides, I'm supposed to be finding things out, not giving information away.'

'Well, you're welcome to all we know,' said Miss Selby.

'Am I?' said Wimsey. 'Tell me, then, how many hundred people in the county, besides Jock, knew that Campbell meant to go up to the Minnoch on Tuesday?'

'You had better ask who did not?' said the doctor. 'He said so here on the Sunday night. He'd been making a preliminary sketch that afternoon. Monday he was going to fish in some wonderful place he wouldn't tell anybody about—'

'I know where it was, all the same,' put in Graham.

'You would. And Tuesday he was going to paint the Minnoch if the weather held. You heard him say so, Sally.'

'I did so,' said Miss Cochran.

'I was here, too,' said Ferguson, 'and I remember it perfectly. I fancy I said something about it to Farren on the Monday morning, because he had a tea-party or something fixed up for Brighouse Bay on Tuesday and said he hoped they wouldn't run into Campbell.'

'I knew, too,' said Strachan. 'My wife and I met him up here on Sunday, as I think I mentioned to Wimsey.'

Wimsey nodded. 'Campbell seems to have been more communicative than usual,' he remarked.

'Och,' said Bob, 'Campbell was not such a bad fellow if you took him the right way. He had an aggressive manner, but I believe it was mostly due to a feeling that he was out of everything. He used to have awful arguments with people—'

'He was an opinionated man,' said the Harbour-master.

'Yes, but that made it all the more amusing. One couldn't take Campbell seriously.'

'Gowan did, for one,' said the doctor.

'Ah, but Gowan takes everything very seriously, and himself most of all.'

'All the same,' said Mrs. Anderson. 'Campbell ought not to have spoken of Gowan as he did.'

'Gowan's away, isn't he? They told me he had gone to London. By the way, Wimsey, what's happened to Waters?'

'I haven't the foggiest. As far as I can make out, he's supposed to be in Glasgow. Did you see anything of him, Ferguson ?'

'No. The police asked me that. Do I take it that Waters is suspected of anything ?'

'Waters was here on Sunday night,' observed the doctor, 'but he didn't stay very long after Campbell came in.'

'You're a great man for facts, doctor. But if Waters was in Glasgow he couldn't have been up at the Minnoch.'

'The odd thing,' said Miss Selby, 'is that nobody saw him in Glasgow. He was supposed to be going by our train, but he didn't, did he, Mr. Ferguson ?'

'I didn't see him. But I wasn't looking out for him particularly. I saw you two get in at Dumfries, and I saw you again with your party at St. Enoch Station. But I went off in rather a hurry. I had some shopping to do before I got down to the show. As a matter of fact, the whole thing was very irritating. Something went wrong with my magneto, otherwise I should have got up early and run over to catch the 7.30 express from Dumfries, instead of waiting for that ghastly 11.22, which stops at every station.'

'Rather than travel by a confirmed stopper,' said Wimsey, 'I'd have waited a little longer and gone by the 1.46.'

'Taking the 10.56 from Gatehouse, you mean ?'

'Or the 11 o'clock 'bus. It gets you in to Dumfries at 12.25.'

'No, it doesn't,' said Strachan. 'That's the Sunday 'bus. The week-day 'bus goes at 10.'

'Well, anyway, I couldn't,' said Ferguson, 'because I'd made an appointment to meet a man at the show at 3.15, and the 1.46 doesn't get in to Glasgow until 3.34. So I had to make a martyr of myself. And the sickening thing was that my man never turned up after all. I found a note at my hotel, saying he'd been called to see a sick relative.'

'Sick relatives ought to be forbidden by law,' said Wimsey.

'Yes; I was damned fed-up. However, I took my mag. along to Sparkes & Crisp, and it's still there, confound it. Something obscure in the armature winding, as far as I could make out – I don't think they knew themselves. And it's practically a new car, too; only done a few thousand. I'm claiming under guarantee.'

'Oh, well,' said Wimsey, consolingly, 'Sparkes & Crisp will provide a nice little alibi for you.'

'Yes; I don't know exactly when I got there, but they'll be able to say. I took a tram up. I should think I got to their place about 3 o'clock. The train was a quarter of an hour late, of course; it always is.'

'It was nearer twenty minutes late,' said Miss Selby, severely. 'We were very much annoyed about it. It cut down our time with Kathleen.'

'Local trains always are late,' said Wimsey. 'It's one of the rules. It's done so that the guard and the engine-driver can step out and admire the station-master's garden at every stop. You know those gardening competitions they have in railway magazines. Well, that's how they're run. The guard gets off at Kirkgunzeon or Brig o' Dee with a yard measure in his hand and measures the prize marrow and says: "Twa fut four inches – that'll no dew, Mr. McGeoch. They've got one at Dalbeattie that beats ye by two inches. Here, George, come and look at this." So the engine-driver strolls over and says, "Och, ay, imph'm, ye'll dew weel tae gie't a mulch o' liquid guano and aspidistra tonic." And then they go back to Dalbeattie and tell them that the marrow at Kirkgunzeon is hauling up on them hand over fist. It's no good laughing. I know they do it. If not, what on earth do they do, hanging everlastingly about at these three-by-four stations ?'

'You ought to be ashamed of yourselves,' said Miss Anderson, 'talking such nonsense, with poor Mr. Campbell lying dead.'

'They're burying him tomorrow, aren't they ?' said Jock Graham, suddenly and tactlessly. 'At Gatehouse. Does one go ? I haven't any wedding garments.'

'Oh, dear,' said Bob. 'Never thought of that. We must go, I suppose. Look odd if we didn't. Besides, I'd like to show respect to the poor fellow. Surely we can go as we are.'

'You can't go in those terrific tweeds, Bob,' said Miss Selby.

'Why not ?' demanded Bob. 'I can feel just as sorry in a check suit as in a frock-coat smelling of moth-balls. I shall go in my ordinary working clothes – with a black tie, naturally. Can you see me in a top-hat ?'

'Dad, you are dreadful,' said Miss Anderson.

'My God!' said Wimsey. 'I hope Bunter has remembered to order a wreath. I expect he has. He remembers everything. Did you decide to send one from the Club, Strachan ?'

'Oh, yes,' said Strachan. 'We all agreed it was the right thing to do.'

'The trouble with Campbell,' said the five-handicap man unexpectedly, 'was that he was a bad loser. A slice off the tee or a foozled approach-shot would put him off his game for the afternoon.'

Having unburdened his mind of this criticism, he retired in obscurity again and spoke no more.

'He was having a one-man show in London this autumn, wasn't he?' said Ferguson.

'I expect his sister will carry on with that,' said the doctor. 'It will probably be a great success.'

'I never know what the doctor means by those remarks,' said young Anderson. 'What's the sister like, by the way? Has anybody seen her?'

'She called here yesterday,' said Mrs. Anderson. 'A nice, quiet girl. I liked her.'

'What did she think about it all?'

'Well, Jock, what could she think? She seemed very much distressed, as you would expect.'

'No idea of who might have done it, I suppose?' suggested Wimsey.

'No – I gathered that she hadn't seen anything of her brother for some years. She's married to an engineer in Edinburgh, and, though she didn't say much, I rather fancy the two men didn't hit it off very well.'

'It's all very unpleasant and mysterious,' said Mrs. Anderson. 'I hope very much it'll all turn out to be a mare's nest. I can't really believe that anybody about here would have committed a murder. I think the police are just anxious to make a sensation. Probably it was only an accident, after all.'

The doctor opened his mouth, but caught Wimsey's eye, and shut it again. Wimsey guessed that his colleague at Newton-Stewart must have said something, and hastened to lead the conversation away on lines which would at the same time convey a warning and possibly also elicit useful information.

'A great deal,' he said, 'depends on how long Campbell actually spent at the Minnoch on Tuesday. We know – at least, Ferguson knows – that he started out about 7.30. It's about twenty-seven miles – say he got up there between 8.30 and 8.45. How long would it take him to do his sketch?'

'Starting from scratch?'

'That's just what one can't be sure of. But say he set out with a blank canvas.'

'Which he probably did,' said Strachan. 'He showed me his

rough sketch in his sketch-book on Sunday, and on Monday he didn't go up.'

'So far as we know,' said Ferguson.

'Exactly. So far as we know.'

'Well, then ?' said Wimsey.

'We haven't seen the picture,' said Bob. 'So how can we tell ?'

'Look here,' said Wimsey. 'I know how we could get a rough idea. Supposing all you fellows were each to start off with a panel that size and a rough charcoal outline – could you kind of fudge something up, imitating Campbell's style as much as possible, while I stood over you with a stop-watch ? We could take the average of your speeds and get a sort of line on the thing that way.'

'Reconstruct the crime ?' said young Anderson, laughing.

'In a sense.'

'But Wimsey, that's all very well. No two men paint at the same rate, and if I, for instance, tried to paint like Campbell, with a palette-knife, I should make an awful muck of it, and get nowhere.'

'Possibly – but then your styles are so very unlike, Ferguson. But Jock can imitate anybody, I know, and Waters said it would be easy to fake a perfectly plausible Campbell. And Bob here is an expert with the knife.'

'I'll be sporting, Lord Peter,' said Miss Selby, surprisingly. 'If it's really going to do any good, I don't mind making a fool of myself.'

'That's the spirit,' said Graham. 'I'm on, Peter.'

'I don't mind having a dash at it,' said Strachan.

'All right, then,' said Bob. 'We all will. Have we got to go up to the scene of the tragedy, old man ?'

'Starting at 7.30 ?' said Miss Selby.

'It's no good getting there too early,' objected Strachan, 'because of the light.'

'That's one of the things we've got to prove,' said Wimsey. 'How soon he could have got going on it.'

'Ugh!' said Bob Anderson. 'It's against my principles to get up in the small hours.'

'Never mind,' said Wimsey. 'Think how helpful it may be.'

'Oh, well – is it tomorrow morning you're thinking of ?'

'The sooner the better.'

'Will you convey us there ?'

'In the utmost luxury. And Bunter shall provide hot coffee and sandwiches.'

'Be sporting,' said Miss Selby.

'If we must—' said Bob.

'I think it's monstrous,' said Ferguson. 'Going over in carloads like that and having a picnic. What will people take us for ?'

'What does it matter what they take us for ?' retorted Graham. 'I think you're absolutely right, Wimsey. Damn it all, we *ought* to do what we can. I'll be there. Come on, Ferguson, don't you let us down.'

'I'll come if you like,' said Ferguson, 'but I do think it's rather disgusting, all the same.'

'Miss Selby, Bob, Strachan, Ferguson, Graham, and me as timekeeper. Coffee and palette-knives for six. Strachan, you'd better run Ferguson and Graham up, and I'll take the Kirkcudbright contingent. I'll get a police witness as well. That's fine.'

'I believe you enjoy it, Lord Peter,' said Mrs. Terrington. 'I suppose you get carried away by these investigations.'

'They are always interesting,' admitted Wimsey. 'Every man is thrilled by his own job. Isn't that so, Mr. Doulton ?' he added, addressing the Harbour-master.

'That's so, my lord. I remember having tae du much the same thing, mony years since, in an inquest upon a sailing-vessel that ran aground in the estuary and got broken up by bumping herself to bits in a gale. The insurance folk thocht that the accident wasna a'tegither straightforward. We tuk it upon oorsels tae demonstrate that wi' the wind and tide settin' as they did, the boat should ha' been well away fra' the shore if they had started at the hour they claimed to ha' done. We lost the case, but I've never altered my opeenion.'

'That estuary can be awkward if you don't know the channels,' said Bob.

'Ay, that's true. But a man of experience, as this skipper was, should no ha' made such a mistake, unless indeed he was drunk at the time.'

'That's a thing that might happen to anybody,' said Wimsey. 'Who were those fellows that were kicking up such a row in the town over the week-end ?'

'Och, they were juist a couple a' English gentlemen fra' the wee yacht that was anchored up by the Doon,' said the Harbour-master, placidly. 'There was nae harm in them at a'. Verra decent, hospitable fellows, father and son, and knew how tae handle a boat. They were aff on Tuesday mornin', makin' their way up the west coast to Skye, they tell't me.'

'Well, they've got fine weather for it,' said the doctor.

'Ay, imph'm. But I'm thinkin' there'll be a bit of a change the nicht. The wind's shiftin', and there's one o' they depressions coming over fra' Iceland.'

'I wish they'd keep their depressions at home,' grumbled Wimsey, thinking of his experiment.

The meeting did not break up till 11 o'clock. Stepping out into the street, Wimsey became immediately aware of the change in the weather. A soft dampness beat on his cheek, and the sky was overcast with a close veil of drifting cloud.

He was about to turn into Blue Gate Close, when he saw, far away at the end of the street, the red tail-lamp of a car. It was difficult to judge distances in the close blackness, but his instinct seemed to tell him that the car was standing before Gowan's house. Possessed by curiosity, he strolled down the street towards it. Presently, straining eyes and ears, he seemed to hear a stir of low voices, and to see two muffled figures cross the pavement.

'Something's happening!' he said to himself, and started to run, noiselessly, on rubber soles. Now he heard distinctly enough the starting of the engine. He redoubed his speed.

Something tripped him – he stumbled and sprawled headlong bruising himself painfully. When he picked himself up, the red tail-light was vanishing round the corner.

The Harbour-master appeared suddenly at his elbow, assisting him to rise.

'It's a fair scandal,' said the Harbour-master, 'the way they doorsteps is built right oot tae the edge o' the pavement. Are ye hurt, my lord? The Council should du something aboot it. I remember, when I was a young man—'

'Excuse me,' said Wimsey. He rubbed his knees and elbows. 'No harm done. Forgive me, won't you? I have an appointment.'

He dashed off in the direction of the police-station, leaving the Harbour-master to stare after him in surprise.

CONSTABLE ROSS

THE next day dawned wild and stormy, with heavy rain and violent squalls of south-west wind. Wimsey's sketching-party was perforce postponed. Nevertheless, the day was not wholly lacking in incident.

The first thing that happened was the sudden return of Constable Ross from Ayr, with a remarkable story.

He had gone out on the previous night to Kilmarnock, to investigate the history of a bicyclist in a burberry, who had been seen to leave Ayr station shortly after 1.48. This trail, however, had petered out. He found the man without the least difficulty. He proved to be a perfectly innocent and respectable young farmer who had come to the station to inquire about some goods lost in transit.

Ross had then made further inquiries in and about the town, with the following result:

The bookstall clerk had seen the passenger in grey pass his bookstall at 1.49, in the direction of the exit. He had not seen him actually leave the station, because of the corner of the bookstall, which cut off his view of the exit.

A taxi-driver, standing just outside the station exit, had seen a young man in a burberry come out with a bicycle. (This was the farmer whom Ross subsequently interviewed.) He also saw a youngish man in a cap and a grey flannel suit come out, carrying a small attaché-case, but without a bicycle. A fare had then hailed him and he had driven away, but he fancied he had seen the man in grey turn into a small side-street. This would be about two minutes after the Stranraer train came in – say, at 1.50.

At about 2.20 a porter who was taking along a truck of luggage to the 2.25 for Carlisle, noticed a man's bicycle standing against a board which displayed time-tables and railway posters, just above the bays on the booking-hall side of the platform. He examined it and found that it had an L.M.S. label for Euston. He knew nothing about it, except that he had a dim impression that it had been there for some little time. Supposing that it was in charge of one of his colleagues and possibly belonged to some passenger who was breaking his journey at Carlisle, he left it where it was. At 5 o'clock, however, he noticed that it was still there, and asked the other porters about it. None of them remembered handling it or labelling it, but since it was there, with its label all in order, he did his duty by it and put it into the 5.20 express for Euston. If the passenger to whom it belonged had travelled by the 2.25, the bicycle would arrive in Euston by the same train as himself, for the 2.25 does not run to Euston, and London passengers would have to change at Carlisle and wait two-and-a-quarter hours till the 5.20 came in to take them on.

This porter, having had his attention particularly directed to the bicycle, had examined it fairly closely. It was a Raleigh, not new and not in very good condition, but with good tyres front and back.

Ross jumped when he heard this description, and eagerly examined all the porters. He completely failed, however, to discover the man who had affixed the Euston label to it, or to get any information about its owner.

The booking-clerk had issued ten tickets to Carlisle by the 2.25 – five third singles, three third returns, a first single and a first return – and two third singles to Euston. He had issued no long-distance bicycle-ticket by that train or by the 5.20, which had carried eight passengers from Ayr. A porter, not the same man who had put the bicycle into the 5.20, remembered a gentleman in a grey suit who had travelled to Carlisle on the 2.25 without luggage; he had asked him some questions about the route, which was via Mauchline. This person did not wear glasses and had said nothing at all about any bicycle, nor had any passenger by the 5.20 mentioned a bicycle.

Constable Ross next endeavoured to trace the man in the grey suit who had vanished down the side-street, but without success. It was a small alley, rather than a street, containing nothing but the back-entrances of some warehouses and a public convenience.

The bookstall clerk, interrogated again, thought he remembered seeing a man in a soft felt hat and a burberry pass the bookstall with a bicycle at about 1.53 from the direction of the booking hall, but had not paid much attention to him. Nobody else had noticed this person at all, as the Stranraer train was just due out again to Glasgow and there was a considerable number of passengers hurrying to catch it.

Two porters, who had seen the last of the luggage into the Glasgow train at 1.54, swore definitely that there was no bicycle in either of the vans.

Constable Ross hardly knew what to make of all this. The description of the bicycle coincided almost exactly with that of the machine taken from the Anwoth Hotel and, rather less closely, with that of Farren's bicycle. But how had it come to bear a Euston label? The bicycle put in at Girvan had been labelled for Ayr by the porter, and this point was verified by the guard who put it out at Ayr. It was quite impossible that it could have been re-labelled at Ayr, during the train's six minutes' wait at that station, for throughout that period one porter or another had been continually on duty beside the case containing labels, and all were prepared to swear that the bicycle had not passed through their hands.

The only possibility was that the bicycle had somehow been re-labelled after the Glasgow train had gone; but it was not labelled by a porter, for none of them remembered it.

What had become of the man in the grey suit?

If he was the same person as the man in the burberry who had been seen by the bookstall clerk wheeling a bicycle at 1.53, he must have put on the burberry somewhere outside (in the public convenience?) and returned via the booking hall. What, then, had become of him? Had he hung about the station till 2.55? If so, where? He had not gone into the refreshment-room, for the girl there was positive that she had seen nobody of the sort. He had not been seen in the waiting-room or on the platform. Presumably he had left the bicycle by the hoarding and then gone out again, or taken some other train.

But which train?

He had not gone on to Glasgow by the 1.54, because it was certain that the bicycle could not have been re-labelled before the train left.

There remained the 1.56 to Muirkirk, the 2.12 and the 2.23 to Glasgow, the 2.30 to Dalmellington, the 2.35 to Kilmarnock and the 2.45 to Stranraer, besides, of course, the 2.25 itself.

Of these seven possibilities, Ross was able to eliminate the 1.56, the 2.30 and the 2.35. Nobody in the least corresponding to the description had travelled by any of them. The 2.45 to Stranraer he thought he could also dismiss. It had the advantage of bringing the murderer (if it was the murderer) back on his tracks – and Ross bore in mind Wimsey's remark that the murderer would probably wish to reappear at home as soon and as plausibly as possible – but it seemed almost inconceivable that anybody should take the trouble to go all the way to Ayr to get rid of a bicycle which could have been dumped so much more readily and easily at some point nearer home.

There remained the two Glasgow trains and the 2.25. The 2.12 to Glasgow was a comparatively slow train, getting in at 3.30; the 2.23 was the Stranraer boat-train, getting in at 3.29. The former had the advantage of getting the traveller away from the station earlier. He made inquiries about both trains, and received, in each case, vague descriptions of men in burberries and grey suits. It depressed him that this style of dress should be so common. He played a little with the idea that the wanted man might have changed his clothes before leaving Ayr, but dismissed the idea. He could not have carried a second suit of clothes as well as a burberry in the little attaché-case, and he could hardly have gone out, bought a suit in the town and taken a room to change in. At least, he *could* have done so, but it would have been unnecessarily risky. In that case he would have had to go by a much later train, and the more time he wasted at Ayr, the more worthless his alibi would be. And if he had not wanted to establish an alibi, what was the meaning of the elaborate proceedings at the Minnoch ? If, then, he had gone on to Glasgow, he could not have arrived there before 3.29 at the earliest, and in all probability would not have travelled later.

There remained the 2.55. He might have been the grey-suited traveller who had travelled to Euston. But if so, why take the bicycle with him, acknowledged or unacknowledged ? He might just as well have left it on the platform at Ayr.

But no! Perhaps the best thing he could have done was to take it with him. He would know that it might be inquired for – as a stolen bicycle at least, if not as a piece of evidence in a murder plot. Euston was larger and farther from the site of the crime than Ayr. A bicycle could be lost very conveniently in London, and so long as he had not been seen to travel with it, he could deny all knowledge of it.

Constable Ross was not entirely satisfied with any of these explanations. It was perfectly possible that the man had not travelled by any train at all. He might still be walking about Ayr. He might have taken a car or a 'bus to anywhere. He felt that the thing was becoming too complicated to tackle single-handed.

Accordingly he decided to return to Newton-Stewart with his report and get further instructions.

The first necessity was obviously to find out what had happened to the bicycle if and when it had got to London. Dalziel put an inquiry through to Euston. The reply came back in an hour's time, a bicycle answering to the description had duly arrived on the 5 a.m. train on Wednesday morning. As it had not been claimed, it had been placed in the left-luggage office to await its owner. It was a Raleigh corresponding to the description issued.

The police scratched their heads about this, and instructed the railway authorities to hold the machine until someone could come and identify it. In the meantime, if anybody called for it, he was to be detained. A call was put through to the London police requesting assistance in this part of the business, though it seemed likely that, if the bicycle was indeed the one which had been stolen, anybody who called for it would be foolish indeed.

'He couldna get it if he did call for 't,' said Constable Ross. 'They'd no gie 't up wi'oot a ticket.'

'Wad they no ?' said Sergeant Dalziel. 'An' if the fellow had got oot o' the train an' purchased a ticket at some other station ? At Carlisle or Crewe or Rugby, maybe ?'

'That's a fact,' said Ross. 'But had he done so, he'd have called for 't earlier. The later he leaves it the mair risky it wad be for him.'

'Ay, we'll be thankful it isna away already,' said Dalziel.

'Imph'm,' said Ross, pleased with himself.

Inspector Macpherson was pleased, too. He had driven over early to Newton-Stewart to lay his time-table before Sergeant Dalziel, and he preened himself.

'It a' fits in fine wi' my theory,' said he. 'If yon's no Farren's bicycle, I'll eat my hat.'

In the meantime, however, a shock was being prepared for Sergeant Dalziel. Full of pride in his own swift efficiency, he had, on his way back from Ayr the previous night, left a set of photographs at Girvan police-station, with instructions that they were to be shown to the porter McSkimming, as soon as he arrived in the morning, to see if he could identify the man in the grey suit. Now the Girvan police rang through to say that the porter had been carried off to hospital during the night, the 'awfu' pain in his stomach' having suddenly developed into acute appendicitis.

A call to the hospital brought the news that the man was being operated upon at that very moment, and would certainly be able to make no statement for some time. Disquieting details were added about 'perforation,' 'threatenings of peritonitis' and 'condition of the heart unsatisfactory.' Dalziel swore, and instantly packed Ross off again with a second set of photographs to show to the station officials at Ayr.

The next blow was directed at Inspector Macpherson, and caught him right on the midriff.

'If yon's no Farren's bicycle,' he had said, 'I will eat my hat.'

The words were scarcely out of his mouth before the telephone bell rang.

'This is the Creetown police speaking,' said a voice. 'We've found yon bicycle o' Mr. Farren's lying abandoned in the hills by Falbae. There's nae doot it's his all right, for his name is written on a label tied to the handle-bars.'

It will be remembered that on the previous evening, the Inspector had dispatched a party to search the neighbourhood of certain disused lead-mines, the scene of an unfortunate disaster a year or two before. These mines consisted of half a dozen or more narrow shafts cut in the hill-granite a few miles east of Creetown. They were reached by following the road to a farm called Falbae. From there a sheep-track or two led to the mines, which were surface-workings only, from thirty to forty feet deep at most. Some of the supporting beams of the cages were still in position, though all the tackle had long since disappeared. The mines had a bad name, particularly since an unhappy girl had thrown herself down one of them, and nobody went near them, except an occasional shepherd. The people of the farm had little occasion to visit the place, and the road ended at the farm. Though the mines were comparatively close to civilisation, they were, for all practicable purposes, as lonely and desolate as though they had been in the middle of a desert.

It was in this ill-omened spot that Farren's bicycle had been found. Macpherson, hastily driving over to investigate, found the Creetown policeman and a number of volunteer assistants clustered round the head of one of the pits. A man was fitting a rope about his waist preparatory to descending.

The bicycle was lying where it had been found – a few hundred yards beyond the farm, and half a mile or so from the nearest pit. It was in good order, though the plated parts were slightly rusty from lying four nights among the bracken. There were no signs of accident or violence. It seemed simply to have been flung down and left when the track became too rough and steep for bicycling.

'Ye've no found the body ?' said Macpherson.

No, they had found no body or clothing, but it seemed only too probable that the unfortunate Farren might be lying at the foot of one of the pits. They were intending – subject to instructions – to explore all the shafts in turn. It might be an awkward job, for one or two of them had water at the bottom. Macpherson told them to carry on and report the moment anything turned up. Then, deeply disappointed and chagrined, he made his mournful way back to Kirkcudbright.

To the Chief Constable fell the unpleasant task of telling Mrs. Farren about the fears they entertained about her husband. She was smiling when she met him at the door, and looked more cheerful than she had been for some days, and Sir Maxwell found it hard to enter upon his story. She took it well, on the whole. He laid stress on the fact that nothing as yet definitely pointed to suicide and that the search was only a matter of precaution.

'I quite understand,' said Mrs. Farren, 'and it is most good of you. You are very kind. I can't really believe that Hugh would do such a dreadful thing. I'm sure it's all a mistake. He is rather eccentric, you know, and I think it's much more likely that he has just wandered off somewhere. But of course you must search the mines. I quite see that.'

The Chief Constable made a few other inquiries, as tactfully as he could.

'Well, yes – if you know that already – I must admit that he was rather in a temper when he went away. Hugh is excitable, and he was upset by something that happened about the dinner. Oh, dear, no – nothing whatever to do with Mr. Campbell. What a ridiculous idea!'

Sir Maxwell felt he could not let this pass. He explained as kindly as possible, that Farren had been heard to make some very unfortunate observations that same evening with reference to Mr. Campbell.

Mrs. Farren then admitted that her husband had, indeed, objected to Campbell's repeated visits to the house.

'But as soon as he came to think it over,' she said, 'he would realise that he was doing me an injustice. He would never go so far as to lay violent hands on himself – or on anybody else. Sir Maxwell, you *must* believe me. I *know* my husband. He is impulsive, but with him everything blows over very quickly. I am as certain as I stand here that he is alive and well, and that he has done nothing rash. Even if – even if you should find his dead body, nothing will persuade me but that he has met with an accident. Anything else is unthinkable – and before long you will come back and tell me that I am right.'

She spoke with so much conviction that Jamieson was shaken in his belief. He said that he very much trusted that events would prove Mrs. Farren right, and took his leave. As he went, Strachan's car passed him at the turn of the lane, and glancing over his shoulder, he saw it stop at Mrs. Farren's door.

'Whatever it is about Farren,' he said, 'Strachan is in it, up to the hilt.'

He hesitated for a moment, and then turned back. He remembered that Macpherson had so far received no reply to his inquiry at Gatehouse about Strachan's whereabouts at 9.15 on Monday night.

'Oh, Mr. Strachan!' he said.

'Oh, good morning, Sir Maxwell.'

'I just wanted to ask you something. I don't know if you've heard this – er – this rather disquieting news about Farren.'

'No. What about him?'

Sir Maxwell explained about the discovery of the bicycle.

'Oh!' said Strachan. 'Yes – h'm – well – that does look rather bad, doesn't it? Farren's a temperamental beggar, you know. I hope there's nothing in it. Does Mrs. Farren know?'

'Yes; I thought it better she should be prepared – just in case—'

'M'm. Is she upset?'

'No; she's being very brave. By the way, my people were trying to get hold of you yesterday evening.'

'Were they? I'm so sorry. We'd all gone down to Sand Green and the girl had her night out. What did you want me for?'

'Just to ask if you happened to be at home on Monday night at a quarter past nine.'

'Monday night? Let me see. No, I wasn't. No. I went up to fish at Tongland. Why?'

'Farren was seen going up the Laurieston Road, and we thought he might have been calling at your place.'

'Not that I know of,' said Strachan. 'But I'll ask my wife. She'll know, or the girl will, if she doesn't. But they never said anything about it, so I don't think he can have called. Poor devil! I should never forgive myself if I thought that he was looking for me and that I might have prevented him from – But we don't know yet that anything has happened to him.'

'Of course not,' said the Chief Constable. 'We'll hope for the best, anyway.'

He turned away homewards.

'Poker-faced man, that,' he muttered to himself. 'I don't trust him. But of course Farren may have nothing to do with all this. This extraordinary story of Wimsey's—'

For Wimsey had, an hour or so earlier, given him a shock beside which all other shocks were a gentle tickling.

BUNTER

THE shock was a staggerer of the first water, and lost nothing of its force by being conveyed in terms of the most melancholy reproach. With bent head Wimsey bowed to the storm, and at the end had so little spirit left in him that he meekly allowed himself to be stripped of his grey flannel suit and sent to attend Campbell's funeral in a black morning-coat, top hat and black kid gloves, to the consternation of his friends and the immense admiration of Mr. McWhan.

The trouble was this. On the Thursday morning, Bunter had asked for and received leave of absence in order to attend the cinema. Owing to Wimsey's having dinner with Inspector Macpherson at Newton-Stewart and then going straight on to Bob Anderson's he had not seen Bunter again until he returned between midnight and one o'clock in the morning after his visit to the police-station.

Then his first words were:

'Bunter! Something's going on at Mr. Gowan's house.'

To which Bunter replied:

'I was about, my lord, to make a similar communication to your lordship.'

'Somebody's just made a moonlight flitting,' said Wimsey.

'I've been round to tell the police. At least,' he corrected himself, 'not moonlight, because there is no moon; in fact, it's beastly dark and I fell over some confounded steps, but the principle is the same and have you got any arnica?'

Bunter's reply was memorable:

'My lord, I have already taken upon me, in your lordship's absence, to acquaint Sir Maxwell Jamieson with Mr. Gowan's project of escape. I have every reason to anticipate that he will be detained at Dumfries or Carlisle. If your lordship will kindly remove your garments, I will apply suitable remedies to the contusions.'

'For God's sake, Bunter,' said Lord Peter, flinging himself into a chair, 'explain yourself.'

'When,' said Bunter, 'your lordship was good enough to acquaint me with the result of Inspector Macpherson's inquiry at Mr. Gowan's house, it came into my mind that possibly a greater amount of information might be elicited from Mr. Gowan's domestic staff by a gentleman's personal attendant than by an officer of the law. With this object in view, my lord, I desired permission to attend the cinematograph performance tonight. There is' – Bunter coughed slightly – 'a young person employed in Mr. Gowan's household of the name of Elizabeth, from whom, in the course of a casual conversation yesterday, I obtained the information that she was to receive permission to spend this evening out. I invited her to attend the cinematograph entertainment in my company. The film was one which I had already seen in London, but to her it was a novelty and she accepted with apparent pleasure.'

'No doubt,' said Wimsey.

'During the course of the performance I contrived to render our relations somewhat more confidential.'

'Bunter! Bunter!'

'Your lordship need be under no apprehension. In short, the young person confessed to me that she had some cause for dissatisfaction with her present situation. Mr. Gowan was kind, and Mrs. Alcock was kind and so was Mr. Alcock, but during the last few days certain circumstances had arisen which had put her into a state of considerable trepidation. I naturally inquired what these circumstances might be. In reply she gave me to understand that her alarm was occasioned by the presence of a mysterious stranger in the house.'

'You paralyse me!'

132

'Thank you, my lord. I pressed the young woman for further particulars, but she appeared apprehensive of being overheard in so public a place. I accordingly waited until the close of the performance, which took place at 10 o'clock, and invited her to take a stroll in the environs of the town.

'Not to trouble you with a long story, my lord, I succeeded at length in eliciting from her the following particulars. The mysterious occurrences of which she complained had commenced to eventuate on Monday last, on which day she had received permission to spend the evening with a sick relative. On returning to the house at half-past 10, she was informed that Mr. Gowan had been suddenly called away to London and had departed by the 8.45 train for Carlisle. She alleges that she would have thought nothing of this circumstance, had not the butler and the housekeeper taken such excessive pains to impress it upon her mind.

'The next day she was further surprised by being expressly forbidden by Mrs. Alcock to enter a certain corridor at the top of the house. This was a corridor leading to some disused rooms and one which, under ordinary circumstances, it would never have occurred to her to enter. Being, however, of the female sex, the prohibition immediately aroused in her a strong spirit of inquiry, and, on the first possible occasion, when she had reason to suppose the rest of the staff occupied downstairs, she went into the forbidden corridor and listened. She heard nothing, but to her alarm detected a faint odour of disinfectant – an odour which immediately connected itself in her mind with the idea of death. Which reminds me, my lord, to suggest that your lordship's injuries—'

'Never mind my injuries. Carry on.'

'The young woman, alarmed as she was, was still more frightened by hearing footsteps ascending the stairs. Not wishing to be caught in an act of disobedience, she hastened to conceal herself inside a small broom-cupboard at the head of the staircase. Peeping through the crack, she observed Alcock, carrying a jug of hot water and a safety-razor, pass along the corridor and enter a room at the end. Convinced that there was a corpse in the house, and that Alcock was on his way to wash and shave it in preparation for burial, she rushed downstairs and indulged in hysterics in the pantry. Fortunately Mrs. Alcock was not at hand, and in time she contrived to control her feelings and go about her duties in the accustomed manner.

'Immediately after lunch she was sent out upon an errand in the town, but she was afraid to communicate her suspicions to anybody. On returning, she was kept fully occupied by various tasks, and was never out of sight of one or the other of her fellow-domestics until bed-time. She spent the night in a condition of nervous apprehension, trying but failing to summon up courage to investigate the mysterious corridor again.

'Early in the morning she began to feel that even the most disagreeable certainty was preferable to agitating suspicions. She got up, crept cautiously past the bedroom of the two Alcocks and went up to the top of the house again. She ventured a little way down the corridor, when she was rooted to the spot by the sound of a hollow groan.'

'Really, Bunter,' said Wimsey, 'your narrative style would do credit to the *Castle of Otranto*.'

'Thank you, my lord. I am only acquainted by repute with the work you mention, but I understand that it enjoyed a considerable vogue in its day. The girl Elizabeth was hesitating whether to shriek or to run away, when she happened to tread upon a loose board, which made a loud noise. Thinking that the sound would awaken the Alcocks, she was preparing to retreat once more to the shelter of the broom-cupboard, when the door at the end of the passage was opened in a stealthy manner and a terrible face looked out at her.'

Bunter appeared to be enjoying the sensation he was producing, and paused.

'A terrible face,' said Wimsey. 'Very well, I've got that. A terrible face. Next, please!'

'The face, as I understand,' pursued Bunter, 'was enveloped in grave-clothes. The jaws were closely bound up, the features were hideous and the lips writhed away from the protruding teeth and the apparition was of a ghastly pallor.'

'Look here, Bunter,' said Wimsey, 'could you not cut out some of the fancy adjectives and say plainly what the face was like ?'

'I had not myself the opportunity of observing the face,' said Bunter, reprovingly, 'but the impression produced on me by the young woman's observations was that of a dark-haired, clean-shaven man with protruding teeth under the affliction of some form of physical suffering.'

'Oh, it was a man, then ?'

'That was Elizabeth's opinion. A lock of hair was visible

beneath the bandages. The eyes appeared to be shut, or partly shut, for, although she was standing in full view, the man said in a muffled tone, "Is that you, Alcock?" She did not reply, and presently the apparition retired into the room and shut the door. She then heard a bell ring violently. She rushed down the passage in blind alarm, encountering Alcock as he issued from his bedroom. Too terrified to think what she was doing, she gasped out: "Oh, what is it? What is it?" Alcock replied: "It must be those dratted mice playing with the bell-wires. Go back to bed, Betty." She then remembered that she deserved rebuke for having gone into the upstairs corridor and retired to her own room to hide her head in the bed-clothes.'

'The best thing she could do,' said Wimsey.

'Precisely, my lord. Thinking the matter over during the fore-noon, she came to the very reasonable conclusion that the person she had seen might, after all, not be a living corpse but merely a sick man. She was, however, quite sure that she had never seen the person's face in her life. She now noticed that food was disappearing at every meal in excess of that consumed by herself and the Alcocks, and this she found encouraging, be-cause, as she observed, dead folks do not eat.'

'True,' replied Wimsey. 'As G. K. C. says, "I'd rather be alive than not".'

'Quite so, my lord. I spoke as encouragingly as possible to the young woman and offered to accompany her back to Mr. Gowan's house. She informed me, however, that she had received permission to spend the night at her mother's.'

'Indeed?' said Wimsey.

'Precisely. I therefore took her home and returned to the High Street, where I observed Mr. Gowan's saloon car standing before the door. It was then five minutes to eleven. It was borne in upon me, my lord, that some person was about to take a surreptitious departure from Mr. Gowan's residence, and that Elizabeth had been given a night's leave of absence in order that she might not be a witness of the proceedings.'

'I think the inference is justifiable, Bunter.'

'Yes, my lord. I took the liberty of concealing myself at the corner of the street contiguous to Mr. Gowan's house where the little flight of steps leads down to the river. Presently a tall figure, closely muffled in a scarf and overcoat with the hat pulled well down to conceal the features, emerged from the doorway. I could not see the features at all, but I am confident that the form was that of a male person. A few words were exchanged in a low tone with the chauffeur, and the impression produced upon my mind was that the speaker was Mr. Gowan himself.'

'Gowan ? Then who was the mysterious stranger ?'

'I could not say, my lord. The car moved away, and, on consulting my watch, I found that the time was three minutes past eleven.'

'H'm,' said Wimsey.

'I formed the opinion, my lord, that Mr. Gowan had, after all, not departed from Kirkcudbright on the Monday evening as Alcock had stated, but that he had remained concealed in his own house in attendance upon the sick person observed by Elizabeth.'

'Curiouser and curiouser,' said Wimsey.

'I returned here,' pursued Bunter, 'and consulted the local timetable. I found that there was a train leaving Dumfries for Carlisle and the South at two minutes past midnight. It appeared conceivable that Mr. Gowan was intending to catch it either at Dumfries or at Castle-Douglas.'

'Did you see any luggage taken out ?'

'No, my lord; but it might have been previously placed in the car.'

'Of course it might. Did you inform the police ?'

'I thought it best, my lord, in view of the delicacy of the circumstances, to communicate directly with Sir Maxwell Jamieson. I hastened to the Selkirk Arms and put in a call from there.'

'You must have passed me,' said Wimsey. 'I had just hared across to the police-station, but Inspector Macpherson wasn't there.'

'I regret extremely that I should have missed your lordship. I informed Sir Maxwell of the circumstances, and I understood him to say that he would immediately telephone to Castle-Douglas and Dumfries, with a view to intercepting Mr. Gowan if he should make his appearance at either of those points, and that he would also circulate a description of the car and its driver.'

'Well, well, well,' said Wimsey. 'For a quiet country place, Kirkcudbright seems to boast a bright lot of inhabitants. They appear and disappear like Cheshire cats. I give it up. Bring forward the arnica and a whiskey-and-soda, and let's get to bed.

All I know is, that it's perfectly useless for me to try and detect things. You're always off the mark before me.'

The real sting of this episode lay in its tail. Inspector Macpherson came in the next day after lunch in an irritable frame of mind. Not only had his rest been broken the previous night by an alarm of burglars at a house on the outskirts of the town, which turned out to be purely fictitious, not only had he thereby missed the scoop about Gowan, but the Chief Constable had bungled matters somehow. Though he had (or so he said) immediately telephoned descriptions of the car and its occupants to Castle-Douglas, Dumfries, Carlisle and all the intermediate stations up to Euston, nothing whatever had been seen of any of them. Inquiries in the Stranraer direction had proved equally useless.

'It's fair rideeculous,' said the Inspector. 'It's pairfectly feasible that the car should ha' stopped on the outskirts of Castle-Douglas or Dumfries tae let Gowan tak' the train on his ain feet, but that they should ha' missed Gowan is no thinkable – and him so conspicuous wi' his big black beard an' a'.'

Wimsey suddenly uttered a loud yelp.

'Oh, Inspector, Inspector! He's done it on us! What dolts and ninnies we are! And now I suppose that damned photograph has been circulated all over the country. Show Bunter the specimen, Inspector. I told you we ought to have done that before we did anything else. This will be the death of us. We shall never hold up our heads again. The specimen, Inspector, the specimen!'

'By God!' said the Inspector, 'I believe your lordship's right. Tae think o' that, noo. An' me sairtain that it was Farren!'

He drew out his notebook and handed the bunch of curly black hair to Bunter.

'My lord,' said the latter, reproachfully, 'it is most regrettable that I did not see this before. Without presuming to speak as an expert, I may say that on several occasions I had the opportunity of examining the beard of a person belonging to the Mohammedan persuasion. You are doubtless aware, my lord, that the strict followers of this sect consider it unlawful to trim the hair of the face, with the consequence that the beard is extremely silky in texture, each hair preserving the natural tapering point.'

Wimsey, without a word, handed Bunter his lens.

'Your lordship has doubtless observed,' pursued Bunter,

'that this specimen conforms in every particular to this description, and having seen Mr. Gowan's beard, I do not hesitate to give it as my personal opinion – subject to expert correction – that Mr. Gowan will now be found to be deprived, in whole or in part, of that facial adornment.'

'I'm afraid you're right, Bunter,' said Wimsey, sadly. 'Now we know who the mysterious stranger was, and what he was suffering from. You'll have to revise your time-scheme, Inspector, and put Gowan in the leading rôle.'

'I must go and send off a corrected description at once,' said the Inspector.

'Just so,' said Wimsey. 'But have you the slightest idea what Gowan looks like without his beard? Inspector, I venture to prophesy that it will be a shock to you. When a man grows a jungle of face-fungus up to his cheek-bones and half-way down his chest, he has generally something to hide. I have known revelations—' he sighed. 'Do you realise, my dear man, that you have never seen *anything* of Gowan, except his eyes and a somewhat exaggerated nose?'

'We'll catch him by his nose,' said the Inspector, without the slightest humorous intention. He bustled away.

'Bunter,' said Wimsey, 'this case resembles the plot of a Wilkie Collins novel, in which everything happens just too late to prevent the story from coming to a premature happy ending.'

'Yes, my lord.'

'The trouble about this, Bunter, is that it completely destroys our theory, and apparently lets out Farren.'

'Quite so, my lord.'

'And unless your friend Betty is lying, it lets out Gowan too.'

'That appears to be the case, my lord.'

'Because, if he was hiding at home all Monday night and Tuesday morning, suffering from an accident, he couldn't have been painting pictures beyond Newton-Stewart.'

'I quite see that, my lord.'

'But is Betty telling the truth?'

'She appeared to me to be an honest young woman, my lord. But you will recollect that it was not until after lunch-time on the Tuesday that she saw Alcock enter the Bluebeard's Chamber, if I may use so fanciful an expression, and that the sick man was not seen by her in person until early on Wednesday morning.'

'True,' said Wimsey, thoughtfully. 'We have no evidence that he was there on Tuesday at all. Alcock will have to be interrogated. And in my opinion, Alcock is a man of considerable resource and sagacity.'

'Exactly so, my lord. And, what is more, Alcock had disappeared also.'

CHIEF INSPECTOR PARKER

THE mystery of the car turned out to have a perfectly simple explanation. It was reported from a small hotel at Brig of Dee, a village a few miles out on the Kirkcudbright side of Castle-Douglas. A visit by the police discovered Messrs. Alcock and Hammond calmly seated at lunch. Their story was a straight-forward one. Mr. Gowan had written from London, suggesting that, in his absence, they should take a holiday, and giving them his permission to use the car. They had decided on a little fishing excursion, and here they were. They had started late, on account of some small repairs which Hammond had had to make to the engine. The muffled-up person who had got in was Alcock himself. Certainly the Inspector could see Mr. Gowan's letter. Here it was, written from Mr. Gowan's club, the Mahlstick, on the club's own paper, and posted in London on the Wednesday.

As for Bunter's story, Alcock denied it altogether. The girl Betty was a foolish and hysterical young person, who imagined a great deal of nonsense. It was perfectly true that Mrs. Alcock had forbidden her to go into the disused part of the house. Betty was a great deal too fond of wasting her time. There were a lot of old magazines kept up there in a box-room, and the girl was always sneaking in there to read them when she ought to be engaged on household duties. Mrs. Alcock had had occasion to speak about it before. As regards the Tuesday, it was a fact that he (Alcock) had gone up there with hot water. One of the dogs had been hurt in a rabbit snare. He had made it a bed in the disused room and washed the wounds out with disinfectant. Mrs. Alcock would show the dog to the police if they cared to call. As for the alleged apparition on Wednesday morning, it was quite obvious that the girl had merely been suffering from nightmare, due to her own ridiculous fancies about corpses. There was no sick person there and never had been. Mr. Gowan had left Kirkcudbright, as previously stated, by car on Monday evening to catch the 8.45. The person whom Bunter had seen entering the car on the Thursday night had been Alcock. Hammond and Mrs. Alcock could confirm all this.

They could, and did, confirm it. The injured dog was produced and found to be actually suffering from a nasty sore in the leg, and Betty, when closely questioned, admitted that she had frequently got into trouble through reading magazines in the box-room.

As against this, there was the evidence of a garage proprietor at Castle-Douglas that a gentleman, giving his name as Rogers, had telephoned the previous evening for a fast car to catch the 12.2 express at Dumfries. He had got ready a 14 h.p. Talbot, which was a new and speedy car, and at about twenty minutes past eleven, the gentleman had walked into the garage. He was tall and had dark eyes and what the proprietor described as a 'rabbity' face. The proprietor had himself driven Mr. Rogers to Dumfries and set him down at the station at four minutes to twelve precisely.

The booking-clerk at Dumfries confirmed this up to a point. He remembered selling a first-class ticket for Euston to a gentleman who had come in just before midnight. He did not remember the gentleman very distinctly – he was much like other gentlemen, but he agreed that he had rather a big nose and stick-out teeth.

The ticket-collector on the train was not helpful. Gentlemen on night-trains tended to be sleepy and muffled-up. Several first-class gentlemen had joined the 12.2 at Dumfries. Certainly he had seen nobody remotely resembling the photograph of Gowan. Was there anybody at all like what Gowan would be if clean-shaven? Well, there now, that was asking something, that was. Had the Inspector any idea what a 'edge-'og would look like without its spikes? No, nor he didn't suppose nobody had, neither. He was a ticket-collector, not a puzzle-picture expert. The booking-clerk at Dumfries expressed a similar opinion, still more forcibly.

Inspector Macpherson, whom this dreary investigation had carried as far as Euston, then turned his attention to the club from which Gowan was supposed to have written. Here the news was a little more cheering. Mr. Gowan had certainly not been staying there. One or two letters had arrived for him, which had been collected by a gentleman presenting Mr. Gowan's card. The gentleman had signed a receipt for them. Might the Inspector see the receipt? Certainly he might. The signature was J. Brown. The Inspector wondered how many J. Browns there might be among London's four million, and turned his weary steps towards Scotland Yard.

Here he asked for Chief Inspector Parker, who received him with more than official cordiality. Any friend of Wimsey's was entitled to Parker's best attention, and the complicated story of Gowan and the spanner, Farren, Strachan and the two bicycles, was sympathetically listened to.

'We'll find Gowan for you all right,' said Parker, encouragingly. 'With the very precise details you have produced for us it ought not to take long. What do you want done with him when we've got him?'

'Weel, noo, Mr. Parker,' said the Inspector, deferentially, 'do ye think we have enough evidence tae arrest him?'

Parker turned this over carefully.

'I take it,' he said, 'that your idea is that Gowan met this man Campbell in the road between Gatehouse and Kirkcudbright and killed him in a quarrel. Then he got frightened and decided to fake up the accident. His first step was to cut off his own very conspicuous beard, in the hope, I suppose, of getting through the Gatehouse end of the business unrecognised. It must have been an awkward bit of barbering. Still, he might have managed to produce a fairly good imitation of a man who hadn't shaved for a fortnight. Then he went through all the movements which you originally ascribed to Farren. He hid the body up the side-lane and drove Campbell's own car back to Gatehouse. Now, why should he have done that?'

'There!' said the Inspector, 'yon's the great deeficulty. Wherefore did he no tak' the corp back wi' him? It was verra weel understandable when we supposed that the murderer was Farren in Strachan's car, because we had the theory that he meant at first tae pit the blame on Strachan, but what for should Gowan du sic a fulish thing?'

'Well, let's see,' said Parker. 'He had to get Campbell's car back somehow. Ferguson might have noticed if the wrong car came in. But he didn't take the body with him on that journey, because, again, Ferguson or somebody might have spotted him with it. Gowan's car was a two-seater. Perhaps the dickey wasn't big enough to hide the corpse properly. He decides that it's better to risk leaving the corpse and his own car in the lane than driving openly back to Gatehouse with a dead man upright in the seat beside him. Very well. Now he's got to get back to the scene of the crime. How ? On foot ? – No, this, I take it, is the point at which the bicycle was pinched from the what-d'ye-call-it hotel.'

'Verra like,' said the Inspector.

'You may have to alter your times a trifle here, but you've still got ample margin. You had 10.20 as the time for Campbell's car to arrive at Standing Stone Pool. Now then. Your man has still got to do the journey back on a bicycle. But he hasn't got to waste time going on foot to Strachan's house. So, if anything, he will get to the scene of the crime a trifle earlier than we supposed. He picks up his own car, puts the bike in the dickey – we've got to allow that – however, it would be pretty dark by that time and probably no one would notice. By the way, I see that this fellow Ferguson says that Campbell's car came in a little after 10 o'clock. Well, that fits your first time-table all right. It means that the murderer brought the car straight away in after the crime. But I see you've made an alteration here.'

'Ay,' said Macpherson. 'We thocht he wad ha' lodged Campbell's car somewhere on the road an' transferred the body tae 't on his second journey. It wad be suspicious like for a second car tae come in tae Campbell's place.'

'True; but if Ferguson is right about his times, that can't be the case. Is Ferguson an exact man ?'

'Ay; they tell me he has a gran' memory for details.'

'Then the murderer *must* have come in a second time with the body in his own car. It's odd that Ferguson shouldn't have heard the second car either come or go.'

'Ay, that's a fact.'

'The second car – when would it have got in ? Between five and six miles on a push-bike – say half-an-hour. That brings it to 10.50. The bicycle put into the dickey and five or six miles back in a fast car – say fifteen minutes at the outside. That gives us 11.5 for the second time of arrival. Ferguson says he went to bed shortly after 10. He must have been asleep, that's all. And still asleep when the car went out again – the murderer's car, I mean. No, that won't do. How and when did Gowan – if he was the murderer – get his car back to Kirkcudbright ? He had to be on the spot in Gatehouse to look after the body and prepare his fake for the next morning. I suppose he *could* have driven his car home to Kirkcudbright during the small hours and then walked or push-cycled back to Gatehouse.'

'Ay, there's nae doot he cud ha' done it. But it wadna' be necessary. The chauffeur Hammond cud ha' driven him over again.'

'So he could. That makes Hammond rather definitely an accomplice. But there's no reason why he shouldn't be. If Gowan committed the murder, all his servants, except possibly Betty, are obviously lying like Ananias, and one degree of guilt more or less makes no difference. Well, that explains that all right, and we've only got to suppose that Gowan carried out the rest of the scheme according to plan, changed over into the London train at Ayr and is now lurking in London till his beard's grown again. And that explains – what would otherwise seem rather odd – why, having faked the murder, he didn't disarm suspicion by showing himself openly in Kirkcudbright.'

'Ay,' said Macpherson, excitedly, 'but dinna ye see it explains naething at a' ? It disna fit the description o' the man in the grey suit that tuk the bicycle tae Ayr. Nor it disna explain Betty's tale to Bunter, nor the muffled-up man escapin' fra' Gowan's hoose at deid o' nicht, nor the rabbity-faced fellow in the train fra' Castle-Douglas tae Euston. An' hoo aboot yon man that came knockin' on Campbell's door o' Monday midnicht ?'

Parker rubbed his jaw thoughtfully.

'It's funny about the description of the man,' he said. 'Perhaps Gowan contrived to disguise himself in some way, with a false fair moustache, or something. And the girl's story may, as Alcock suggests, be partly imagination. Gowan may have returned to Kirkcudbright on Tuesday afternoon instead of going straight through to London, though I can't think why he should, and the letter sent from the Mahlstick certainly suggests that he was in London on the Wednesday. And the rabbity man may be somebody different altogether. And I'm inclined to think that the man who knocked at midnight *was* somebody different altogether.'

'But,' said the Inspector, 'if that man gaed into the hoose and found Campbell dead and Gowan there, why hasna he come forward tae say so ?'

'Possibly he was after no good,' suggested Parker. 'He may, as you previously remarked, have been a lady. Still, I admit that there are awkward gaps in the story. I think we'd better get on the tracks of Gowan and the rabbity man separately, and try to find out definitely which way Gowan really went. And when we do catch Gowan, I think perhaps we'd better not arrest him, but merely detain him on the ground that he can give information. After all, Inspector, we don't even know for an absolute certainty that it was he who met Campbell on the road. There may be other people with black beards.'

'There's nae ither *artist* wi' a black beard like yon,' said Macpherson, stubbornly. 'Not in a' the district.'

'Hell! yes,' said Parker. 'He's got to be an artist, of course. Well, anyhow, we'll detain Gowan.'

Inspector Macpherson thanked him.

'And now there's this man Farren,' went on Parker. 'Do you want him too ? Supposing he's not down a mine.'

'I'm thinkin' he did ought tae be found,' said the Inspector. 'He was heard tae utter threats – an' forbye, he's disappeared, which in itself is distressin' tae his family an' friends.'

'True. Well, we'll make inquiries for him as a lost, stolen or strayed. That will do no harm. But I daresay you've got him up your end somewhere. Who else is there ? The Englishman – what's his name ? – Waters. How about him ?'

'I'd forgot Waters,' replied Macpherson, frankly. 'I canna see how he comes intae 't at a'.'

'Nor do I,' said Parker. 'Well, we'll leave him out. And of course we're watching that bike at Euston to see if anybody's fool enough to come for it. And you'd better send somebody down to identify it, because it may not be the right one at all. Is that all ? Suppose now we go and have a drink after all this talking ? Oh, by the way, can you tell me what school Gowan went to ? No ? Oh, well, it doesn't matter. He's probably in the reference-books.'

The Inspector still seemed a little unhappy.

'What is it ?' said Parker.

'Ye havena—' he began. And then added, impulsively, 'if we canna find somethin' sune, I'm thinkin' ye'll be hearin' officially fra' the Chief Constable.'

'Oh!' said Parker. 'But I don't see any need for that. You have lost no time, and you seem to me to be doing very well. We have to give you help at this end, of course – just as you would help me if one of my pet-lambs escaped to Scotland – but surely there's no call for us to take over the management of the case. It seems to be a matter in which the local man has all the advantages on his side.'

'Ay,' said the Inspector, 'but it's an awfu' big job.'

He sighed heavily.

LORD PETER WIMSEY

'STRACHAN!' said Lord Peter Wimsey.

Mr. Strachan started so violently that he nearly pitched himself and his canvas into a rock-pool. He was perched rather uneasily on a lump of granite on the Carrick shore, and was industriously painting the Isles of Fleet. There was a strong wind and the menace of heavy storm, which together were producing some curious cloud effects over a rather fretful-looking sea.

'Oh, hullo, Wimsey!' he said. 'How on earth did you get here?'

'Drove here,' said Wimsey. 'Fresh air and that kind of thing.' He sat down on a convenient knob of rock, settled his hat more firmly on his head and pulled out a pipe, with the air of a man who has at last found an abiding-place.

Strachan frowned. He did not much care for spectators when he was painting, but Wimsey was working away in a leisurely manner with his tobacco-pouch, and appeared impervious to nods and winks.

'Very windy, isn't it?' said Strachan, when the silence had lasted some time.

'Very,' said Wimsey.

'But it's not raining,' pursued Strachan.

'Not yet,' said Wimsey.

'Better than yesterday,' said Strachan, and realised at once that he had said a foolish thing. Wimsey turned his head instantly and said brightly:

'Tons better. Really you know, you'd think they'd turned on the water-works yesterday on purpose to spoil my sketching-party.'

'Oh, well,' said Strachan.

'Well, perhaps it was rather a wild idea,' said Wimsey, 'but it appealed to me rather. That's rather nice,' he added, 'how long have you been on that?'

'About an hour,' said Strachan.

'You use very big brushes. Broad, sweepin' style and all that. Campbell used the knife a lot, didn't he?'

'Yes.'

'Is it quick work with a knife?'

'Yes, generally speaking, it is.'

'Do you work as fast as Campbell?'

'I shouldn't work quite as fast as he would with a knife, if you mean that, because I should fumble it a bit, unless I had practice with it first. But using my own methods, I could probably produce a finished sketch nearly as fast as he could.'

'I see. What do you call an ordinary time for a finished sketch?'

'Oh – well, what size of sketch?'

'About the size you're working on now.'

'I shall have done everything I want to this in another half-hour – or perhaps a little bit longer. Provided the whole show doesn't carry away first,' he added, as a fresh gust came drumming off the sea, making the easel vibrate and rock, in spite of the heavy stone slung between its legs.

'Oh, you're well ballasted. But I wonder you don't use a sketching-box on days like this.'

'Yes, I don't know why I don't, except that I never have done and am not used to it. One gets into habits.'

'I suppose one does.'

'I'm rather methodical, really,' said Strachan. 'I could lay my hands on any of my tools in the dark. Some people seem to like muddle, and all their stuff chucked into a satchel anyhow. I lay everything out before I begin – tubes of colour in the same order on my tray, dipper just here, spare brushes hung on there – even my palette is always made up in the same order, though not always with the same colours, of course. But, roughly speaking, it follows the order of the spectrum.'

'I see,' said Wimsey. 'I'm not methodical myself, but I do admire method. My man, Bunter, is a marvel in that way. It is such a grief to him to find all kinds of odds and ends bulging my pockets or chucked helter-skelter into the collar-drawer.'

'Oh, I'm terrible about drawers, too,' said Strachan. 'My tidiness begins and ends with my painting. It's just a habit, as I said before. I haven't a tidy mind.'

146

'Haven't you ? Aren't you good at dates and figures and time-tables and all that sort of thing ?'

'Not the least. Hopelessly unobservant. I haven't even got a good visual memory. Some people can come back from a place and make a picture of it with every house and tree in its place, but I have to see things before I can draw them. It's a drawback in a way.'

'Oh, I could do that,' said Wimsey. 'If I could draw, I mean. F'r instance – take the road between Gatehouse and Kirkcudbright. I could make a plan of that, here and now, with every corner, every house, practically every tree and gate on the road marked. Or if you drove me along it blindfold, I could recite to you exactly what we were passing at every moment.'

'I couldn't do that,' said Strachan. 'I've been over it hundreds of times, of course, but I'm always seeing things I hadn't noticed before. Of course I get the fun of having perpetual surprises.'

'Yes; you're safeguarded against boredom. But sometimes an eye for detail is a good thing. If you want to tell a good, plausible, circumstantial lie, for example.'

'Oh!' said Strachan. 'Yes, I suppose it would be – under those circumstances.'

'Your little story of the golf-ball on the links, for example,' said Wimsey. 'How much better it would have been if surrounded and supported by stout, upstanding, well-thought-out details. It wasn't a fearfully good lie to start with, of course, because it really left rather *too* much time unaccounted for. But since you stood committed to it, you should have made more of it.'

'I don't know what you mean,' said Strachan, stiffly. 'If you doubt my word—'

'Of course I doubt it. I don't believe it for a moment. Nor would anybody. For one thing, you didn't tell your wife the same story you told me. That was careless. If you're going to tell a lie, it should always be the same lie. Then you omitted to mention what hole you were playing when it happened. There never was a man telling a golfing story who didn't buttress it about with every kind of geographical and historical detail. That was poor psychology on your part. Thirdly, you said you were up at the golf-course all morning, quite forgetting that there might be plenty of witnesses to say you'd never been near the place, and that, as a matter of fact, you'd instructed Tom Clark to roll the greens that morning. He was on the ninth, as a matter of fact, between 10 and 11 o'clock, and can swear that you didn't come in, and if you'd gone up later, you'd hardly have called it "after breakfast". Besides—'

'Look here,' said Strachan, with a lowering brow, 'what the devil do you mean by talking to me like this ?'

'I'm just wondering,' said Wimsey, 'whether you cared to suggest any other explanation for that black eye of yours. I mean, if you liked to give it to me now, and it happened to be – well, say, anything in the nature of a domestic fracas, or anything, I – er – I might not need to pass it on, you see.'

'I don't see at all,' said Strachan. 'I think it's damned impertinence.'

'Don't say that,' pleaded Wimsey. 'Look here, old man, your midnight revels are nothing to me. If you were out on the tiles, or anything—'

'If you take that tone to me, I'll break your neck.'

'For God's sake,' cried Wimsey, 'don't use any *more* threats.'

Strachan looked at him, and slowly flushed a deep crimson from brow to throat.

'Are you accusing me,' he demanded, thickly, 'of having anything to do with murdering Campbell ?'

'I'm not accusing anybody,' said Wimsey, lightly, 'of murdering him – yet.' He suddenly scrambled to his feet, and stood poised on the rock, looking out away from Strachan over the sea. The clouds had blown together into one threatening mass, and the waves were lipping along cold and yellow, showing snarling little teeth of foam. 'But I do accuse you,' he said, turning suddenly and leaning back against the wind to keep his balance, 'I do accuse you of knowing a good deal more about it than you have told the police. Wait! Don't be violent. You fool! *It's dangerous to be violent.*'

He caught Strachan's wrist as the blow glanced past his ear.

'Listen, Strachan, listen, man. I know I look tempting, standing here like this. Damn it, that's what I did it for. I'm a smaller man than you are, but I could chuck you into eternity with a turn of the wrist. Stand still. That's better. Don't you *ever* think two minutes ahead ? Do you really suppose you can settle everything by brute force in this blundering way ? Suppose you *had* knocked me down. Suppose I had split my head open, like Campbell. What would you have done then ? Would you be better off, or worse off ? What would you have done with the body, Strachan ?'

The painter looked at him, and put the back of his hand up against his forehead with a sort of desperation in the gesture.

'My God, Wimsey,' he said, 'you deadly devil!' He stepped back and sat down on his camp-stool, shaking. 'I meant to kill you then. I've got such a hell of a temper. What made you do that?'

'I wanted to see what sort of a temper you had got,' said Wimsey, coolly. 'And you know,' he added, 'as a matter of fact, if you had killed me, you would have run very little risk. You had only to go away and leave me, hadn't you? My car would have been here. Everybody would have thought I'd just been blown off my feet and cracked my skull – like Campbell. What evidence would there have been against you?'

'None, I suppose,' said Strachan.

'You think that?' said Wimsey. 'Do you know, Strachan, I almost wish I had let you knock me over – just to see what you would do. Well, never mind. It's starting to rain. We'd better pack up and go home.'

'Yes,' said the other. He was still very white, but he started meekly to put his painting materials together. Wimsey noticed that, in spite of his obvious agitation, he worked swiftly and neatly, evidently following out some habitual order of working. He secured the wet canvas in a carrier, mechanically putting in the canvas-pins and pulling the straps tightly, transferred the brushes to a tin case and the palette to a box and then collected the tubes of paint from the ledge of the easel.

'Hullo!' he said, suddenly.

'What's up?' said Wimsey.

'The cobalt's not here,' said Strachan, dully, 'it must have rolled off.'

Wimsey stooped.

'Here it is,' he said, extracting it from a clump of heather. 'Is that the lot?'

'That's the lot,' said Strachan. He laid the tubes in their box, folded up and strapped the easel and stood, as though waiting for orders.

'Then we'd better make tracks,' said Wimsey, turning up his coat-collar, for the rain had started to come down heavily.

'Look here,' said Strachan, still motionless in the downpour, 'what are you going to do?'

'Go home,' said Wimsey. 'Unless' – he looked hard at Strachan – 'unless there's anything you want to tell me.'

'I'll tell you this,' said Strachan. 'One of these days you'll go too far, and somebody *will* murder you.'

'I shouldn't be in the least surprised,' said Lord Peter, pleasantly.

MRS. SMITH-LEMESURIER

ALL this time there was a gentleman who was feeling rather hurt and neglected, and that was the young constable who had so signally failed in interviewing Mr. Jock Graham. This young man, whose name was Duncan, was keen about his profession, and he was acutely aware that he was not being given a proper chance. Graham had laughed at him; Sergeant Dalziel, importantly rushing about after bicycles and railway-tickets, had callously ignored his suggestions and left him to deal with drunks and motoring offences. Nobody took P.C. Duncan into his confidence. No matter. P.C. Duncan would pursue a line of his own. Perhaps, when he had shown them what he could do, they would be sorry.

There was no doubt at all in Duncan's mind that Jock Graham's movements required investigating. There were rumours. Hints were dropped in bars. Fishermen had been seen to nudge one another and fall suddenly silent when Graham's name was mentioned. Unfortunately, it is hardly possible for a local policeman in a country place to snoop about, wheedling information out of the inhabitants after the manner of Sherlock Holmes. His features are known. He is a marked man. Duncan played a little with the idea of getting himself up (when off duty) as an aged clergyman or a Breton onion-seller, but a glance in the mirror at his stalwart frame and round, ruddy cheeks was enough to rob him of his self-confidence. He envied the Scotland Yard detective, who, lost among a multitudinous population and backed by a powerful force, can go about, impenetrable and unknown, hob-nobbing with thieves in the East End or with dukes and millionaires in Mayfair night-clubs. Alas! in Creetown and Newton-Stewart he had only to poke his nose round the door to be known and avoided.

He made persistent inquiries, cajoling and even threatening one or two people who appeared to know more than they should. Unhappily, the Scottish peasant has a remarkable talent for silence when he likes and, unhappily, also, Jock Graham was a popular man. After several days of this kind of thing, Duncan did, however, contrive to unearth one piece of definite information. A farmer who was passing along in a cart towards Bargrennan at 11.30 on the Tuesday morning, had seen a man walking along the farther side of the Cree as though coming from the scene of the crime. The man had immediately ducked down as though to escape observation, but not before the farmer had definitely recognised him as Graham. But further than this, Duncan succeeded only in hearing and raising rumours. A journalist on the *Glasgow Clarion*, to whom he had rather rashly said more than he ought, came out with an unfortunate article, and P.C. Duncan received a severe rebuke from his harassed superiors.

'An' if Graham was as guilty as sin,' said Sergeant Dalziel angrily – this occurred on the same day that the porter at Girvan developed appendicitis, and the Sergeant was quite ready to take it out of somebody – 'what for wad ye be tellin' him that he's suspectit, an' givin' him the chance to make up an alibi ? Wull ye look at this, noo ?' He flapped the *Clarion* before Duncan's unhappy eyes. '"Reason to suppose that the crime was committit by an artist." Isna yon precisely the fact that we was wishfu' tae conceal frae the suspecks ? "Weel-known airtist interviewed by oor correspondent." Whae tell't yae tae send yon fellie speirin' round at Graham's place ? If ye canna lairn discretion, Charlie Duncan, ye wad du better tae fin' some ither profession.'

However, this indiscretion had its consequences. On the Saturday morning, Sergeant Dalziel was seated in his office when a lady was ushered in, demurely dressed in a black costume and close-fitting hat. She smiled nervously at the Sergeant, and murmured that she desired to make a statement in connection with Campbell's murder.

Dalziel knew the lady well enough. She was Mrs. Smith-Lemesurier, an 'in-comer' of some three years' standing in Newton-Stewart, and giving herself out to be the widow of an African civil servant. She lived, simply and inexpensively, in a small converted cottage, with a French maid. Her manner was plaintive and artless, her age rather more than it appeared, and young men who knew no better were apt to see in her a refreshing revelation of an unfashionable womanliness. Why she should have chosen to settle in this out-of-the-way spot was never explained. Mrs. Smith-Lemesurier herself was accustomed to say that the rents in Scotland were so low, and that she had to do the best she could with her poor little income. It did not matter where she lived, she would add, sadly; since her husband's death she was all alone in the world. Lord Peter Wimsey had been introduced to her the previous year at a small sale of work which was being held in connection with the Episcopalian Church. He had afterwards expressed the coarse opinion that the lady was 'out for blood.' This was ungrateful, since Mrs. Smith-Lemesurier had devoted herself to him very charmingly throughout what must have been to him a tedious afternoon, and had sold him a green silk sachet with 'Pyjamas' embroidered upon it with her own hands. 'I can't give money,' said Mrs. Smith-Lemesurier, smiling shyly up at him, for she was a dainty little person, 'but I can give my work, and it's the intention that counts, isn't it?'

Sergeant Dalziel placed a chair for his visitor, and softened his rugged tones as he inquired what he could do for her.

Mrs. Smith-Lemesurier hunted in her vanity-bag for some time, and eventually produced the cutting from the *Glasgow Clarion* which had brought P.C. Duncan so much trouble and reproof.

'I just wanted to ask,' she said, raising her speedwell-blue eyes pleadingly to the policeman's face, 'whether there is any foundation for – for the dreadful insinuations in this.'

Sergeant Dalziel read the paragraph through as carefully as though he had never seen it before, and replied cautiously:

'Ay, imph'm. That's as may be.'

'You see,' said Mrs. Smith-Lemesurier, 'it says that the m-m-murder must have been committed by an artist. Wh-what makes them say that?'

'Well,' said the Sergeant, 'I'll no be sayin' that there mightna be some evidence tae point in that direction.'

'Oh!' said the lady. 'I hoped – I thought – I fancied perhaps this reporter was making it all up out of his own head. They are terrible people, you know. Did he really get that idea from – from the police?'

'I couldna verra weel say,' replied the Sergeant. 'He'll maybe ha' caught it fra' some ither irresponsible pairson.'

'But the police do think that?' she insisted.

'I'll no be sayn' so,' said Sergeant Dalziel, 'but seein' as the

152

deceased was an airtist himsel' and that the most of his friends was airtists, there is always the possibeelity.'

Mrs. Smith-Lemesurier fumbled with the clasp of her bag.

'And then,' she said, 'it goes on to mention Mr. Graham.'

'Ay, it does so,' said the Sergeant.

'Surely, surely' – the blue eyes again sought the Sergeant's – 'it can't be that you – that you actually suspect Mr. Graham of this dreadful thing ?'

Sergeant Dalziel cleared his throat.

'Och, weel noo,' said he, 'there is always some groonds for suspeecion when a crime is committed an' a pairson willna state juist whaur he was at the time. I wadna say that there was what they ca' a violent presumption of guilt, but there's groonds for what we may ca' a general suspeecion.'

'I see. Tell me, officer – supposing – supposing anybody were to clear your mind of this – general suspicion against Mr. Graham – it wouldn't be necessary to – to – to make the explanation public ?'

'That depends,' said Dalziel, eyeing his visitor rather more closely, 'on the nature of the explanation. If it was such as tae remove a' possibeelity of this gentleman's bein' consairned, an' if it was weel supportit by proofs, an' provided that the maitter never cam' tae trial, there wad be nae need tae mak' onything public at a'.'

'Ah! then, in that case – oh, Mr. Dalziel, I can rely on your discretion, can't I ? It's such a dreadful thing to have to tell you – just consider – but I'm sure you will understand – in my sad, lonely position – I – oh! I don't know how to say it.'

Mrs. Smith-Lemesurier dragged out a wispy handkerchief and temporary veiled the light of the speedwell eyes.

'Come, noo,' said the Sergeant, gently, 'there's no call tae fash yoursel'. We hear an awful' lot o' things, in oor profession, that we niver think twice on. Forbye,' he added, helpfully, 'I'm a mairrit man.'

'I don't know that that doesn't make it worse,' bleated Mrs. Smith-Lemesurier. 'But I'm sure,' she added, peeping hopefully up over the edge of the handkerchief, 'you're a kind, understanding man, and wouldn't make it worse for me than you could help.'

''Deed, no,' said the Sergeant. 'Dinna fash yersel', Mrs. Smith-Lemesurier. Juist tell me a' aboot it, as if I micht be your feyther.'

'I will, thank you, I will. Mr. Graham would never say any-thing, of course, he's too kind and too chivalrous. Mr. Dalziel – he couldn't tell you where he was on Monday night – because – he was – with me.'

Mrs. Smith-Lemesurier paused with a little gasp. Sergeant Dalziel, for whom this revelation held by this time no element of surprise, nodded paternally.

'Ay, imph'm, is that so ? That's a verra guid reason for him tae keep silence, a verra satisfactory reason indeed. Can ye tell me, Mrs. Smith Lemesurier, at whit time Mr. Graham came tae your hoose and left ye again ?'

The lady squeezed the filmy handkerchief between her small, plump hands.

'He came to dinner, at about 8 o'clock. And he left me again after breakfast. That would be a little after 9.'

The Sergeant made a note on a slip of paper.

'And did naebody see him come or gae ?'

'No. We were – very careful.'

'Ay. How did he come ?'

'I think he said a friend had given him a lift into Newton-Stewart.'

'Whit friend wad that be ?'

'I don't know – he didn't say. Oh, Mr. Dalziel, shall you have to find out ? My maid can tell you when he arrived. Is it necessary to bring this other person into it ?'

'Maybe no,' said the Sergeant. 'An' he went aff again after 9 o'clock ? Your maid can witness that tu, I'm thinkin'.'

'Yes, of course.'

'An' he was in the hoose a' the time ?'

'He – he was never out of my sight,' moaned Mrs. Smith-Lemesurier, again overcome by the painfulness of this confession.

The Sergeant looked at her shaking shoulders and hardened his heart.

'An' whit makes ye think, ma'am, that this story provides Mr. Graham wi' an alibi for the murder o' Campbell, that was fund wi' his heid dunted in at 2 o'clock o' Tuesday afternoon ?'

Mrs. Smith-Lemesurier gave a little shriek.

'Oh!' she stared at him wildly. 'I didn't know. I thought – look at that horrid newspaper. It said Mr. Graham refused to state where he was the previous night. I don't understand. I imagined – oh! don't, don't say it doesn't clear him after all!'

'I'll no gae sae far as tae say that,' said the Sergeant, 'but ye'll see for yersel' that it disna cover a' the groond. Mr. Graham was twa days missin'. Ye dinna ken whaur he went after he left your hoose ?'

'No – no – I've no idea. Oh, my God! Why did I ever come here ? I made so certain that it was an alibi for the Monday night you wanted.'

'Well, that's a' tae the guid,' said the Sergeant, comfortingly. 'It's verra like, when he kens that the Monday nicht is accountit for, he'll tell us aboot the ither maitter. Noo, I'll juist rin ye back tae your hoose in my car and get a wee word fra' your maid, by way o' corroboration. Dry your eyes, ma'am. I'll no say a word mair than is necessary. It's verra courageous of ye tae ha' come tae me wi' your story, an' ye can coont upon ma' discretion.'

The maid's story agreed word for word with that of the mistress – as, indeed, the Sergeant had expected it would. He did not care for the woman – a sly foreign creature, he thought her – but he could not shake her on any essential point.

The whole episode was disquieting. No sooner had that infernal paragraph appeared in the paper than he had expected an alibi to be produced. He had said as much to the unhappy Duncan. But why this particular alibi ? The woman's story was not improbable in itself, given Jock Graham and given Mrs. Smith-Lemesurier, only – why the alibi for the Monday night only ? He read the newspaper cutting again. '– Mr. J. Graham, the distinguished artist, who laughingly refused to state where he had been between Monday night and Wednesday morning.' No; nobody could have deduced from that that Monday night was the crucial period. Wimsey must have been talking. God knew what he had been blurting out in the course of his unofficial inquiries. If it was not Wimsey—

If it was not Wimsey, then nothing but guilty knowledge could possibly account for that alibi, so neatly covering the time of Campbell's death. And if Jock Graham had guilty knowledge, then what became of the beautiful theory about Farren, and the hopeful imbroglio about the bicycle ?

The Sergeant groaned aloud. He might have groaned still more deeply if he had known that Inspector Macpherson and Chief Inspector Parker of Scotland Yard were at that very moment engaged in destroying the beautiful Farren theory in favour of a Gowan theory.

His eye fell upon an object lying on his desk. It was a grey felt hat – the sole treasure-trove that the search party had so far brought back from Falbae. It was not Farren's. Mrs. Farren and Jeanie had both repudiated it. It bore no name. It was just another puzzle. He turned it about in his hands discontentedly.

The telephone rang. Sergeant Dalziel lifted the receiver. The speaker was the police-superintendent at Glasgow.

'We've got a man here who says he is Mr. Waters of Kirkcudbright. Are you still wanting him ? He was just boarding the Dumfries train.'

'Whit account does he gie o' himsel' ?'

'Says he's just off a yachting expedition. He made no attempt to deny his identity. What shall we do with him ?'

'Detain him,' said Sergeant Dalziel, desperately. 'I'll be along on the next train.'

'I'll tak nae mair chances,' he added to himself, as he hurriedly prepared for his journey. 'I'll detain the whole bluidy lot o' them.'

WATERS' STORY

To his great surprise, the Sergeant found Wimsey at the Glasgow police-station before him. He was waiting placidly in the Superintendent's office, with his hands clasped over his walking-stick and his chin on his hands, and he greeted the Sergeant with exasperating cheerfulness.

'Hullo – ullo – ullo!' he said. 'So here we are again.'

'An' hoo did yew get here ?' snapped Dalziel, his Galloway accent very pronounced and sharpening his u's almost to the point of menace.

'In a rather roundabout way,' said Wimsey, 'but, generally speaking, by train. I spent last night in Campbell's cottage. Arrived in Glasgow by the 2.16 to see Picture Exhibition. Distressed fellow-countryman wires to Kirkcudbright that he is in the hands of the children of Amalek and will I come and disentangle him. Faithful valet sends wire on to Picture Exhibition. Intelligent attendant at Exhibition identifies me and delivers wire. Like a mother-eagle I fly to the place where distressed fellow-countryman, like wounded eaglet, bleeds, metaphorically speaking. You know my friend, Superintendent Robertson ?'

'Oh, yes,' said the Superintendent, 'Sergeant Dalziel has been over about this matter before. Well, now, Sergeant, you'd probably like to see this man Waters straight away. He's told his story to us, but you had best hear it from himself. Forbes, just bring Waters in here again.'

After a few moments the door opened, to admit an exceedingly dishevelled and exceedingly angry Waters, dressed in a grubby waterproof and very grubby sweater and flannel trousers. His untidy hair was pushed up into a dissipated-looking comb by a linen bandage which half covered one eye, and gave him a rake-helly and piratical appearance.

'Good Lord, man!' exlaimed Wimsey, 'what the devil have you been doing to yourself ?'

'Doing to myself ?' retorted Waters. 'What the devil have all you people been doing ? What's all this damned fuss about ? What's all this tripe about Campbell ? What in thunder do these damned idiots mean by arresting me ? What the hell has it all got to do with me, anyhow ?'

'My dear man,' said Wimsey, breaking in before the Sergeant could speak, 'your eloquence is extremely impressive, but not more so than your appearance, which is, if I may say so, picturesque in the extreme. Your absence from your usual haunts has been causing acute distress to your friends – a distress and anxiety which the manner of your return is doing nothing to allay. Before embarking on any discussion about Campbell or any other extraneous subject, will you so far relieve the agony of mind of a sympathising compatriot as to say where you have been, why you have not written and why you appear to have been indulging in a free fight, with extensive damage to your handsome façade ?'

'I never knew such a lot of silly fuss about nothing,' grumbled Waters. 'I've been yachting with a bloke, that's all – old Tom Drewitt of Trinity, as a matter of fact. We were running up the west coast, and he was going to put me off at Gourock on Thursday, only we fell in with a bit of bad weather and had to run across and hang round the Irish coast for a couple of days while it blew itself out. I don't know if you fancy hugging a lee shore full of rocks in a sou-westerly gale. All I can say is, we didn't. I daresay I am a bit untidy – so'd you be, after five days in Tom's dirty little wind-jamming beast of a boat. I've no skin left on my hands, and it's not the fault of that young lout of Tom's that I'm still alive. He got the wind up – Tom ought to have stuck to the tiller himself. Boom came across and nearly cracked my head open. Tom wanted me to go on with him this morning up to Skye, but I wasn't having any. I told him he could damn well put me off at Gourock and if ever I sailed with him again it would be when that cub of his was drowned and out of harm's way.'

'See here, noo,' put in Sergeant Dalziel. 'Let's get a' this story correct. Ye say ye started oot wi' this man Drewitt on his yacht. When did ye go aboard, sir ?'

'Look here, why all this ?' said Waters, appealing to Wimsey.

'Better tell him what he wants to know,' said Wimsey. 'I'll explain later.'

'Oh, all right, if you say so. Well, I'll tell you exactly what happened. Last Monday night I was in bed and asleep, when I heard some fool chucking stones at my window. I went down, and there was Drewitt. You remember Drewitt, Wimsey ? Or was he before your time ?'

'I never knew any Trinity men,' said Wimsey. 'The Jews have no dealings with the Samaritans.'

'Of course, you were at Balliol. Well, it doesn't matter. Anyway, I let Drewitt in and gave him a drink. It was about 11 o'clock at night, I think, and I was rather fed-up at being rousted out, because I meant to go up to Glasgow by the 8.45, and I wanted my beauty-sleep. Besides, I felt rather bloody. You remember, Wimsey – I'd had that scrimmage with Campbell at the McClellan Arms. By the way, what is this story about Campbell ?'

'Tell you later, old man. Carry on.'

'Well, I told Drewitt I was going to Glasgow, and he said he'd got a better idea than that. Why not come with him ? He was running up that way, and if I wasn't in a hurry I might just as well join him and do a bit of fishing and get the sea-air. It was lovely weather and his boat, *Susannah*, he calls her, could make the voyage in two or three days, or we could muck about a bit longer if we wanted to, and if the wind didn't hold, we could fall back on the auxiliary motor. Well, it sounded all right, and it didn't matter to me when I got to Glasgow, so I said I'd think about it. So then he said wouldn't I go with him anyhow and have a look at the *Susannah*. He'd got her lying off the Doon.'

'That's right,' said Wimsey to Dalziel. 'There was a boat there on Monday night, and she went off Tuesday morning.'

'You seem to know all about it,' said Waters. 'Well, I thought I might as well have the run. It seemed the best way of getting Drewitt out of the house, so I put on a coat and went up with him. He'd hired a car from somewhere or other and he ran me along. He wanted me to go aboard and meet his whelp, but I didn't want to do that. I hadn't made up my mind, you see. So he brought me back again and dropped me at the corner of the road where it turns off to Borgue. He'd have come all the way, only I wouldn't let him, because I knew I'd have to ask him in again and give him another drink, and I'd had quite as much as I wanted already. So I walked back into Kirkcudbright, and left it with him that I'd think it over, and if I wasn't on board at half-past 9, he wasn't to wait any longer, because I shouldn't be coming and he'd miss the tide.

'Well, I didn't really intend to go, but I turned in and had a good sleep and next morning when Mrs. MacLeod called me, the weather looked damn good, and I thought why not, after all? So I had my breakfast and got my bike out and pushed off.'

'Ye didna tell Mrs. McLeod whaur ye were gaein'.'

'No, there wasn't any need. She knew I was going to Glasgow and might be away some days, and it was no concern of hers how I went. As a matter of fact she was out at the back somewhere, and I didn't see her. I bicycled up to the Doon, signalled to Drewitt and he took me off.'

'What did you do with your bicycle?' asked Wimsey.

'I just shoved it into a little shed-place there is up there, among the trees. I'd often put it there before when I was painting or bathing off the Doon, and it never came to any harm. Well, that was that. As I was saying, we had rather bad luck with the weather and one thing and another, and we didn't get to Gourock till this morning.'

'Did ye no touch onywhere?'

'Yes – I can give you the itinerary if you want it. We dropped down the estuary with the morning tide, passing the Ross Light some time before 10. Then we held on across Wigtown Bay, passing Barrow Head fairly close in. We had a good south-easterly breeze and made the Mull about tea-time. Then we followed the coast northwards, passing Portpatrick at about 7 o'clock, and anchored for the night in Lady Bay, just outside

Loch Ryan. I can't give you more details than that, as I'm no yachtsman. That was Tuesday. On Wednesday we lazed about and did a bit of fishing, and then, about lunch-time, the wind started to haul round to the south-west and Drewitt said he thought we'd better run across to Larne instead of carrying on up to Gourock as we intended. We put in at Larne for the night and took some beer and stuff aboard. On Thursday it was fine enough, but blowing rather a lot, so we sailed up to Ballycastle. It was a bally place, too. I began to think I was wasting my time, I was sick, too. Friday was a foul beast of a day, raining like hell and blowing. However, Tom Drewitt seemed to think it was the kind of day he liked to be out in. Said he didn't care how it blew, provided he had plenty of sea-room or words to that effect. We staggered across to Arran, and I was sick all the time. That was the day I got this crack on the head, curse it. I made Tom put in somewhere under the lee of the island, and in the night the wind dropped, thank God! This morning we got up to Gourock and I shook the dust of the beastly boat off my feet. No more sailing-boats for me, thank you. For complete boredom and physical misery, commend me to a small sailing-vessel in a gale of wind. Have you ever tried cooking fish on a dirty little oil-stove, with your knees above your head? Oh, well, perhaps you enjoy that sort of thing. I don't. Nothing but fish and corned beef for four days – that's not my idea of amusement. Go on up the coast, indeed! Not on your sweet life, I told him. I got off that damned old wherry as quick as I bloody well could, and went on by train to Glasgow and got a hot bath and a shave, and my God! I needed them. And I was just starting off to catch the 5.20 to Dumfries, when these police imbeciles came along and collared me. And now, *do* you mind telling me what it's all about?'

'Did ye no see a newspaper all those four days?'

'We saw a *Daily Mail* at Larne on Thursday morning and I got an *Express* in Glasgow this afternoon, but I can't say I read them very carefully; why?'

'The story tallies all right, what?' said Wimsey, nodding to the Sergeant.

'Ay, imph'm. It tallies well enough, only for the evidence of this man Drewitt.'

'He'll have to be found, of course,' said the Glasgow Superintendent. 'Where will he be just now, Mr. Waters?'

'Oh, God knows!' said Waters, wearily. 'Somewhere off

Kintyre, I should imagine. Don't you believe what I'm telling you?'

'Of course; why not?' said the Superintendent. 'But you see, sir, it's our duty to obtain corroboration of your statement if possible. Did Mr. Drewitt carry a wireless set on board?'

'Wireless set? The filthy canoe hadn't so much as a spare frying-pan,' said Waters, crossly. 'Do you mind telling me what I'm accused of?'

'Ye're no accused of onything at all,' said the Sergeant. 'If I'd been accusin' ye of onything,' he added, cannily, 'I would ha' warned ye that ye'd no need tae be answerin' my questions.'

'Wimsey, I can't make head or tail of all this. For God's sake, what is all this mystery?'

'Well,' said Wimsey, consulting the Superintendent by a look, and receiving a nodded permission to speak, 'you see, it's like this, old horse. Last Tuesday morning they found Campbell lying dead in the Minnoch with a nasty crack in his head, made with a blunt instrument. And as you had last been seen with your ten fingers on his throat, threatening to do him in, we rather wondered, you know, what had become of you and all that.'

'My God!' said Waters.

'Noo, that,' remarked Sergeant Dalziel to Wimsey, some time later, when Waters had retired to write agitated letters and telegrams addressed to the *Susannah* at various possible and impossible ports, 'that is a verra inconvenient piece of evidence. Naiturally, we'll be findin' this felly Drewitt, an' naiturally the baith o' them will be in the same story tegither. But even supposin' Waters went on board at the Doon as he said – an whae's tae tell that? – he may ha' bin pit ashore again at any point.'

'Wait a minute,' said Wimsey. 'How about the body? He couldn't very well have taken that on board with him.'

'Ay, that's so. That's verra true. But supposin' Drewitt runs him up in the night tae the Minnoch—'

'No,' said Wimsey. 'You're forgetting. The man who threw stones at the window may have been Campbell or he may have been Drewitt. He can't have been both. And somebody came back to Waters' bedroom that night and ate his breakfast in the morning. He can't have been Campbell, and it's extremely unlikely that it was Drewitt, so it must have been Waters. He couldn't have got up to the Minnoch and back again in the time.'

'But Drewitt might ha' cairrit the corpse away for him.'

'That depends. He'd have had to know the country pretty well to find the right place in the dark. And when was all this planned ? If the man at the window was Campbell, how did Waters get into communication with Drewitt ? If Drewitt was the man at the window, when and where was Campbell murdered ? Hang it all, Sergeant, you can't have it both ways. If Waters went on board when he said he did, he's got his alibi. Otherwise, I freely admit that there may be a flaw in the thing. It's perfectly possible that the *Susannah* may have picked him up at some point or other on the Tuesday night. Suppose, for example, that Waters knew beforehand that the boat would be at Lady Bay that night. He could have hired a car somewhere and picked the *Susannah* up there, and the rest of the tale could have been concocted between them. The point you've got to prove is that Waters went aboard the *Susannah* on the Tuesday morning. There are cottages down at the Doon. Surely to goodness somebody must have seen him.'

'That's a fact,' said the Sergeant.

'And the bicycle should be there, too.'

'Aweel,' said Dalziel, resignedly, 'I can see there'll be no kirk for me the morn. It's awfu', the wark there is in a case the like o' this. An' there's no train back tae Newton-Stewart the nicht.'

'No more there is,' said Wimsey. 'Life's just one damn thing after another.'

'It is that,' said Sergeant Dalziel.

FARREN'S STORY

GILDA FARREN sat, upright as a lily-stalk, in the high-backed chair, spinning wool. Her dress was mediaeval, with its close bodice and full, long skirt, just lifted from the ground by the foot that swayed placidly upon the treadle. It had a square neck and long, close-fitting sleeves, and it was made of a fine cream-coloured serge which gave her an air of stately purity. Besides, it had the advantage of not showing the fluff of white wool which settles all over the spinning-woman and tends to give her the appearance of a person who has slept in her clothes. Lord Peter Wimsey, seated rather closely beside her, to avoid the draught from the whirling wheel, noted this detail with sardonic appreciation.

'Well, Mrs. Farren,' he said, cheerfully, 'we shall have the truant husband back now.'

The long hands seemed to falter for a moment in feeding the flock to the spindle, and the thread ran fine and thickened again.

'What makes you think that ?' asked Mrs. Farren, never turning her red-gold head.

'All-stations call,' said Wimsey, lighting another cigarette. 'Nothing agitating, you know. Anxious friends and relations, and all that.'

'That,' said Mrs. Farren, 'is a very great impertinence.'

'I admit,' said Wimsey, 'that you don't seem frightfully anxious. If it isn't rude to ask, why aren't you ?'

'I think it is rather rude,' said Mrs. Farren.

'Sorry,' said Wimsey, 'but the question remains. Why aren't you ? Abandoned bicycle – dangerous old mine – indefatigable police with ropes and grappling-hooks – empty chair – deserted home – and a lady who sits spinning an even thread. It might be thought puzzling.'

'I have already said,' replied Mrs. Farren, 'that I consider all that story about mines and suicide to be absurd. I am not responsible for the foolish ideas of country policemen. I resent this inquisitiveness about my private affairs extremely. The police I can forgive, Lord Peter, but what business is it of yours ?'

'None whatever,' said Wimsey, cheerfully. 'Only, if you cared to tell me the facts, I might be able to quell the riot.'

'What facts ?'

'You might tell me, for instance,' said Wimsey, 'where the letter came from.'

The right hand paused and fumbled in its task. The thread whisked out of the left-hand thumb and finger and wound itself up sharply on the spindle. Mrs. Farren uttered a little exclamation of annoyance, stopped the wheel, and unwound the thread again.

163

'I beg your pardon,' she said, when she had made the join in the wool. She re-started the wheel with a light touch of the hand. 'What was that you said?'

'I said you might tell me where the letter came from.'

'What letter?'

'The letter your husband wrote you on Thursday.'

'If,' said Mrs. Farren, 'the police have been tampering with my correspondence, they can probably give you all the information you want – unless, of course, they also dislike interference.'

Her breath was coming short and angrily.

'Well,' replied Wimsey, 'as a matter of fact they omitted that simple precaution. But since you admit the existence of the letter—'

'I admit nothing of the sort.'

'Come now,' said Wimsey. 'You are not one of Nature's gifted liars, Mrs. Farren. Up to Thursday, you were genuinely frightened and anxious about your husband. On Friday you were pretending to be anxious, but you were not. Today I suggest that you received a letter from your husband on Friday morning, and you leap to the conclusion that the police have been investigating your correspondence. Therefore you did receive a letter. Why deny it?'

'Why should I tell you anything about it?'

'Why indeed? I have only to wait a day or two and I shall get the answer from Scotland Yard.'

'What has Scotland Yard to do with it?'

'Surely, Mrs. Farren, you must know that your husband is, or may be, a valuable witness in the Campbell case?'

'Why?'

'Well, you know, he went off from here looking for Campbell. He was last heard of inquiring for Campbell in Gatehouse. It would be interesting to know if he did meet Campbell – wouldn't it?'

'Lord Peter Wimsey!' Mrs. Farren stopped the wheel and turned indignantly to face him. 'Have you ever thought how contemptible you are? We have received you here in Kirkcudbright as a friend. Everybody has shown you kindness. And you repay it by coming into the houses of your friends as a police-spy. If there is anything meaner than a man who tries to bully and trap a woman into betraying her husband, it is the wife who falls into the trap!'

'Mrs. Farren,' said Wimsey, getting up, with a white face, 'if it is a question of betrayal, then I beg your pardon. I shall say nothing to the police about the letter or about what you have just said. But in that case I can only say again – and this time as a warning – that they have sent out an all-stations call from London and that from today your correspondence *will* be watched. In telling you so, I am possibly betraying official secrets and making myself an accessory after the fact to a murder. However—'

'How dare you ?'

'To be frank with you,' said Wimsey, taking the question at its face-value, 'I do not think I am running any very great risk. If I did, I might be more cautious.'

'Do you dare to suggest that I believe my husband to be guilty of murder ?'

'If I must answer that, then – I think you have thought so. I am not sure that you do not think so now. But I thought it possible that you believed him innocent, in which case, the sooner he returns to give an account of himself, the better for himself and for everybody.'

He took up his hat and turned to go. He had his hand on the latch when she called him back.

'Lord Peter !'

'Think before you speak,' he said hastily.

'You – you are quite mistaken. I am sure my husband is innocent. There is another reason—'

He looked at her.

'Ah!' he said. 'Stupid of me. It is your own pride that you are sheltering now.' He came back into the room, treading gently, and laid his hat on the table. 'My dear Mrs. Farren, will you believe me when I say that all men – the best and the worst alike – have these moments of rebellion and distaste ? It is nothing. It is a case for understanding and – if I may say so – response.'

'I am ready,' said Gilda Farren, 'to forgive—'

'Never do that,' said Wimsey. 'Forgiveness is the one unpardonable sin. It is almost better to make a scene – though,' he added, thoughtfully, 'that depends on the bloke's temperament.'

'I should certainly not make a scene,' said Mrs. Farren.

'No,' said Wimsey. 'I see that.'

'I shall not do anything,' said Mrs. Farren. 'To be insulted was enough. To be deserted as well—' Her eyes were hard and angry. 'If he chooses to come back, I shall receive him, naturally. But it is nothing to me what he chooses to do with himself. There seems to be no end to what women have to endure. I should not say as much as this to you, if—'

'If I didn't know it already,' put in Wimsey.

'I have tried to look as though nothing was the matter,' said Mrs. Farren, 'and to put a good face on it. I do not want to show my husband up before his friends.'

'Quite so,' said Wimsey. 'Besides,' he added, rather brutally, 'it might look as though you yourself had failed in some way.'

'I have always done my duty as his wife.'

'Too true,' said Wimsey. 'He put you up on a pedestal, and you have sat on it ever since. What more could you do?'

'I have been faithful to him,' said Mrs. Farren, with rising temper. 'I have worked to keep the house beautiful – and to make it a place of refreshment and inspiration. I have done all I could to further his ambitions. I have borne my share of the household expenses –' Here she seemed suddenly to become aware of a tinge of bathos and went on hurriedly, 'You may think all this is nothing, but it means sacrifice and hard work.'

'I know that,' replied Wimsey, quietly.

'Is it my fault that – just because this house was always a peaceful and beautiful place – that unhappy man should have come to me to tell me his troubles? Is that any reason why I should be outraged by vile suspicions? Do *you* believe there was anything more than sympathy in my feelings for Sandy Campbell?'

'Not for a moment,' said Wimsey.

'Then why couldn't my husband believe it?'

'Because he was in love with you.'

'That is not the kind of love I recognise as love. If he loved me he should have trusted me.'

'As a matter of fact,' said Wimsey, 'I quite agree with you. But everybody has his own ideas about love, and Hugh Farren is a decent man.'

'Is it decent to believe vile things of other people?'

'Well – the two things often go together, I'm afraid. I mean, virtuous people are generally rather stupid about those things. That's why bad men always have devoted wives – they're not stupid. Same with bad women – they usually have their husbands on a lead. It oughtn't to be like that, but there it is.'

166

'Do you consider yourself a decent man when you talk like that?'

'Oh dear no,' said Wimsey. 'But I'm not stupid. My wife won't have that to complain of.'

'You seem to imagine that infidelity is a trifle, compared with —'

'With stupidity. I don't quite say that. But the one can cause quite as much upheaval as the other, and the trouble is that it's incurable. One of those things one has to put up with. I shan't necessarily be unfaithful to my wife, but I shall know enough about infidelity to know it when I see it, and not mistake other things for it. If I were married to you, for example, I should know that under no circumstances would you ever be unfaithful to me. For one thing, you haven't got the temperament. For another, you would never like to think less of yourself than you do. For a third, it would offend your aesthetic taste. And for a fourth, it would give other people a handle against you.'

'Upon my word,' said Mrs. Farren, 'your reasons are more insulting than my husband's suspicions.'

'You're quite right,' said Wimsey. 'They are.'

'If Hugh were here,' said Mrs. Farren, 'he would throw you out of the window.'

'Probably,' said Wimsey. 'In fact, now that I've put it to you in the right light, you can see that his attitude towards you is rather a compliment than otherwise.'

'Go and see him,' said Mrs. Farren fiercely. 'Tell him what you have been saying to me – if you dare – and see what he says to you.'

'With pleasure,' said Wimsey, 'if you will give me his address.'

'I don't know it,' said Mrs. Farren, shortly. 'But the post-mark was Brough in Westmorland.'

'Thank you,' said Wimsey, 'I will go and see him – and, by the way, I shall not mention this to the police.'

At an early hour on Monday morning, a large black Daimler car, with an outsize bonnet and racing body, moved in leisurely silence down the main street of Brough. The driver, glancing carelessly from side to side through his monocle, appeared to be about to pull up at the principal hotel; then, suddenly changing his mind, he moved forward again, and eventually stopped the car before a smaller inn, distinguished by the effigy of a spirited bull, careering ferociously in an emerald green meadow beneath a bright summer sky

He pushed open the door and strode in. The innkeeper was polishing glasses, and bade him a polite good morning.

'A fine morning,' said the traveller.

'Ay, so 'tis,' agreed the innkeeper.

'Can you give me a bit of breakfast ?'

The innkeeper appeared to turn this suggestion over in his mind.

'Hey, mother!' he bellowed at last, turning towards an inner door, 'canst a' give breakfast to t' gentleman ?'

His shout brought out a comely woman in the middle forties who, after looking the gentleman over and summing him up, reckoned that she could, if a dish of eggs and Cumberland ham would suit the gentleman.

Nothing could be better, in the gentleman's opinion. He was ushered into a parlour full of plush-covered chairs and stuffed birds, and invited to take a seat. After an interval, a sturdy young woman appeared to lay the table. After a further interval came a large and steaming tea-pot, a home-baked loaf, a plate of buns, a large pat of butter and two sorts of jam. Finally, the landlady reappeared, escorting the ham and eggs in person.

The motorist complimented her on the excellence of the food and fell to with an appetite, mentioning that he had just come down from Scotland. He made a few sensible observations on the curing of hams, and gave an intelligent account of the method used in Ayrshire. He also inquired particularly after a certain kind of cheese peculiar to the district. The landlady – in whom the monocle had at first raised some doubts – began to think that he was a more homely body than he appeared at first sight, and obligingly offered to send the girl round to the shop to procure a cheese for him.

'I can see you know the town, sir,' she observed.

'Oh, yes – I've been through here lots of times, though I don't think I've ever pulled up here before. You're looking very smart and all that – got the old Bull repainted, I see.'

'Ah, you noticed 'en, sir. Well, that was nobbut finished yesterday. 'Twas done by a painter gentleman. He came walking into t' bar Thursday and says to George, "Landlord," he says, "the signboard would do wi' a bit paint. If I make 'ee a fine new bull for 'en, will 'ee let me have a room cheap ?" George, he didn't know what to think, but t' gentleman says, "I'll make 'ee a fair offer. Here's my money. Gie me my food and lodging and I'll do my best by t' bull, and if tha likes 'en

168

when a's done, tha canst allow what tha likes for 'en on t' bill."
On walking-tour, a' said a' was, and a' had one of these little
boxes full of paints wi' 'en, so that we could see a' was an artist.'

'Funny,' said the motorist. 'Had he any luggage?'

'A little bag-like – nothing much. But anybody could see a'
was a gentleman. Well, George didn't know what to think.'

From what the traveller had seen of George, this seemed very
probable. There was a kind of stolid dignity about George which
suggested that he disliked being flurried.

Apparently, however, the mysterious artist had then and there,
with a piece of black stuff, sketched on the back of an envelope
a bull so rampant, so fierce, so full of fire and vigour, as to
appeal very strongly to George's agrarian instincts. After some
discussion, the bargain was struck, the old bull taken down and
the paints brought out. On Thursday the new bull had made his
appearance on one side of the sign, head down and tail up,
steam issuing from his nostrils, and the painter had explained
that this represented the frame of mind of the hungry traveller
bellowing for his food. On Friday, a second bull was drawn and
coloured on the other side, sleek, handsome and contented,
having fed well and received the best of treatment. On Saturday,
the sign had been set out to dry in the wash-house. On Sunday,
the painter had applied a coat of varnish on both sides and set
the board back in the wash-house. On Sunday night, the varnish,
though still a little tacky, seemed to be dry enough to allow of
the sign's being put in place, and there it was. The painter had
taken his departure on foot on Sunday afternoon. George had
been so pleased with the bull that he had refused to take any
money at all from the gentleman, and had given him an intro-
duction to a friend of his in a neighbouring village, who also had
a sign that needed renewal.

The motorist listened with great interest to this story and
carelessly inquired the painter's name. The landlady produced
her visitors' book.

''Tis wrote here,' said she. 'Mr. H. Ford of London, but by
a's speech you'd ha' taken 'en for a Scotsman.'

The motorist looked down at the book, with a slight smile
twisting the corners of his long mouth. Then he pulled a
fountain-pen from his pocket and wrote, beneath the signature
of Mr. H. Ford:

'Peter Wimsey. Kirkcudbright. Good baiting at the Bull.'

Then, getting up and buckling the belt of his leather coat, he observed, pleasantly:

'If any friends of mine should come inquiring for Mr. Ford, be sure you show them that book, and say I left my compliments for Mr. Parker of London.'

'Mester Parker?' said the landlady, mystified, but impressed. 'Well, to be sure, I'll tell 'en, sir.'

Wimsey paid his bill and went out. As he drove away he saw her standing, book in hand, under the signboard, staring at the bull which capered so bravely on the bright green grass.

The village mentioned by the landlady was only about six miles from Brough, and was reached by a side-turning. It possessed only one inn, and that inn had no sign, only an empty iron bracket. Wimsey smiled again, stopped his car at the door and passed into the bar, where he ordered a tankard of beer.

'What's the name of your inn?' he asked, presently.

The landlord, a brisk Southerner, grinned widely.

'Dog and Gun, sir. The sign's took down to be repainted. Gentleman a-workin' on it now in the back garden. One of these travelling painter chaps – gentleman, though. Comes from over the Border by his way o' talkin'. Old George Wetherby sent him on here. Tells me he's made a good job o' the old Bull in Brough. Working his way down to London, by what I can make out. Very pleasant gentleman. Real artist – paints pictures for the London shows, or so he tells me. My sign won't be any the worse for a dab o' fresh paint – besides, it amuses the kids to watch him muckin' about.'

'Nothing I like better myself,' said Wimsey, 'than to hang round while another fellow does a spot of work.'

'No? Well, that's so, sir. If you like to step into the garden, sir, you'll see him.'

Wimsey laughed and wandered out, tankard in hand. He dodged under a little archway, covered with a tangle of faded ramblers, and there, sure enough, squatting on an upturned bucket with the signboard of the Dog and Gun propped on a kitchen-chair before him, was the missing Hugh Farren, whistling cheerfully, as he squeezed out paint upon his palette.

Farren's back was turned towards Wimsey and he did not turn his head. Three children watched, fascinated, as the thick blobs of colour oozed out on to the board.

'What's that, mister?'

'That's the green for the gentleman's coat. No – don't pinch it, or you'll get it all over you. Yes, you can put the cap on. Yes, that's to keep it from drying up. Yes, put it back in the box . . . That's yellow. No, I know there isn't any yellow in the picture, but I want it to mix with the green to make it brighter. You'll see. Don't forget the cap. What? Oh, anywhere in the box. White – yes, it's a big tube isn't it? You'll see, you have to put a little white into most of the colours – why? Well, they wouldn't come right without it. You'll see when I do the sky. What's that? You want the dog made white all over? No, I can't make it a picture of Scruggs. Why not? Well, Scruggs isn't the right sort of dog to take out shooting. Well, he's not, that's why. This has got to be a retriever. All right, well, I'll put in a liver-and-white spaniel. Oh, well, it's rather a pretty dog with long ears. Yes. I daresay it is like Colonel Amery's. No. I don't know Colonel Amery. Did you put the cap on that white paint? Dash it! if you go losing things like that I'll send you back to Mother and she'll spank you. What? Well, the gentle-man has a green coat because he's a gamekeeper. Possibly Colonel Amery's gamekeeper doesn't, but this one does. No. I don't know why gamekeepers wear green coats – to keep them warm, I expect. No. I haven't got any brown paint same as that tree-trunk. I get that by mixing other colours. No, I've got all the colours I want now. You can put 'em away and shut the box. Yes, I can tell pretty well how much I want before I start. That's called a palette knife. No, it isn't meant to be sharp. It's meant for cleaning your palette and so on. Some people use a knife to paint with. Yes, it's nice and wiggly, but it won't stand too much of that kind of treatment, my lad. Yes, of course you can paint with a knife if you want to. You can paint with your fingers if it comes to that. No, I shouldn't advise you to try. Yes, well, it makes a rougher kind of surface, all blobs and chunks of paint. All right. I'll show you presently. Yes, I'm going to begin with the sky. Why? Well, why do you think? Yes, because it's at the top. Yes, of course that blue's too dark, but I'm going to put some white in it. Yes, and some green. You didn't know there was any green in the sky? Well, there is. And sometimes there's purple and pink too. No, I'm not going to paint a purple and pink sky. The gentleman and the dogs have only just started out. It's morning in this picture. Yes, I know, on the other side they're coming home with a lot of birds and things. I'll put a pink and purple sunset into that if you're good and don't ask too many questions. No, be a good girl and don't joggle my arm. Oh, Lord!'

'Hullo, Farren!' said Wimsey. 'Finding the young idea a bit too eager for information, eh?'

'My God!' said the painter. 'Wimsey, by all that's holy! How did you get here? Don't say my wife sent you!'

'Not exactly,' said Wimsey. 'And yet, now you mention it, I believe she did do something of the sort.'

Farren sighed.

'Come on,' he said. 'Spit it out and get it over. Run away to your mother, bairns. I've got to talk to this gentleman.'

'Look here,' said Wimsey, when they were alone. 'I want to say, first of all, that I haven't the faintest right to ask questions. But I'd be damned glad if you'd tell me exactly what you've been up to since Monday night.'

'I suppose my conduct is being harshly criticised at Kirkcudbright,' said Farren. 'Deserting the home, and all that?'

'Well, no,' said Wimsey. 'Your wife has stuck to it that there's nothing unusual in your disappearance. But – as a matter of fact – the police have been hunting for you everywhere.'

'The police? Why in the world— ?'

'I think I'll smoke a pipe,' said Wimsey. 'Well, the fact that you were talking rather wildly about suicide and other things, don't you know. And then your bicycle being found close to those old mines up beyond Creetown. It – suggested things, you see.'

'Oh, I'd forgotten about the bicycle. Yes, but surely Gilda – I wrote to her.'

'She isn't worried about that, now.'

'I suppose she must have been rather anxious. I ought to have written earlier. But – damn it! I never thought about their finding that. And – by Jove! old Strachan will have been in a bit of a stew.'

'Why Strachan, particularly?'

'Well, surely he told people – didn't he?'

'Look here, Farren, what the devil are you talking about?'

'About Monday night. Poor old Strachan! He must have thought I'd really gone and done it.'

'When did you see Strachan, then?'

'Why, that night, up by the mines. Didn't you know?'

'I don't know anything,' said Wimsey. 'Suppose you tell me the story right end foremost.'

'All right. I don't mind. I suppose you know that I had a bit of a row that night with Campbell. Oh! that reminds me, Wimsey. Didn't I see something funny in the paper about Campbell? Something about his being found dead?'

'He's been murdered,' said Wimsey, abruptly.

'Murdered? That wasn't what I saw. But I haven't looked at a paper for days. I only saw – when was it? – Wednesday morning, I think – something about "well-known Scottish painter found dead in a river."'

'Oh, well, it hadn't got out then. But he was bumped off, as a matter of fact, some time on Monday night or Tuesday morning – up at the Minnoch.'

'Was he? Serve the beggar right. Oh, by the way, I seem to see something behind this. Am I supposed to have done it, Wimsey?'

'I don't know,' said Wimsey, truthfully. 'But there is a feeling that perhaps you ought to come forward and say something. You were looking for him, you know, on Monday night.'

'Yes, I was. And if I'd met him, there would have been murder done. But as a matter of fact, I didn't meet him.'

'You can prove that?'

'Well – I don't know that I can if it comes to that. This isn't serious, is it?'

'I don't know. Let's have the story, Farren.'

'I see. Well. Well, I came home about six o'clock on Monday and found that blighter making love to my wife. I was fed up, Wimsey. I hoofed him out and I dare say I made a bit of an ass of myself.'

'Wait a minute. Did you actually see Campbell?'

'He was just making off when I came in. I told him to clear out, and then I went in and spoke my mind. I told Gilda I wouldn't have that fellow there. She stuck up for him, and that annoyed me. Mind you, Wimsey, I haven't a word against Gilda except that she can't and won't understand that Campbell is – was – a poisonous sort of hound and that she was making me a laughing-stock. She's got an idea about being kind and sympathetic, and she can't see that that sort of thing doesn't work with fellows like Campbell. Dash it all, I *know* the blighter was crazy about her. And when I tried, quite nicely, to point out that she was making a fool of herself, she got on her high horse and – Damn it, Wimsey! I don't want to talk like a pig about my wife, but the fact is, she's too good and too full of ideals to understand what the ordinary man is like. You do see what I mean?'

'Perfectly,' said Wimsey.

'Because my wife really is a wonderful woman. Only – well, I daresay I said a lot of silly things.'

'I know exactly the sort of thing you said,' observed Wimsey. 'She didn't tell me, but I can imagine it. You stormed about, and she told you not to have coarse ideas, and you got hotter, and she got colder, and you said things you didn't mean in the hope of bringing her to your arms, so to speak, and then she said you were insulting and burst into tears, and then you worked yourself into half-believing the accusations you'd only made to annoy her, and then you threatened murder and suicide and went out to get drunk. Bless your soul, you're not the first and won't be the last.'

'Well, you've got it about right,' said Farren. 'Only I really did begin to believe it at the time. At least, I believed Campbell was out to do all the mischief he could. I did get drunk I had one or two in the town, and then I barged off to Gatehouse to find Campbell.'

'How did you miss him in Kirkcudbright? He was at the McClellan Arms all the time.'

'I never thought of that. I just hared off to Gatehouse. He wasn't in his cottage, and Ferguson yelled out to me. I thought of having a row with Ferguson, but I wasn't as drunk as all that. Then I went and had a few more. Somebody told me they'd seen Campbell go out to Creetown, so I went after him.'

'No, you didn't,' said Wimsey. 'You went up the road to the golf-links.'

'Did I? Oh, yes so I did. I went to find Strachan, but he was out. I left a note or a message for him, I think; to tell the truth, I'm not very clear about it. But I think I told him I was going to Creetown to do Campbell in and cut my own throat. Some rot or other. . . . I say, poor old Strachan! He must have had a time! Did he show that note to the police?'

'Not that I know of.'

'Oh, no, I suppose he wouldn't. Strachan's a good sort. Well, I went over to Creetown. The pubs were shut when I got there, but I went in and got hold of a man there – by Jove, no, I suppose he wouldn't have come forward, either. Well, never mind the man – I don't want to get him into trouble. The point is that I raised a bottle of whiskey after closing-time.'

174

'Yes ?'

'Well, I'm a bit vague about the next part of it, but I know I remember going up into the hills, with some vague idea of chucking myself down one of the pits. I wandered round. I remember wheeling the damned bike over the rough stuff – and then, damn it all, I came to the mouth of one of the mines. Nearly fell into it. I sat down and moralised a bit on the brink, with the help of the whiskey. I must have been damned drunk. I don't know how long that lasted. Well, then, presently I heard somebody shouting and I shouted back. I felt like that. Somebody came up, and started talking. It was old Strachan. At least, my impression is that it was Strachan, but I freely admit that I may be mixing things up a bit. I know he talked and talked and tried to get hold of me, and I struggled and fought him. It was a lovely fight, I do know that. Then I knocked him down and started to run. I ran like hell. My God! it was fine. Drink takes me in the head, you know; my legs are always all right. I simply bounced over the heather, and the stars bounced along with me. Good God! I remember that now. I don't know how long it went on. And then I lost my footing and went rolling away down a slope somewhere. I suppose I fetched up all right at the bottom, because, when I woke, it was well on in the morning, and I was lying in a sort of hollow among the bracken, quite snug and cosy and without so much as a head-ache.

'I didn't know where I was. But I didn't care. I just felt that nothing mattered at all. I didn't want to go home. I didn't care a hang about Campbell. I just felt as if all the cares of the world had tumbled off my back and left me alone in the sunshine. I walked straight ahead. I was getting damned hungry by that time, because I'd had no dinner the night before, but there wasn't so much as a shepherd's hut in sight. I walked and walked. The place was full of wee burns and I had plenty to drink. After hours and hours I struck a road and walked along, not meeting anybody. And then, some time about mid-day, I crossed a bridge and knew where I was. It was the place they call New Brig o' Dee, on the New Galloway Road. I hadn't really come so very far. I expect I must have made a bit of a circle, though I thought I was keeping the sun on my right all the time.'

'The sun moves, you know,' said Wimsey, 'or appears to.'

'Yes – I don't think I realised how long I'd been going. Anyhow, I got there, and started to walk towards New Galloway. I met some sheep and a few cows and carts, and at last a fellow with a lorry overtook me. He took me as far as New Galloway, and I got something to eat there.'

'What time was that?' asked Wimsey, quickly.

'Oh, it must have been nearly three. Then I wondered what to do with myself. I'd got about ten pounds in my pocket and my one idea was that I didn't want to go back. I was finished. Done. I wanted to go gipsying. I didn't give a damn if I never saw the Tolbooth spire again. I saw an empty lorry labelled with the name of a Glasgow firm on it, and I bargained with the man to take me to Dumfries. They were going that way.'

'What was the name of the firm?'

'Eh? Oh, I don't know. There were two very decent fellows on it and we talked about fishing.'

'Where did they put you off?'

'Just before we got to Dumfries. I wanted to think a bit, you see. It was a question whether I'd take the train there or put up in some pub or other. I was afraid of running into some of our crowd at the station. Besides, some of the railway people there would have known me. I often go to Dumfries. That was the trouble about the pub idea too. ... I don't know if I can explain how I felt, Wimsey. It was as if I'd escaped from something and was afraid of being – well, bagged. I mean, if I had met anyone who knew me, I should have fudged up some tale about fishing or painting and made everything sound quite ordinary, and then I should have gone home. You see. It wouldn't have been the same if I'd had to make up an elaborate deception about it. You're not free when you have to tell lies to escape. It's not worth it. I can't possibly make you understand that.'

'Why not?' said Wimsey. 'It would be like buying a week-end wedding-ring.'

'Yes – just as tedious as if it was 22-carat. And signing the hotel register and wondering if the reception-clerk believed you. Wimsey, you're rich and there's nothing to stop you from doing what you like. Why do you trouble to be respectable?'

'Just because there's nothing to stop me from doing what I like, probably. I get my fun out of it.'

'I know you do,' said Farren, looking at him in a puzzled way. 'It's odd. You create an illusion of liberty. Is it money? Or is it being unmarried? But there are plenty of unmarried men who don't—'

'Aren't we wandering slightly from the matter in hand ?' said Wimsey.

'Perhaps. Well – I went into a little inn – a one-horse little place – and had a drink in the four-ale bar. There was a young fellow there with a bike and side-car. He said he was going through to Carlisle. That gave me an idea. I asked him if he'd take me and he said he would. He was a decent bloke and didn't ask any questions.'

'What was his name ?'

'I didn't ask, nor did he. I said I was on a walking tour and that my belongings were waiting for me in Carlisle. But he didn't seem to bother. I never met such a reasonable man.'

'What was he ?'

'I gathered that he had something to do with the second-hand motor trade and was taking the bike in part-exchange for something. I shouldn't have known that, only he apologised for its internals not being in perfect trim. In fact, something went wrong with them on the road, and I had to hold an electric torch for him while he put it right. He didn't seem to have many ideas beyond plugs and things. He didn't talk. Said he'd been thirty-six hours on the road, but I needn't worry, because he could drive in his sleep.'

Wimsey nodded. He knew the helots of the second-hand-motor trade. Grim, silent, cynical, abroad at all hours and in all weathers, they are men accustomed to disillusionment and disaster. To deliver their melancholy screws to their customers and depart before inconvenient discoveries are made; to scramble home with their surprise-packets of old iron before the patched radiator bursts or the clutch gives way – this is their sole preoccupation. Always dog-tired, dirty and prepared for the worst, habitually hard-up and morose, they are not likely to be inquisitive about stranded travellers who offer to pay for a lift.

'So you got to Carlisle ?'

'Yes. I slept most of the time, except, of course, when I was holding the torch. I enjoyed the bits when I was awake. Not knowing who he was made it better. Do you know, I hadn't been in a side-car before. It's not like a car. Cars fascinate me, too, though the only two or three times I tried to drive one I didn't get much kick out of it. I like being driven – and this side-car business gets my imagination. The power is outside you, and you are pulled along – in tow, so to speak. Like being eloped with. You seem to notice the strength of the machine more than you do in a car. Why is that ?'

Wimsey shook his head.

'Perhaps I was imagining things. Well, anyhow, we got to Carlisle in the morning and I had some grub in a sort of tea-shop place. Then, of course, I had to decide on something. I bought a clean shirt and some socks and a toothbrush and so on, and a knapsack to shove them into. It was only then that I thought about money. I'd have to cash a cheque somewhere. But that meant telling people where I was. I mean, the bank people would have to ring up Kirkcudbright and all that. I thought it would be more fun to pay my way. I'd still got enough to buy paints with, so I went into an art-dealers' and got a box and a palette and some brushes and colours—'

'Winsor & Newton, I observe,' said Wimsey.

'Yes. You can get them easily in most places, you know. I usually get my stuff from Paris, but Winsor & Newton are perfectly reliable. I thought I'd make my way down into the Lake Country and paint little pictures for tourists or something. It's fearfully easy. You can knock off two or three in a day – hills and water and mists, you know – and idiots will give you ten bob a time, if the stuff's sentimental enough. I knew a man who always paid for his holidays that way. Didn't sign 'em in his own name, naturally. It's a form of mass-production.'

'Hence the idea of a Mr. H. Ford ?'

'Oh, you've been to the Bull at Brough ? Yes – the idea rather tickled me. Well, after I'd bought the paints I had just about enough left to bribe another lorry-driver. But I didn't. I found a man with a Riley – Oxford fellow – a frightfully good sort. He was heading south and told me I could go as far as I like with him and damn paying for it. He talked all right. His name was John Barrett and he was just fooling around amusing himself. Didn't know where he was going. Had just got the new car and wanted to see what she could do. Damn it, he did, too. I was never so frightened in my life.'

'Where did he live ?'

'Oh, London, somewhere. He told me the place, but I can't remember it now. He asked a lot of questions, too, but I just said I was a travelling artist and he thought it was a fearfully good wheeze. I didn't mind telling him that, because by that time it was true, you see. He asked what one could make out of it and all that, and I gave him all the stuff I'd had from my

178

friend, and he asked me where I'd been last and I said in Galloway. It was just as easy as that. But when we got to Brough, I said I'd get off there. I felt I was too young to die – just as I was starting off on an adventure, too. He was a bit disappointed, but he wished me luck and all that. I went to the Bull, because it looked less grand than the other place, and that was where I got the idea about the sign. Good thing I did, too, because the weather turned nasty the next day, and I hadn't altogether reckoned with that when I made my plan about doing the hills and lakes and things. So that was that, and here I am.'

Farren took up his brushes again and renewed his assault upon the Dog and Gun.

'Very jolly,' said Wimsey. 'But you know, it all boils down to this, that you can't produce a single witness to say where you were between Monday night and Tuesday afternoon at 3 o'clock.'

'Oh! no – I'd forgotten about all that. But, I mean, all this isn't serious, really? And, after all, I've got a perfectly natural, straightforward explanation.'

'It sounds natural enough to me, perhaps,' said Wimsey, 'but whether the police will take that view—'

'Damn the police! I say, Wimsey—'

The shadow of something cold and deadly crept into the painter's eyes.

'Does this mean I've got to go back, Wimsey?'

'I'm afraid,' said Wimsey, 'I'm very much afraid—' He was looking back over Farren's shoulder at the back door of the inn, from which two squarely-built men in tweeds were emerging. Farren, catching the infection of uneasiness, turned his head.

'My God,' he said. 'It's all up. Bagged. Trapped. Prison.'

'Yes,' said Wimsey, almost inaudibly. 'And you won't escape this time – ever.'

STRACHAN'S STORY

'BICYCLES?' said Inspector Macpherson. 'Dinna ye talk tae me o' bicycles. I'm fair fed up wi' the name o' them. Wad ye believe that there could be sic a stour aboot twa-three bicycles? Here's ane o' them at Euston and anither up at Creetoon, and as if that wasn't enough, here's Waters' bicycle vanished and naebody kens whether we should arrest Waters for murder or make a sairch for a bicycle-thief.'

'It's very trying,' said Wimsey. 'And I suppose nobody saw Waters go aboard at the Doon ?'

'An' if onybody had seen him,' said the Inspector, wrathfully, 'wad I be fashin' masel' the noo ? There's a mon saw anither mon wadin' across the sand, but he was half a mile off, an' whae's tae sae it was Waters ?'

'I must say,' said Wimsey, 'that I never in all my life heard of such an unconvincing bunch of alibis. By the way, Inspector, did you check up that story of Ferguson's ?'

'Ferguson ?' said the Inspector, in the resentful accents of a schoolboy burdened with too much homework. 'Oo, ay, we havena forgot Ferguson. I went tae Sparkes & Crisp an' interviewed the employees. There was twa of them remembered him weel eneuch. The lad doonstairs in the show-room couldna speak with sairtainty tae the time, but he recognised Ferguson from his photograph as havin' brocht in a magneto on the Monday afternoon. He said Mr. Saunders wad be the man tae see tae that, and pit a ca' through on the house telephone tae Mr. Sparkes, an' he had the young fellow in. Saunders is ane o' they bright lads. He picked the photograph at once oot o' the six I showed him an' turned up the entry o' the magneto in the daybook.'

'Could he swear to the time Ferguson came in ?'

'He wadna charge his memory wi' the precise minute, but he said he had juist come in fra' his lunch an' found Ferguson waitin' for him. His lunch time is fra' 1.30 tae 2.30, but he was a bit late that day, an' Ferguson had been waitin' on him a wee while. He thinks it wad be aboot ten minutes tae three.'

'That's just about what Ferguson made it.'

'Near eneuch.'

'H'm. That sounds all right. Was that all Saunders had to say ?'

'Ay. Forbye that he said he couldna weel understand whit had happened tae the magneto. He said it looked as though some yin had been daein' it a wilfu' damage.'

'That's funny. That would be the mechanic's report, of course. Did you see the mechanic at all ?'

The Inspector admitted that he had not done so, not seeing what bearing it could have upon the case.

'Was you thinkin', maybe,' he suggested, 'that some felonious body was interested in seein' that Ferguson didna take oot his car that mornin' ?'

'Inspector,' said Wimsey, 'you are a mind-reader. I was thinking exactly that.'

Farren had returned to Kirkcudbright. His dream of escape had vanished. His wife had forgiven him. His absence was explained as a trifling and whimsical eccentricity. Gilda Farren sat, upright and serene, spinning the loose white flock into a strong thread that wound itself ineluctably to smother the twirling spindle. The story had been told to the police. Sir Maxwell Jamieson shook his head over it. Short of arresting Farren, they must remain content with his story or else disprove it. And they could not very well arrest Farren, for they might want to arrest Waters or Gowan or Graham or even Strachan, all of whose stories were equally odd and suspicious. It would be preposterous to arrest five people for one crime.

The porter at Girvan was still desperately ill. He had – out of pure perversity, no doubt – developed peritonitis. The Euston bicycle had been duly identified as the property of young Andrew of the Anwoth, but what evidence was there that it had any connection with Campbell ? If Farren were the murderer it had obviously no connection with it at all, for Farren could not have taken the Ayr train at Girvan and been in New Galloway at 3 o'clock. And that part of Farren's story was true, anyway, for they had checked it. No, Farren, like the rest, must have rope given him. So Farren sat sulkily in his studio and Mrs. Farren span – not a rope, perhaps, but fetters at any rate – in the sitting-room with the cool blue curtains.

The Chief Constable took upon himself the task of interviewing Strachan, who received him with politeness, but without enthusiasm.

'We have obtained a statement from Mr. Farren,' said Sir Maxwell, 'with reference to his movements on Monday night and Tuesday morning, which required your corroboration.'

'Indeed,' said Strachan. 'In what way ?'

'Come,' said the Chief Constable, 'you know very well in what way. We know, from Mr. Farren's story, that you have not told us all the facts about your own movements at that time. Now that Mr. Farren has given his explanation, you have no longer any reason for reticence.'

'I don't altogether understand this,' said Strachan. 'Mr.

Farren, as I am told, went for a holiday trip to England and has returned. Why should I answer any questions about his private affairs ? To what is the inquiry directed ?'

'Mr. Strachan,' said the Chief Constable, 'I do most earnestly beg you not to take up this attitude. It can do no good and only creates difficulties and, if I may say so, suspicion. You are perfectly well aware that we are inquiring into the circumstances of Mr. Campbell's murder, and that it is absolutely necessary for us to obtain information about all the persons who saw Mr. Campbell shortly before his death. Mr. Farren saw him at 6 o'clock on Monday week, and he has given us an account of his movements since that time. This account requires your corroboration. If you can give it, where is the point of refusing ?'

'The point is,' said Strachan, 'that Mr. Farren is going about at liberty, and that therefore, presumably, you have nothing against him. In that case, I am not bound to answer any impertinent queries about his behaviour or his personal affairs. If, on the other hand, you intend to accuse him or me of anything criminal, it is your duty to say so, and also to warn us that we are not obliged to answer your questions.'

'Of course,' said Sir Maxwell, smothering his annoyance, 'you are not in any way bound to answer if you think that by so doing you will incriminate yourself. But you cannot prevent us from drawing the natural conclusion from your refusal.'

'Is that a threat ?'

'Certainly not. It is a warning.'

'And if I thank you for the warning and still decline to make a statement ?'

'In that case, well—'

'In that case your only alternative is to arrest me and charge me with murder, or with complicity. Are you prepared to go as far as that ?'

The Chief Constable was not by any means prepared, but he replied, curtly:

'You will have to take your chance of that.'

Strachan paused, tapping his fingers on the table. The clock on the mantelpiece ticked loudly, and the voice of Myra floated in from the garden, playing at tig with her mother and the nurse.

'Very well,' said Strachan, at last. 'What does Farren say that wants my corroboration ?'

Sir Maxwell Jamieson was annoyed again at the obviousness of this trap.

'I am afraid that won't do, Mr. Strachan,' he said, a little acidly. 'It will be better, I think, that you should begin from the beginning and give me your own account of what happened.'

'What do you call the beginning?'

'Begin by saying where you were on Monday afternoon.'

'On Monday afternoon? I was out, painting.'

'Whereabouts?'

'Up at Balmae. Would you like proof of that? I can show you the canvas, but of course that won't bear visible signs of having been painted on Monday. However, I daresay somebody saw the car. I stuck it in a field and walked down to the edge of the cliff. Subject of the painting, Ross Island. Price, when finished, 50 guineas.'

'What time did you leave there?'

'About half-past seven.'

'Did the light remain good as long as that?'

'Good heavens!' said Strachan. 'Are the police going to display intelligence about art? No, it didn't, but I had taken my dinner out with me. The dinner consisted of cold meat sandwiches, baps, brown bread, cheese and tomatoes, with a bottle of Worthington. To entertain myself during the orgy I had a book – a very nice book, all about a murder committed in this part of the country. *Sir John Magill's Last Journey*, by one Mr. Crofts. You should read it. The police in that book called in Scotland Yard to solve their problems for them.'

Sir Maxwell took this information without wincing, and merely demanded:

'Did you then return to Gatehouse?'

'I did not. I went on to Tongland.'

'Passing through Kirkcudbright?'

'Not being in an aeroplane, obviously I had to pass through Kirkcudbright.'

'I mean, at what time?'

'At about 8 o'clock.'

'Did anybody see you?'

'I have no doubt they did. It is my experience that one never passes through Kirkcudbright or anywhere else without being seen by at least half a dozen people.'

'You did not stop at all?'

'I did not.'

'You went on to Tongland. And there?'

'I fished. Total bag, one trout, three-quarters of a pound, one ditto, seven ounces, and three that were too young to leave home.'

'Did you see anybody there?'

'I don't know that I did. The keeper knows me, but he wasn't there. But I dare say some busybody or other noticed me.'

'When did you leave Tongland?'

'Round about 11 o'clock, I think. The fish seemed to have lost enthusiasm, and so did I.'

'And then?'

'Then I went home like a good boy. I got back some time round about midnight.'

'You could produce witnesses to that, of course?'

'Of course. My wife and my servant. But naturally they would swear to anything I told them to swear to.'

'No doubt,' said Sir Maxwell, unmoved by this sarcasm. 'What then?'

'I went out again in the car.'

'Why?'

'To look for Farren.'

'What made you do that?'

'I found a note from him waiting for me.'

'Have you still got that note?'

'No, I burnt it.'

'What was in it?'

'He told me that he was going to commit suicide. I thought I ought to follow him and stop him.'

'Did he say where he was going?'

'No, but I thought he would probably go up into the hills by Creetown. We had sometimes discussed the question of suicide, and the old mines up there seemed to have a kind of attraction for him.'

'I see. You went straight over to Creetown?'

'Yes.'

'Are you quite sure, Mr. Strachan?'

'Yes, of course.'

Sir Maxwell was a cautious man, but there was something guarded in Strachan's tone which warned him that this was a lie, and a sudden illumination moved him to risk a bluff.

'Then you would be very surprised if I told you that your

car had been seen on the road between the Anwoth Hotel and Standing Stone Pool between midnight and 12.30 ?'

Strachan was obviously not prepared for this.

'Yes,' he said, 'I should be surprised.'

'It is surprising,' rejoined the Chief Constable, 'but, as you say, there is always some busybody about. Anyway, now that you are reminded of it, you do recollect going in that direction ?'

'Well, yes. I had forgotten about it for the moment; I went – I thought—'

'You went to Campbell's house, Mr. Strachan. As a matter of fact, you were seen there. Why did you go ?'

'I thought possibly I might find Farren there.'

'Why ?'

'Oh, well – he didn't like Campbell very much, and I thought – it struck me as just possible that he might have had the idea of getting an explanation or something from Campbell.'

'That was an odd thing for you to think, was it not ?'

'Not very. After all, it's no good pretending that Campbell and he were on good terms. They had had a quarrel that evening—'

'Yes, but you didn't know that at the time, Mr. Strachan. You tell me that you went straight through from Balmae to Tongland without stopping or speaking to anybody in Kirkcudbright.'

'No, that's true. But of course, if Farren wanted to commit suicide, I could put two and two together.'

'I see. It was just a guess. There was nothing in Mr. Farren's note to suggest that he might be going to see Mr. Campbell ?'

'Nothing whatever.'

'Mr. Strachan, I must warn you that if you persist in concealing the truth, you may involve yourself in very serious trouble. We know the contents of the note.'

'Oh!' Strachan shrugged his shoulders. 'If you know, why ask me ?'

'We are asking you for independent corroboration, Mr. Strachan, and I must say that you are making things very difficult for Mr. Farren and for us by this attitude.'

'Well, if Farren has told you— Very well, then, the note did mention Campbell, and I went along to see if Farren was there, and, if not, to warn Campbell.'

'To warn him ? You took Mr. Farren's threats very seriously then ?'

'Well, not very seriously. But they are both excitable men, and I thought that there might be a great deal of unpleasantness if they met in that mood, and possibly a really nasty row.'

'Did you deliver the warning?'

'The house was empty. I knocked two or three times and then, as everything was dark, I went in.'

'The door was open, then?'

'No, but I knew where to find the key.'

'Was that a thing everybody knew?'

'How should I know? I only knew that I'd often seen Campbell hang it up, after locking the door, on a particular nail hidden behind the gutter-spout.'

'I see. So you went in?'

'Yes. Everything was quite clean and tidy and it didn't look as though Campbell had been in. There were no supper-dishes or anything about, and he wasn't in bed, because I went upstairs to see. I left a note for him on the table and came away again, relocking the door and putting the key back where I found it.'

Only by a great effort of self-control did the Chief Constable keep from showing the staggering effect of this piece of news. He succeeded in asking in matter-of-fact tones:

'What exactly did you say in the note?' As Strachan seemed to hesitate, he added, with more assurance than he felt:

'Try to make your recollection more precise this time, Mr. Strachan. As you see, we are sometimes able to check these items.'

'Yes,' said Strachan, coolly. 'As a matter of fact, I've been rather wondering why I haven't heard about the note before.'

'Have you? Didn't you take it for granted that Campbell had received it and destroyed it?'

'I did at first,' said Strachan, 'and that was why I thought all this fuss about Monday night so unnecessary. If Campbell came in after I was there, then he was alive long after I saw him. He had his breakfast, didn't he? At least, I understood so – and I supposed he had seen the note then and got rid of it.'

'But you don't think that now?'

'Well, if you've got the note, he obviously didn't. And if you'd found it on his dead body, you'd surely have mentioned it before this.'

'I did not say,' said Sir Maxwell, patiently, '*when* the note had come into our possession.'

For some reason, this remark appeared to unnerve Strachan, and he remained silent.

'Well, now,' said the Chief Constable, 'do you mind telling me what was in the note? You have had plenty of time to think it over.'

'To invent something, you mean? Well, I'm not going to invent, but I can't undertake to remember it word for word. I think I said something like this: "Dear Campbell, – I am rather anxious about F. He is in a highly-wrought-up state and is threatening to do you some injury. However much he may have to complain of your behaviour – and you know best about this – I think it advisable to put you on your guard." It was something like that, and I signed it with my initials.'

'You thought it worth while to write that note about a friend of yours to a man you personally disliked – and you still say you did not take Farren's threats seriously?'

'Well, you never know. I was thinking more of Farren than of Campbell. I didn't want him to get into trouble – an action for assault, or anything of that kind.'

'It still seems to me a fairly strong step to take, Mr. Strachan. How often had Farren seriously threatened to harm Campbell?'

'He had occasionally expressed himself in rather a reckless manner.'

'Had he ever attacked him?'

'N–no. There was a slight fuss once—'

'I seem to remember hearing something about a quarrel – about six months ago, was it?'

'About that. But it didn't amount to anything.'

'In any case, you thought the matter of enough importance to write the note to a man as notoriously indiscreet and fiery-tempered as Campbell. That speaks for itself, doesn't it? What happened next?'

'I went up to Creetown in my car and turned off up the hill road. I left the car where the road ends just beyond Falbae, and went along on foot calling Farren as I went. There was no moon, but it was starlight and I had my torch with me. I know that road pretty well. At least, it isn't a road, but a sort of shepherd's path. When I got close to the old mines I began searching about carefully. Presently I thought I saw something move and I shouted again. Then I saw that there really was a

187

man there. He ran away and I followed him and caught him up. I said, "My God, Farren, is that you?" and he said, "What the hell do you want?" So I caught hold of him.'

'Was it Farren?'

Strachan seemed to hesitate again, but finally replied, 'Yes, it was.'

'Well?'

'Well I argued with him for some time and tried to persuade him to come home. He absolutely refused and started to move off again. I took him by the arm, but he struggled with me and in the confusion he hit me in the face and knocked me down. By the time I had scrambled up again he had got away from me, and I could hear him scrambling over some stones in the distance. I ran after him. It was pretty dark, of course, but the sky was quite clear and one could see moving objects like lumps of grey shadow. I caught glimpses of him now and again when he came up on the sky-line. You know that place – all dips and hillocks. I was getting pretty well winded and I was thinking about him and didn't look where I was going. I tripped over a bunch of stuff and found myself falling head-first – over the edge of the world, it seemed to me. I bumped and banged against what felt like baulks of timber, and finally brought up against something. I was completely knocked out of course. Anyhow, when I came to my senses I found myself at the bottom of a pretty deep place with black darkness rising up all round me and a patch of starlight at the top. I felt round very cautiously and tried to get up, but the moment I was on my feet, I went all sick and giddy and lost consciousness again. I don't know how long that lasted. It must have been a good many hours, because when I came to myself again it was broad daylight, and I was able to see where I was.'

'One of the old shafts, I suppose.'

'Yes, Lord! it was a place! I don't suppose it was more than forty feet deep, but that looked quite enough to me, and it went sheer up like a chimney, with a little square of light twinkling away at the top; it seemed a mile off. It was narrow, fortunately. By spread-eagling myself I could get a grip on the sides and hoist myself painfully up by inches, but it was slow work, and my head was so swimmy and my legs so weak that I simply tumbled down again after the first two or three attempts. I yelled and yelled, hoping against hope that somebody might hear me, but the place was as silent as the grave. I was extraordinarily lucky not to have broken a leg or an arm. If I had, I suppose I should have been down there now.'

'No,' said the Chief Constable. 'We should have brought you up on Friday or Saturday.'

'Ah! – well, by that time I don't suppose I should have been in any condition to worry about it. Well, after resting a bit more I got my head and legs under better control, and gradually wormed my way up. It was a slow job, because the sides were smooth and didn't give much foothold or handhold, and sometimes I'd lose purchase and slip down a few feet. Fortunately there were horizontal beams across the sides at intervals, and I was able to catch on to them and give myself a bit of a breather from time to time. I kept on hoping that the people at the farm would find my car and come to look for me, but if they did see it, they probably thought I was fishing or picnicking somewhere and attached no importance to it. I clawed my way up – happily I'm on the tall and hefty side – and at last – God! it was a relief – I found myself at the top and hooked an arm out on to the blessed grass. There was an awful tussle with that last foot or so – I thought I should never heave myself over the edge, but I managed it somehow. I dragged my legs out after me, feeling as though they were made of solid lead, and then I just rolled over and lay gasping. Ugh!'

Strachan paused, and the Chief Constable congratulated him.

'Well, I lay there for a bit. It was a gorgeous day, very windy and sunny, and I tell you that the world looked good to me for a bit. I was quivering like a blanc-mange, and hungry and thirsty – ye gods!'

'What time do you think that was?'

'I couldn't be sure, because my watch had stopped. It's a wrist-watch, and must have got a bump in the fall. I rested a bit – half an hour, perhaps – and then I pulled myself together and tried to find out where I was. The mines were scattered about a good bit, and I couldn't recognise the place. However, presently I found a burn and had a drink and stuck my head in the water. After that I felt better, only I discovered that I'd collected a magnificent black eye when Faren punched me in the face, and of course I was wrenched and bruised from head to foot. The back of my head still has a lump on it like an egg; I suppose that was what knocked me out. The next thing was to find the car. I calculated that I must be nearly two miles from Falbae, and decided that if I followed the flow of the burn, I must be going in the right direction, so I set off downstream. It was damned hot, and I'd lost my hat. Did you find it, by the way?'

'Yes, but we didn't know what to make of it. It must have got knocked off in your rough-and-tumble with Farren, and at first we thought it was his, but Mrs. Farren said it wasn't, so we didn't know quite what to think.'

'Well, now you know. The fact that you found it there ought to prove my story pretty well, don't you think?'

The Chief Constable had been thinking that very thing, but at the sharply triumphant note in Strachan's voice, a doubt shot through him. What would have been easier than to drop a hat at a suitable place, any time between Tuesday and Friday, as a foundation for this highly dramatic story?

'Never mind what I think, Mr. Strachan,' said he. 'Go on. What did you do next?'

'Well, I kept on down the burn, and after a time I came in sight of the road and the car. It was just where I had left it, and the dashboard clock made it a quarter past twelve.'

'Didn't you see anybody on the way back?'

'Well, yes – I did see one man. But I – well, I lay doggo till he had passed.'

'Why?'

Stranchan looked rather uncomfortable.

'Because – well, because I wasn't exactly ready to answer questions. I didn't know what had become of Farren. I realised that it looked as though I'd been in the wars, and if Farren's body was going to be found down a hole or anything it might look rather queer for me.'

'But surely —'

'Yes, I know just what you're going to say. But surely, if I thought that, I ought to have told somebody and got a search-party going. But don't you see, it was perfectly possible that Farren had come to his senses and gone quietly home. It would have been perfectly idiotic to start a rumpus and make a scandal all about nothing. It seemed to me that the best thing I could do was to get back quietly and find out what really had happened. I had a beast of a time starting up the car. I'd left the lights on the night before, with the idea of finding it again, and the batteries had run down. I had to swing her over with the starting-handle, and it was heavy work. Those Chrysler 70's have rather a big engine. Still, I managed to get her going after about a quarter of an hour—'

'Surely you could have got help from the farm.'

Strachan made a gesture of impatience.

'Haven't I told you that I didn't want to attract attention? As a matter of fact, I was afraid all the time that somebody would hear me and come up to see what was happening. But they didn't. Probably they were all at their dinner. I had an old cap and a motoring coat in the car, so I tidied myself up as best I could, and got on to the back road – the one through Knockeans. It crosses the Skyre Burn just beyond Glen and comes out by Anwoth Auld Kirk. I got back home about half-past one.'

The Chief Constable nodded.

'Was your family alarmed by your being out all night?'

'No. I forgot to say that when I got Farren's note I rang up and told my wife that I'd been called away and that I didn't want anything said about it.'

'I see. What did you do when you got home?'

'I rang up the McClellan Arms in Kirkcudbright and asked them kindly to send a message up to the Farrens to say, would Mr. Farren ring me up about a fishing appointment. The call came through in about half an hour's time, when I'd had a bath and felt rather better. Mrs. Farren had come down and said Hugh wasn't at home and could she take a message? I told her to say absolutely nothing to anybody for the moment, but that I would come over and see her after lunch, as I had something rather important to tell her. She gave a bit of a gasp, and I said, had Hugh come home last night, and to answer only yes or no. She said, No. And I said, Had there been any sort of trouble with Campbell? and she said, Yes. So I told her to say nothing about that either, and I would come over as soon as I could.'

'How much did you tell your wife about all this?'

'Only that Farren had got himself into a state of mind and left home, and that she was on no account to say anything to anyone about it, or about my having come home so late and in such a pickle. When I'd made myself reasonably presentable, I had some lunch. I needed it by that time.'

'I expect you did. Did you, in fact, go over to Kirkcudbright afterwards?'

'No, I didn't.'

'Why not?'

There was something about the Chief Constable's dogged 'Why?' and 'Why not?' that was irritating as well as disquieting. Strachan shifted awkwardly in his seat.

'I changed my mind about it.'

'Why?'

'I was going to go, of course.' Strachan appeared to lose the scent for a moment and then went off on a fresh cast. 'We dine in the middle of the day on account of my little girl. We had roast jiggot of mutton. It wasn't ready till past two o'clock. That was later than our usual time, of course, but they'd kept it back with the idea that I might turn up. I wanted that mutton, and I didn't want to appear unusual before the servant. So we took our time over dinner and hadn't finished till nearly three. About a quarter past three it would be before I was ready to start. I went down to open the gate for the car. I saw Tom Clark coming down from the golf-course. Just opposite my gate he met the Gatehouse policeman. They didn't see me, because of the hedge.'

The Chief Constable made no comment. Strachan swallowed hard and continued.

'The constable said, "Is the Provost up at the golf-course?" Clark said, "Ay, he is that." The constable said, "He's wanted. Mr. Campbell's been found lying dead at Newton-Stewart." After that they moved farther up the road, and I didn't hear any more. So I went back to the house to think about it.'

'What did you think about it?'

'I couldn't make up my mind what to think about it. I couldn't see how it was going to affect me. But I didn't feel that it was quite the moment to go up to the Farrens'. It might cause comment. At any rate, I wanted time to consider.'

'Was that the first you had heard about Campbell?'

'Of course it was. Why, the news had only just come through.'

'Did it surprise you?'

'Naturally.'

'But you didn't rush out as anybody else would have done and demand details?'

'No.'

'Why?'

'What the devil do you mean, why? I didn't, that's all.'

'I see. When Lord Peter Wimsey called later in the evening, you still hadn't been over to Kirkcudbright?'

'No.'

'He brought the news of Campbell's death to your wife. Had she heard about it before?'

'No. I didn't know any particulars and I thought it better not to mention it.'

'Did you tell Lord Peter that you knew about it already?'

'No.'

'Why not?'

'I thought my wife would think it odd that I'd said nothing about it to her.'

'Was anything said about your black eye?'

'Yes. I gave a – er – fictitious explanation.'

'Why?'

'I didn't see what business it was of Wimsey's.'

'And what did your wife think of that explanation?'

'I don't see what business that is of yours.'

'Were you at that time of the opinion that Farren had committed a murder?'

'There wasn't any question of murder at that time.'

'Precisely, Mr. Strachan. That is what makes your behaviour appear so odd. You went over and saw Mrs. Farren late that night?'

'I did.'

'What did you say to her?'

'I told her the events of the previous night.'

'Was that all? You did not, for example, say that you expected a charge of murder to be preferred against Farren and that she was to be very careful what she said to the police?'

Strachan's eyes narrowed.

'Isn't that one of those questions which you are not supposed to ask, nor I to answer?'

'Have it your own way, Mr. Strachan.' The Chief Constable got up. 'You seem to be well acquainted with the law. You know, for example, that an accessory to murder after the fact is liable to the same punishment as the principal?'

'Certainly I do, Sir Maxwell. I also know that you are not allowed to use threats, either overt or implicit, in interrogating a witness. Is there anything further I can do for you?'

'Nothing, thank you,' said the Chief Constable, politely.

Indeed, he thought, as he drove back to Kirkcudbright, Strachan had done quite enough. If the story about the note left on Campbell's table were true – and he was inclined to believe it – then Strachan had shattered the whole elaborate theory that the police had been building up. For what it meant was clearly this. Either Campbell had been alive after Strachan's visit – in which case there had been no murder on the Gatehouse-Kirkcudbright road – or else some other person, hitherto unknown, had entered the cottage after midnight, and that person was undoubtedly the murderer.

There was, of course, the possibility that there never had been any note, and that Strachan had found Campbell at home and killed him. This agreed with Ferguson's evidence. But in that case, why invent the tale about the note at all, unless to throw suspicion on Farren? That was ridiculous, because the only reasonable explanation of Strachan's conduct otherwise was that he was either shielding Farren or in league with him.

Some other person – some other person. Who could that be? So far, Ferguson's story had been amply borne out. The first arrival of the car with the body, the second arrival of Strachan – if a third person had arrived, how unfortunate that Ferguson should not have heard him come! Ferguson—

Ferguson.

Yes, well what about Ferguson?

He, of all people, could have entered Campbell's cottage unnoticed. He had only to walk round and open the door with that convenient key, which he must have seen Campbell hide a hundred times.

But then, that was absurd. Not only had Ferguson got an alibi – the Chief Constable did not set any undue value on alibis – but this theory left one huge question unanswered. *Where had Campbell been when Strachan came in*? If Strachan had found him there, why should he not have said so?

Suppose Strachan had found Campbell lying there dead – killed by Ferguson at some earlier moment. What then? Was Strachan in league with Ferguson?

Here was a real idea at last. All their difficulties had arisen from supposing that only one artist had been concerned in the crime. Ferguson could have committed the murder and established an alibi by going to Glasgow, while Strachan remained behind to concoct the faked accident and paint the picture.

All that story about fighting Farren and tumbling down a mine was very thin. Strachan had been up at Newton-Stewart all that time. His return by the by-road between Creetown and Anwoth Kirk could probably be proved, and agreed reasonably well with the time necessary for taking the body to the Minnoch, painting the picture and making his escape.

Only – why bring Farren into it ? Could Strachan not have invented some better excuse for being out all night than one which involved his best friend ? One, too, which was so suspicious in itself ? It argued a degree of cold-blooded villainy that one would hardly expect from Strachan.

A clever fellow, though. One who saw the drift of your questions before you asked them. A keen, canny, cautious devil. A man who could think a plan like this out beforehand.

Clever, to think of taking that hat up to Falbae and leaving it there on the edge of the mine-shaft. But he had shown his triumph a bit too openly there.

The Chief Constable felt more satisfied than he had done for some time. He unbent so far as to go and look for Wimsey, to tell him all about it. But Wimsey was not at home.

GRAHAM'S STORY

'I DO wish, Wimsey,' said Waters, irritably, 'you would get something to do. Why not go fishing, or take the car out for a run ? I can't paint properly with you snooping round all the time. It puts me off my stroke.'

'I'm sorry,' said Wimsey. 'It fascinates me. I think the most joyous thing in life is to loaf round and watch another bloke doing a job of work. Look how popular the men are who dig up London with electric drills. Duke's son, cook's son, son of a hundred kings – people will stand there for hours on end, with their ear-drums splitting – why ? Simply for the pleasure of being idle while other people work.'

'Very likely,' said Waters. 'But the row fortunately prevents them from hearing the workmen's comments on their behaviour. How would you like me to sit round and watch you detecting things ?'

'That's different,' said Wimsey. 'The essence of detection is secrecy. It has no business to be spectacular. But you can watch me if you like.'

'Right-ho! You run away and do some detecting, and I'll come and watch you when I've finished this panel.'

'Don't disturb yourself,' said Wimsey, pleasantly. 'You can watch me now. There's no charge.'

'Oh! are you detecting now?'

'Like anything. If you could take the top of my head off, you would see the wheels whizzing round.'

'I see. You're not detecting me, I hope.'

'Everybody always hopes that.'

Waters glanced at him sharply and uneasily, and laid his palette aside.

'Look here, Wimsey – you're not suggesting anything? I've told you all about my movements, and I suppose you believe me. The police may be excused for seeing nothing but the obvious, but I should have thought that you at least had common sense. If I had been murdering Campbell, surely I should have taken care to provide myself with a better alibi.'

'It depends on how clever you are,' replied Wimsey, coolly. 'You remember Poe's bit about that in *The Purloined Letter*. A very stupid murderer doesn't bother about an alibi at all. A murderer one degree cleverer says, "If I am to escape suspicion I must have a good alibi." But a murderer who was cleverer still might say to himself, "Everyone will expect the murderer to provide a first-class alibi; therefore, the better my alibi, the more they will suspect me. I will go one better still; I will provide an alibi which is obviously imperfect. Then people will say that surely, if I had been guilty, I should have provided a better alibi. If I were a murderer myself, that is what I should do."'

'Then you would probably come to a sticky end.'

'Very likely; because the police might be so stupid that they never got beyond the first step in the reasoning. It's a pity about that bicycle of yours, isn't it?'

Waters took up his palette again.

'I don't want to discuss this stupid business.'

'Nor do I. Go on painting. What a lot of brushes you've got. Do you use them all?'

'Oh, no!' said Waters, sarcastically. 'I keep them there for swank.'

'Do you always keep everything in this satchel? It's just like a woman's vanity-bag, all higgledy-piggledy.'

'I can always find things when I want them.'

'Campbell used a satchel, too.'

'Then that was a bond of union between us, wasn't it?' Waters snatched the satchel, rather impatiently, out of Wimsey's hands, ferreted out a tube of rose madder, dabbed some paint on his palette, screwed up the tube and tossed it back into the bag again.

'Do you use rose madder ?' said Wimsey, inquisitively. 'Some people say it's such an awkward colour.'

'It's handy sometimes – if you know how to use it.'

'Isn't it supposed to be rather fugitive ?'

'Yes – I don't use much of it. Have you been taking an art course ?'

'Something like it. Studying different methods and all that. It's very interesting. I'm sorry I never saw Campbell at work. He—'

'For God's sake, don't keep harping on Campbell!'

'No ? But I so well remember your saying that you could do a perfectly good imitation of Campbell if you liked. That was just before he was bumped off – do you remember ?'

'I don't remember anything about it.'

'Well, you were a bit tight at the time, and I don't suppose you meant it. There's a bit about him in the *Sunday Chronicle* this week. I've got it somewhere. Oh, yes – it says he is a great loss to the artistic world. "His inimitable style," it says. Still, I suppose they have to say something. "Highly individual technique": that's a good phrase. "Remarkable power of vision and unique colour-sense placed him at once in the first rank." I notice that people who die suddenly generally seem to be in the first rank.'

Waters snorted.

'I know that fellow who does the *Sunday Chronicle* stuff. One of the Hambledon gang. But Hambledon *is* a painter. Campbell took Hambledon's worst tricks and made a style out of them. I tell you—'

The door of the studio burst open and Jock Graham tumbled in, breathless.

'I say is Wimsey here ? Sorry, Waters, but I must speak to Wimsey. No, it's all right. I don't want to take him away. Wimsey, old man, I'm in the most ghastly hole. It's too awful. Have you heard about it ? It's only just been sprung on me.'

'Go to, go to,' said Wimsey, 'you have heard what you should not. Put on your nightgown, look not so pale. I tell you yet again. Campbell's dead; 'a cannot come out on's grave.'

'I wish he could.'

'Wake Duncan with thy knocking ? I would thou couldst.'

'Oh, stop drivelling, Wimsey. This really is damnable.'

'O horror, horror, horror,' pursued Wimsey, staggering realistically into a corner, 'tongue nor heart cannot conceive nor name it. Where got'st thou that goose-look ?'

'Goose is right enough,' said Graham. 'That's exactly what I'm looking like just now.'

'Geese are made to be plucked,' said Wimsey, eyeing him shrewdly, 'and so are you.'

'Was that a lucky shot, or did you mean it ?'

'What is all this about ?' asked Waters, peevishly.

'I don't mind your knowing,' said Graham. 'It'll be all over the county in half a moment if something isn't done about it. My God!' He wiped his forehead and dropped heavily into the nearest chair.

'Well, well,' said Wimsey.

'Listen! You know all this fuss there is about Campbell. That constable fellow, Duncan—'

'I told you Duncan came into it somewhere.'

'Shut up! That fool came asking questions about where I'd been on Tuesday and so on. I never took the thing seriously, you know. I told him to run away and play. Then something got into the papers—'

'I know, I know,' said Wimsey. 'We can take that part as read.'

'All right. Well – you know that female at Newton-Stewart – the Smith-Lemesurier woman ?'

'I have met her.'

'God! so have I. She got hold of me this morning—'

'Jock! Jock!'

'I couldn't make out what she was driving at first of all. She hinted and smiled and languished at me and said that whatever I had done wouldn't make any difference to her friendship, and talked about honour and sacrifice and God knows what, till finally I had almost to shake it out of her. Do you know what she's done ?'

'Oh, yes,' said Wimsey, cheerfully. 'All is known. A lady's reputation has been sacrificed on the altar of affection. But, dear old boy, we do not blame you. We know that, rather than compromise a noble woman, you would have gone to the scaffold with your lips locked in a chivalrous silence. I do not know which is the nobler soul – the woman who without a thought of self – I seem to be dropping into blank verse.'

'My dear Wimsey, don't say you ever thought for one moment that there was a word of truth in it.'

'Frankly, I never did. I have known you do many rash things, but I gave you credit for seeing through Mrs. Smith-Lemesurier.'

'I should hope so. But what on earth am I to do?'

'It's awkward,' said Wimsey, 'it's awkward. Short of admitting where you really were that night, there is nothing for it but to accept the sacrifice, and with the sacrifice, the lady. And I greatly fear the lady means matrimony. Still, that's a thing that overtakes most of us, and most of us survive it.'

'It's blackmail,' groaned Graham. 'And after all, what have I done to deserve it? I tell you that beyond a passing compliment or so I've never – dash it all!'

'Not so much as a squeeze of the hand?'

'Well, possibly a squeeze of the hand. I mean to say, hang it, one must be civil.'

'Or a kiss or so – meaning no harm?'

'No, no, Wimsey. I never went as far as that. I may be a bad cad, but I have some instincts of self-protection. No, really.'

'Well, never mind,' said Wimsey, consolingly. 'Perhaps the love will come after marriage. When you look at her over the coffee-pot and say to yourself, "To this noble woman's pure affection I owe my life and freedom," your heart will reproach you for your coldness.'

'Life and freedom be damned! Don't be a fool. Just imagine how frightful it was. I had to be absolutely brutal before I could get away.'

'Did you repulse the dear little woman?'

'Yes, I did. I told her not to be a damned idiot, and she burst into tears. It's appalling. What those people there will think—'

'What people, where?'

'At the hotel. She walked in there and asked for me, and I left her howling on the drawing-room sofa. God knows what she's telling people! I ought to have seen her off the premises, but I – my God, Wimsey, she frightened me. I fled for my life. People ought to be had up for making scenes in public places. That old padre who's staying there barged in in the middle, just as the waterworks were in full play. I'll have to leave the place!'

'You don't seem to have played your cards very well.'

'I shall have to go and make it right with the police, of course.

But what's the good? Nobody will ever believe that there wasn't something in it.'

'How true that is! What are you going to say to the police?'

'Oh, I shall have to tell them where I was. That part's O.K. But don't you see that the mere fact of that woman's having trotted out that tale will be proof enough that I'd given cause for it? She's absolutely got me taped, old man. Scotland isn't big enough to hold both of us. I shall have to go to Italy or somewhere. The more I prove that story to be a lie, the more obvious it will be that she couldn't have told such a lie unless we were on terms of the most damnable intimacy.'

'Isn't life difficult?' said Wimsey. 'It all shows how careful one should be to tell the police everything at the first possible moment. Had you only been frank with that zealous young constable, all this would have been avoided.'

'I know, but I didn't want to get anybody into trouble. You see, Wimsey, the fact is, I was out poaching with Jimmy Fleeming, up at Bargrennan. I thought it would be good fun. We were netting the pool just below the fall.'

'Oh, were you? That's the Earl of Galloway's water.'

'Yes. We were out all Monday night. We had a damn good time, only I had more whiskey than was good for me. But that's by the way. There's a little sort of hut-place up there. It belongs to one of the men on the estate. We camped there. I wasn't feeling altogether so good on the Tuesday, so I stayed up there and on Tuesday night we had another go at it, because Monday had produced more fun than fish. We did rather well on Tuesday. Some of these fellows are damn good sorts. I get a lot more kick out of that crowd than I do out of what's called our own class. Jimmy Fleeming has an amazing collection of good stories. And the sidelights you get on the lives of respectable citizens! Besides, men like that know a damn sight more than ordinary educated people. What they don't know about fish, flesh and fowl isn't worth knowing. And they're all damn good friends of mine. It makes me sick to think of giving them away to the police.'

'You are an ass, Graham,' said Wimsey. 'Why the hell didn't you come and tell me about it in the first place?'

'You'd have had to tell the police.'

'Oh, I know – but that could have been squared. Are these fellows prepared to give evidence now?'

'I haven't said anything to them. How could I? Dash it, I'm

not such a swine as to go and ask them. I've no doubt they'd back me up, but I can't ask them to. It isn't done.'

'The best thing you can do,' said Wimsey, 'is to go straight to Sir Maxwell Jamieson and cough it all up. He's very decent, and I bet he'll see that your friends don't suffer. By the way, you're sure they can answer for you on Tuesday as well as Monday night ?'

'Oh, yes, Jimmy and another bloke were hanging round most of Tuesday morning off and on. But that doesn't matter a damn. The thing I want to get clear is this business about Monday night.'

'I know. But Tuesday morning is what's going to interest the police.'

'Good Lord, Wimsey – this rot about Campbell isn't serious, really ?'

'That's what I say,' struck in Waters, grimly. 'We seem to be in the same boat, Graham. I am supposed to have faked an alibi, suborned my friends and played merry hell generally. As far as I can see, Wimsey, Graham is just as clever a murderer as I am. However, no doubt you are the super-detective who can see through both of us. We can't both be guilty, anyhow.'

'Why not ?' said Wimsey. 'You may be accomplices for all I know. Of course, that makes you not quite so clever, because the best murderers don't have accomplices, but one can't always expect perfection.'

'But really and truly, Wimsey, what is the evidence about the murder, if it is one ? Everybody seems to be full of mysterious hints, but you can't get out of anybody why it is murder, or when it is supposed to have happened, or what it was done with or why, or anything about it – except, according to the papers, that it was done by an artist. What's the point ? Did the assassin leave his finger-prints behind in paint, or what ?'

'I can't tell you,' said Wimsey. 'But I don't mind saying this, that the whole thing turns upon how quickly Campbell could have got that sketch done. If I could have had that painting-party we planned—'

'By Jove, yes! We never did that stunt,' said Graham.

'Look here, let's do it now,' said Wimsey. 'Both you and Waters claim to be able to imitate Campbell's style. Start off now and do something and I'll time you. Half a jiff! I'll run round to the police-station and borrow the sketch for you to copy. It won't be quite the same thing, but it will give us an idea.'

Inspector Macpherson released the canvas without demur, but without enthusiasm. He seemed, indeed, so much depressed that Wimsey paused to ask what was the matter with him.

'Maitter eneugh,' said Macpherson. 'We've found a mon that saw Campbell's car goin' up tae the Minnoch on Tuesday mornin', an' the time-table's a' went tae hell.'

'No!' said Wimsey.

'Ay. There's yin o' the men as is workin' at the road-mendin' on the Newton-Stewart road, an' he saw the car wi' Campbell in 't – that'll be the pairson that was got up tae luik like Campbell – pass the New Galloway turnin' on the road betune Creetoon and Newton-Stewart at five an' twenty meenuts tae ten. He disna ken Campbell, but he described the car an' the hat and cloak, an' he tuk parteecular notice o't because it was goin' fast an' nearly ran him doon as he was comin' away on his bicycle tae deliver a message for the foreman.'

'Five-and-twenty to ten,' said Wimsey, thoughtfully. 'That's a bit on the late side.'

'Ay. We was calculatin' on him startin' oot at 7.30 fra' Gatehouse.'

'Oh, I don't mind that,' said Wimsey. 'He must have cleared off before Mrs. Green came, and parked the body somehow, though why he should have taken such a risk I don't know. It's the other end of the business that's worrying me. At that rate he wouldn't be up at the Minnoch much before ten. We reckoned that to catch the train at Girvan, he'd have to start off again at about 11.10. He'd have to be pretty quick with his picture.'

'That's so, he would that. But there's more to it. We've found a man that passed yon bicyclist on the way tae Girvan, an' it's juist impossible that he could have caught the train at all!'

'Don't be ridiculous,' said Wimsey, 'he must have caught it, because he did catch it.'

'That's so, but it must ha' been anither man a'tegither.'

'Well, then,' said Wimsey. 'If it was another man altogether it wasn't our man at all. Do be logical.'

The Inspector shook his head, just as a constable knocked at the door, and, putting his head in, announced that Sergeant Dalziel was here with Mr. Clarence Gordon to see the Inspector.

'Here's the verra man,' said Macpherson. 'Ye'd better wait an' see what he has to say.'

Mr. Clarence Gordon was a stout little gentleman with a pronounced facial angle, who pulled his hat off in a hurry at the sight of Wimsey.

'Be covered, be covered,' said that gentleman, graciously. 'I fancy you may be asked to make a sworn statement.'

Mr. Gordon spread out his hands deprecatingly.

'I am thure,' he said, pleasantly, 'that I thall be only too willing to athitht the polithe in any way and to thwear to vat ith nethethary. But I athk you, gentlemen, to take into conthiderathon the interrupthon to my bithneth. I have come from Glathgow at conthiderable inconvenienth—'

'Of course, of course, Mr. Gordon,' said the Inspector. 'It's verra gude of ye.'

Mr. Gordon sat down, and spreading the four fat fingers of his left hand upon his knee, so as to display to full advantage a handsome ruby ring, raised his right hand, by way of adding emphasis to his statement and began:

'My name ith Clarenth Gordon. I am a commerthial traveller for the firm of Moth & Gordon, Glathgow – ladieth' dretheth and hothiery. Here ith my card. I travel thith dithrict on alternate Mondayth, thpending the night at Newton-Thtewart and returning on Tuethday afternooth by the Bargrennan road to Girvan and Ayr where I have many good cuthtomerth. Latht Tuethday week I thtarted from Newton-Thtewart in my limouthine ath uthual after an early lunth. I patht Barrhill at a little after half-patht twelve. I remember theeing the train go out of the thtathion jutht before I got there. That ith how I know the time. I had patht through the village when I thaw a bithyclitht in a grey thuit riding very fatht along the road in front of me. I thay to mythelf: "There ith a man in a great hurry in the middle of the road – I mutht blow my horn loudly." He ith vobbling from thide to thide, you underthtand, with hith head down. I thay to mythelf again, "If he ith not careful, he will have an acthident." I blow very loud, and he hearth me, and drawth to the thide of the road. I path him, and I thee hith fathe very vite. That ith all. I do not thee him again, and he ith the only bithyclitht I thee on all that road till I get to Girvan.'

'Half-past twelve,' said Wimsey. 'No – later – the train leaves Barrhill at 12.35. You're right, Inspector, that can't be our man. It's twelve miles, good, from Barrhill to Girvan, and the man

203

with the grey suit – our man, I mean – was there at 1.7. I don't think he could possibly do it. Even a good bicyclist could hardly manage twenty-four miles an hour over twelve miles along that road – not on the Anwoth Hotel bicycle, anyhow. You would want a trained man on a racing machine. You are quite sure, Mr. Gordon, that you didn't pass another bicyclist farther along the road ?'

'Not a tholitary one,' replied Mr. Gordon, earnestly, raising all his fingers protestingly and sawing the air, 'not a thingle thoul on a bithycle at all. I thould have notithed it, becauth I am a very careful driver, and I do not like puth-thyclithtth. No, I thee nobody. I take no notith of thith man at the time, of courthe. But on Thunday my vife tellth me, "Clarenth, there wath a call come through on the vireleth for travellerth by the Bargrennan road to thay if they thaw a bithyclitht lath Tueth-day week. Did you hear it ?" I thay, "No, I am travelling all the week and I cannot alwayth be lithening to the vireleth." Vell, my vife tellth me what it ith, and I thay, "Vell, when I have time I go to tell the polithe what I have theen. And here I am. It ith very inconvenient and not good for bithneth, but it ith my duty ath a thitithen. I tell my firm – the both ith my brother be helped." Tho I came, and here I am and that ith all I – and he thay, "Clarenth, you mutht tell the polithe. It cannot know."'

'Thank you verra much, Mr. Gordon; ye have given us some valuable information an' we're much obliged tae ye. Now, there's juist one other thing. Could ye tell us if the man ye saw is one o' these, sir ?'

The Inspector spread the six photographs out on the table, and Mr. Clarence Gordon bent dubiously over them.

'I hardly thaw the man, you know,' he said, 'and he vore thpectacleth, and there ith no photo here with thpectacleth. I do not think it wath thith one, though.' He set Strachan's photograph aside. 'That man hath a military look, and I thould thay he vould be a big, heavy man. Thith wath not a very big man, the man I thaw. And he did not have a beard. Now *thith* man' – Mr. Gordon gazed at the photograph of Graham very intently – 'thith man hath very remarkable eyeth, but with thpectacleth he might be anybody. You thee ? Thpectacleth vould be a good dithguithe for him. Thith one it might be altho, but he hath a mouthtathe – I cannot remember if the man I thaw had one. It wath not a big one, if he had. Thith might be he and tho might thith or thith. No, I cannot tell.'

'Never mind, Mr. Gordon, ye have done verra weel, an' we're greatly obliged to ye.'

'I may go now ? I have my bithneth to conthider.'

The Inspector released him and turned to Wimsey.

'Not Strachan and not Gowan,' he said. 'Gowan's a verra big man.'

'Not the murderer at all, apparently,' said Wimsey. 'Another red herring, Inspector.'

'The place is fair lousy wi' red herrings,' mourned Inspector Macpherson. 'But it's a miracle to me that yón bicycle should ha' got itself tae Euston an' have no connection wi' the crime. It's no reasonable. Where did the Girvan man come from ? And he had the grey suit and the spectacles an' a'. But – twelve miles in thirty minutes – I'm wonderin' could it no be done after all ? If ony of our men was trained as an athlete—'

'Try *Who's Who*,' suggested Wimsey – 'it may throw some light on their hideous pasts. I must run away now. I've got two artists straining at the leash. Cry havoc! and let slip the dogs of war. It's curious how blank verse seems to come natural to me today. It just shows how blank my mind is, I suppose.'

On returning he found that Waters had supplied Graham with canvas, palette, knife and brushes and was arguing cheerfully with him about the rival merits of two different kinds of sketching easel.

Wimsey stood Campbell's sketch up on the table before them.

'Oh, that's the subject, is it ?' said Graham. 'H'm. Very characteristic. Almost ultra-characteristic, don't you think, Waters ?'

'That's exactly what one expects from the Campbells of this world,' said Waters. 'The trick degenerates into a mannerism, and they paint caricatures of their own style. As a matter of fact, it's apt to happen to anybody. Even Corot, for instance. I went to a Corot exhibition once, and 'pon my soul, after seeing a hundred or so Corots gathered together, I began to have my doubts. And he was a master.'

Graham picked the canvas up and carried it across to the light. He frowned and rubbed the surface with a thoughtful thumb.

'Funny,' he said, 'the handling isn't altogether. . . How many people have seen this, Wimsey ?'

'Only myself and the police, so far. And the Fiscal, naturally.'

'Ah! – well! Do you know, I should have said – if I didn't know what it was—'

'Well ?'

'I should almost have thought I had done it myself. There's a slight flavour of pastiche about it. And there's a sort of – just look at those stones in the burn, Waters, and the shadow under the bridge. It's rather more cold and cobalty than Campbell's usual style.' He held it away at arm's length. 'Looks as though he'd been experimenting. There's a lack of freedom about it, somehow. Don't you think so ?'

Waters came up and stared over his shoulder.

'Oh, I don't know, Graham. Yes, I see what you mean. It looks a bit fumbled here and there. No, not quite that. A little tentative. That's not the word, either. Insincere. But that's exactly what I complain of in all Campbell's stuff. It makes its effect all right, but when you come to look into it, it doesn't stand up to inspection. I call that a thoroughly Campbellish piece of work. A poor Campbell, if you like, but full of Campbellisms.'

'I know,' said Graham. 'It reminds me of what the good lady said about *Hamlet* – that it was all quotations.'

'G. K. Chesterton says,' put in Wimsey, 'that most people with a very well-defined style write at times what looks like bad parodies of themselves. He mentions Swinburne, for instance – that bit about "From the lilies and languors of virtue to the raptures and roses of vice." I expect painters do the same. But of course I don't know a thing about it.'

Graham looked at him, opened his mouth to speak, and shut it again.

'Well, chuck it here,' said Waters. 'If we've got to copy the beastly thing, we'd better start. Can you see all right there ? I'll put the paints on the table here. And please don't throw them on the floor in your usual dirty way.'

'I don't,' said Graham, indignantly. 'I collect them neatly in my hat, if I'm not wearing it, and if I am, I lay them handily in the grass. I'm not always fumbling about for them in a satchel among my sandwiches. It's a miracle to me that you don't eat your colours and put the bloater-paste on the canvas.'

'I never keep sandwiches in my satchel,' retorted Waters. 'I put them in my pocket. The left-hand pocket. Always. You may think I'm not methodical, but I always know where to find everything. Ferguson puts tubes in his pockets, and that's why his handkerchiefs always look like paint-rags.'

'That's better than going round with crumbs in your clothing,' said Graham. 'To say nothing of the time when Mrs. McLeod thought the drains were wrong, till she traced the stink to your old painting-coat. What was it ? Liver-sausage ?'

'That was an oversight. You don't expect me to go about like Gowan, carrying a sort of combined picnic-basket and sketching-box, with a partition for each colour and a portable kettle, do you ?'

'Oh, Gowan ? That's pure swank. Do you remember the day I pinched his box and filled all the partitions up with wee fush ?'

'That was a good riot,' said Waters, reminiscently. 'He couldn't use the box for a week because of the fishy smell. And he had to stop painting, because it put him out to have his arrangements upset. Or so he said.'

'Oh, Gowan's a man of method,' said Graham. 'I'm like a Waterman pen – I function in any position. But he has to have everything just so. Never mind. Here I am, like a fish out of water. I don't like your knife, I don't like your palette and I simply loathe your easel. But you don't imagine trifles like that are going to put me off. Not on your life. Have at it. Are you standing by with the stop-watch, Wimsey ?'

'Yes. Are you ready ? One, two, three – go !'

'By the way, I suppose we can't expect you to tell us whether the object of all this is to incriminate us ? I mean, do we get hanged for being quick or for being slow ?'

'I haven't worked it out yet,' said Wimsey, 'but I don't mind telling you that the less you dawdle the better I shall be pleased.'

'It's not altogether a fair test,' said Waters, mashing up his blue and white to the colour of a morning sky. 'Copying a canvas isn't the same thing as painting direct. It's bound to be rather quicker.'

'Slower,' said Graham.

'Different, anyhow.'

'It's the technique that's a nuisance,' said Graham. 'I don't feel handy with so much knife-work.'

'I do,' said Waters. 'I use the knife myself quite a lot.'

'I used to,' said Graham, 'but I've chucked it lately. I suppose we needn't follow every scratch and scrape exactly, Wimsey ?'

'If you try to do that,' said Waters, 'it will certainly make you slower.'

'I'll let you off that,' said Wimsey. 'I only want you to get somewhere about the same amount of paint on the canvas.'

The two men worked on in silence for some time, while Wimsey fidgeted restlessly about the studio, picking things up and putting them down and whistling tuneless fragments of Bach.

At the end of an hour, Graham was a little farther advanced than Waters, but the panel was still incomplete as compared with the model.

After another ten minutes Wimsey took up his stand behind the painters and watched them with a maddening kind of intentness. Waters fidgeted, scraped out something he had done, put it in again, cursed and said:

'I wish you'd go away.'

'Nerves cracking up under the strain,' commented Wimsey, dispassionately.

'What's the matter, Wimsey? Are we behind time?'

'Not quite,' said Wimsey, 'but very nearly.'

'Well, you can reckon on another half-hour as far as I'm concerned,' said Graham, 'and if you flurry me it'll probably be longer still.'

'Never mind, do the thing properly. Even if you upset my calculations, it doesn't matter. I shall probably be able to get round it somehow.'

The half-hour dragged to an end. Graham, glancing from the model to the copy, said, 'There, that's the best I can make it,' threw down his palette and stretched himself. Waters glanced across at his work and said, 'You've beaten me on time,' and painted on. He put in another fifteen minutes or so and announced that he had finished. Wimsey strolled over and examined the results. Graham and Waters rose and did likewise.

'Not bad efforts, on the whole,' suggested Graham, half-shutting his eyes and retiring suddenly on to Wimsey's toes.

'You've got that stuff on the bridge very well,' said Waters. 'Thoroughly Campbellian.'

'Your burn is better than mine and better than Campbell's, if it comes to that,' replied Graham. 'However, I take it that intrinsic artistic merit is not important in this particular case.'

'Not a bit,' said Wimsey. He seemed to have suddenly grown

more cheerful. 'I'm frightfully obliged to you both. Come and have a drink. Several drinks. I rather want to celebrate.'

'What ?' said Waters, his face going very red and suddenly white again.

'Why ?' said Graham. 'Do you mean to say you've got your man ? Is it one of us ?'

'Yes,' said Wimsey. 'I mean. I think I've got the man. I ought to have known long ago. In fact, I never was in very much doubt. But now I know for certain.'

GOWAN'S STORY

'A CALL for you from London, sir,' said the constable.

Inspector Macpherson took up the receiver.

'Is that Inspector Macpherson of Kirk-kud-brite ?' demanded London in ladylike tones.

'Ay,' said Inspector Macpherson.

'One moment, please.'

A pause. Then, 'You're through,' and an official voice:

'Is that Kirkcudbright Police Station ? Is that Inspector Macpherson speaking ? This is Scotland Yard. One moment, please.'

A shorter pause. Then:

'Is that Inspector Macpherson ? Oh, good morning, Inspector. This is Parker – Chief Inspector Parker of Scotland Yard. How are you ?'

'Fine, thank you, sir. An' hoo's yersel' ?'

'Blooming, thanks. Well, Inspector, we've found your man for you. He's come across with quite an entertaining story, but it's not quite the story you want. It's certainly important. Will you come and have a look at him or shall we send him up to you, or shall we just send the story and keep an eye on him ?'

'Well, what does he say ?'

'He admits meeting Campbell on the road that night and fighting with him, but he says he didn't kill him.'

'That's only tae be expectit. What does he say he did wi' him ?'

A long chuckle rippled over the four hundred miles of wire.

'He says he didn't do anything with him. He says you've got it all wrong. He says he was the dead body in the car.'

'What ?'

'He says he was the body – Gowan was.'

'Och, tae hell wi' 't!' exclaimed the Inspector, oblivious of etiquette, Parker chuckled again.

'He says Campbell knocked him out and left him there.'

'Does he so, sir ? Weel, I'm thinkin' it'll be best I should come an' see him. Can ye keep him till I come ?'

'We'll do our best. You don't want him charged ?'

'No, we'd better no charge him. The Chief Constable has thocht o' a new theory a'tegither. I'll be takin' the next train.'

'Good. I don't think he'll object to waiting for you. As far as I can make out, there's only one thing he's really scared of, and that's being sent back to Kirkcudbright. Right; we'll expect you. How's Lord Peter Wimsey ?'

'Och, he's jist awfu' busy wi' yin thing an' anither. He's a bright lad, yon.'

'You can trust his judgment, though,' said Parker.

'I ken that fine, sir. Will I bring him with me ?'

'We're always glad to see him,' said Parker. 'He's a little ray of sunshine about the old place. Invite him by all means. I think he would like to see Gowan.'

But Lord Peter Wimsey refused the invitation.

'I'd adore to come,' he said, 'but I feel it would be mere self-indulgence. I fancy I know what story he's going to tell.' He grinned. 'I shall be missing something. But I can really be more useful – if I'm useful at all, that is – this end. Give old Parker my love, will you, and tell him I've solved the problem.'

'Ye've solved the problem ?'

'Yes. The mystery is a mystery no longer.'

'Wull ye no tell me what ye've made o't ?'

'Not yet. I haven't proved anything. I'm only sure in my own mind.'

'An' Gowan ?'

'Oh, don't neglect Gowan. He's vitally important. And remember to take that spanner with you.'

'Is't Gowan's spanner to your way of thinkin' ?'

'It is.'

'An' them marks on the corpse ?'

'Oh, yes, that's all right. You can take it those marks come from the spanner.'

'Gowan says—' began the Inspector.

Wimsey looked at his watch.

'Away with you and catch your train,' he said, cheerfully. 'There's a surprise waiting for you at the end of the journey.'

When Inspector Macpherson was shown into Parker's room, there was a dejected-looking man seated on a chair in the corner. Parker, after greeting the Inspector warmly, turned to this person and said:

'Now, Mr. Gowan, you know Inspector Macpherson, of course. He's very anxious to hear your story from yourself.'

The man raised a face like the face of a sulky rabbit, and Inspector Macpherson, wheeling suddenly round upon him, fell back with a startled snort.

'Him ? Yon's no the man.'

'Isn't he ?' said Parker. 'He says he is, anyhow.'

'It's no Gowan,' said Macpherson, 'nor onything like him. I never saw yon ferrety-faced fellow in my life.'

This was more than the gentleman in question could put up with.

'Don't be a fool, Macpherson,' he said.

At the sound of his voice, the Inspector appeared to suffer a severe internal upheaval. The man got up and came forward into the light. Macpherson gazed in speechless bewilderment at the cropped black hair, the strong nose, the dark eyes, which gazed with an expression of blank astonishment from beneath a forehead denuded of eyebrows, the small, pinched mouth, with the upper teeth protruding over the lower lip, and the weak little chin which ran helplessly away to a long neck with a prominent Adam's-apple. The whole appearance of the apparition was not improved by a ten days' growth of black beard, which imparted a suggestion of seediness and neglect.

'It's Gowan's voice, right enough,' admitted the Inspector.

'I think,' said Parker, smothering his amusement, 'that you find the removal of the beard and moustache a little misleading. Put on your hat, Mr. Gowan, and wrap your scarf about your chin. Then, perhaps—'

The Inspector gazed with a kind of horror, as this metamorphosis was accomplished.

'Ay,' he said, 'ay, ye're right, sir, an' I'm wrang. But losh! –
I beg your pardon, sir, but I couldna' ha' believed—'

He stared hard, and walked slowly round the captive as if
still unable to credit his own eyes.

'If you've quite finished making an ass of yourself, Macpherson,' said Mr. Gowan coldly, 'I'll tell you my story and get away.
I've other things to do than fool around in police-stations.'

'That's as may be,' said the Inspector. He would not have
spoken in that tone to the great Mr. Gowan of Kirkcudbright,
but for this unkempt stranger he felt no sort of respect. 'Ye have
given us an awfu' deal o' trouble, Mr. Gowan, an' them servants
o' yours will find theirsel's afore the Fiscal for obstructin' the
pollis in the performance o' their duty. Noo I'm here tae tak'
yer statement and it is ma duty tae warn ye—'

Gowan waved an angry hand, and Parker said:

'He has been already cautioned, Inspector.'

'Verra gude,' said Macpherson, who by now had regained his
native self-confidence. 'Noo, Mr. Gowan, wull ye please tell me
when an' where ye last saw Mr. Campbell that's deid, an' for
why ye fled fra' Scotland in disguise ?'

'I don't in the least mind telling you,' said Gowan, impatiently, 'except that I don't suppose you'll be able to hold your
tongue about it. I'd been fishing up on the Fleet—'

'A moment, Mr. Gowan. Ye wull be speakin' o' the events of
the Monday, I'm thinkin'.'

'Of course. I'd been fishing up on the Fleet, and I was driving
back from Gatehouse to Kirkcudbright at about a quarter to
ten when I nearly ran into that damned fool Campbell at the
S-bend just beyond the junction of the Kirkcudbright road with
the main road from Castle-Douglas to Gatehouse. I don't know
what the man thought he was doing, but he had got his car
stuck right across the road. Fortunately it wasn't at the most
dangerous bit of the bend, or there would probably have been a
most unholy smash. It was on the second half, where the curve
is less abrupt. There's a stone wall one side and a sunk wall the
other.'

Inspector Macpherson nodded.

'I told him to get out of the way and he refused. He was
undoubtedly drunk and in a very nasty mood. I'm sorry, I know
he's dead, but it doesn't alter the fact that he always was one of
Nature's prize swine, and that night he was at his very worst.
He got out of his car and came up to me, saying that he was

just about ready for a row, and if I wanted one I could have one. He jumped on my running-board and used the foulest language. I don't know now what it was all about. I had done nothing to provoke him, except to tell him to take his cursed car out of the way.'

Gowan hesitated for a moment.

'I want you to understand,' he went on, 'that the man was drunk, dangerous and – as I thought at the moment – half off his rocker. He was a great, broad-shouldered, hefty devil, and I was jammed up behind the steering-column. I had a heavy King Dick spanner beside me in the pocket of the car and I grabbed hold of it – purely in self-defence. In fact, I only meant to threaten him with it.'

'Is this the spanner?' interjected Macpherson, producing the instrument from his coat pocket.

'Very likely,' said Gowan. 'I don't profess to know one spanner from another as a shepherd knows his sheep, but it was a similar spanner at any rate. Where did you find that?'

'Go on with your statement, please, Mr. Gowan.'

'You're very cautious. Campbell had got the door of the car open, and I wasn't going to sit there to be hammered into a jelly without defending myself. I pushed out from behind the wheel into the passenger's seat and stood up, with the spanner in my hand. He aimed a blow at me and I landed him one with the spanner. It caught him on the cheek-bone, but not very heavily, because he dodged it. I should think it must have marked him, though,' added the speaker, with appreciation.

'It did that,' said Macpherson, dourly.

'I can't pretend to be sorry to hear it. I jumped out at him, and he got me by the legs and we both rolled out into the road together. I hit out with the spanner for all I was worth, but he was about three times as strong as I was. He got his hands round my throat as we struggled, and I thought he was going to choke me. I couldn't shout and my only hope was that someone would come along. But by a damned bit of luck the road was absolutely deserted. He let go my throat just in time not to strangle me altogether and sat on my chest. I tried to get another one in with the spanner, but he snatched it out of my hand and threw it away. I was horribly impeded all this time by having my driving-gloves on.'

'Ah!' said the Inspector.

'Ah, what?'

'That explains a lot, doesn't it?' said Parker.

'I don't follow you.'

'Never mind, Mr. Gowan. Carry on.'

'Well, after that—'

Gowan seemed now to have got to the most distasteful part of his story.

'I was in a pretty bad way by this time,' he said, apologetically, 'half-choked, you know. And whenever I tried to struggle, he lammed me in the face. Well, he – he got out a pair of nail-scissors – and he was calling me the most filthy names all this time – he got out his scissors—'

A twinkle – unsuppressible – gleamed in the Inspector's eye.

'I think we can guess at what happened then, Mr. Gowan,' said he. 'Forbye we found a nice wee hantle of black beard by the roadside.'

'The damned brute!' said Gowan. 'He didn't stop at the beard. He took off hair, eyebrows – everything. As a matter of fact, I didn't know that till later. His final blow knocked me out.'

He felt his jaw-bone tenderly.

'When I came to,' he went on, 'I found myself in my own car in a sort of grass lane. I couldn't think where I was at first, but after a bit I made out that he'd run the car up a sort of cart-way just off the road. There's an iron gate that you go through. I daresay you know the place.'

'Ay.'

'Well – I was in a hell of a state. I felt frightfully ill. And besides – how on earth could I show myself in Kirkcudbright like that? I didn't know what to do, but I had to do something. I jammed my hat on, wound a scarf round the lower part of my face, and hared home like hell. It was lucky I didn't meet much on the road, because I was all to pieces – couldn't control the car. However, I got home – somewhere about a quarter past ten, I think.

'Alcock was a brick. Of course I had to tell him everything and he concocted all the plot. He got me up to bed without meeting his wife or the girl, and gave me first-aid for cuts and bruises and a hot bath, and then he suggested that I should pretend I'd gone off to Carlisle. Our first idea was to say I was ill, but that would have meant visitors and fuss, and we should have had to have had the doctor in, and square him. So that night we decided to pretend I'd gone to Carlisle by the 11.8 from Dumfries. Of course, we never supposed there'd be any inquiry, and we didn't think it worth while to send the car out specially. My housekeeper was roped into the conspiracy, but we thought it better not to trust the girl. She would be certain to talk. It was her night out, as it happened, so she wouldn't need to know when I came in, or anything, and the only person who'd know anything would be Campbell. He might talk, of course, but we had to risk that, and, after all, when he came to his senses, he might realise that he'd be letting himself in for a charge of assault if he wasn't careful. Anyway, anything was better than going about in Kirkcudbright and being commiserated.'

Gowan wriggled on his chair.

'Quite so, quite so,' said Parker, soothingly. He passed the back of his thumb carelessly down his own profile as he spoke. It was irregular, but the chin was reassuringly prominent. He was clean-shaven and could, he felt, stand it reasonably well.

'Next day,' said Gowan, 'we heard the news about Campbell's death. Naturally, we never thought but that it was an accident, but we did realise that it was just possible somebody might want to ask me whether I'd seen him the evening before. It was then that Alcock had his bright idea. Hammond had actually been over to Dumfries the evening before at about 8.45 to do an errand, and Alcock suggested that he should tell everybody that I'd taken the 8.45 to Carlisle. Hammond was quite game to back up the story, and as people would have seen the car go, it all looked quite plausible. Of course there was the chance that I'd been seen driving home later than that, but we thought we could bluff that out as mistaken identity. Apparently the question didn't crop up?'

'Oddly eneugh,' said Macpherson, 'it didna. At least, not while a gude bit later.'

'No. Well, Alcock was marvellous. He suggested that I should send a letter off by Tuesday afternoon's post, addressed to a friend in London – you know, Chief Inspector, Major Aylwin, through whom you got on my track – enclosing a letter from me to Alcock with directions that it was to be posted immediately. The letter was written as from my club, telling Alcock that he and Hammond could take the saloon and go for a holiday, as I should be detained for some time in Town. The idea was that they should smuggle me away with them in the car and drop me just outside Castle-Douglas, in time to catch the train to Town. I knew that I should never be recognised there without

215

my beard, though, of course, Hammond or the car might have been identified. The letter duly came back to Alcock by the second post on Thursday, and we carried out the rest of the plan that night. Did it work?'

'Not altogether,' said Macpherson, drily. 'We made oot that part o't pretty weel.'

'Of course, all this time I hadn't the faintest idea that Campbell had been murdered. Alcock must have known, I suppose, and it would really have been better if he'd told me. But he knew, too, of course, that I couldn't have had anything to do with it, and I shouldn't think it ever occurred to him that I could be suspected. I had so obviously left Campbell in the rudest of health and spirits.'

He made a wry face.

'There's not much else to say. I felt horribly groggy all Tuesday and Wednesday, and I had gravel-rash all over my face. The brute had rolled me on the rough ground, blast him! Alcock was a splendid nurse. He got the wounds clean and put healing stuff on them. Regular professional touch he had at it, the old scout. Wouldn't touch me without washing himself elaborately in Lysol – took my temperature three times a day and all that. I believe he rather enjoyed it. On Thursday night I'd practically healed up, and was perfectly fit to travel. I got to Town without any trouble, and have been living all this time with Major Aylwin, who has been extremely decent to me. I only hope I shan't be wanted in Kirkcudbright just at present. When Mr. Parker turned up this morning – by the way, Mr. Parker, how did you spot me?'

'Pretty easily,' said Parker, 'when we'd written to your old school and got a photograph of you without your beard. We found the porter who had taken your luggage at Euston, the taxi-driver who had taken you to Major Aylwin's flat, and the porter of the flats, who all recognised you. After that, you know, we had only to ring the bell and walk in.'

'Good God!' said Gowan. 'I never thought about those old photographs.'

'The men hesitated a bit at first,' said Parker, 'till we had the bright notion of painting out the eyebrows as well. That made the appearance so – pardon me – peculiar, that they identified you with little cries of satisfaction.'

Gowan flushed.

'Well,' he said, 'that's my statement. Can I go home now?'

Parker consulted Macpherson by a look.

'We'll have the statement put in writing,' he said, 'and perhaps then you will sign it. After that, I see no reason why you shouldn't go back to Major Aylwin's, but we shall ask you to keep in touch with us and not change your address without letting us know.'

Gowan nodded, and later, when the statement had been typed out and signed, took his departure, still with the same startled look upon his eyebrowless face.

FARREN : FERGUSON : STRACHAN

THE Procurator-Fiscal had called a council of war, Sir Maxwell Jamieson had brought Lord Peter with him. Inspector Macpherson was there by right of office and so was Sergeant Dalziel. Dr. Cameron was there, to see that nothing was suggested which would conflict with the medical evidence. In addition, Constable Ross and Constable Duncan were present by invitation. This was magnanimous on the part of their superiors, to whom Duncan had contrived to give a good deal of trouble, but there was a feeling that, in this confused and disconcerting case, even the opinion of a subordinate might be worth hearing.

The Fiscal opened the discussion by requesting the Chie-Constable to state his views, but the latter demurred. He sugs gested that the police might, perhaps, put forward their theorie-with greater freedom if they were not previously biased by hearf ing his opinion. The result of this was a polite contest for second place between Macpherson and Dalziel, which was eventually won by Macpherson, on the ground that, as the body had actually been discovered in the Newton-Stewart district, Dalziel had, so to speak, the premier claim upon it.

Dalziel rather nervously cleared his throat.

'Weel noo, my lord, Mr. Fiscal, Sir Jamieson and gentlemen,' he began, somewhat influenced in his opening by the recollection of the procedure at Football Club dinners, 'it wad appear tae be uncontrovairtible that this puir gentleman met his death some time Monday night by the use of a blunt instrument, an' that his boady was conveyed tae the place whaur it was found. Forbye I'm thinkin' we're a' agreed that the pairson as kill't him wull ha' been an airtist. Lord Peter Wimsey havin' pointed oot that the vera handsome piece o' pentin' foond at the locus o' the crime must ha' been projuiced by the murderer himself. Owin' tae the careful inquiries o' Inspector Macpherson, we are able tae state that a' the airtists in this district can be accountit for durin' the period covered by the crime, forbye five, or maybe six, which is Mr. Farren, Mr. Gowan, Mr. Waters in Kirkcudbright, an' Mr. Strachan, Mr. Graham an' possibly Mr. Ferguson in Gatehouse. A' these six airtists had a motive for killin' the deceased, in so far as they had bin kent tae utter threats against him, and moreover, by a remairkable coincidence, no yin o' them possesses a satisfactory alibi for the haill period under consideration.

'A' six o' them hae made statements claimin' tae exonerate themsel's, an' if we agree that the guilt lies betune the six o' them, yin or mair o' them must be tellin' lees.

'Noo, takin' everything intae consideration, I am of the opeenion that oor inquiries should be directit tae the movements o' Mr. Farren, and for why? Because he had a much bigger motive for murder than the lave o' them. He seems tae ha' considered that the deceased was payin' too much attention tae Mistress Farren. I'm sayin' nae word against the leddy, but that was the idea this Farren had got intae his heid. I canna credit that ony gentleman wad murder anither for twa-three words about a bit picture, or for a wee difference of opeenion consairnin' a game o' gowf, or a couple troot or a quarrel aboot nationalities. But when it's a maitter o' a man's domestic happiness, there, tae my thinkin', ye have a gude cause for murder.

'We ken weel that Farren set oot fra Kirkcudbright that night wi' the fixed intention o' findin' Campbell an' doin' him some damage. He gaed doon tae the cottage, where he was seen by Mr. Ferguson an' he gaed up to Mr. Strachan's hoose, an' by his ain confession he left a letter tae say as he was away tae find Campbell an' hae't oot wi' him. After this, he disappears till we find him at 3 o'clock on the Tuesday afternoon on the New Galloway road.

'Noo, the Inspector and me thocht first of a' that Farren had murdered Campbell on the road betune Gatehouse and Kirkcudbright, an' we were puzzled how he cam' there and why he should ha' carried on that queer way wi' Campbell's car. We were obleeged tae bring Mr. Strachan intil't. But noo we see as there was no necessity for a' they whigmaleeries. We ken noo that 'twas Mr. Gowan as met Campbell on the road an' was assaulted by him, an' that Campbell gaed away hame in his ain car as was likely eneugh. We ken likewise, fra' Mr. Ferguson's and Mr. Strachan's evidence, that either Campbell was alive after midnight or that some ither pairson entered the cottage. It is my belief that yon ither pairson was Farren, as had been lyin' in wait for Campbell in the vicinity o' the cottage.'

'Just a minute,' put in Sir Maxwell. 'I take it you accept Strachan's statement as far as the note and his subsequent visit to the cottage are concerned.'

'Ay, sir, I do that. Bein' friendly wi' Mr. Farren, he wadna hae inventit sic a tale, an' it agrees fine wi' Farren's ain statement. I'll tell ye what I think wull ha' been the way o't. I've got it a' writ doon here on a bit paper.'

The Sergeant wrestled with the pocket of his tunic and produced a fat notebook, from which he extracted a rather grubby sheet of paper, folded extremely small. He spread this out on the table, flattening it with the palm of a broad hand, and, having thus reduced it to order, passed it to the Fiscal, who, settling his glasses more firmly on his nose, read aloud as follows:

Case against Farren

Monday.

6 p.m.	Farren at Kirkcudbright. Finds Campbell in the house. Quarrel with Mrs. Farren.
7 p.m.	Farren proceeds by bicycle to Gatehouse.
8 p.m.	Farren arrives at Standing Stone cottage asking for Campbell, and is seen by Ferguson.
8–9.15 p.m.	Farren in various public-houses, using threats against Campbell.
9.15 p.m.	Farren goes to Strachan's house and leaves note (on bicycle).
9.25 till after dark.	Farren in hiding, probably somewhere on the Lauriston or Castramont Road.
9.45 p.m.	Campbell meets Gowan when returning from Kirkcudbright.
10.20 p.m.	Campbell returns to Standing Stone Cottage with car. Heard by Ferguson.
10.20 p.m.– 12 midnight.	Some time during this period Farren proceeds to Campbell's cottage on

	bicycle. Lets himself in and kills Campbell. Hides body. (Note: Ferguson presumably asleep.) Farren goes out, locking door. Remains in hiding, perhaps in garage.
12 midnight	Strachan arrives in car (heard by Ferguson). Enters by means of key. Leaves note and departs.

Monday 12 midnight–Tuesday 7.30 a.m. Farren re-enters cottage, destroys Strachan's note, puts body in car, matures plan of escape, puts bicycle and painting materials in car, prepares and eats Campbell's breakfast.

7.30 a.m.	Farren, disguised as Campbell, starts out from Gatehouse in Campbell's car. Seen by Ferguson.
9.35 a.m.	Farren in Campbell's car seen by workman passing turning to New Galloway road between Creetown and Newton-Stewart.
10 a.m.	Farren arrives at Minnoch with body.
10–11.30 a.m.	Farren paints picture.
11.30 a.m.	Farren throws body into Minnoch and departs on bicycle, using the side road from Bargrennan to Minnigaff. (Note: conjectural; no witness as yet produced.) Eight or nine miles.
12.30 p.m.	Farren arrives at Falbae. Leaves bicycle in vicinity of disused mine.
12.30–3 p.m.	Farren walks by New Galloway road to Brig o' Dee; eleven miles: but he may easily have taken a lift from a passing motorist.
	The rest of Farren's movements as per his statement.

'That,' said the Fiscal, looking round over the tops of his glasses, 'appears to me a very plausible and workmanlike conjecture.'

'It's damned good,' said Wimsey.

'Really,' said Sir Maxwell, 'it seems to cover almost everything, and almost shakes me in my own convictions. It is so beautifully simple.'

'Is it no,' said Macpherson, 'a wee thing too simple? It disna tak' intae account the remairkable episode o' the bicycle that was sent fra' Ayr tae Euston.'

Sergeant Dalziel, modestly elated by the applause of the three most distinguished persons in the company, was encouraged to dissent from his superior's view.

'I dinna see,' said he, 'why yon bicycle should be took intae account at a'. I see no necessity tae connect it wi' the maitter o' Campbell. If onybody was tae steal a bicycle fra' the Anwoth, and if, some gate, it was sent tae Lunnon by a mistake, that's yin thing, but what for should we suppose the murderer wad gae oot o' his way tae indulge in such antics, when there's anither explanation that's plain an' simple ?'

'Yes,' said the Fiscal, 'but why should a man take the trouble to steal a bicycle from Gatehouse to go to Ayr, when he could easily have gone the whole way by train ? I'll not deny there's something very mysterious about the story of the bicycle.'

'Ay,' said Macpherson, 'an' how do ye account for the surprisin' length o' time ta'en to get fra Gatehoose tae the New Galloway road ? It's only seventeen mile by the high road when a's said an' dune.'

Dalziel looked a little dashed at this, but Wimsey came to his assistance.

'Farren told me,' he said, 'that he had only driven a car two or three times in his life. He may have got into some difficulty or other. Suppose he ran out of petrol, or got a blocked feed or something. He would probably first of all have a shot at doing something himself – sit about pressing the self-starter or peering hopefully under the bonnet – before he could prevail on himself to ask anybody for help. Possibly he merely ran out of petrol, and had to shove the car down a side-road somewhere and walk to the nearest garage. Or suppose he went by the old road past Gatehouse Station and got into difficulties up there. An inexperienced driver might waste a lot of time.'

'It's possible,' said Macpherson, with a dissatisfied air. 'It's possible, I wadna go farther than that.'

'By the way,' said the Chief Constable, 'on your theory, Dalziel, how do you account for Strachan's hat and the tale he told about meeting Farren up at Falbae ? Because, if your version is correct, that must have been pure invention.'

'I account for't this way,' said Dalziel. 'I think it's a fact that Mr. Strachan searched for Farren at Falbae as he said, an' didna find hide nor hair on him. An' it may verra weel be that he tummel't intae the mine as he says he did. But I think that, no findin' him, he was feart Farren had been up tae mischief, an' when he heard o' the findin' o' Campbell's boady, he juist added a wee word or twa tae his story, tae gie Farren some kind of an alibi. 'Deed an' I'm thinkin' 'tis gude proof o' my theory that Strachan still evidently suspects Farren. Ye ken fine yersel', Sir Maxwell, that he was awfu' saircumspect in tellin' ye his tale and wadna ha' tell't ye a single word o' Farren's note if ye hadna persuadit him ye kenned the truth a'ready.'

'Ay,' said the Chief Constable, 'but I had my own notion about that.'

'Well, let's hear your notion, Sir Maxwell,' said the Fiscal.

'I was wishful,' said Sir Maxwell, 'to let the police have their say first but perhaps my idea does come in better at this point. Of course, the very first thing that struck me was the obvious collusion between Farren and Strachan to conceal something, but I looked at it in rather a different way. In my opinion, it was Strachan that had the guilty knowledge, and his difficulty was to protect himself without implicating Farren too much. Farren, by his behaviour and his threats and his disappearance, provided an almost perfect screen for Strachan, and it is, I think, very much to Strachan's credit that he was so unwilling to make use of it.

'Now, the weak point of your story, Dalziel, if I may say so, seems to me to occur at the moment of the murder itself. I simply cannot believe that, if it took place as you say at the cottage, between midnight and morning, it could have done so without disturbing Ferguson. Campbell was a powerful man, and, unless he was battered to death in his sleep, there would have been a noise and a struggle. Given the characters of all the people concerned, I cannot bring myself to believe that this was a case of a midnight assassin, creeping stealthily up to Campbell's bedroom and felling him with one blow, before he had time to cry out. It is, in particular, exceedingly unlike what one might expect from Farren. On the other hand, if there was a noisy fight, I cannot understand why Ferguson heard nothing of it. It was August, the windows would be wide open, and, in any case, besides the actual noise of the quarrel, there would be a great deal of going to and fro in the night, taking the corpse out to the car and so on, that Ferguson could scarcely have failed to hear.

'My theory is this. I think Farren's story is true. It is too absurd and whimsical a story not to be true, and all Farren's alleged actions are exactly the sort of daft thing Farren would do. I feel sure that Farren isn't the man to plan out an elaborate fake like the planting of the body and the painting of the picture. The man who did that was perfectly cool and unemotional, and he would have known a great deal better than to go and lose himself in that suspicious way immediately afterwards. No. Depend upon it, the man who committed the crime would take the very first opportunity of reappearing in his usual haunts.

'The way I see it is this. Strachan got that note from Farren and went down to the cottage as he said. When he got there, one of two things happened, and I am not perfectly sure which. I *think* Campbell opened the door to him and I think that he went in and had an interview with Campbell which ended in a violent quarrel and struggle. I think Ferguson was awakened by the noise, and came down just at the moment when Strachan had knocked Campbell down and killed him. Or possibly he arrived to find Strachan and Campbell fighting together, and then himself struck the blow which finished Campbell. There is the third possibility that the situation was reversed, and that Strachan came in to find Campbell already dead and Ferguson standing over him red-handed. I think that is rather less likely, for a reason I'll explain later.

'In any case, I'm sure we have this situation – the two men at the cottage with Campbell's dead body and one at least of them guilty of killing him. Now, what would they do next ? It is quite conceivable that, if only one of them had a hand in it, the other should at first threaten to inform the police, but there might be difficulties about that. Both men were well known to have quarrelled previously with Campbell, and the accused man might very well threaten to bring a counter-accusation. In any case, I fancy they realised that they were both of them in an exceedingly awkward position, and decided to help each other out if possible.

'Which of the two had the idea of faking the accident I don't know, of course, but I should imagine it would be Strachan. He is a man of particularly quick and keen intellect – just the sort that can think well ahead and foresee the consequences of his actions. The first bold outline of the idea would probably be his, but Ferguson no doubt helped, with his remarkable memory for details.

'They would hope, naturally, that the whole thing would be accepted as pure accident, but they would remember that, if once a murder was suspected, they would need alibis to cover

223

the whole period from midnight to the following mid-day. Obviously, they couldn't both have alibis for the whole period, but they might do equally well by dividing the time. Eventually they decided that Strachan was to establish the alibi for the night hours, while Ferguson did everything necessary in connection with the body, and that Ferguson would then establish his alibi for the next morning, while Strachan painted the picture.'

The Chief Constable paused and looked round to see how his audience were taking this. Encouraged by a little hum of appreciative surprise, he took up his tale again.

'The reason why they worked it that way is, I think, that Ferguson had already announced his intention of going to Glasgow in the morning, and that any sudden change of plan might appear odd. They now had to think of some alibi which Strachan could reasonably put forward at that hour of the night, and the best thing they could think of was that he should carry out his original intention of going after Farren.'

'But,' interposed the Fiscal, 'was not that a very difficult and uncertain plan on which to rely ? It was a hundred to one against his meeting Farren. Would it not have been simpler to knock up some person with a suitable story ? He could, for instance, have communicated to somebody his fears about Farren, and even taken that person with him as a witness to his alibi.'

'I don't think so,' said Sir Maxwell. 'That point occurred to me also, but when I came to think the matter over, I saw that Strachan's plan was about the best he could have adopted in the circumstances. For one thing, I believe that it would have been awkward for him to present himself in public at that moment. I think that he had already received that blow in the eye which he afterwards accounted for in another manner. That is why I said I felt pretty sure that Strachan took part in the struggle with Campbell, even though he may not have struck the fatal blow himself. Moreover, suppose he did knock somebody up to inquire about Farren, and suppose that somebody kindly offered to accompany him in his search ? He would then, as the Fiscal truly says, have an unimpeachable witness to his alibi – certainly he would. But what if he could not get rid of the witness in time to do the very important job he had to do the next morning ? What reason could he possibly give for abandoning his search for Farren and rushing away to Newton-Stewart ? And how could he prevent people from knowing where he was going, if once he got a hue-and-cry started? Whatever happened, he had to get up to the Minnoch early the next morning, and he had to do it in secret.

'As a matter of fact, I don't think his plan turned out as he intended. Indeed, it went very near to miscarrying altogether. I feel sure his original intention was to find Farren and bring him home – either to Kirkcudbright or to his own house at Gatehouse. He could then have explained his black eye as being due to a fall sustained in his search at Falbae.'

'But,' objected Wimsey, who had been following all this argument with a keenness which his half-drooped eyelids scarcely veiled, 'he'd still have to trundle off to the Minnoch next morning, wouldn't he, old thing?'

'Yes,' said Sir Maxwell, 'so he would. But if he had dropped Farren at Kirkcudbright, he could easily have driven straight away again from there. He would hardly be expected to stay and make a third in the conjugal reunion. Then he could have gone off where he liked – perhaps leaving some sort of reassuring message for Mrs. Strachan. Or similarly, if he had taken Farren to Gatehouse, he could then have gone off for the ostensible purpose of reassuring Mrs. Farren about her husband. When he was once away, he could always be detained somewhere, by engine-trouble or what not. I see no great difficulty about that.'

'All right,' said Wimsey. 'I pass that. Roll on, thou deep and dark blue ocean, roll.'

'Well then, Strachan drove off in search of Farren, leaving Ferguson to pack the body up and do all the necessary things about the house. And by the way, I may as well say at this point that I don't think any of you have paid sufficient attention to these things that were done about the house. The man who did them must have known a great deal about Campbell's manner of living. He must have known exactly when to expect Mrs. Green, for example, and the way Campbell behaved when at home – whether he was tidy or untidy, for instance, and what sort of breakfast he usually had, and all that kind of thing. Otherwise, Mrs. Green would have noticed that something out of the ordinary had happened. Now, how could Farren or Waters or Gowan or Graham be aware of all these domestic details? The man who would know them was Ferguson, who was his next door neighbour and employed the same daily woman. He would be the one person who might habitually see Campbell having breakfast and puttering about the house; and what he didn't know from his own observation he'd be sure to get from Mrs. Green in the course of her daily gossip.'

'That's a damned good point, Chief,' said Wimsey, with the detached air of an Eton boy applauding a good stroke by a Harrow captain. 'Damned good. Of course. Mrs. Green would be full of information. "Och. Mr. Campbell's an awfu' mon wi' his pyjammers. Yesterday he was leavin' them in the coal-hole an' them only jist back fra' the laundry. An' today I'm findin' them in the stoojo an' him usin' them for a pentin'-rag." One learns a lot about one's neighbours by listening to what is called kitchen-talk.'

'Ay, that's so,' said Macpherson, a little doubtfully.

Sir Maxwell smiled. 'Yes,' he said, 'when I came to think the matter over, that struck me very forcibly. But to go on with Strachan. There's no doubt he did find Farren, and there, I admit, he was rather lucky, though perhaps the chances against his doing so were not quite a hundred to one. After all, he had an extremely good idea where Farren was likely to be found, and he knew the ground about Falbae pretty well.'

'Ay, that's so,' said Dalziel, 'but whit wad he ha' done, sir, if Farren really had throwed himsel' doon the mine?'

'That would have been rather unfortunate for him, I admit,' said the Chief Constable. 'In that case, he would have had to forgo his alibi for the early morning. All he could have done would be to leave some object or objects at Falbae to show that he had been there – his hat, for example, or his overcoat – and carry out his painting job at the Minnoch as early as possible, returning later to give the alarm and start the search for Farren. He could explain that he had been searching in some other place in the interim. It wouldn't have been so good, but it would have been fairly good, especially as the subsequent discovery of Farren's body would have been a very good witness to the truth of his story. However, he did find Farren, so we need not bother about that.

'Unhappily, however, the plan came rather unstuck at this point. Farren, instead of coming quietly, escaped, and Strachan tumbled into a mine. This very nearly prevented Strachan from carrying out his part of the plot at all. He did fall down, he did have a job to extricate himself – though it didn't take him quite as long as he said it did – and that was why he was so late in

226

getting up to the Minnoch. If his plan had worked out properly, he no doubt hoped to be back with Farren at, say, 3 o'clock in the morning, and then go straight on to pick up the car and the body where Ferguson had left them ready for him.'

'And where would that be ?' asked the Fiscal.

'I can't say exactly, but the idea would be for Ferguson to drive Campbell's car up to some suitable spot – say by the old road through Gatehouse Station to Creetown – and leave it there to be picked up and taken on by Strachan. Ferguson would then return on a bicycle—'

'What bicycle ?' said Wimsey.

'Any bicycle,' retorted the Chief Constable, 'except, of course, the Anwoth Hotel bicycle that we've heard so much about. It's not difficult to borrow bicycles in these parts, and he would have had plenty of time to bring it back and leave it where he found it. Ferguson would be back, say, at 7 o'clock, in good time to eat his own breakfast and catch the omnibus for Gatehouse Station.'

'He must have been full of breakfast by that time,' observed the Fiscal, 'having already eaten Campbell's.'

'My dear man,' said the Chief Constable, rather irritably, 'if you had committed a murder and were trying to get away with it, you wouldn't let a trifle like a second breakfast stand in your way.'

'If I had committed a murder,' replied the Fiscal, 'I would feel no appetite even for one breakfast.'

The Chief Constable restrained any expression of feeling at this frivolous comment. Macpherson, who had been jotting words and figures in his notebook, struck in at this point.

'Then I take it, sir, this'll be your time-table for the crime.'

Case against Ferguson and Strachan

Monday.

    9.15 p.m. Farren leaves note at Strachan's house.

  10.20 p.m. Campbell returns home after encounter with Gowan.

12 midnight or thereabouts Strachan returns home and finds note.

Tuesday.

  12.10 a.m. (say). Strachan goes to Campbell's cottage; is joined by Ferguson. Murder is committed.

227

12.10–12.45	(say). Plan of fake accident evolved. Strachan starts for Falbae, taking Campbell's hat and cloak, painting materials, etc., in car.
2–3 a.m.	During this period Strachan and Farren meet and Farren escapes.
3.30 a.m.	(say). Strachan falls down mine.
4 a.m.	(say). Ferguson arrives at some spot on old road from Gatehouse Station to Creetown, with Campbell's car containing body and bicycle. Leaves car hidden.
5–6 a.m.	Ferguson returns on bicycle to Gatehouse by old road.
9 a.m.	Strachan extricates himself from mine and finds his car.
9.8 a.m.	Ferguson takes the train to Dumfries.
9.20 a.m.	Strachan arrives at rendezvous transfers himself to Campbell's car. Hides own car. Disguises himself.
9.35 a.m.	Strachan disguised as Campbell seen by workman passing turning to New Galloway.
10 a.m.	Strachan arrives at Minnoch. Plants body and paints picture.
11.15 a.m.	Strachan finishes picture.

Here Macpherson paused.

'How will Strachan get back tae his car, sir ? 'Tis fourteen mile gude. He culdna du't on his twa feet ?'

'Farren's bicycle,' replied the Chief Constable, promptly. 'You should have made him pick that up at Falbae. Of course, if his original plan hadn't gone wrong, he would either have borrowed another bicycle or had time to go on foot, but under the circumstances, with Farren's machine lying ready to hand, he would take advantage of it.'

'Ay, sir; but ye have an answer tae everything.' Macpherson shook his head soberly and returned to his time-table.

12.45 p.m.	Strachan returns on Farren's bicycle to Creetown; abandons bicycle. Transfers to own car.
1.15 p.m.	Strachan returns to Gatehouse by Skyre Burn road.

'That,' said the Fiscal, who had been checking this time-table with the Chief Constable's report of his interview with Strachan, 'agrees very well with Strachan's statement to you.'

'It does' replied Sir Maxwell 'and what is still more important, it agrees with the facts. We have found a man who distinctly remembers seeing Strachan passing along the Skyre Burn road between 1 o'clock and 1.20. Moreover, we have traced his telephone-call to the McClellan Arms, and it was put through at 1.18 precisely.'

'You realise,' said Wimsey, 'that you've only allowed him an hour and a quarter for painting that picture. I had two of the slickest men in the district working on it, and the quicker painter of the two couldn't get the result under an hour and a half.'

'That's true,' said the Chief Constable, grimly, 'but he wasn't painting for his life, you know.'

'I wad like tae be sairtain o' that,' said a voice. Everybody was surprised. P.C. Duncan had sat so silent that they had almost forgotten his existence.

'Is that so?' said the Chief Constable. 'Well, Duncan, you're here to give us your opinion. Suppose we have it now.'

The policeman shifted on his chair and glanced uneasily at Dalziel. He had an obscure idea that he was going to let himself in for a wigging, but he stuck manfully to his guns, and opened fire with a flourish.

GRAHAM : GOWAN : WATERS

'THEM twa theories,' said P.C. Duncan, 'is jist fine, an' I'm no sayin' the contrair', but, mon! they're jist awfu' complicated. It mak's ma heid spin only tae think o' them. I wadna wish tae be puttin' masel' forrit, but I wad like fine tae know how Sir Maxwell Jamieson thinks that yon plan could ha' been a' talked oot in three-quarters o' an hour.'

'Well,' replied Sir Maxwell, 'those times are very elastic. Provided we get Strachan up to Falbae before it's too light for tumbling into mines, I don't mind how late you make him start.'

'But no matter for that,' put in the Fiscal, seeing that Duncan looked a little discouraged. 'If you have a better and simpler idea to offer, by all means put it forward.'

'I was jist thinkin', then,' said Duncan, 'and beggin' your pardon, Dr. Cameron, whether it was not, after all, possible that the mon was kill't the same day he was found. Ye'll no be offended, doctor?'

'Not at all,' said Dr. Cameron, heartily. 'Speak out your mind, man. This business of speaking to the precise time of death is not so easy as ye'd think by reading detective novels. In my experience, the older a medical man gets, the less willing he is to make *ex cathedra* pronouncements, and the more he learns that Nature has her own way of confounding self-confident prophets.'

'Ay,' said Duncan. 'I've jist been readin' a wee buik aboot the subject. It's a gran' buik, an' it was gied me by my feyther for my last birthday. My feyther was an' awfu' weel-eddicated mon for his station in life, an' he wad always be tellin' me that studyin' was the road tae success.'

He laid a large, square, brown-paper parcel on the table as he spoke, and slowly untied the stout string with which it was secured.

'This here,' said he, as the last knot yielded and the paper was turned back to disclose the 'wee buik' – a formidable volume nine inches long by six inches across and thick in proportion – 'this here is ca'ed *Forensic Medicine and Toxicology* by Dixon Mann, an' there's gran' readin' in it for a man in oor profession. Noo, there's a passage here as I'd like tae get your opinion on, doctor. I've pit a wee bit paper tae mark the place. Ay, here 'tis, page thirty-seven. This is aboot the death-stiffenin'.'

'Rigor mortis,' said the doctor.

'Ay, that's what it is, only here it's ca'ed Cay-day-verrio Rigeedity, but 'tis that same rigor he means. Yon's jist his difficult name for't. Noo, here's whit this man says, an' he'll be a great authority, for my puir feyther paid a terrible deal o' money for the buik. "Under ordinary circumstances the' – och, dear! – the s-k-e-l-e-t-a-l, the skeeleetal muscles begin tae stiffen, in fra' fower tae ten hours after death." Fower tae ten hours. Noo, that'll gie us whit ye might ca' a margin o' six hours error in estimatin' the time o' death. Wull't no, doctor?'

'Other things being equal,' said the doctor, 'yes.'

'Ay, an' here again: "It is fully developed," that is, the rigor,

230

ye onnerstand, "in fra' twa tae three hours." That'll gie us anither hour's margin.'

'Well, yes.'

'Ay, "This condition last for a period varyin' from a few hours tae six or eight days." There's a terrible big difference there, doctor!'

'So there is,' said Dr. Cameron, smiling slightly, 'but there are other things to be taken into consideration besides rigor mortis. You'll not be suggesting the body was six or eight days old?'

'Not at all, doctor. But it gaes on tae say, "Twenty-four tae forty-eight hours may be regarded as the average duration of ca-da—" that is, o' this rigor. Ye'll allow, maybe, that this great authority isna so varra preceese tae twa-three hours. Noo, then, doctor, when ye saw this corpse at 3 o'clock o' the afternoon, how stiff was he?'

'He was quite stiff,' replied the doctor. 'That is, to employ the stately language of your great authority, the cadaveric rigidity was fully established. This made it probable that the man had then been dead not less than six hours and probably – taking the appearance of the bruises, etc., into account – considerably longer. Taking Mr. Dixon Mann's pronouncement as the basis of a diagnosis, you will see that it would allow death to have taken place as much as thirteen hours earlier – ten hours to start the rigor and three to develop it fully. That is, the death might have taken place as late as 9 a.m. or as early as midnight, and the body would still have been stiff at 3 p.m., without its being necessary to presume anything abnormal in the onset or development of the rigor.'

'Ay, but—' began Macpherson, hastily.

'Ay, that's jist what I—' began Duncan, at the same moment.

'One minute,' said the doctor. 'I know what ye're about to say, Inspector. I'm not fully allowing for the case that the rigor might have been completely established some time before I saw it. Supposing the rigor had come on slowly and had been fully developed, say, at 1 o'clock. That would make it possible that the death took place as early as 10 p.m. the day before. I told you before that that was not impossible.'

Macpherson gave a satisfied grunt.

'Campbell was a man in vigorous health,' went on the doctor, 'and he died from a sudden blow. If you'll consult that authority of yours a bit farther on, Duncan, you'll see it says that, under

231

those conditions, the onset of cadaveric rigidity is likely to be slow.'

'Ay, doctor,' persisted the policeman, 'but ye'll see also that when the subject is exhausted an' depressed in his physical strength, the rigidity may come on verra quick. Noo, I was thinkin' that yon Campbell must ha' passed an awfu' exhaustin' nicht. He was fightin' wi' Mr. Waters at 9 o'clock or thereabouts, he was fightin' again wi' Mr. Gowan at 9.45, an' he had his inside fu' o' whuskey forbye, which is weel known tae be depressin' in its effects – that is,' he added hastily, catching a slight grin on Wimsey's face, 'after the high speerits o' the moment is wore off. Then he's away oot airly in the mornin' wi'oot his breakfast, as was established by examination o' his insides, an' he drives his car twenty-seven mile. Wad he no be sufficiently exhausted wi' a' that tae stiffen up quick when he was killed ?'

'You seem to have thought this out, Duncan,' said the doctor. 'I see I shall have to be careful, or I shall be caught tripping. I will only say this. The average duration of rigor mortis is from twenty-four to forty-eight hours. Campbell's body was rigid when I saw it on Tuesday afternoon at 3 o'clock, and it was still rigid on Wednesday night when it was put into its coffin. On Thursday evening, when I examined it in the presence of a number of you gentlemen, the rigidity had entirely passed off. That gives a fairly average duration for the rigor. In general, a quick onset is followed by a short duration, and a slow onset by a long duration. In this case, the duration appeared average to slow, and I conclude that the onset would also have been average to slow. That is why I finally gave it as my considered opinion that the most probable time of death was somewhere round about midnight, and this agreed with the general appearance of the body and the bruises.'

'How about the contents of the stomach ?' asked Sir Maxwell.

'The contents of the stomach was whiskey,' said the doctor, drily, 'but I'm not saying how late on Monday night the deceased would be drinking whiskey.'

'But,' said Duncan, 'supposin' the murder didna take place till 9 o'clock or so on the Tuesday, that wad shorten the duration of the rigor.'

'Well, of course,' said the doctor. 'If he didn't die till Tuesday morning, that might bring the duration of the rigor down to a little over thirty-six hours. I can only speak to the period between 3 p.m. on Tuesday and 7 p.m. on Wednesday, when I handed it over to the undertaker.'

'Well, the point appears to be,' said the Fiscal, 'that, though the appearances suggest to you a death round about midnight, you may be in error to the extent of an hour or two either way.'

'That is so.'

'Could you be in error to the extent of eight or nine hours ?'

'I would not like to think so,' replied the doctor, cautiously, 'but I would not say it was impossible. There's very few things impossible in Nature, and an error in diagnosis is not one of them.'

'Weel,' said Dalziel, eyeing his subordinate with some disfavour, 'ye hear what the doctor says. He'll no say it is impossible an' that's mair nor ye could ha' expectit, an' you tae be questionin' his great experience, with your rigor mortis an' your auld feyther, an' your wee buik an' a'. 'Tis tae be hoped ye can gi'e a gude reason for your presumption. Ye'll kindly excuse him, doctor. Duncan is a gude lad, but he's ower zealous.'

Duncan, thus stimulated, began again, blushing hotly all over his face.

'Weel, sirs, the point I started from was this, that oot of a' six suspects there's not one that's been proved to ha' been nigh the place where the corpse was found, only Mr. Graham. But we've evidence that Graham was actually seen at Bargrennan the verra morning o' the murder. An', what's mair, he admits tae't himsel'.'

'That's a fact,' said the Fiscal. 'You've got in here in your notes that this man Brown saw Graham walking along the banks of the Cree just below Bargrennan at half-past eleven on Tuesday morning. He says that Graham was going upstream, and that when he saw Brown approaching, he scrambled quickly down the bank as though to avoid observation. That certainly looks like a suspicious circumstance.'

'Ay,' said Duncan, excitedly. 'An' when Graham is questioned, what does he say ? First of a', he refuses tae state whaur he's been. An' that, mind you, before there's ony suspicion gi'en oot that Campbell's death was mair nor an accident. That's yin thing. Secondly, as sune as it's known through the papers that it may be a case o' murder, he comes forrit wi' a fause alibi for the Monday nicht only.'

'Stop a moment, Duncan,' said Sir Maxwell. 'If, as you seem to suppose, Graham did not commit the murder till Tuesday

233

morning, there would be no point in his bringing forward an alibi for Monday night. He'd know it would not cover him.'

'Ay, that's so,' said Duncan, screwing up his ingenuous face into an expression of the most concentrated cunning, 'but it was the leddy brought forrit the alibi, an' why? Because it had been pit aboot – I'm no sayin' by whom – that the murder was maist probably committed o' the Monday nicht. Then the leddy – that kens fine Graham did the murder but isna sae weel informed as tae the time – fa's heid ower heels intae the trap. She says, "He couldna' ha' done 't; he was wi' me." Mr. Dalziel asks her sharp and sudden. "How long was he wi' you?" She says, "Till past 9 o'clock," knowing verra weel that if she was tae say till 12 o'clock or some such hour, the next question wad be, "Did nae-body see him leavin' the hoose?" – which, wi' a' the folks astir in the toon is no verra probable. Verra gude. Then Graham hears on't an' says tae himsel', "I maun du better than that. Likely enough I was recognised by that fellow up yonder. I'll say I was the haill of they two nichts and days up at Bargrennan poachin' wi' Jimmy Fleeming an' Jimmy'll bear me oot." An' that's when he comes in wi' his second alibi.'

'Jimmy Fleeming does bear him out, as far as I can see,' observed the Fiscal, turning over his papers.

'Och, ay,' said Duncan, 'Jimmy Fleeming's the biggest leear in the Stewartry. Forbye, Graham is weel likit by that poachin' lot. There's no a man among them that wadna swear to a wee lie or so tae protect Graham.'

'That's true enough,' said Macpherson. 'An' there's no need for them tae be tellin' sic a big lie, neither. They'd be up half the nicht wi' their poachin' an' sleepin' half the day. What's tae hinder Graham walking off an' committin' his murder – ay, an' pentin' his bit picture – wi'oot them knowin'? He wad say he's ta'en a wee walk, maybe. Or maybe they'd be sleepin' and never notice when he comed or gaed?'

'Your idea, Duncan, is that Campbell came up to the Min-noch – when, exactly?'

'That's clear enough,' said Wimsey. 'We've got to take Fergu-son's times, because, on this assumption, there's no reason for doubting them. Starting at 7.30, and driving at an ordinary speed, he wouldn't be likely to do the twenty-seven miles in much under an hour. Say he arrives there at 8.30 and sits down and gets his painting things out. Graham taking his morning walk, gets along there at, say, 8.45. They quarrel, and Campbell is knocked into the river and killed. At 9 o'clock, summer time, Graham might reasonably begin to do his painting, it takes him an hour and a half. We know that, because we've seen him do it – at least, I have. That brings us to half-past ten. But we know he was still there at five past eleven, so we'll have to give him till then. That's quite likely, because if, when I saw him, he was merely copying his own painting, he'd probably do it quicker than if it was his effort. As soon as he's finished, and the road is free of inquisitive passers-by, he strolls back to his sleeping friends, who will subsequently be ready to swear that they never took their eyes off him the whole time. That's your theory, isn't it, Duncan ?'

'Ay, that's it,' said Duncan, gratified.

'It's not a bad one, either, as far as it goes,' went on his lordship, with the air of a man sampling a glass of old port. 'It has at least three snags, but I dare say they could be demolished with a little goodwill. First, the doctor has got to be all wrong in his calculations, but, as he doesn't seem to mind that, neither need we. Secondly, who ate Campbell's breakfast ? Well, we can suppose that, having drunk rather deeply the night before, he nevertheless courageously cooked his egg and rasher and, having cooked them, didn't like the look of them and shot them into the fire. Or we can suppose – though I should hate to do so – that Mrs. Green ate them herself and said she hadn't. Or we can suppose that Campbell ate them, was promptly sick, and filled up the void with whiskey. Any one of those suppositions would account for the conditions as found, eh, doctor ?

'Then there are the marks of tar on Campbell's Morris, which we put down to bicycle-tyres, but they might quite well have been due to something else. I pointed them out in the first place, but I wouldn't be bigoted about them on that account. They're not significant enough to wreck a theory on.

'The big snag in Duncan's ingenious reconstruction is the man who saw the car pass the New Galloway turning at 9.45. I'm afraid Duncan hasn't accounted for him at all. Still, we can say he was mistaken. If a doctor can be mistaken, so can an honest workman. He didn't see the number of the car, so it may have been another Morris.'

'But the piled-up stuff under the rug at the back,' said the Chief Constable, 'and the driver's conspicuous cloak. You can't get away from them.'

'Can't I ?' said Wimsey. 'You don't know me. I could get

away from a galloping fire-engine. You'd been advertising for a Morris car driven by a man in a loud cloak, with a pile of luggage behind, hadn't you? Well, you know what happens when you advertise for things. A man sees something that corresponds to part of the description and imagines the rest. Probably twenty Morris cars drove over the main road from Castle-Douglas to Stranraer that morning and probably half of those had luggage in them. Several of them may have been driven by gentlemen whose dress was more noisy than discriminating. Your man had no very particular reason to notice the car at the time, except that he shot out on it unexpectedly. If the truth was known, he was probably riding carelessly himself. The car got in his way and annoyed him, and if he can persuade himself that he had an encounter with a desperado fleeing from justice, he's not going to stick at remembering a few things that weren't there. There are plenty of people who are always ready to remember more than they saw.'

'That's awfu' true,' sighed Macpherson.

'I will tell you a thing I like about this theory of Duncan's,' said the Fiscal. 'It makes it appear likely that the crime was unpremeditated. It is more likely that Graham, coming suddenly upon Campbell like that, should quarrel with him and knock him down than that anybody should contrive a scheme to carry a dead body all those miles and plant it in so awkward a place.'

'The place was more or less forced on the murderer, was it not, by Campbell's expressed intention of painting there that day?'

'But he might be supposed to have changed his mind, Sir Maxwell.'

'To an innocent man,' said Macpherson, acutely, 'that supposition wad present no difficulty at all. But a murderer might weel be ower particular, even tae the point o' riskin' the miscarriage of his plans by an unnecessary verisimilitude.'

'Well, Inspector,' said the Chief Constable, 'I can see that you are not altogether satisfied with any of our theories. Let us have yours.'

The Inspector brightened. This was his moment. He felt convinced that he, and no other person, had the right sow by the ear, and was, indeed, extremely grateful to Dalziel, Sir Maxwell and Duncan for having produced such inferior animals and refrained from spoiling his market.

'The Sergeant said just noo,' said he, 'that Jimmy Fleeming

was the biggest leear in the Stewartry. Weel, I ken three that's bigger leears than him, an' that's Gowan and his pack of English servants. An' ye'll mind that they three are the only pairsons that's proved oot o' their own mouths tae be leears, exceptin' Strachan an' his bit tale aboot a gowf-ball.

'I believe Gowan killed Campbell when they met on the road, an' I dinna credit one word o' that story aboot his beard.

'Noo, I've written doon the course o' events as I see them, an' I'll ask ye tae read it out for me, Mr. Fiscal, seein' as ye're better accustomed tae speakin' in public than I am.'

With these words, the Inspector handed over a neatly-written manuscript which he produced from his breast-pocket, and leaned back with the shy smile of a poet attending a public reading of his own works.

The Fiscal adjusted his glasses and, in a clear voice, proceeded to do justice to—

The Case against Gowan

The evidence of the girl Helen Macgregor is that Campbell met with another motorist, since proved and admitted to be Gowan, on the Gatehouse-Kirkcudbright road at about 9.45 on Monday night. That there was a quarrel, and that one of the parties then placed the inanimate body of the other party in the two-seater car and drove off with it in the direction of Gatehouse. That she then became frightened and ran home. This story was subsequently substantiated by the finding of a spanner, bearing Campbell's finger-prints, close to the locus of the alleged assault, and by the discovery of car-tracks tending to show that a car had been driven into a grass lane, through a gate some fifty yards from the said locus.

In my opinion, the crime is to be reconstructed as follows.

Having killed Campbell in the struggle, Gowan's first consideration was to remove the corpse to a place where it would not be seen by a passer-by. This he effected by placing it in his own car, driving up to the gate, and dumping the body inside. He selected his own car for this purpose because it was the nearest to Gatehouse and could be more readily shifted by him. If he had put the body at once in Campbell's car, he would have had to move his own car first, to get the other past, and someone might have arrived while he was so doing. If such a person had found Campbell's car obstructing the road and had ascertained upon investigation that it contained a dead body it would have a very suspicious appearance.

He then brought up Campbell's car, drove it through the gate, placed the body in it and deposited it at some distance up the lane. He then proceeded on foot to his own car, turned it and returned in it to Kirkcudbright. He could accomplish this, driving *like hell* (the last two words were carefully ruled out) in a reckless manner in rather under five minutes. Say at 10.10. The girl Helen saw him when he passed her house.

He would find Hammond on duty and would urge him to return with him at once. On reaching the scene of the crime at, say, 10.20, he would proceed on foot to the Morris car and drive it out of the lane in the direction of Gatehouse, while Hammond would return with the two-seater to Kirkcudbright.

Gowan could be back with the Morris at Standing Stone cottage at, say, 10.30. (Note: Ferguson gives the time as 10.15, but he only says 'about.')

Gowan then conceives the plan of simulating an accident to Campbell. Since his black beard would make it impossible to impersonate Campbell, he shaves this off with Campbell's razor, carefully cleaning the same, and destroying the hair in the fire, except a portion which he reserved for another purpose.

When Strachan arrived, Gowan was in hiding some place or other, probably in the garage. On Strachan's departure, he returned to the cottage in a stealthy manner, destroyed the note and proceeded with his preparations.

At 7.30 he would start out with the car, disguised in Campbell's clothes and carrying the corpse, the painting materials and the bicycle, which he would have taken from the Anwoth Hotel. Now we have to account for the long time taken by him to arrive at the New Galloway road, where he was seen by the workman. In my opinion he proceeded to some town or village not yet ascertained, and there instructed Hammond to meet him at some point with the two-seater. In my opinion this would be a locality in the neighbourhood of Pinwherry. Inquiries have been set on foot to trace this telephone message within an area of thirty miles round about Gatehouse.

At this point the Chief Constable interrupted the reading.

'Could not the call be readily traced at the Kirkcudbright end?' he inquired.

'No, no,' said Wimsey, before Macpherson could speak.

'Hammond would have been instructed to go somewhere else to get it. A desperate fellow like Gowan isn't going to take all this trouble only to trip up on a trifle like a telephone-call, eh, Macpherson?'

'That's so,' said the Inspector. 'That's jist exactly what was in my mind.'

'Then why did he not tell Hammond what to do when they were together, and avoid the telephone call altogether?' demanded Sir Maxwell.

'He hadn't made his plan then,' said Wimsey. 'How fretful you people are! Do give the man time to think. His first idea is, "Let's get the body away off this road that I'm known to have driven along. I'll plant it somewhere. I don't know where. I'll think it out and 'phone you tomorrow at 8 o'clock. Go to Lauriston or Twynholm (or Kamschatka or Timbuctoo or whatever was the handiest place) and I'll put the call through to you there." After all, you've got to explain the delay on the road somehow. Ferguson is a liar, Strachan fell down a mine, Farren – let me see; oh, yes – Farren was a poor hand with a car and Gowan made a telephone call. Please go on with the reading, Fiscal.'

Gowan then proceeded to the site on the Minnoch and painted his picture. This would occupy him till about 11.30. He then mounted the bicycle and rode along the road to Pinwherry and Girvan to the spot selected by him. It would be just as he had passed Barrhill that he was observed by Mr. Clarence Gordon. Mr. Gordon said that the bicyclist was not a very tall man, but Gowan would not look so tall if he was bent down over a bicycle and pedalling fast. Without his beard, Gowan would not be recognisable from his photograph. Hammond would meet him with the two-seater some place between Barrhill and Girvan, and he would be provided with any necessary tackle for securing the bicycle to the car. They would drive together to just this side of Girvan, where Hammond would alight, take the bicycle and proceed to Ayr, contriving whether by design or mischance to lose the bicycle in the station. It will be remembered that the person travelling with the bicycle was said to speak like an Englishman. Gowan then proceeded with the car to some point from which he could write and dispatch his letter to Major Aylwin. He would not wish to make his appearance in Kirkcudbright without his beard so that he probably did not return till that night. Efforts are being made to trace the movements of the car during this period.

239

With reference to the portions of beard discovered on the Gatehouse-Kirkcudbright road. It would occur to Gowan and his confederates that the fact of murder might be suspected and his own movements investigated. In that case the shaving-off of his beard and his disappearance to London might present a suspicious appearance. They therefore concocted a story to fit the case, and planted the portions of hair by the roadside in order to support this invention. This was the story subsequently told by Gowan at Scotland Yard, which was very misleading, on account of containing so large a proportion of facts. The details of Gowan's escape from Kirkcudbright occurred exactly as related in his statement. This is the case against Gowan as presented by me.

(*Signed*) JOHN MACPHERSON,
Inspector of Police.

'Ingeniouser and ingeniouser,' said Wimsey. 'There are a good many details that need verification, but the whole thing is very pretty indeed. What a shocking set of crooks these English servants are! Not even murder will turn them from their feudal devotion to the man who pays!'

The Inspector flushed.

'Ye're tryin' tae make a fool of me, my lord,' he said, reproachfully.

'Indeed, no,' replied his lordship. 'One thing in your story pleases me particularly, and that is that you have bravely tackled the business of the bicycle at Euston, which everybody else has fought shy of.'

At this point, Constable Ross cleared his throat in so pointed a manner that everyone turned to look at him.

'I perceive from your manner, Ross,' said his lordship, 'that to you also the word bicycle has not been devoid of significance. With the permission of these other gentlemen, I should greatly like to hear your version of the matter.'

The constable looked at the Chief Constable for his approval, and receiving a nod, embarked upon his theory.

'The thing that's in my mind,' said he, 'is this man Waters. Here's a man wi' a verra unsatisfactory alibi, which is no capable o' proof. We have not yet established communication wi' this man Drewitt an' his sailing-yacht –'

'Just a moment, Ross,' broke in the Chief Constable. 'We got a wire in from him this morning from Arisaig. We just missed him at Oban. He wires, "Waters joined us at Doon 8.30 Tuesday morning. Left yacht Gourock Saturday. Writing." He has also, I understand, made a confirmatory statement to the police.'

'Aye,' said Ross, not in the least disconcerted, 'ay, imph'm. But we dinna ken what kind o' a man is this Drewitt. He'll be for backing up Waters ony gait, tae my thinkin'. He may swear till he's black in the face Waters went aboard at the Doon, but the fact remains that naebody saw him to speak to, an' the bicycle has clean disappeared. In my opinion, yon bicycle is doon in the deep waters betune Arran an' Stranraer, an' ye'll never see it mair till it rises oot o' the sea tae bear witness at the great Day of Judgment. Unless,' he added, with some sacrifice of picturesqueness, 'ye sairch for't wi' deep-sea tackle.'

'What's your idea, then, Ross?'

'Well, Sir Maxwell, 'tis this, an' 'tis awfu' clear an' simple tae my thinkin'. Here's Campbell, fou' as a puggie an' looking for trouble. He has a row wi' Waters an' says it'll no end there. He's aff away to Gatehouse, an' he meets Gowan an' gets the better o' him. "That's fine," thinks he, "it's my night the night." He's away home an' he gets drinkin' again, and he thinks to himsel', "What for wad I no drag that bastard Waters" (beggin' your pardon) "oot o' his bed an' finish wi' him now?" He gets his car oot again an' starts away. Ferguson will be asleep an' no hearin' him. He admits himsel' he didna hear Strachan gae, an' what for wad he ha' heard Campbell? He drives ower tae Kirkcudbright an' chucks stones at Waters' window. Waters looks oot, sees him an' thinks, "We'll no have a row in the street." He lets him in an' they talk a bit, an' yin or t'ither o' them says, "We'll away up tae the stoojo an' fight it oot." They do so, an' Campbell's kilt.

'Waters is in an awfu' pickle and doesna ken what tae do. He's comin' oot o' the stoojo in a distracted condition when he meets his friend Drewitt, that's visitin' there wi' his hired car. "Drewitt," says he, "I'm in awfu' trouble. I've killt a man," he says, "an' I dinna ken what tae do. It was a fair fight," he says, "but they'll bring it in murder an' I'll be hangit." Then they puts their heids tegither an' makes a plan. Drewitt's away tae Mrs. McLeod's for tae impairsonate Waters. An' ye'll mind,' added Constable Ross, forcibly, 'that Mrs. McLeod never set eyes on her lodger fra' the time he went oot a little after midnicht. She *heard* him come upstairs, she heard him ca' oot when she brought up the water, an' when she came in fra' the back o' the hoose, he'd eaten his breakfast and away.'

'Drewitt would be takin' an awfu' risk,' said Macpherson.

241

'Ay, but murderers maun tak' risks,' said Ross. 'In the meantime, Waters is away wi' Campbell's car an' his bicycle at the same time that Drewitt entered the hoose. Then he does a' the same things as we've suggested for the other suspects. He's away wi' the body at 7.30. I'm thinkin' he'll ha' ta'en the auld road through Gatehouse Station an' he'll maybe have had engine trouble in that lonely place, or burst a tyre an' had tae change the wheel. The road's wicked wi' the ruts and the stones thereabouts. Ony gait, he passes the New Galloway turnin' at 9.35 an' arrives at the Minnoch at 10. He pents his picture, throws the body into the burn and makes off on his bicycle. He has plenty o' time, for he'll no be able tae carry oot the rest o' his plan before nightfall. He hides up in the hills, an' it's here he'll be cursin' himsel', for he'll ha' forgot tae bring wi' him the sandwiches that was found in Campbell's satchel. Ay, he'll be fine an' empty before night. When 'tis safe for him tae move, he rides his bicycle tae the appointed meetin'-place wi' Drewitt.

'Drewitt will ha' been workin' up the coast, like he said. It will ha' been Drewitt as was seed tae go aboard at the Doon, an' after that, the course o' the yacht will agree wi' Waters' statement. In the night, she'll make across fra' Lady Bay tae Finnart Bay, an' pick up Waters that's ridden doon by the high road fra' Pinwherry. They take the bicycle on board an' return tae lie up in Lady Bay. After that they hae only tae carry oot their original sailing plan, an' land Waters at Gourock on Saturday mornin', after sinkin' the bicycle some place where it'll no be easy found. Man! it's as plain as the nose on your face.'

'But—' said the Chief Constable.

'But—' said the Inspector.

'But—' said the Sergeant.

'But—' said Constable Duncan.

'Imph'm,' said the Fiscal. 'All these theories are very interesting, gentlemen, but they are all conjectural. I congratulate you all extremely upon your ingenuity and hard work, but to say which theory is the most probable is a harder choice than that between Portia's caskets. It appears to me that all are worth being followed up, and that the next step is to prosecute inquiries which may tend to confirm either one or the other of them. The movements of all cars upon the roads in the district must be checked with the greatest possible care. The man Drewitt must be interviewed and closely questioned, and the persons living about Finnart Bay and Lady Bay must be asked whether they observed anything of the movements of the yacht. At least we can feel certain that one among the five theories presented to us must be the true one, and that is something. Do you not think so, Lord Peter?'

'Yes, Wimsey,' said the Chief Constable. 'You told the Inspector the other day that you had solved the problem. Are you in a position to give a casting vote? Which of our suspects is the murderer?'

THE MURDERER

'THIS,' said Lord Peter Wimsey, 'is the proudest moment of my life. At last I really feel like Sherlock Holmes. A Chief Constable, a Police Inspector, a Police Sergeant and two constables have appealed to me to decide between their theories, and with my chest puffed like a pouter-pigeon, I can lean back in my chair and say, "Gentlemen, you are all wrong."'

'Damn it,' said the Chief Constable, 'we can't *all* be wrong.'

'You remind me,' said Wimsey, 'of the steward who said to the Channel passenger, "You can't be sick here." You can all be wrong and you are.'

'But we've suspected everybody,' said Sir Maxwell. 'See here, Wimsey, you're not going to turn round now and say that the crime was committed by Mrs. Green or the milkman, or somebody we've never heard of? That would be in the very worst tradition of the lowest style of detective fiction. Besides, you said yourself that the murderer was an artist, and you even picked out those six artists yourself. Are you going back on that now?'

'No,' said Wimsey, 'I wouldn't do anything quite so mean as that. I'll qualify my original statement. You are all wrong, but one of you is less wrong than the rest. Still none of you has got the right murderer, and none of you has got the whole of the method right, though some of you have got bits of it.'

'Don't be portentous and tiresome, Wimsey,' said Sir Maxwell. 'There is a serious side to this matter. If you possess any information that we do not, you ought to let us have it. In fact, you ought to have let us have it at once, instead of wasting our time like this.'

'I did let you have it at once,' said Wimsey. 'I let you have it on the day of the crime, only you keep on forgetting it. And I haven't really been holding anything up my sleeve. I had to wait till all the suspects were roped in before I could be certain of my theory, because at any moment something might have turned up to unsettle it. And I haven't actually proved it now, though I'll undertake to do it any time you like.'

'Come, come,' said the Fiscal, 'please tell us what it is you're wanting to prove, and you shall be given every opportunity.'

'Right-ho! I will be good. Now we'll have to go back to the discovery of the body. The crucial point of the whole problem was there, and I pointed it out to you, Dalziel, and that was the thing that made us sure from the start that Campbell's death was murder and no accident.

'You remember how we found the body. It was lying in the burn, cold and stiff, and on the easel up above there was a picture, half-finished, together with a palette, a satchel and a painting-knife. We went through all the belongings of the dead man, and I said to you, "There's something missing, and if we can't find it, it means murder," You remember that, Dalziel?'

'I mind it fine, Lord Peter.'

'In Campbell's satchel we found nine tubes of oil colour – vermilion, ultramarine, two chrome yellows, viridian, cobalt, crimson lake, rose madder and lemon yellow. But there was no flake white. Now, as I explained to you at the time, it is absolutely impossible for a painter in oils to make a picture without using flake white. It is the fundamental medium which he uses to mix with his other colours to produce various shades of light and shadow. Even a man like Campbell, who used a great deal of pure colour, would as soon think of setting out to paint without flake white as you would to set out to catch trout without a cast. And in any case, the proof that Campbell had been using flake white that morning was proved by the picture itself, which contained huge masses of white cloud, wet and fresh and just laid on.

'A glance at the palette confirmed this. It had seven blobs of colour on it, in this order: White, cobalt, viridian, vermilion, ultramarine, chrome yellow and rose madder.

'Well, you know how we searched for that missing tube of colour. We turned out Campbell's pockets, we scoured every inch of the ground and we lifted – or rather, you lifted, because I'd made tracks like a sensible man – every stone in that confounded stream, right down to the bridge. I told you the tube would

244

probably be a big one, but that it might, of course, be nearly empty and therefore rather light. If it had been anywhere about, I think we may take it that you would have found it.'

'Ay,' said Dalziel, 'ye may confidently assume that, my lord.'

'Very well, then. There was, of course, the faint possibility that, after Campbell's death, someone had come up and removed the tube, but we felt that to be too fantastic for consideration. Why should anybody steal just that one thing and nothing else? And then, there was the condition of the body, which suggested that death had occurred a good deal earlier than the amount of work on the picture would lead one to suppose. And by the way, doctor, I may as well relieve your mind and say at once that, in spite of Duncan's able and ingenious special pleading, your estimate of the time of death was perfectly sound.'

'I'm glad to hear it.'

'Yes. Well, the question was, what had happened to the flake white? Taking all the appearances into consideration, I formed the opinion that (a) Campbell had been murdered, (b) the murderer had painted the picture, (c) he had for some reason taken the flake away with him.

'Now, why should he take it away? It would be the silliest possible thing for him to do, since its absence would instantly arouse suspicion. He must have taken it by mistake, and that meant that he must have automatically put it in the place where he was accustomed to put tubes of colour while painting. He hadn't put it in any of the ordinary places – on the ground, or in a box, or in the satchel or on the tray attached to the easel. He must have bestowed it about his person somewhere, and a pocket was the likeliest place. So that from that moment I felt we ought to look about for a painter with the untidy habit of dropping paints into his pockets.'

'You didn't mention that,' said Dalziel, reproachfully.

'No, because I was afraid – forgive me – that if I had, you might possibly go and make inquiries about it, and if once the murderer had his attention drawn to this unfortunate habit of his, there would be an end of the habit and the inquiry. Besides, several painters might have the same habit. Or I might be entirely mistaken about the whole thing – it was a slender clue, and I might be straining it too far. I thought my best plan was to snoop about the studios and watch people at work and find out what their habits were. That was obviously a job which I, as a private person, could do better than any official. But I gave you the pointer, Dalziel, and put it into your report. Anybody could have come to the same conclusion as I did. Why didn't anybody?'

'Never mind why we didn't, Wimsey,' said Sir Maxwell. 'Go on with your story.'

'The next thing,' said Wimsey, 'was – why all this elaborate fake with the picture? Why should a murderer hang round the place of the crime painting pictures? Obviously, to disguise the fact that Campbell had been killed at – well, whatever time he was killed. Say the previous night. That meant that the murderer hadn't got a good alibi for the previous night or whenever it was. But if he wanted to make it look as though Campbell had been killed that morning, it meant that he must be preparing himself a cast-iron alibi for that particular morning. So I decided that I knew four things about the murderer already: (1) he was an artist, or he couldn't have painted the picture, (2) he had a habit of putting paints in his pocket, (3) he had a weak alibi for the actual time of death, (4) he would have a good alibi for Tuesday morning.

'Then came the discovery of the tar-marks on the car. That suggested that the alibi had somehow been worked out with the aid of a bicycle. But I couldn't get farther than that, because I didn't know when Campbell was killed, or when he was supposed to have started out for the Minnoch, or how long the picture would take to paint, or any details of that kind. But what I did know was that Campbell had been a quarrelsome kind of devil, and that at least six artists in the district had been going about shouting for his blood.

'Now the confusing thing about this case was that of these six artists, five had disappeared. Of course it isn't in the least unusual for five artists to be away from the district at the same time. There was the Exhibition at Glasgow, to which several people had gone, including Ferguson. There was fishing, which often takes people out at night – there were hundreds of perfectly legitimate things they might have been doing. But the fact remained that those five people were not available for inquiries. You can't sit round and watch a man painting when you don't know where he is. The only man I could get hold of at once was Strachan, and when I came to look into his case, it appeared that his alibi was anything but satisfactory, not only for the Monday night but for the Tuesday morning as well; to say nothing of his having a black eye and a generally dilapidated appearance.

'So that was how the case stood then. Graham, vanished;

Farren vanished; Waters vanished; Gowan gone to London; Ferguson, gone to Glasgow; Strachan, at home, but obviously telling lies.

'Strachan, I may say, I almost absolved at once, though I thought it possible that he had some guilty knowledge of some kind. I was looking for a murderer with a good alibi, and Strachan's was about as bad and clumsy as it could be. Graham, Farren and Waters had to wait; they might turn up with excellent alibis; I couldn't tell. Only I had expected something more obvious and immediate. The two most suspicious people, from my point of view, were Ferguson and Gowan, because they had alibis supported by outside people. But if Gowan's alibi was sound, it covered the night as well as the morning; therefore the man who best fulfilled all the conditions was Ferguson. He had an alibi of exactly the kind that I expected. It covered the morning only; it was watertight in every joint; and it was established by people like station-masters and bus-conductors, who could have no possible reason for lying about it. If Ferguson had really travelled by the 9.8 train from Gatehouse to Dumfries, he *could not* have painted the picture.

'Well, then the rest of the people began to filter along. Graham turned up with no explanation at all, and he gave me a bad jolt; because Graham is the one man of the six who has, not only imagination, but the same *kind* of imagination as my own. I could see Graham working out that train of thought about the alibi and saying to himself that any alibi would be suspect, and that the biggest proof of innocence would be to have none. I believe that at that point I suspected Graham more than anybody else. He said he could imitate Campbell's style of painting – went out of his way to demonstrate it, too. I had an awful feeling that we should never be able to pin Graham down to anything. His manner was perfect. He took exactly the right line about the thing. And he didn't mean to commit himself until he knew what he had got to meet.

'Then Ferguson came back, with plenty of witnesses to show that he had really been to Glasgow, and told us a story which gave us at last a few real times to go upon. I am sure that all the times he gave us were perfectly correct, by the way, and that he didn't fall asleep or miss anything. I barged in on him and studied his method of painting and all that, and got him settled in my mind.

'That was the day we began to get a line on that bicycle busi-

247

ness at Ayr. Now, I don't want to be rude to anybody, but I do think that bicycle ought to have been taken into account in any explanation of the crime. The whole affair was so extremely odd that it could hardly be an accident or a coincidence. It didn't throw any light on the personality of the murderer, of course, because, though it was a Gatehouse bicycle, that merely meant that the crime had been worked from Gatehouse, which was overwhelmingly probable in any case. It was a great pity that that unfortunate porter at Girvan should have crocked up when he did. If he could have identified one of those photographs, he might have spared us a lot of trouble.

'Thursday – what did I do on Thursday? Of course, yes – we got the story of the row on the Gatehouse-Kirkcudbright road, and the spanner and the black hair. We rather tripped up on that, Macpherson. If we'd been a bit quicker, we could have caught Gowan before he eloped and saved several railway-fares to London. It was my fault, because I was taken up with my painting idea, and went round to Bob Anderson's to propose a sort of reconstruction up at the Minnoch. I was going to cart a lot of painters up there and set them to paint in Campbell's manner and see how long it took them. Graham and Strachan and Ferguson were there. They all agreed to try, except that Ferguson thought the idea wasn't in very good taste. But the weather spoilt that plan.

'What happened then? Oh, yes. I went over to the Carrick shore and watched Strachan painting, and he started to knock me into the sea, but thought better of it. By that time it was clear enough that he was either concealing something or shielding somebody, and the probability was that he was mixed up in Farren's disappearance. I'd seen him over at Mrs. Farren's, you know, on the Tuesday night, when I was inspecting Waters' studio and observing what a handy place the lane was for a car-park.

'Saturday, I didn't do much, but Waters came back and we got that remarkable story from Mrs. Smith-Lemesurier. I was still uncertain about Graham. It was far too stupid a story for him to put up, but, as Duncan pointed out, the lady might have lost her head and concocted it without reference to him.

'On Sunday I bullied Mrs. Farren into telling me where to find her husband. I ran him to earth on Monday and had a look at his painting methods, just before the official sleuths came along. So now I had only three more of my painters to inspect. After

248

that, the Chief Constable got Strachan's story, but I knew all I needed to know about Strachan by that time.

'My final job was to get hold of Graham and Waters and put them on to copying Campbell's painting. That killed four birds with one stone. It told me how they both used their colours, it gave me the time-factor I wanted to make my theory complete and, as it happened, they gave me, in conversation, the information I wanted about Gowan. That was why, Inspector, I told you that I didn't need to go and see Gowan.

'Now what you are all panting to know is – what did these six people do with their colours?

'Gowan, it appeared, was a fearfully spick and span fellow. He couldn't paint without having everything just so. He had a place for everything and everything in its place. He was the last person in the world to put paints in his pockets. And besides, to tell you the truth, I feel sure that he couldn't have produced that imitation of Campbell's style. He is too set in his methods. Nor do I think he would have the brains to carry out the fake from first to last. All the clever part of his little disappearance was planned and executed by Alcock, who has the makings of a very fine schemer indeed.

'Waters habitually chucks his paints into a satchel. Consequently, with Campbell's satchel handy, he would naturally have chucked them into it. And though he boasted of being able to imitate Campbell, he was slow at copying him, and his imitation was not extraordinarily good. But yet it wasn't bad enough to look like a deliberate attempt to do it badly. And neither he nor Graham looked in the least as though they had any unpleasant associations with the picture.

'Graham – well, Graham is a very clever man. *He* knew straight away that the painting wasn't Campbell's. He didn't exactly say so, in so many words, but he noticed differences in the style and remarked upon them. That might, of course, have been the culminating point in his scheme of over-reaching me, but I was pretty sure it wasn't. He seemed genuinely puzzled and suspicious. He also said that when painting out of doors, he put his tubes either on the ground or in his hat, and Waters bore him out in this. Neither Graham nor Waters showed any tendency to drop paints into their pockets. I watched them for an hour and a half, without surprising so much as a half-checked movement.

'Farren uses a sketching-box and is particular about putting each tube back in its place immediately after use. I can't say what he would do when he hadn't a box handy, but while I was at Mrs. Farren's I inspected the pockets of his old painting-jacket, and found that they had no tubes in them and no marks of paint on the lining. Besides, I eliminated Farren the moment I found that he had no alibi for Tuesday morning. The whole point of the fake was to support an alibi. If it didn't do that, it wasn't worth doing.

'Strachan lays his colours out on the tray of his easel, always in the same order, and he makes up his palette in a uniform order, too – the order of the spectrum. Now Campbell's palette was not made up like that, and the tubes of paint were all in the satchel – except, of course, the flake white. While watching Strachan, I took the opportunity to abstract a tube of cobalt, but he missed it instantly when he came to pack up, though he was all of a dither at the time, on account of the things I'd been saying to him. He wasn't the man to go off with an incriminating tube of flake white in his pocket.

'And now we come to Ferguson. Ferguson always puts paints in his pocket; I saw him do it. Ferguson gets his colours from Roberson's, but he had a pound tube of Winsor & Newton on his table; I saw and handled it. It was Ferguson's mania for a particular kind of bluish shadow-tint that puzzled Jock Graham in the faked picture. Ferguson, and nobody else, faked that picture and established that alibi.

'Wait a minute. There are one or two other points about Ferguson that I want to make. He is the one man with the alibi that it was the aim and object of the murderer to establish by means of the fake. He is known to have a remarkable visual memory for details. It was Ferguson who objected to the painting expedition to the Minnoch. And I take off my hat to Sir Maxwell Jamieson for affirming, in the face of all probability, that Ferguson was the man with the special knowledge to produce all the right appearances at the cottage to deceive Mrs. Green.'

There was a short silence when Wimsey had finished this long speech, which he delivered with an unaccustomed sobriety of style, and then Sir Maxwell said:

'That is all very well, Wimsey, and it sounds very convincing, but unless you can break down Ferguson's alibi, it goes for nothing at all. We know that he – or somebody – went from Gatehouse to Dumfries with the 9.8 and on to Glasgow. The ticket was clipped at three points on the journey, and given up at Glasgow. And besides, Ferguson was seen at Glasgow by those magneto people, and by Miss Selby and Miss Cochran. Are you suggesting that he had an accomplice to impersonate him, or what '

'No. He hadn't an accomplice. But he was a student of detective literature. Now, I'll tell you what I propose to do, with your permission. Tomorrow is Tuesday again, and we shall find all the trains running as they did on the morning of the alibi. We will go down to the cottage tonight and reconstruct the whole course of events from beginning to end. I will undertake to show you exactly how the thing was worked. If I break down at any point, then my theory breaks down. But if I get through, I will not only prove that the thing is possible but also that it was done that way.'

'Ye canna say fairer than that,' said Inspector Macpherson.

'The only thing is,' said Wimsey, 'that we must get Ferguson out of the way. If he sees what we're doing, he'll bolt.'

'Let him,' said Macpherson, grimly. 'If he bolts, we'll ken fine that he's guilty.'

'Good idea,' said Wimsey. 'Now, look here, we shall want a smallish, heavyish man to be Campbell. All you police blokes are too big. I'm afraid it will have to be you, Sir Maxwell.'

'I don't mind,' said that stout soldier, gamely, 'provided you stop short at throwing me into the burn.'

'I won't do that, but you'll have to do some very uncomfortable motoring, I'm afraid. Then we shall want two observers, one to stay with the corpse and the other to keep an eye on me. They will get a lot of strenuous exercise. How about you, Fiscal?'

'No, no,' said that gentleman, 'I'm over old for traipsing about the country.'

'Then it had better be Inspector Macpherson and the Sergeant. You can come as a passenger, Fiscal, if you like. Then we shall want a bicycle, since the real bicycle is still patiently sitting at Euston, waiting for somebody to be fool enough to claim it; eggs and bacon for everybody, and an extra car to carry the observers.'

The Inspector undertook to procure all the necessary commodities.

'Ross and Duncan,' he added, 'can watch Ferguson. Ye understand. Whatever place he goes, ye'll shadow him, an' if he tries tae bolt, ye'll arrest him.'

'That's the spirit,' said Wimsey. 'Sir Maxwell, you will start out from Kirkcudbright after the pubs close, and you'll be waiting at the S-bend at 9.45. You, Macpherson, can take the observation car and play Gowan's part in the business, but instead of returning to Kirkcudbright, you will follow the Chief Constable down to Gatehouse, so as to be ready to act Strachan's part when the time comes. You, Dalziel, will cling to me and watch me like a cat watching a mouse-hole. You, Fiscal, will do as you like. And we'll all start by having a very good dinner, for we've got a strenuous bit of work before us.'

LORD PETER WIMSEY

'HULLO!' said Ferguson.

'Hullo!' said Wimsey. 'This is the Procurator-Fiscal and this is Sergeant Dalziel of Newton-Stewart, whom I fancy you've met before. We are making a little experiment in connection with Campbell's death and we want to use your house, if we may. It's a good place to observe from, don't you know ?'

'I trust we will not be putting you out, Mr. Ferguson,' added the Fiscal, courteously.

'Not at all,' said Ferguson. 'Come in. What exactly do you want to do ?'

'We are going to reconstruct the events of Monday night,' said Wimsey, 'and we want you to tell us if we go wrong at any point.'

'Oh, certainly, with pleasure. When does the show start ?'

Wimsey looked at his watch.

'Eight o'clock. It ought to be starting now. Will you do Farren, Dalziel, or shall I ? You'd better, because then I can stay here under the Fiscal's eye.'

'Verra gude,' said Dalziel, and departed.

'Where were you sitting, Ferguson, when Farren arrived ?'

'Here,' said Ferguson, indicating an arm-chair by the fire.

'Good; then will you sit there again and do whatever it was you did that night ? The Fiscal shall take the opposite corner and I will sit here between you.'

'Who are you supposed to be?' asked Ferguson, with polite interest.

'Nobody just yet. Later on, I'm going to be the murderer. It's one of those things I've always wanted to be. Hullo! that sounds like the racket beginning.'

A series of heavy thumps testified to Dalziel's conscientious attack on Campbell's door.

'Carry on, Ferguson,' said Wimsey.

Ferguson, his face a little set and pale in the light of the petrol-gas lamp, moved across to the window and drew back the curtain.

'Who's that?' he shouted. 'For God's sake stop making that filthy row. Oh, it's you, Farren. What's the matter?'

'Whaur's that —— —— Campbell?' roared the Sergeant at the top of his lungs. 'Beggin' yer pardon, sir, but my orders is tae reprojuice the conversation as reported. Where's Campbell gone?'

'Campbell? I haven't seen him all day. I haven't the faintest idea where he is. What do you want him for?'

'I'm wantin' tae twist his guts oot,' yelled the Sergeant with relish. 'I'll no have the b—— hangin' roond after my wife. Jist yew show me whaur tae find the lousy —— an' I'll blow his bloody brains oot.'

'You're drunk,' said Ferguson.

'I may be drunk an' I may no be drunk,' retorted Dalziel with spirit, 'it's no matter to you. I'm not too drunk tae ken a dirty —— when I find him makin' love tae my wife. Where is the bastard?'

'Don't be a fool, Farren. You know perfectly well Campbell's not doing anything of the sort. Pull yourself together and forget it. Go and sleep it off.'

'Go an' so-and-so yerself,' vociferated the Sergeant. 'Leastways, that's what it's set doon fer me tae say. Ye're a couple o' what's-his-names the baith o' ye!'

'Oh, go and hang yourself!' said Ferguson.

'Ay, that's jist what I'm goin' tae do,' said Dalziel. 'I'm away tae hang masel' jist noo, but I'll ha'e the life o' Campbell first.'

'Oh right-oh! hang yourself by all means, but don't come making that bloody row. Go and do it somewhere else, for Christ's sake.'

There was a pause. Ferguson remained at the window. Then a plaintive voice inquired from outside:

'What'll I do now, sir ? My directions is tae hang aboot a bit.'

'You kick the door violently,' said Ferguson, 'and walk round to the back and make a noise there. Then you come back and let off a lot of foul language and go off on your bicycle.'

'Is that right, sir ?'

'Just about right,' said Ferguson. 'An excellent performance. I congratulate you.'

'Will I go away, now ?'

'Put the bicycle in its place,' said Wimsey, joining Ferguson at the window, 'and then come back here.'

'Verra gude,' said Dalziel. His red tail-lamp moved away to the gate and vanished behind the hedge.

'The worthy Sergeant is enjoying himself,' said Ferguson. 'His choice of language is not quite as good as Farren's, though.'

'Our presence probably cramped his style a bit,' said Wimsey. 'Eight-fifteen. The next act doesn't take place till after ten. What shall we do, Fiscal ? Play cards or tell stories? Or would you like me to read aloud to you ? Ferguson has a fine collection of detective novels.' He strolled over to the shelves. 'Hullo, Ferguson, where's that thing of Connington's *The Two Tickets Puzzle* ? I was going to recommend that to the Fiscal. I think he'd like it.'

'I've lent it to the padre at the Anwoth,' replied Ferguson.

'What a pity! Never mind. Here's an Austin Freeman. He's always sound and informative. Try this one, *The Eye of Osiris*. Great stuff. All about a mummy. Or Kennedy's *Corpse on the Mat* – that's nice and light and cheerful, like its title. Or if you're fed up with murders, try the new Cole, *Burglars in Bucks*.'

'Thank you,' said the Fiscal, in an austere voice, belied by the twinkle behind his glasses. 'I have brought the latest number of *Blackwood* to while away the time.'

'Crushed again!' said Wimsey. 'Ah! here's Dalziel. Come on, Sergeant. I'll take you on at dominoes for ha'-penny points. I'm a great dab at dominoes.'

Ferguson took up a book and sat down by the fire. Wimsey produced a box of dominoes from his pocket and slung them out on the table. The Sergeant pulled a chair in beside him. The Fiscal turned over the pages of *Blackwood*.

The silence became oppressive. The flutter of leaves, the click of the dominoes, and the ticking of the clock sounded unnaturally loud. Nine o'clock struck. Wimsey paid the Sergeant fourpence and the game went on.

Ten o'clock struck.

'This is where you start getting ready for bed, isn't it, Ferguson?' said Wimsey without taking his eyes from the table.

'Yes.' Ferguson pushed back his chair and got up. He wandered round the room, putting away a newspaper here and a book there. Once or twice he dropped things and had to pick them up. He walked over to the shelf and selected a book, then poured out a glass of whiskey and soda. He drank this slowly, standing by the mantelpiece.

'Do I put out the light?' he asked, when he had finished.

'Did you put out the light?'

'Yes.'

'Put it out then.'

Ferguson turned off the petrol-gas. The light dimmed and sank. The mantle glowed redly for a moment or two, and faded gradually out.

'Do I go to bed?' came the voice from the dark.

'Did you go to bed?'

'Yes.'

'Go to bed then.'

Ferguson's footsteps passed slowly out of the door and up the stairs.

'My God,' said Wimsey, softly. 'I had my revolver ready. Listen!'

The hum of a car came down the lane. It drew nearer, louder. The car was turning in at the gate. The headlights flashed across the window and passed. Wimsey got up.

'Do you hear that, Ferguson?' he called up the stairs.

'Yes.'

'What is it?'

'Campbell's car.'

'Can you see it?'

'I'm not looking at it. But I know the sound of the engine.'

Wimsey went out into the yard. The engine was still running noisily, and the driver appeared to be finding some difficulty in backing into the shed.

'What the bloody hell are you doing, Campbell?' shouted

255

Wimsey. 'Mind where you're going, you drunken ass. You'll have that wall down again.'

The reply was an outburst of very military language. Wimsey retorted, and a handsome slanging-match ensued. Sergeant Dalziel, stealing up the stairs in his stockinged feet, found Ferguson hanging with head and shoulders out of the bedroom window.

The voices of the men wrangling below came up loudly. Then there was a leap and a scuffle. Two dark bodies swayed backwards and forwards. Then came a crash and a heavy fall, followed by a most realistic groan.

'Was that the way it was, Mr. Ferguson ?'

Ferguson turned so sharply that he hit his head a crash against the window-frame.

'How you startled me!' he said. 'No, not in the least. I heard nothing of that kind. Nothing like that happened at all.'

'Och weel,' said the Sergeant philosophically. 'We'll maybe be mistaken. An' by the way, Mr. Ferguson, I was tae ask ye no tae gae tae yer bed jist noo, because we'll be wantin' the room for the pairpose of observation.'

'What am I to do then ?'

'Ye'll jist come doon an' sit wi' the Fiscal in the back room.'

'I don't know what you're getting at,' said Ferguson, yielding to the Sergeant's clutch upon his arm, 'but you've got it all wrong, you know. And if I'm not to get any rest tonight, I think I'd better go over and ask for a bed at the Anwoth.'

'That's no a bad idea, sir,' replied the Sergeant, 'but we'll ask ye tae bide here till 12 o'clock. I'll jist run over tae the hotel an' tell them tae expect ye.'

'Oh, I can do that, Sergeant.'

'I'll no be pittin' ye tae the trouble, sir,' replied Dalziel, politely. He had used his torch to guide them down the stairs and now led his victim into the studio, where the Fiscal was once more placidly reading *Blackwood* by the light of a candle.

'Sit ye doon, sir,' he urged pleasantly. 'I'll be back in a crack. Ah! here's Inspector Macphairson comin' in wi' the observation car. He'll be company for ye.'

In a very few moments the Inspector came in.

'Whit's happened ?' asked the Sergeant, eagerly.

'His Lordship is carryin' on terrible over the corp,' said the Inspector with a grin, 'tryin' tae revive it wi' whuskey.'

'Will ye bide here a moment, Inspector, while I rin over tae the Anwoth tae bespeak a room for Mr. Ferguson?'

Macpherson glanced from the frail figure of the Fiscal to Ferguson, kneading his handkerchief into a ball between his clammy hands. Then he nodded. The Sergeant went out. There was a long silence.

Sergeant Dalziel went no farther than the gate, where he flashed his torch. The bulky form of Constable Ross rose silently out of the hedge. Dalziel dispatched him to the hotel with a whispered message, and then went to see what was happening in the yard.

Here he found the Chief Constable extended flat on the ground, apparently receiving frantic first-aid from Wimsey.

'Is he deid yet?' asked Dalziel sympathetically.

'As mutton,' replied the murderer, sadly. 'I daresay we ought to have spun the riot out a bit longer, but the great thing is that he's dead. What's the time? Half-past ten. That's good enough. He breathed stertorously for a few minutes, and then, you know, he died. How did Ferguson take it?'

'Badly' replied the Sergeant 'but he denies it.'

'Naturally he would.'

'He's away tae the Anwoth for a quiet night.'

'Then I hope he'll sleep well. But we shall want him here till 12.'

'Ay, I've settled that.'

'Good. Carry on now. I'm supposed to be thinking out my plan of escape.'

The Sergeant waited for the return of P.C. Ross, and then went back to Ferguson's house to announce that all was well.

'How did your bit go, sir?' he asked the Inspector.

'Fine – the time worked out beautifully. We allowed five minutes for the struggle and five for the hair-cuttin' business.'

'Did anyone pass ye?'

'Not a solitary soul.'

'That was gude luck. Weel, I'll away tae his lordship.'

'Ay.'

'But this is all wrong, you know Inspector,' protested Ferguson. 'A thing like that couldn't have happened without my hearing it.'

'It'll maybe have taken place in the road,' said the Inspector, diplomatically, 'but it's mair convenient tae du't in private.'

'Oh, I see.'

The Sergeant returned to the yard to find Wimsey laboriously hoisting the Chief Constable on his back. He carried the inert body into the garage and dumped it on the floor, rather heavily. 'Hi!' said the corpse. 'You shut up,' said Wimsey, 'you're dead, sir. I couldn't drag you. It might leave marks.'

He stood looking down on the body.

'No blood,' he said, 'thank God there's no blood. I'll do it. I must do it. I must think, that's all. Think. I might pretend to be out fishing. But that's no good. I've got to have a witness. Suppose I just leave him here and pretend that Farren did it. But Farren may have gone home. He'll be able to prove he wasn't here. Besides, I don't want to get Farren into trouble if I can help it. Can't I make it look like an accident.'

He went out to the car.

'Better put this in,' he said, 'Farren might come back. If he does, I've got him. Or he's got me. One or the other. No, that won't do. Anyway, I can't count on it. The accident's the thing. And an alibi. Wait!'

He backed the car into the garage and switched the lights out.

'Whiskey's the next move, I think,' said he. He picked up the bottle from where he had left it. 'Probably, Dalziel, I did my thinking in the cottage, but just for the moment I'll do it in the garage. I'll just fetch a couple of glasses and the water-jug.'

A smothered shout from the garage indicated at this point that the corpse was growing restive.

'All right, corpse,' yelled Wimsey, cheerfully. 'I'm getting drinks.'

He fetched the glasses and the water, Dalziel moving dog-like at his heels, and brought the whole consignment back to the garage.

'We'll all have a drink,' he said. 'Corpse, you may sit up. Now, listen. It's difficult for me to think this plan out aloud now, because I know beforehand what it's going to be. But I know that when I was detecting it, it took me about an hour to hit on the general outline of it, and a bit more to fill in the details. So we'll give Ferguson all that time to play with. At about half-past eleven I shall begin to get to work. Meanwhile I think I'll make out a list of the things I've got to do. It would be fatal to forget anything.'

He switched on the lights again, then switched them off.

'Better not do that. Can't run the risk of letting the batteries run down. Lend me your torch, Dalziel. I don't want to do it at the cottage, under Ferguson's nose. He might, of course, betray himself and confess, but he might not. Besides, I'd rather he didn't really. I've set my heart on this reconstruction.'

He pulled a notebook out of his pocket and began to write. The Chief Constable and the Sergeant passed the whiskey bottle from hand to hand and conversed in whispers. Eleven o'clock struck from the church tower. Wimsey went on writing. At a quarter-past eleven, he read his notes through very carefully, and stowed them away in his pocket. After ten minutes more, he stood up.

'I'm supposed to have made my plans now,' he said, 'more or less, that is. Now I've got to start work. I've got to sleep in two beds tonight, so I'll start with Ferguson's. Dalziel, you must be getting ready to be Strachan.'

The Sergeant nodded.

'And the corpse had better stay here. Cheerio, folks. Leave a drink or two in the bottle for me.'

The corpse and the Sergeant stood for a moment at the door and watched Wimsey's dark figure cross the yard. It was dark, but not pitch-dark, and they saw him slip through the door. Presently the light of a candle flickered in the bedroom. Dalziel moved away, got into the observation car and started it up.

'Ferguson!'

Wimsey's voice sounded a little hoarse. Ferguson rose and went to the foot of the stairway.

'Come up here.'

Ferguson went up rather reluctantly, and found Wimsey with his shoes off, and in his shirt-sleeves standing by the bed.

'I'm going to lie down and have a rest. I want you to wait here with me till something happens.'

'This is a silly game.'

'It is, rather. I'm afraid. But you'll soon be out of it.'

Wimsey got into bed and drew the clothes over him. Ferguson took a chair by the window. Presently the noise of an approaching car was heard. It stopped at the gate, and footsteps passed hurriedly across the yard.

Knock, knock, knock.

Wimsey consulted his watch. Ten minutes after midnight. He got out of bed and stood close behind Ferguson, almost touching him.

'Look out of the window, please.'

Ferguson obeyed. A dark form stood on Campbell's threshold.

It knocked again, stepped back and looked up at the windows, walked round the house and came round to the door again. Then it moved aside and seemed to fumble behind the window shutter. Then came the scrape of a key being fitted into a lock. The door opened, and the figure went in.

'Is that right?'

'Yes.'

They watched again. There came a flash of light on the side window of the downstairs room. Then it passed away and presently appeared in the bedroom, the window of which faced Campbell's. It moved as though it were being flashed about the room; then vanished. After a little time it reappeared downstairs and remained stationary.

'Is that right?'

'Not quite. It was matches, not a torch.'

'I see. How did you know that, by the way? I thought you only heard this person come and didn't see anything.'

He heard the hiss of Ferguson's breath. Then:

'Did I say that? I didn't mean to give quite that impression. I heard the door open and saw the light upstairs. But I didn't actually see the person who came.'

'And you didn't see him come out again?'

'No.'

'And you had no idea who it was?'

'No.'

'And you saw nobody else that night?'

'Nobody.'

'And you saw Campbell go off in his car at 7.30 next morning?'

'Yes.'

'Right. Then you can hop it now, if you want to.'

'Well I think I will . . . I say Wimsey!'

'Yes?'

'Oh nothing! Good night!'

'Good night.'

'He nearly told me then' said Wimsey. 'Poor devil!'

Ferguson went out of the house and out of the gate. Two stealthy shadows crept out from the hedge and followed him.

Wimsey waited at the window till he saw Dalziel leave the next-door cottage and carefully lock the door behind him replacing the key in its hiding-place. When the hum of the car had died away in the distance, he ran hastily down the stairs, and across to the garage.

'Corpse!' he cried.

'Yessir!' said the corpse, smartly.

'While that ghastly blighter was nosing round – I – in my role as murderer you understand – had an awful thought. All this time you're getting stiff. If I leave you like that I shall never be able to pack you into the back of the car. Come out, sir, and be arranged in a nice hunched-up position.'

'Don't you dump me in the car earlier ?'

'No, or you wouldn't look natural. I lay you out on the floor to set. Now, where's that blighter Dalziel ? I hope he hasn't buzzed zealously off to Falbae. No. Here he comes. Dalziel, help me to arrange the corpse exactly as it looked when it was found. It had the arms folded round in front, I think, and the head tucked down on them – no! not as far as that – we mustn't cover up the bruise on the temple. That's here. Now the legs bundled up sideways. Right. Hold that. That's beautiful.'

'Do I stay like this all night ?' asked Sir Maxwell, dolefully.

'No – but remember the pose. We shall want it tomorrow. We'll consider that done. Now we lock the garage door and take the key, for fear of other visitors. Now we go across to Campbell's place. Hullo, Fiscal! come to see the fun ? And Macpherson ? That's the ticket.

'Now we find the key and open the door, locking it, I think, behind us. We shut the shutters and light up. My God! what's this ? A note. *Look out for F.* Great Jehoshaphat! – Oh, no, of course, it doesn't mean me – it means Farren. Now – do we use that or destroy it ? Better destroy it. It's an accident we're staging, not a murder. We don't want the slightest suggestion of violence. Besides – must be decent to Farren. Campbell is alive till 7.30 tomorrow, so he found this and read it. When did he come in, though ? After 12, of course, since Strachan can say he wasn't here earlier. Yes, but how do I know how many people saw him come in at 10.15 ? Must say one thing or the other. Better suggest he came in and then went out again while I was asleep. On foot, perhaps, so that I didn't hear the car. Damn Strachan! What did he want to come poking his nose in for, anyhow ?'

'Well, now – Campbell's bed and Campbell's pyjamas. I don't think we put on the pyjamas. We shake them out – Tuesday's wash-day, so they've had a week's use, and we've only got to sprawl them about on the floor to make 'em look natural. Basin – dirty water – wash the hands and face. That does that and leaves the towel untidy. Bed. Must get into that. Horrid business, lying in bed when you can't and mustn't sleep, but it's got to be done. And one can think.

'One can read, too. I've provided some literature. Got it out of Ferguson's place just now. L.M.S. Time Table. Great work of literature. Style slightly telegraphic, but packed with interest. Road-map, too also from next-door. Does the bed look sufficiently towsled yet? No, I'll give it half an hour – rather a restless half-hour, I'm afraid.'

The restless half-hour over, the murderer crawled out of bed, dragging half the clothes with him.

'I think that's fairly convincing. Now. Throw dirty water into slop-pail and dirty a fresh lot. Shaving brush? Toothbrush? Damn it, no. Must do them later on, or they'll dry up. But I can go down and pack up the painting kit and lay two breakfast-tables. And meanwhile, you know, I can still be thinking out my plan. There's a horrible hole in it at present and one place where I simply must trust rather to luck. By the way, my present intention, I may tell you, is to catch the 12.35 at Barrhill. But that absolutely depends on my getting away in good time from the Minnoch. Let's pray there won't be many people about.'

'But ye didna gae tae Barrhill.'

'No; I think something happened to make me change my mind.' Wimsey was busily sorting out crockery. 'You'll remember that my over-mastering necessity is to get to Glasgow somehow. I have announced my intention of going, and I shall be feeling morbidly nervous about making any change of plan. If you only knew how my brain is spinning at the moment. There! there's Campbell's breakfast all laid out ready: tea-pot, cup and saucer, two plates, knife, fork, bread, butter, sugar. Milk! I must remember to take Campbell's milk in in the morning, by the way; I know when to expect it, you see. Eggs, rasher and frying-pan laid out in the kitchen. Now, over to my own house. Same business here. I believe I had kippers for breakfast actually, but it doesn't matter. For my own convenience I will make it a boiled egg.'

He chattered on as he laid the breakfast-materials out. Then suddenly, as though struck by a sudden thought, he dropped the saucepan on the kitchen floor.

'Curse it! I was nearly forgetting. All this alibi depends on my going by train from Gatehouse. But I told a whole lot of people yesterday that I was going to drive to Dumfries and take the 7.35 train from there. Why should I change my mind? It will look so funny. The car. Something wrong with the car. Something the local people can't be supposed to put right in a hurry. Of course – mag. trouble. Yes – I can work that, and it'll probably help my alibi, too. Steady, old man. Loads of time. Be sure you finish one thing properly before you start another. Right. Breakfast's ready. Now then. I've done my bed, but I haven't done the water and things. Do that now. Pyjamas – there! One lot dirty water. Two lots dirty water. Happy thought. Clean socks and shirt to go to Glasgow in, and respectable suit. You must imagine that I'm doing all this. Must be a grey flannel suit, to match those bags of Campbell's. Here it is, as a matter of fact, hanging up. I won't put it on, but we might have a look at the pockets. Hullo, Macpherson, here you are! See the smear of white paint on the lining of the left-hand jacket pocket? Careless. careless. A little benzine rids us of this guilt. Well, well, well.'

He went swiftly through the motions of changing his garments, while the police, with satisfaction, examined the grey flannel jacket. Play-acting was all very well, but this had the appearance of solid evidence.

Presently Wimsey indicated that the change of clothes was supposed to be accomplished.

'I am spending the night in Glasgow,' he went on, 'so I must pack an attaché-case. Here it is. Clean pyjamas, shaving-tackle, toothbrush. Better shave now, to save time. Five minutes for a shave. In they go. What else? Oh, a burberry. Absolutely essential. But I shall want to use that first. And a soft felt hat *Voilà*! A clean collar, no doubt. There it is. And the magneto will have to go in. That will just about fill the case. Now we go over the way again.'

He led them back to Campbell's cottage, where, after putting on a pair of thin gloves, he carefully checked and repacked all the articles contained in Campbell's painting-outfit, which had been brought over by Dalziel from the police-station for that purpose.

'Campbell would take some grub with him,' observed the murderer thoughtfully. 'I'd better cut some. Here is a ham in the cupboard. Bread, butter, ham, mustard. And a small whiskey-flask, considerably left in full view. I think I shall be right in filling it up. Splendid. Now we go out and detach the mag. from our own car. Gently does it. Up she comes. Now we've got to damage her somewhere. I won't do it really, but we'll suppose it done. Wrap her up neatly in brown paper. Careful man, Ferguson. Always keeps odd bits of string and paper and stationery handy in case they're wanted. Right. Now we'll put this in the attaché-case so that we don't forget it. We shall want an extra cap for when we cease to be Campbell. We'll put that in the pocket of Campbell's cloak. Oh, yes. And this pair of spectacles will be a good aid to disguise. They're Campbell's, but happily they are just sun-glare glasses with plain lenses, so that's O.K. We'll put those in our pocket. Now then, we're all fit and ready.

'Now comes the moment when we have to trust to a stroke of luck. We've got to go out and find a bicycle. It may take a bit of time, but the odds are that if it isn't down one close it'll be down the next. Put out the lights. Lock both doors and take the keys away. We can't risk any more Strachans paying visits while we're away.'

Suiting the action to the words, Wimsey left the cottages and walked briskly away down the road, closely followed by his observers. 'I told you there'd be walking exercise,' said Wimsey. 'You people had better take the car. I shall have the bike to come back on.'

As the cortège arrived opposite the Anwoth Hotel, a bulky form came cautiously up to meet it.

'He's in there, all right,' said P.C. Ross. 'Duncan's watching the other entrance and we've got the Gatehouse policeman sittin' in the back garden tae see that he doesna get oot by the windows. Here's your bicycle, my lord.'

'Wonderful!' said Wimsey. 'Hit it the very first shot. Anybody'd think it had been left there on purpose. No' – as the constable obligingly struck a match. 'No lights. I'm supposed to be stealing this, my dear man. Good night – or rather, good morning. Wish us luck.'

It was a little after two when Wimsey got back to the cottage with the bicycle.

'Now,' he said, when he had deposited the bicycle in the garage, 'we can have a rest. Nothing further happens till about 5 o'clock.'

The conspirators accordingly rolled themselves up in rugs

and coats and disposed themselves on chairs and hearth-rugs, the couch being voted to the Fiscal in right of seniority.

The Chief Constable, being an old soldier, slept promptly and soundly. He was awakened a little before five by a clashing of pots and pans.

'Breakfast for the observers is served in the kitchen,' said Wimsey's voice in his ear. 'I am going up to finish off the bedrooms.'

At a quarter past five this job was finished, Campbell's toothbrush and shaving-brush and both sets of soap and towels left wet and the proper appearances produced. Wimsey then came in to cook and eat his solitary eggs and bacon in Campbell's front room. The tea-pot was left on the hob to keep warm.

'I don't know,' said Wimsey, 'whether he left the fires going or re-lit them. He did one or the other, and it doesn't matter a hoot. Now, corpse, it's time I packed you into the car. I probably did it earlier, but you'd have been so uncomfortable. Come and take up your pose again, and remember you're supposed to be perfectly rigid by now.'

'This may be fun to you,' grumbled Sir Maxwell, 'but it's death to me.'

'So it is,' said Wimsey. 'Never mind. Ready ? Up you go!'

'Eh!' said Macpherson, as Wimsey seized the Chief Constable's cramped and reluctant body and swung it into the back seat of the Morris, 'but your lordship's wonderful strong for your size.'

'It's just a knack,' said Wimsey, ruthlessly ramming his victim down between the seat and the floor. 'I hope you aren't permanently damaged sir. Can you stick it ?' he added, as he pulled on his gloves.

'Carry on,' said the corpse, in a muffled voice.

Wimsey slung in the painting outfit – stool, satchel and easel – followed it with Campbell's cloak and hat, and piled the bicycle on top, securing it with a tow-rope which he produced from a corner of the garage, and tucking a large rug round and over his awkward load.

'We'll let the easel stick out a bit,' he remarked. 'It looks innocent and explains the rest of the load. Is that right ? What's the time ?'

'A quarter to six, my lord.'

'Right; now we can start.'

'But ye've no eaten Ferguson's breakfast, my lord.'

'No; that comes later. Wait a bit. We'd better lock the doors again. Right-ho!'

He drew a cloth cap closely down upon his head, muffled himself unrecognisably in a burberry and muffler, and climbed into the driving-seat.

'Ready? Right. Let her go!'

The car with its burden moved gently out into the pale light of the morning. It bore round to the right at the end of the lane and took the direction of Gatehouse Station. The observation car swung in behind and followed it.

Upwards the road climbed steadily, mounting triumphantly past the wooded beauty of Castramont, ever higher over the lovely valley of the Fleet. Through the trees and out on to the lofty edge of the moor, with the rolling hills lifting their misty heads upon the right. Past the quarry and up still farther to the wide stretch of heather and pasture. Sheep stared at them from the roadside, and scurried foolishly across their path. Partridges, enjoying their last weeks of security, rose whirring and clattering from among the ling. Over to the north-east, white in the morning, the graceful arches of the Fleet viaduct gleamed pallidly. And ahead, grim and frowning, stood the great wall of the Clints of Dromore, scarred and sheer and granite-grey, the gate of the wilderness and guardian-barrier of the Fleet.

The little cottage by the level crossing seemed still asleep and the gates stood open. The cars passed over the line and, avoiding the station entrance, turned sharp away to the left, along the old road to Creetown. Here, for some distance, the way was flanked on either side by a stone wall, but, after a few hundred yards, the walls came to a stop. Wimsey held up a warning hand, stopped, turned his car, with some bumping, over the grass, and drove it well behind the shelter of the wall on the left. The police-car halted in the middle of the road.

'What noo?' asked Macpherson.

Wimsey alighted and peered cautiously under the rug.

'Still alive, Sir Maxwell?'

'Only just.'

'Well, I think you might come out now and have a stretch. You won't be needed again till 9 o'clock. Sit down comfortably with the Fiscal and have a smoke.'

'And what do the others do?'

'They walk back with me to Gatehouse,' said Wimsey, with a grim smile.

'Mayn't we bring the car?' said Macpherson, mournfully.

'You can if you like, but it would be more sporting to cheer me with a little pleasant conversation. Damn it! I've *got* to walk.'

Eventually it was arranged that Macpherson should walk with Lord Peter, while Dalziel brought the car along behind in case the station-omnibus proved to be crowded. Telling the Fiscal to see that the corpse behaved itself, Wimsey waved a cheerful hand and started off with Macpherson to trudge the six-and-a-half miles back to Gatehouse.

The last mile was the most awkward, for the road was getting busy, and they had to be continually diving over walls and under hedges to avoid observation. At the last moment they were nearly caught in the lane by the paper-boy, who passed whistling, within a foot of them while they crouched behind a convenient hawthorn-bush.

'Damn the paper-boy,' said Wimsey. 'Ferguson, of course, would have been expecting him. In any case, he probably did all this earlier, but I didn't want to keep the corpse out all night. A quarter to eight. We've cut it rather fine. Never mind, Here goes.'

They took the remainder of the lane at a run, unlocked Campbell's door, hid the key, performed the motions of taking in the milk and emptying part of it down the sink, took in and opened letters and newspapers, and dashed back to Ferguson's cottage. Here Wimsey took in Ferguson's milk, boiled his egg and made his tea, and sat down to his breakfast with an air of simple enjoyment.

At 8 o'clock, the rotund form of Mrs. Green was seen waddling down the lane. Wimsey looked out of the window and waved a friendly hand to her.

'Better warn her, Macpherson,' he said. 'If she goes into Campbell's place, she'll have a fit.'

Macpherson hurried out, and was seen to vanish into the next-door cottage with Mrs. Green. Presently he returned, smiling broadly.

'Verra gude, my lord,' he said, 'she's tellt me it a' luiks fine: jist precisely as it did the mornin' Campbell was missin'.'

'Good,' said Wimsey. He finished his breakfast, packed the burberry into the attaché-case, and made a tour of inspection round the house, to make sure that nothing looked suspicious. With the exception of the mysterious remains of four extra breakfasts in the kitchen, everything seemed normal. He strolled out, met Mrs. Green in the front of the cottages, had a word with her, mentioning that he was catching the station 'bus and strolled down to the end of the lane.

Shortly after 8.30, the pant of the omnibus was heard coming along the road. Wimsey flagged it and got in. The police car followed on behind, much to the interest of the other passengers in the omnibus.

At 9 o'clock, or a little after, 'bus and car drew up in the station yard. Wimsey alighted and came across to the car.

'I want you, Inspector, to come across to the train with me. When the rain has gone, come out and join Dalziel here. Then get out on to the road and pick up the other car.'

The two officers nodded, and Wimsey strolled into the station with the Inspector at his heels. He spoke to the station-master and booking-clerk and bought a first-class return to Glasgow. After a few minutes, the train was signalled, and a general exodus took place to the opposite platform. The station-master marched across, carrying the staff under his arm; the signalman came down from his lofty perch and crossed also, to perform the duties of a porter. The passengers from the 'bus streamed across the line, followed by the 'bus-conductor on the look-out for return passengers with parcels. The booking-clerk retired into his office and took up a paper. Wimsey and the Inspector crossed over with the other passengers.

The train came in. Wimsey wrung the Inspector's hand affectionately, as though he were not going to see him again for a month, and stepped into the first-class compartment which the porter was holding open for him. The station-master exchanged staffs and a pleasantry or two with the guard. A crate of poultry was wheeled along and dumped into the van. It suddenly occurred to Macpherson that this was all wrong. He ought to have been travelling with Wimsey. He darted to the carriage-window and looked in. The compartment was empty. The whistle blew. The guard waved his flag. The porter, with great bustle, urged Macpherson to 'stand away'. The train moved out. Macpherson, left gazing up and down the line, perceived that it was empty.

'By God!' said Macpherson, slapping his thigh. 'In at one side and oot at t'ither. The auldest dodge in the haill bag o' tricks.' He ran precipitately across the line and joined Dalziel.

'The cunning wee b—!' he exclaimed affectionately. 'He's did it! Did ye see him come across ?'

Dalziel shook his head.

'Is that what he did? Och, the station buildin's is between us. There's a path through the station-master's garden. He'll ha' come by that. We'll best be movin'.'

They passed up the station entrance and turned along the road. In front of them went a small grey figure, walking briskly. It was then ten minutes past nine.

LORD PETER WIMSEY

THE corpse was repacked into the car. Wimsey put on Campbell's hat and cloak, again wrapping a muffler closely about his chin so that very little of his features was visible beneath the flapping black brim. He backed the car out on to the road and drove gently away towards Creetown. The road was stony, and Wimsey knew that his tyres were a good deal worn. A puncture would have been fatal. He kept his speed down to a cautious twenty miles an hour. He thought as he drove how maddening this slow progress must have been to Ferguson, to whom time had been so precious. With a real corpse in the back seat, it must have been a horrible temptation to go all out at whatever risk.

The road was completely deserted, except for the wee burn which chuckled along placidly beside them. Once he had to get down to open a gate. The burn, deserting the right-hand side of the road, ran under a small bridge and reappeared on their left, glimmering down over stones to meander beneath a clump of trees. The sun was growing stronger.

Between twenty and twenty-five minutes past nine they came down at the head of the steep little plunge into Creetown, opposite the clock-tower, Wimsey swung the car out to the right into the main road, and encountered the astonished gaze of the proprietor of the Ellangowan Hotel, who was talking to a motorist by the petrol-pump. For a moment he stared as though he had seen a ghost – then he caught sight of Macpherson and Dalziel, following in the second car with the Fiscal, and waved his hand with an understanding smile.

'First incident not according to schedule,' said Wimsey. 'It's odd that Ferguson shouldn't have been seen at this point – especially as he would quite probably have liked to be seen. But that's life. If you want a thing, you don't get it.'

He pressed his foot on the accelerator and took the road at a good thirty-five miles an hour.

Five miles farther on, he passed the turn to the New Galloway road. It was just after half-past nine.

'Near enough,' said Wimsey to himself. He kept his foot down and hurried along over the fine new non-skid surface which had just been laid down and was rapidly making the road from Creetown to Newton-Stewart one of the safest and finest in the three kingdoms. Just outside Newton-Stewart, he had to slow down to pass the road-engine and workers, the road-laying having now advanced to that point. After a brief delay, bumping over the new-laid granite, he pushed on again, but instead of following the main road, turned off just before he reached the bridge into a third-class road running parallel to the main road through Minnigaff, and following the left bank of the Cree. It ran through a wood, and past the Cruives of Cree, through Longbaes and Borgan, and emerged into the lonely hill-country, swelling with green mound after green mound, round as the hill of the King of Elfland; then a sharp right-turn and he saw his goal before him – the bridge, the rusty iron gate and the steep granite wall that overhung the Minnoch.

He ran the car up upon the grass and got out. The police-car drew up into the shelter of a little quarry on the opposite side of the road. When the observers came up with him, Wimsey was already rolling back the rug and pulling out the bicycle.

'Ye've made verra gude time,' observed the Inspector. 'It's jist on 10 o'clock.'

Wimsey nodded. He ran up on to the higher ground and surveyed the road and the hills to left and right. Not a soul was to be seen – not so much as a cow or a sheep. Though they were only just off a main road and a few hundred yards from a farm, the place was as still and secret as the heart of a desert. He ran down again to the car, flung the painting-kit upon the grass, opened the door of the tonneau and clutched ruthlessly the huddled form of the Chief Constable who, more dead than alive after his disagreeable journey, hardly needed to feign the stiffness which was cramping him in every limb. Hoisted in a dismal bundle on Wimsey's back, he made a last lurching stage

270

of his progress, to be dumped with a heavy thud on the hard granite, at the edge of the incline.

'Wait there,' said Wimsey, in a menacing tone, 'and don't move, or you'll fall into the river.'

The Chief Constable dug his fingers into a bunch of heather and prayed silently. He opened his eyes, saw the granite sloping sharply away beneath him, and shut them again. After a few minutes, he felt himself enveloped in a musty smother of rug. Then came another pause, and the sound of voices and heartless laughter. Then he was deserted again. He tried to imagine what was happening and guessed, rightly, that Wimsey was secreting the bicycle somewhere. Then the voices came back, and a few muttered curses suggested that somebody was setting up an easel with unpractised hands. More laughter. Then the rug was twitched from his head and Wimsey's voice announced, 'You can come out now.'

Sir Maxwell retreated cautiously on hands and knees from the precipice, which, to his prejudiced eyes, appeared to be about two hundred feet in depth, rolled over and sat up.

'Oh, God!' he said, rubbing his legs. 'What have I done to deserve all this?'

'I'm sorry, sir,' said Wimsey. 'If you had been really dead, you know, you wouldn't have noticed it. But I didn't like to go as far as that. Well, now we've got an hour and a half, I ought to paint the picture, but, as that is beyond me, I thought we might have a little picnic. There's some grub in the other car. They're just bringing it up.'

'I could do with something to drink,' said Sir Maxwell.

'You shall have it. Hullo! Somebody's coming. We'll give them a start. Get under the rug again, sir.'

The distant clack of a farm-lorry was making itself heard in the distance. The Chief Constable hurriedly snatched up the rug and froze. Wimsey sat down before the easel and assumed brush and palette.

Presently the lorry loomed into sight over the bridge. The driver, glancing across with natural interest at the spot where the tragedy had taken place, suddenly caught sight of the easel, the black hat and the conspicuous cloak. He gave vent to one fearful yell and rammed his foot down on the accelerator. The lorry went leaping and crashing forward, scattering the stones right and left in its mad progress. Wimsey laughed. The Chief Constable sprang up to see what was happening and laughed too. In a few minutes the rest of the party joined them, so agitated with laughter that they could scarcely hold the parcels they were carrying.

'Och, mon!' said Dalziel, 'but that was grand! That was young Jock. Did ye hear the skelloch he let oot? He's away noo tae tell the folks at Clauchaneasy that auld Campbell's ghaist is sittin' up pentin' pictures at the Minnoch.'

'I trust the poor lad will come to no harm with his lorry,' observed the Fiscal. 'He appeared to me to be driving at a reckless pace.'

'Never mind him,' said the Chief Constable. 'Lads like that have nine lives. But I'm dying of hunger and thirst, if you are not. Half-past five is a terrible hour for breakfast.'

The picnic was a cheerful one, though it was a little disturbed by the return of Jock, supported by a number of friends, to view the phenomenon of a ghost in broad daylight.

'This is getting rather public,' said Wimsey.

Sergeant Dalziel grunted, and strode down to warn the spectators off, his stalwart jaws still champing a wedge of veal and ham pie. The hills returned to their wonted quiet.

At 11.25 Wimsey rose regretfully.

'Corpse-time,' he said. 'Here, Sir Maxwell, is the moment when you go bumpety-bump into the water.'

'Is it?' said the Chief Constable, 'I draw the line there.'

'It would make you rather a wet-blanket on the party,' said Wimsey. 'Well, we'll suppose it done. Pack up, you languid aristocrats, and return to your Rolls-Royce, while I pant and sweat upon this confounded bicycle. We had better take away the Morris and the rest of the doings. There's no point in leaving them.'

He removed Campbell's cloak and changed the black hat for his own cap, then retrieved the bicycle from its hiding-place, and strapped the attaché-case to the carrier. With a grunt of disgust he put on the tinted spectacles, threw his leg across the saddle and pedalled furiously away. The others packed themselves at leisure into the two cars. The procession wound out upon the Bargrennan road.

Nine and a half miles of crawling in the wake of the bicycle brought them to Barrhill. Just outside the village, Wimsey signalled a halt.

'Look here,' said he. 'Here's where I have to guess. I guess that Ferguson meant to catch the 12.35 here, but something went wrong. It's 12.33 now, and I could do it. The station is just down that side-road there. But he must have started late and missed it. I don't know why. Listen! There she comes!'

As he spoke, the smoke of the train came in view. They heard her draw up into the station. Then, in a few minutes, she panted away again.

'Well on time,' said Wimsey. 'Anyway, we've missed her now. She's a local as far as Girvan. Then she turns into an express, only stopping at Maybole before she gets to Ayr. Then she becomes still more exalted by the addition of a Pullman Restaurant Car, and scorns the earth, running right through to Paisley and Glasgow. Our position is fairly hopeless, you see. We can only carry on through the village and wait for a miracle.'

He remounted and pedalled on, glancing back from time to time over his shoulder. Presently, the sound of an overtaking car made itself heard. An old Daimler limousine, packed with cardbord dress-boxes, purred past at a moderate twenty-two or three miles and hour. Wimsey let it pass him, then, head down and legs violently at work, swung in behind it. In another moment, his hand was on the ledge of the rear window, and he was free-wheeling easily in its wake. The driver did not turn his head.

'A-ah!' said Macpherson, 'It's our friend Clarence Gordon, by Jove! And him tellin' us he'd passed the man on the road. Ay, imph'm, an' he wad be tellin' nae mair nor less than the truth. We'll hope his lordship's no killt.'

'He's safe enough,' said the Chief Constable, 'providing his tyres hold out. That's a very long-headed young man, for all his blether. At this rate, we'll be beating the train all right. How far is it to Girvan?'

'Aboot twelve miles. We ought tae pass her at Pinmore. She's due there at 12.53.'

'Let's hope Clarence Gordon keeps his foot down. Go gently, Macpherson. We don't want to overtake him.'

Clarence Gordon was a careful driver, but acted nobly up to expectation. He positively put on a spurt after passing Pinwherry, and as they attacked the sharp rise to Pinmore, they caught sight of the black hinder-end of the train labouring along the track that ran parallel and close to the road. As they topped the hill, and left the train behind them, Wimsey waved his hat. They span merrily along, bearing to the left and winding down towards the sea. At five minutes past one, the first houses of

273

Girvan rose about them. The pursuer's hearts beat furiously as the train now caught them up again on their right and rushed past them towards Girvan Station. At the end of the town, Wimsey let go his hold on the car, sprinting away for dear life to the right down the station road. At eight minutes past he was on the platform, with three minutes to spare. The police force, like the ranks of Tuscany, could scarce forbear to cheer. Leaving Dalziel to arrange for the safe keeping of the cars, Macpherson ran to the booking office and took three first-class tickets to Glasgow. As he passed Wimsey on the platform, he saw him unstrapping the attaché-case and heard him cry to the porters in an exaggerated Oxford accent: 'Heah! portah! label this bicycle for Ayr.' And as he turned from the booking-window the porter's urgent voice came right in his ear:

'One first and a bicycle-ticket to Ayr, and make it quick, laddie. I must be gettin' back tae my gentleman.'

They tumbled out on to the platform. The bicycle was being bundled into the rear van. They leapt for their carriage. The whistle blew. They were off.

'Gosh!' said Wimsey, wiping his face. And then: 'Damn this thing, it's like a fly-paper.'

In his left hand, concealed by the hat which he had removed for the sake of coolness, he held something which he now displayed with a grin. It was a luggage-label for Euston.

'Simple as shelling peas,' he said laughing. 'I pinched it while he was wheeling the bike off to the van. All ready gummed, too. They do things handsomely on the L.M.S. Fortunately the pigeon-hole was labelled, so I didn't have to hunt for it. Well, that's that. Now we can take a breather. There's nothing else till we get to Ayr.'

After a stop at Maybole to collect the tickets, the train ran merrily along to Ayr. Almost before it drew up at the platform, Wimsey was out of the train. He ran back to the rear van, with Macpherson hurrying at his heels.

'Let me have that bicycle out, quick,' he said to the guard. 'You'll see it there. Labelled to Ayr. Here's the ticket.'

The guard, who was the same man whom Ross had interviewed previously, stared at Wimsey, and appeared to hesitate.

'It's a' richt, guard,' said Macpherson, 'I'm a police officer. Let this gentleman have what he wants.'

The guard, with a puzzled look, handed out the bicycle,

receiving the ticket in exchange. Wimsey pressed a shilling into his hand and hurried with the bicycle along the platform to a point near the station entrance where the end of the bookstall masked him from the view both of the guard and of the booking-clerk. Dalziel, seeing that Macpherson was involved in explan-ations with the guard, followed Wimsey quietly, and was in time to see him moisten the Euston luggage-label with an expansive lick and clap it on to the bicycle over the Ayr label. This done, Wimsey marched briskly out, attaché-case in hand, and plunged down the little side-street and into the public convenience. In less than a minute he was out again, minus spectacles, his cap exchanged for the soft felt hat, and wearing the burberry. Passengers were now dashing through the booking-hall to catch the Glasgow train. Wimsey joined them and purchased a third-class ticket to Glasgow. Dalziel, panting on his heels, purchased four. By the time he had paid for them, Wimsey was gone. The Chief Constable and the Fiscal, waiting near the hoarding at the head of the side-bays, received a cheerful wink from Wimsey as he strolled up and planted the bicycle against the hoarding. They were probably the only people who noticed this man-oeuvre, for the Pullman Car had by now been attached to the train, and the platform was filled with passengers, porters and luggage. Wimsey, his hands before his face lighting his cigar-ette, wandered away towards the head of the train. Doors slammed. Dalziel and Macpherson skipped into a compartment. Wimsey followed. The Chief Constable and the Fiscal did likewise. The guard shouted 'Right away!' and the train moved out again. The whole business had occupied exactly six minutes.

'There's another good bicycle gone west,' said Wimsey.

'No,' said Macpherson. 'I saw what ye'd be after an' I warned a porter tae send it back tae Gatehouse. It belongs tae the con-stable, and he wad not care tae be wantin' it,' he added, thriftily.

'Splendid, I say – it's all gone rather prettily so far, don't you think ?'

'Charmingly,' said the Fiscal, 'but you're not forgetting, Lord Peter, that this train doesn't get into St. Enoch till 2.55, and that, according to these motor-people – er – Sparkes & Crisp – Mr. Ferguson was in their show-rooms at ten minutes to three ?'

'That's what they say,' replied Wimsey, 'but Ferguson didn't say that. He said "About three". I fancy, with luck, we may be able to reconcile those two statements.'

'And how about that other ticket you've got there ?' put in

Sir Maxwell. 'That's the thing that's been worrying me. The ticket from Gatehouse to Glasgow.'

'It doesn't worry *me*,' said Wimsey, confidently.

'Oh, well,' said the Chief Constable, 'if you're pleased, we're pleased.'

'I have not enjoyed anything so much for a long time,' said the Fiscal, who seemed quite unable to get over his delight in the excursion. 'I ought to be sorry to see the net closing round this poor Mr. Ferguson, but I must admit that I find myself a prey to excitement.'

'Yes – I'm sorry for Ferguson too,' answered Wimsey. 'I wish you hadn't reminded me, sir. But it can't be helped, I'd be sorrier still if it was Farren, for instance. Poor beggar! This business will tie him by the leg for ever, I'm afraid. Opportunity doesn't come twice. No; the only thing that's really worrying me is the possibility of this train's getting in late.'

The train, however, ran most creditably to time, and drew into St. Enoch at 2.55 to the minute. Wimsey was out of it at once and led his party along the platform at a great pace.

As they passed the entrance to the station hotel, he turned to Sir Maxwell.

'I suggest,' he said, 'though I don't absolutely know, that it was at this point that Ferguson caught sight of Miss Cochran and Miss Selby and their party. They were probably just emerging from their lunch, and he guessed that their friends had come along to meet their train at Glasgow.'

He broke off to wave frantically to a taxi. The whole five of them crammed into it, and Wimsey directed the driver to set him down in the street where Messrs. Sparkes & Crisp had their showrooms.

'And drive like blazes,' he added.

At five minutes past three he tapped on the glass. The driver pulled up and they all scrambled out on to the pavement. Wimsey paid off the taxi and headed off at a brisk pace for the motor show-rooms a few yards away.

'Don't let's all go in in a bunch,' he said. 'Come with me, Sir Maxwell, and the others can drift in afterwards.'

Messrs. Sparkes & Crisp possessed the usual kind of establishment, filled with tall show-cases exhibiting motoring gadgets. On the right was a counter, where a lad was earnestly discussing with a customer the rival merit of two different brands of shock-absorber. Through an archway appeared a glittering array of motor-cycles and side-cars. A frosted-glass door on the left appeared to lead to an inner office.

Wimsey darted silently in with Sir Maxwell and disappeared behind a show-case. The lad and the customer continued their discussion. After about a minute, Wimsey emerged again and strode wrathfully to the counter.

'See here, sonnie,' he said, peremptorily, 'do you want to do any business today, or don't you? I've got an appointment and I can't wait here all afternoon.' He looked at his watch. 'I've been hanging about here for the last ten minutes.'

'Very sorry, sir. What can I do for you?'

Wimsey brought out his brown-paper parcel from the attaché-case.

'You're agents for these magnetos?'

'Yes, sir. That will be our Mr. Saunders. Excuse me one minute, sir. Call him down, sir.'

The youth dashed to the frosted-glass door, leaving Wimsey to endure the furious stare of the specialist in shock-absorbers.

'Will you come this way, sir?'

Wimsey, attaching his party to him with a glance, plunged through the door and was conducted to a small office where 'our Mr. Saunders' sat, in company with a typist.

Mr. Saunders was a fresh-faced young man with the Eton-and-Oxford manner. He greeted Wimsey like one welcoming an old schoolfriend after many years' absence. Then he glanced beyond him to Sergeant Dalziel, and his breezy gusto seemed to suffer a slight diminution.

'Look here, old horse,' said Wimsey, 'you've seen this magneto before, I fancy?'

Mr. Saunders looked at the magneto and its number rather helplessly, and said:

'Yes, yes, oh, yes, to be sure. Quite. Number XX/47302. Yes. When did we have Number XX/47302 through our hands, Miss Madden?'

Miss Madden referred to a card-index file.

'It came in for repairs a fortnight ago, Mr. Saunders. It belongs to Mr. Ferguson of Gatehouse. He brought it in himself. Defect in armature winding. Returned to him the day before yesterday.'

'Yes – exactly. Our fellows at the shops reported a defect in the armature winding. Quite. I hope it is quite O.K. now, Mr. – er—'

'After that,' said Wimsey, 'you may remember getting a visit from my friend here, Sergeant Dalziel.'

'Oh, absolutely,' said Mr. Saunders. 'Quite so. You're very well, I hope, Sergeant ?'

'You told him then,' said Wimsey, 'that Mr. Ferguson came in here about ten minutes to three.'

'Did I ? Oh, yes – I remember. Mr. Crisp called me in. You remember, Miss Madden ? Yes. But I didn't say that. Birkett said that – the young man in the show-room, don't you know. Said the customer had been waiting ten minutes. Yes. I didn't see the chappie when he came in, you know. I found him waiting when I got back from lunch. I was a little late that day, I think. Yes. Lunching with a customer. Business, and all that sort of thing. Yes. Mr. Crisp rather hauled me over the coals, I remember. Ha, ha!'

'When exactly *did* ye come in, Mr. Saunders ?' asked the Inspector grimly.

'Oh, well – must have been about three o'clock, I'm afraid. Yes. Half an hour late. Business, of course. Mr. Crisp—'

'Wull ye no speak the truth, mon ?' said Inspector Macpherson, irritated.

'Eh ? Oh – well – as a matter of fact, I may have been a minute or two later. I – I rather avoided looking at the clock, I'm afraid. What time did I come in, Miss Madden ?'

'A quarter past three, Mr. Saunders,' said Miss Madden concisely. 'I remember the occasion perfectly.'

'By jove, was it ? Well, I thought it must have been somewhere about three or a little after. What a memory you've got, Miss Madden.'

Miss Madden smiled faintly.

'There you are, Inspector,' said Wimsey. 'Difference between five minutes to and five minutes past. All the difference, isn't it ?'

'Ye may have tae swear tae this in a court of law, Mr. Saunders,' said the Inspector, sourly. 'So I'll trouble ye no tae forget it again.'

'Oh, I say, really ?' said Mr. Saunders, in some alarm. 'Look here, shall I have to say who I was lunching with ? Because, as a matter of fact, it wasn't exactly business. At least, it was private business.'

'That will be your own concern, Mr. Saunders. Ye may like tae know that we're investigatin' a murder.'

'Oh, I *say*! Of course, I didn't know that. Mr. Crisp just

asked me when I came in. I said, about three – because it really was that, you know, more or less. Of course, if I'd known, I should have asked Miss Madden. She has such a wonderful memory for details.'

'Ay,' said the Inspector, 'and I wad advise ye tae cultivate the same yersel'. Gude mornin' tae ye.'

The investigators were shown out by Mr. Saunders, who burbled unconvincingly all down the passage.

'It's not much good questioning this fellow Birkett, I suppose,' said Sir Maxwell. 'He probably spoke in perfect good faith. He'd be ready to swear today that he'd kept you waiting, Wimsey.'

'Probably. Well, now, we've got to be up at the Exhibition at four. Not much time. However, I noticed a jobbing printer's on the way up here. I daresay we shall find what we want there.'

He led them at a quick pace along the street, and darted into a small printing-works.

'I want to buy a few metal types,' he said. 'Rather like these. Must be this size, and as near in character as you can supply them.' He produced a sheet of paper.

The foreman scratched his head.

'That'll be 5 point,' he said. 'The nearest thing to it wad be Clarendon caps. Ay, we can gi'e ye that, if ye wasn't wantin' a great weight o't.'

'Oh, dear, no. I only want five letters – S – M and L – A and D and a complete set of figures.'

'Will monotype castings do ye ?'

'I'd rather have foundry-metal if you have it. I want to use them as punches for a small piece of leather-work.'

'Verra gude.' The Foreman went to a case of type, extracted the required letters and figures and wrapped them up in a screw of paper, mentioning a small price.

Wimsey paid for them and put the little parcel in his pocket.

'By the way,' he said, 'did you have a gentleman in here, asking for the same thing a fortnight ago ?'

'No, sir. I wad mind it weel eneugh. Na, na, it wad be a rather uncommon transaction. I havena been askit for sic a thing since I cam' tae this business, an' that's twa year next January.'

'Oh, well, it doesn't matter. Thanks awfully. Good morning.'

'Better get a trade directory, Inspector, and count out all the printers. And – yes – wait, – the people who sell book-binding materials. Ferguson must have got these – unless, of course, he brought them with him, which isn't very likely.'

Dalziel departed on this errand, while the rest took a taxi and hurried away to the Exhibition, which they reached a few minutes before four. Here they dallied till half-past four, making a hasty tour of all the rooms, and noting one or two striking pictures in each.

'There,' said Wimsey, as they passed the turnstile again. 'Now, if we were to meet any inquisitive friends on the doorway, we could persuade them that we had visited the whole show and used our brains. And now we had better make tracks for a quiet place. I suggest a hotel bedroom.'

LORD PETER WIMSEY

IN a remote bedroom in one of Glasgow's principal hotels, Wimsey unwrapped his little parcel of types, together with Ferguson's safety-razor, and a small hammer, which he had purchased on the way.

Then, gathering his audience about him, he brought out from his pocket the outward half of his first-class ticket from Gatehouse to Glasgow.

'Now, gentlemen,' said he, 'we come to the crucial point of our investigation.

'If you had read that excellent work of Mr. Connington's, to which I drew your attention, you would have found that it contained an account of how a gentleman forged a clip-mark on his railway ticket, by means of a pair of nail-scissors.

'That was on an English line. Now, the Scottish railway authorities, possibly out of sheer tiresomeness, and possibly with the laudable idea of making the way of a ticket-forger hard, are not content with a simple triangular clip.

'The other day I travelled – at great inconvenience to myself – from Gatehouse to Glasgow by the 9.8 a.m. train. I found that the brutal ticket-collectors actually inflicted three ferocious punches on my poor little half-ticket. The first was at Maxwelltown, where they produced a horrible set of indented letters and numerals, thus: $^{LMS}_{42D}$. At Hurlford, they were content to take a large bite out of the ticket – not a simple triangular snip, but

280

a disgusting thing like a squat figure 1. Ferguson would probably have seen these marks, and having the artist's eye and a remarkable visual memory, would no doubt be able to reproduce these things from memory. Personally, I took the precaution of drawing the mark left by the clipper. Here it is: ⌐. Then, at Mauchline, they went all cautious again, and disfigured the ticket with another cipher-code $\frac{LMS}{23A}$. Now, gentlemen, with your permission and these instruments, we will proceed to forge the punch-marks on this ticket.'

He took up the safety-razor, detached the blade, and, laying the ticket down on the marble-topped washstand, proceeded to cut the Hurlford clip-mark out of the pasteboard.

This done, he laid the ticket on the blotting-pad provided by the hotel, placed the type-metal figure 2 carefully just above the edge of the ticket, and delivered a smart tap with the hammer. The figure appeared, when the type was lifted, sharply incised on the face of the ticket, which, on being turned over, showed a thicker and blunter version of the figure in relief on the reverse.

'Eh, mon!' exclaimed Macpherson, 'but ye're ower clever tae be an honest mon.'

Wimsey added the figure 3 and an A, taking care to keep the feet of the letters parallel – a task easily accomplished by setting the beard of the type in line with the edge of the pasteboard. Then, with careful attention to spacing and uprightness, he punched in the letters LMS over the 23A. This completed the Mauchline punch-mark. In the third place he forged the $\frac{LMS}{42D}$ for the Maxwelltown mark, and laid his tools aside with a sigh of satisfaction.

'It's a wee bit groggy here and there,' he said, 'but it would probably pass on a casual inspection. Now, there's only one thing to do, and that is, to get it back into the hands of the railway company. I'd better take only one witness to this. We don't want to create a sensation.'

The Inspector was chosen to accompany him, and, taking a taxi, they bustled down to St. Enoch Station. Here Wimsey inquired, in a fussy manner, for the collector who had been on duty when the 2.16 came in from Dumfries. The man was pointed out to him at one of the barriers. Wimsey, wreathing his features into a kind of peevish smile, approached him with an air of worried kindliness.

'Oh, good evening. I think you were at the barrier when I came in on the 2.16 this afternoon. Now, do you know that you let me get past without giving up my ticket? Yes, yes, he-he! I might have been defrauding the company and all that. I really think you ought to be more careful. Yes. I'm a shareholder on this line, and my cousin is a director, and I *do* think it's dreadfully careless. There'd be an inquiry when they found a ticket short at the audit-office, of course, but, you know, he-he. I could have escaped by that time, couldn't I? Tut, tut – no wonder dividends go down. But I don't want you to get you into trouble, my good fellow, so I've brought you the ticket, and if I were you I'd just slip it in with the others and say no more about it. But you'll be more careful in future, won't you?'

During this harangue, which was poured out all in one breath, allowing no time for reply, the ticket-collector's face changed gradually from weary courtesy to astonishment and from astonishment to anger.

'Eh, sir,' said the man, the moment he could get a word in edgeways, 'I dinna ken what ye'll be up to, but I'll no be had twice that way within the fortnight.'

Inspector Macpherson here intervened.

'My mon,' said he, 'I'm a police-officer, an' I'll trouble ye tae attend tae me. Have ye had this same thing happen tae ye before?'

The ticket-collector, now thoroughly alarmed, excused himself, stammered and then let out the whole story.

He had been on duty just about this time exactly a fortnight earlier. A gentleman had come, just as Wimsey had done, and produced a ticket, explaining that he had somehow slipped through the barrier without having to give it up. He (the collector) had examined the ticket, and seen that it had been properly clipped at Maxwelltown, Hurlford and Mauchline, and he had seen no reason to doubt the passenger's story. Not wishing to be reprimanded for negligence, he had thanked the gentleman, taken the ticket and carried it to the clerk who was making up that day's tickets for dispatch to the audit-office. The clerk had obligingly added the ticket to the appropriate bundle, and no more had been heard about it. The collector was sorry, but in view of the fact that the ticket appeared perfectly in order in every way, he had not thought he could be doing any harm. On being shown the photograph of Ferguson, the collector rather tentatively identified him as the passenger who had brought back the ticket.

The clerk confirmed the collector's story, and all that remained was to visit the audit-office and obtain a view of the ticket itself. This, owing to the fact that there had already been one police inquiry about it, was fortunately still in existence. A careful examination showed a slight difference between the form of lettering and that of the correctly-punched tickets in the same bunch, and also that, whereas the figures purporting to have been punched on it at Mauchline were $\frac{LMS}{23A}$ the other tickets bore the cipher $\frac{LMS}{23B}$. It was explained that in each case the letter following the numerals denoted the particular collector who clipped the tickets on that train, each man having his own pair of clippers. The Mauchline numbers ranged from 23A to 23G. Therefore, while in itself the punch-mark $\frac{LMS}{23A}$ was perfectly correct and in order it was suspicious that collector A should have punched only that one ticket out of all the tickets punched on that train. The previous inquiry had, of course, merely been directed to ascertain that the ticket had actually reached Glasgow, and therefore no special attention was paid to the punch-marks. Now, however, it was evident enough that the punch-marks were forgeries, very neatly executed.

On their return to the hotel, Wimsey and the Inspector were met by Dalziel, with additional confirmation. A man corresponding to Ferguson's description had, on the Tuesday in question, visited a firm that sold book-binders' tools, and purchased a set of letter-punches, similar in character and size to the letter on the tickets. He had explained that he was doing a little amateur book-binding, and wanted the punches for the spines of a set of volumes, which were to be labelled SAMUEL, 1, 2, 3 and 4 – this series containing all the letters and numbers necessary for faking the ticket-punches. The case against Ferguson was complete.

Wimsey was rather silent as they took the last train back from Glasgow.

'You know,' he said. 'I rather liked Ferguson, and I couldn't stick Campbell at any price. I rather wish—'

'Can't be helped, Wimsey,' said the Chief Constable. 'Murder is murder, you know.'

'Not always,' said Wimsey.

They came back to find Ferguson under arrest. He had endeavoured to take out his car – had found the magneto missing and had then attempted to make a bolt for the railway-station. Ross and Duncan had then thought it time to intervene. He had made no reply when arrested and cautioned, and was then in the Newton-Stewart police-station, awaiting examination. On being confronted with the forged tickets, he gave in, and, despite the warnings of the police, decided to tell his story.

'It wasn't murder,' he said. 'I swear to God it wasn't murder. And I told you the truth when I said it didn't happen in the least like your reconstruction.

'Campbell came back at 10.15, just as I said. He barged into my place and began boasting about what he had done to Gowan and what he was going to do to Farren. He had been drinking again after he came in. He used filthy expressions to me and told me he was going to have it out with me, once and for all. He was damnably offensive, I tell you, it wasn't murder. It was Campbell's night to howl, and he got what was coming to him.

'I told him to get out of my house. He wouldn't go, and I tried to push him out. He attacked me, and there was a struggle. I'm stronger than I look, and he wasn't sober. There was a rough and tumble, and I got a heavy punch in on his jaw. He went over and caught his head on the rounded top of the studio stove. When I went to pick him up, he was dead. That was at 11 o'clock.

'Well, I was frightened. I knew I'd often threatened to do him in, and I'd got no witnesses. Here he was, in my house, dead, and I had certainly used force to him first.

'Then I began to think that I might make it look like an accident. I needn't go into the details. You seem to know them all. My plan worked perfectly, with one exception, and I got over that, and as a matter of fact, it did me good. I meant to start from Barrhill, but I missed the train, and then I hung on to old Ikey-Mo, which made my alibi much better, because it didn't look, on the face of it, as though I could have got to Girvan in time, especially when I'd heard from Jock Graham that you knew I couldn't have started from the Minnoch before 11.30.

'It was bad luck, of course, that the body was found quite so soon. I knew there might be trouble over that rigor mortis business. Was that what put you on to the idea of murder in the first place?'

'No,' said Wimsey. 'It was your habit of putting paints in your pocket. Did you realise that you had carried off Campbell's flake-white?'

'I didn't notice it till I got back home. But it never occurred to me that anybody would spot that. I suppose you were the intelligent sleuth, Wimsey. I'd have taken it up to the Minnoch and dropped it somewhere, only that you had seen it the day you came to the studio. That was the first real fright I got. But afterwards I thought I could rely on the alibi. I was rather proud of that ticket-forgery. And I hoped you would overlook the possibilities of Ikey-Mo.'

'There's only one thing I don't understand,' said the Chief Constable, 'why didn't you start out earlier from the Minnoch? There wasn't any need to do such a lot to the painting.'

Ferguson smiled faintly.

'That was a big bloomer. You reconstructed the events of the night, and you know what a lot I had to do? Well – I forgot one thing. I forgot to wind up my watch, which I usually do at bedtime. I was going to pack up my painting things, after I'd done a goodish bit, when I heard a lorry coming along. I waited for that to go by and looked at my watch. It said half-past ten. I thought I could easily give it another half-hour. I didn't want to hang about at Barrhill for fear of being recognized. I estimated another half-hour, and looked at my watch again. It was still half-past ten.

'That put me into a panic. I booted the body over the bank and packed up as though the devil was after me. That must have been how I came to overlook the flake-white. I scorched away as fast as I could, but that bicycle I borrowed was too small for me and geared rather low. A beast. I missed the train by a hair's-breadth – it was just moving out of the station as I got to the station turn. I rode on in a kind of desperation – and then that car came along and I thought I was saved. But apparently I wasn't.

'I'm sorry. I didn't mean to kill Campbell. And I still say, and say again, it was not murder.'

Wimsey got up.

'Look here, Ferguson.' he said. 'I'm damned sorry, and I always thought it couldn't really be murder. Will you forgive me?'

'I'm glad,' said Ferguson. 'I've felt like hell ever since. I'd really rather stand my trial. I'd like to tell everybody that it wasn't murder. You do believe that, don't you?'

'I do,' said Wimsey, 'and if the jury are sensible people, they'll bring it in self-defence or justifiable homicide.'

The jury, after hearing of Mr. Gowan's experiences, took a view mid-way between murder and self-defence. They brought it in manslaughter, with a strong recommendation to mercy, on the ground that Campbell was undoubtedly looking for trouble, and the beard of Samson was not sacrificed altogether in vain.

NEL BESTSELLERS

T046 133	HOW GREEN WAS MY VALLEY	Richard Llewellyn	£1.00
T039 560	I BOUGHT A MOUNTAIN	Thomas Firbank	95p
T033 988	IN THE TEETH OF THE EVIDENCE	Dorothy L. Sayers	90p
T038 149	THE CARPETBAGGERS	Harold Robbins	£1.50
T040 917	TO SIR WITH LOVE	E.R. Braithwaite	75p
T041 719	HOW TO LIVE WITH A NEUROTIC DOG	Stephen Baker	75p
T040 925	THE PRIZE	Irving Wallace	£1.65
T034 755	THE CITADEL	A.J. Cronin	£1.10
T042 189	STRANGER IN A STRANGE LAND	Robert Heinlein	£1.25
T037 053	79 PARK AVENUE	Harold Robbins	£1.25
T042 308	DUNE	Frank Herbert	£1.50
T045 137	THE MOON IS A HARSH MISTRESS	Robert Heinlein	£1.25
T040 933	THE SEVEN MINUTES	Irving Wallace	£1.50
T038 130	THE INHERITORS	Harold Robbins	£1.25
T035 689	RICH MAN, POOR MAN	Irwin Shaw	£1.50
T037 134	EDGE 27: DEATH DRIVE	George G. Gilman	75p
T037 541	DEVIL'S GUARD	Robert Elford	£1.25
T042 774	THE RATS	James Herbert	80p
T042 340	CARRIE	Stephen King	80p
T042 782	THE FOG	James Herbert	90p
T033 740	THE MIXED BLESSING	Helen Van Slyke	£1.25
T037 061	BLOOD AND MONEY	Thomas Thompson	£1.50
T038 629	THIN AIR	Simpson & Burger	95p
T038 602	THE APOCALYPSE	Jeffrey Konvitz	95p

NEL P.O. BOX 11, FALMOUTH TR10 9EN, CORNWALL

Postage charge:

U.K. Customers. Please allow 25p for the first book plus 10p per copy for each additional book ordered to a maximum charge of £1.05 to cover the cost of postage and packing, in addition to cover price.

B.F.P.O. & Eire. Please allow 25p for the first book plus 10p per copy for the next 8 books, thereafter 5p per book, in addition to cover price.

Overseas Customers. Please allow 40p for the first book plus 12p per copy for each additional book, in addition to cover price.

Please send cheque or postal order (no currency).

Name ....

Address ....

....

Title ....

While every effort is made to keep prices steady, it is sometimes necessary to increase prices at short notice. New English Library reserve the right to show on covers and charge new retail prices which may differ from those advertised in the text or elsewhere.